T0113134

GOLDEN AGE
LOCKED ROOM
MYSTERIES

OTTO PENZLER, the creator of American Mystery Classics, is also the founder of the Mysterious Press (1975); MysteriousPress.com (2011), an electronic-book publishing company; and New York City's Mysterious Bookshop (1979). He has won a Raven, the Ellery Queen Award, two Edgars (for the *Encyclopedia of Mystery and Detection*, 1977, and *The Lineup*, 2010), and lifetime achievement awards from NoirCon and *The Strand Magazine*. He has edited more than 70 anthologies and written extensively about mystery fiction.

GOLDEN AGE LOCKED ROOM MYSTERIES

OTTO PENZLER, EDITOR

AMERICAN MYSTERY CLASSICS

Penzler Publishers
New York

Published in 2022 by Penzler Publishers
58 Warren Street, New York, NY 10007
penzlerpublishers.com

Distributed by W. W. Norton

Cover image: Andy Ross
Cover design: Mauricio Diaz

Paperback ISBN 978-1-61316-329-0
Hardcover ISBN 978-1-61316-328-3
eBook ISBN 978-1-61316-330-6

Library of Congress Control Number: 2022902497

Printed in the United States of America

9 8 7 6 5 4 3 2 1

CONTENTS

INTRODUCTION

Among aficionados of detective fiction, the term "locked room mystery" has become an inaccurate but useful catchall phrase meaning the telling of a crime that appears to be impossible. The story does not require a hermetically sealed chamber so much as a location with an utterly inaccessible murder victim. A bludgeoned, stabbed, or strangled body in the center of pristine snow or sand is just as baffling a location as a lone figure on a boat at sea, a solo airplane, or the classic locked room.

Like so much else in the world of mystery fiction, readers are indebted to Edgar Allan Poe for the invention of the locked room mystery, which happened to be the startling core of the first pure detective story ever written, "The Murders in the Rue Morgue," initially published in the April 1841 issue of *Graham's Magazine*. In this ground-breaking tale, two women are heard to be screaming and a group of neighbors race up the stairs to their apartment. They break down the locked door, the key still in the lock on the inside, to find the savagely murdered mother and daughter. The windows are closed and fastened, egress through the fireplace chimney impassable, and no loose floorboards or secret passages. Of course, the police are baffled (just as readers were then, and continue to be today, a hundred and seventy years after its original appearance). Only the detective, C.

Auguste Dupin, sees the solution, establishing another of the mainstays of the detective story: the brilliant amateur (often replaced in later stories by the private eye) who is smarter than both the criminal and the official police.

The locked room mystery, or impossible crime story, is the ultimate manifestation of the cerebral detective story. It fascinates the reader in precisely the same way that a magician is able to bring wonderment to his audience. What he demonstrates appears to be impossible. After all, young ladies, no matter how attractive and scantily clad, don't just disappear, or turn into tigers, or get sawed in half. Yet we have just seen it happen, right before our very focused eyes.

Be warned. As you read these astoundingly inventive stories, you will inevitably be disappointed, just as explanations of stage illusions exterminate the spell of magic that we experienced as we watched the impossible occur. Impossible crimes cannot be impossible, as the detective will quickly point out, because they have happened. Treasure has been stolen from a locked and guarded room or museum or library, in spite of the constant surveillance by trained policemen. A frightened victim-to-be has locked, bolted, and sealed his home because the murderer has warned him that he will die at midnight, and a brigade of officers in a cordon surrounding the house cannot prevent it.

If the mind of a diabolical genius can invent a method of robbery or murder that appears to be insoluble, then surely there must be a mind of equal brilliance that is able to penetrate the scheme and explain its every nuance. That is the detective's role and, although he appears to be explaining it all to the police and other interested parties, he is, of course, describing the scenario to the reader. The curtain that has masked the magic, that has screened the illusion, is raised, and all returns to ordinary mechanics, physics, and psychology—the stuff of everyday life.

Therefore, if you want to maintain the beauty of a magic show, refuse to listen to a magician who is willing to explain how he performed his illusion. Similarly, if the situations in these locked room mysteries have provided a delicious frisson of wonder, stop reading them as soon as you reach the denouement.

No, of course you can't do that. It is human nature to want to *know*, and the moment of clarity, when all is revealed, brings a different kind of satisfaction. Admiration replaces awe. The legerdemain achieved by the authors of the stories in this volume is, to use a word that has sadly become cheapened by overuse, awesome.

While it is true that Poe invented the locked room story (although Robert Adey, in the introduction to his monumental bibliography, *Locked Room Murders*, gives credit to a pioneering effort by the great Irish novelist Sheridan Le Fanu, claiming the honor of first story for "A Passage in the Secret History of an Irish Countess," which appeared in the November 1838 issue of *Dublin University Magazine* and was later reprinted in the posthumously published *The Purcell Papers* in 1880), there can be no argument that the greatest practitioner of this demanding form was John Dickson Carr.

Not only did Carr produce 126 novels, short stories, and radio plays under his own name and as Carter Dickson, but the range of seemingly impossible murder methods he created was so broad and varied that it simply freezes the brain to contemplate. In perhaps the most arrogant display of his command of the locked room mystery, he has his series detective, Dr. Gideon Fell, deliver a lecture to a captivated audience in his 1935 novel *The Three Coffins* (published in England as *The Hollow Man*). In this display of erudition, Fell spends fifteen pages enumerating all the ways in which a locked room does not turn out to be impenetrable after all, and in which the impossible is clearly explained. He offers scores of ideas for solutions to the most challenging puzzles in the mystery genre, tossing off in rapid succession a greater cornucopia of invention than most mystery writers will conceive in a lifetime. When he has concluded his seemingly comprehensive tutorial, he informs the attendees that none of these explanations are pertinent to the present case and heads off to conclude the investigation.

Many solutions to the feats of prestidigitation in this collection will have been covered in Fell's lecture, but the sheer inventive genius of many of the contributors will have exceeded even Carr's tour-de-force. In his brilliant history of the mystery genre, *Murder for Pleasure* (1941), Howard Haycraft warned writers of detective fiction to stay away from the locked room puzzle because "only a genius can invest it with novelty or interest today." It should be pointed out that, however well-intentioned the admonition, nearly half the stories in this volume were written after the publication date of that cornerstone history and appreciation of the literature of crime.

The locked room mystery reached its pinnacle of popularity during the Golden Age of detective fiction between the two world wars. This is when Agatha Christie flourished, and so did Dorothy L. Sayers, Ellery Queen, Clayton Rawson, R. Austin Freeman, Margery Allingham, and, of course, Carr. In those years, the emphasis, particularly in England, was on the creation and solution of a puzzle. Readers were more interested in *who* dunnit, and *how* dunnit, whereas in the more modern era a greater focus has been placed on *why* dunnit. Murder—the taking of another person's life—was a private affair and its solution demanded a ritual that was largely followed by most writers. The book or short story generally began with a fairly tranquil community (even if that community was in a big city, such as London or New York) in which all the participants knew each other. A terrible crime, usually murder, occurred, rending the social fabric. The police came to investigate, usually a single detective rather than an entire team of forensic experts, and either he (there were precious few female police officers in the detective stories of that era) would solve the mystery or show himself to be an abject fool, relying on a gifted, and frequently eccentric, amateur to arrive at a conclusion. Clues were placed judiciously throughout the story as the author challenged the reader to solve the case before the protagonist did. The true colors of the least likely suspect were then revealed and he or she was taken into custody, returning the community to its formerly peaceful state.

Many current readers don't have the patience to follow the trail of clues in a detective story in which each suspect is interviewed (interrogated is a word for later mysteries), each having doubt cast on their alibis, their relationships with the victim, and their possible motives, until all the suspects are gathered for the explanation of how the crime was committed, who perpetrated it, and it why they did it. It is not realistic and was never intended to be. It is entertainment, as all fiction is . . . or should be. Dorothy L. Sayers pointed out that people have amused themselves by creating riddles, conundrums, and puzzles of all kinds, with the apparently sole purpose being the satisfaction they give themselves by deducing a solution. Struggling with a Rubik's cube is a form of torment eliciting a tremendous sense of achievement and joy when it is solved. This is equally true of reading a good detective story, the apotheosis of which is the locked room puzzle, with the added pleasure of becoming involved with fascinating, occasionally memorable, characters, unusual backgrounds, and, when the sun is shining most brightly, told with captivating prose.

Don't read these stories on a subway train or the back seat of a car. They want to be read when you are comfortably ensconced in an easy chair or a bed piled high with pillows, at your leisure, perhaps with a cup of tea or a glass of port. Oh, heaven!

—OTTO PENZLER

ELSEWHEN
Anthony Boucher

Can a mystery writer have a greater tribute than to have the world's largest gathering of crime fiction aficionados named in his honor? Although William Anthony Parker White (1911-1968), better known under the pseudonyms he used for his career as a writer of both mystery and science fiction, Anthony Boucher and H.H. Holmes, may not be as famous as a few other Golden Age detective writers, such as Ellery Queen, John Dickson Carr, and Erle Stanley Gardner, the annual convention is called the Bouchercon. Of course, the Anthony Awards are also named for him.

Under his real name, as well as under his pseudonyms, White established a reputation as a first-rate critic of opera and literature, including general fiction, mystery, and science fiction. He also was an accomplished editor, anthologist, playwright, and an eminent translator of French, Spanish, and Portuguese, becoming the first to translate Jorge Luis Borges into English.

He wrote prolifically in the 1940s, producing at least three scripts a week for such popular radio programs as *Sherlock Holmes*, *The Adventures of Ellery Queen* and *The Case Book of Gregory Hood*. He also wrote numerous science fiction and fantasy stories, reviewed books in those genres as H.H. Holmes for the *San Francisco Chronicle* and *Chicago Sun-Times*, and produced notable anthologies in the science fiction, fantasy, and mystery genres.

As Boucher (pronounced like voucher), he served as the long-time mystery reviewer of *The New York Times* (1951-1968, with eight hundred fifty-two columns to his credit) and *Ellery Queen's Mystery Magazine* (1957-1968). He was one of the founders of the Mystery Writers of America in 1946.

"Impossible" crime stories are a joy to read and very challenging to write, but Boucher gave himself a real challenge when he set "Elsewhen" in the future, combining his skills as a science fiction writer as well as a constructor of first-rate mystery plots. Even with a time machine, you will find this a classic, fair-play mystery story.

"Elsewhen" was originally published in the December 1946 issue of *Street & Smith's Detective Story Magazine*; it was first collected in *Far and Away* (New York, Ballantine, 1955).

Elsewhen
Anthony Boucher

"MY DEAR Agatha," Mr. Partridge announced at the breakfast table, "I have invented the world's first successful time machine."

His sister showed no signs of being impressed. "I suppose this will run the electric bill up even higher," she observed.

Mr. Partridge listened meekly to the inevitable lecture. When it was over, he protested, "But, my dear, you have just listened to an announcement that no woman on earth has ever heard before. Never before in human history has anyone produced an actual working model of a time-traveling machine."

"Hm-m-m," said Agatha Partridge. "What good is it?"

"Its possibilities are untold." Mr. Partridge's pale little eyes lit up. "We can observe our pasts and perhaps even correct their errors. We can learn the secrets of the ancients. We can plot the uncharted course of the future—new conquistadors invading brave new continents of unmapped time. We can—"

"Will anyone pay money for that?"

"They will flock to me to pay it," said Mr. Partridge smugly.

His sister began to look impressed. "And how far can you travel with your time machine?"

Mr. Partridge buttered a piece of toast with absorbed concentration, but it was no use. His sister repeated the question: "How far can you go?"

"Not very far," Mr. Partridge admitted reluctantly. "In fact," he added hastily as he saw a more specific question forming, "hardly at all. And only one way. But remember," he went on, gathering courage, "the Wright brothers did not cross the Atlantic in their first model. Marconi did not launch radio with—"

Agatha's brief interest had completely subsided. "I thought so," she said. "You'd still better watch the electric bill."

It would be that way, Mr. Partridge thought, wherever he went, whomever he saw. "How far can you go?" "Hardly at all." "Good day, sir." People cannot be made to see that to move along the time line with free volitional motion for even one fraction of a second is as great a miracle as to zoom spectacularly ahead to 5900 A.D. He had, he could remember, felt disappointed at first himself—

The discovery had been made by accident. An experiment which he was working on—part of his long and fruitless attempt to re-create by modern scientific method the supposed results described in ancient alchemical works—had necessitated the setting up of a powerful magnetic field. And part of the apparatus within this field was a chronometer.

Mr. Partridge noted the time when he began his experiment. It was exactly fourteen seconds after nine thirty. And it was precisely at that moment that the tremor came. It was not a serious shock.

To one who, like Mr. Partridge, had spent the past twenty years in southern California it was hardly noticeable. But when he looked back at the chronometer, the dial read ten thirteen.

Time can pass quickly when you are absorbed in your work, but not so quickly as all that. Mr. Partridge looked at his pocket watch. It said nine thirty-one. Suddenly, in a space of seconds, the best chronometer available had gained forty-two minutes.

The more Mr. Partridge considered the matter, the more irresistibly one chain of logic forced itself upon him. The chronometer was accurate; therefore it had registered those forty-two minutes correctly. It had not registered them here and now; therefore the shock had jarred it to where it could register them. It had not moved in any of the three dimensions of space; therefore—

The chronometer had gone back in time forty-two minutes, and had registered those minutes in reaching the present again. Or was it only a matter of minutes? The chronometer was an eight-day one. Might it have been twelve hours and forty-two minutes? Forty-eight hours? Ninety-six? A hundred and ninety-two?

And why and how and—the dominant question in Mr. Partridge's mind—could the same device be made to work with a living being?

It would be fruitless to relate in detail the many experiments which Mr. Partridge eagerly performed to verify and check his discovery. They were purely empirical in nature, for Mr. Partridge was that type of inventor who is short on theory but long on gadgetry. He did frame a very rough working hypothesis—that the sudden shock had caused the magnetic field to rotate into the temporal dimension, where it set up a certain—he groped for words—a certain negative potential of entropy, which drew things backward in time. But he would leave the doubtless highly debatable theory to the academicians. What he must do was perfect the machine, render it generally usable, and then burst forth upon an astonished world as Harrison Partridge, the first time traveler. His dry little ego glowed and expanded at the prospect.

There were the experiments in artificial shock which produced synthetically the earthquake effect. There were the experiments with the white mice which proved that the journey through time was harmless to life. There were the experiments with the chronometer which established that the time traversed varied directly as the square of the power expended on the electromagnet.

But these experiments also established that the time elapsed had not been twelve hours nor any multiple thereof, but simply forty-two minutes. And with the equipment at his disposal, it was impossible for Mr. Partridge to stretch that period any further than a trifle under two hours.

This, Mr. Partridge told himself, was ridiculous. Time travel at such short range, and only to the past, entailed no possible advantages. Oh, perhaps some piddling ones—once, after the mice had convinced him that he could safely venture himself, he had a lengthy piece of calculation which he wished to finish before dinner. An hour was simply not time enough for it; so at six o'clock he moved himself back to five again, and by working two hours in the space from five to six finished his task easily by dinner time. And one evening when, in his preoccupation, he had forgotten his favorite radio quiz program until it was ending, it was simplicity itself to go back to the beginning and comfortably hear it through.

But though such trifling uses as this might be an important part of the work of the time machine once it was established— possibly the strongest commercial selling point for inexpensive home sets—they were not spectacular or startling enough to make the reputation of the machine and—more important—the reputation of Harrison Partridge.

The Great Harrison Partridge would have untold wealth. He could pension off his sister Agatha and never have to see her again.

He would have untold prestige and glamor, despite his fat and his baldness, and the beautiful and aloof Faith Preston would fall into his arms like a ripe plum. He would—

It was while he was indulging in one of these dreams of power that Faith Preston herself entered his workshop. She was wearing a white sports dress and looking so fresh and immaculate that the whole room seemed to glow with her presence.

"I came out here before I saw your sister," she said. Her voice was as cool and bright as her dress. "I wanted you to be the first to know. Simon and I are going to be married next month."

Mr. Partridge never remembered what was said after that. He imagined that she made her usual comments about the shocking disarray of his shop and her usual polite inquiries as to his current researches. He imagined that he offered the conventional good wishes and extended his congratulations, too, to that damned young whippersnapper Simon Ash. But all his thoughts were that he wanted her and needed her and that the great, the irresistible Harrison Partridge must come into being before next month.

Money. That was it. Money. With money he could build the tremendous machinery necessary to carry a load of power—and money was needed for that power, too—that would produce truly impressive results. To travel back even as much as a quarter of a century would be enough to dazzle the world. To appear at the Versailles peace conference, say, and expound to the delegates the inevitable results of their too lenient—or too strict?—terms. Or with unlimited money to course down the centuries, down the millennia, bringing back lost arts, forgotten secrets—

"Hm-m-m!" said Agatha. "Still mooning after that girl? Don't be an old fool." He had not seen Agatha come in. He did not quite see her now. He saw a sort of vision of a cornucopia that would give him money that would give him the apparatus that would give him his time machine that would give him success that would give him Faith.

"If you must moon instead of working—if indeed you call this work—you might at least turn off a few switches," Agatha snapped. "Do you think we're made of money?"

Mechanically he obeyed.

"It makes you sick," Agatha droned on, "when you think how some people spend their money. Cousin Stanley! Hiring this Simon Ash as a secretary for nothing on earth but to look after his library and his collections. So much money he can't do anything but waste it! And all Great-uncle Max's money coming to him too, when we could use it so nicely. If only it weren't for Cousin Stanley, I'd be an heiress. And then—"

Mr. Partridge was about to observe that even as an heiress Agatha would doubtless have been the same intolerant old maid. But two thoughts checked his tongue. One was the sudden surprising revelation that even Agatha had her inner yearnings, too. And the other was an overwhelming feeling of gratitude to her.

"Yes," Mr. Partridge repeated slowly. "If it weren't for Cousin Stanley—"

By means as simple as this, murderers are made.

The chain of logic was so strong that moral questions hardly entered into the situation.

Great-uncle Max was infinitely old. That he should live another year was out of the question. And if his son Stanley were to pre-decease him, then Harrison and Agatha Partridge would be his only living relatives. And Maxwell Harrison was as infinitely rich as he was infinitely old.

Therefore Stanley must die, and his death must be accomplished with a maximum of personal safety. The means for that safety were at hand. For the one completely practical purpose of a short-range time machine, Mr. Partridge had suddenly realized, was to provide an alibi for murder.

The chief difficulty was in contriving a portable version of the machine which would operate over a considerable period of time. The first model had a traveling range of two minutes. But by the end of the week, Mr. Partridge had constructed a portable time machine which was good for forty-five minutes. He needed nothing more save a sharp knife. There was, Mr. Partridge thought, something crudely horrifying about guns.

That Friday afternoon he entered Cousin Stanley's library at five o'clock. This was an hour when the eccentric man of wealth always devoted himself to quiet and scholarly contemplation of his treasures. The butler, Bracket, had been reluctant to announce him, but "Tell my cousin," Mr. Partridge said, "that I have discovered a new entry for his bibliography."

The most recent of Cousin Stanley's collecting manias was fiction based upon factual murders. He had already built up the definitive library on the subject. Soon he intended to publish the definitive bibliography. And the promise of a new item was an assured open-sesame.

The ponderous gruff joviality of Stanley Harrison's greeting took no heed of the odd apparatus he carried. Everyone knew that Mr. Partridge was a crackpot inventor.

"Bracket tells me you've got something for me," Cousin Stanley boomed. "Glad to hear it. Have a drink? What is it?"

"No thank you." Something in Mr. Partridge rebelled at accepting the hospitality of his victim. "A Hungarian friend of mine was mentioning a novel about one Bela Kiss."

"Kiss?" Cousin Stanley's face lit up with a broad beam. "Splendid! Never could see why no one used him before. Woman killer. Landru type. Always fascinating. Kept 'em in empty gasoline tins. Never could have been caught if there hadn't been a gasoline shortage. Constable thought he was hoarding, checked the tins, found corpses. Beautiful! Now if you'll give me the details—"

Cousin Stanley, pencil poised over a P-slip, leaned over the desk. And Mr. Partridge struck.

He had checked the anatomy of the blow, just as he had checked the name of an obscure but interesting murderer. The knife went truly home, and there was a gurgle and the terrible spastic twitch of dying flesh.

Mr. Partridge was now an heir and a murderer, but he had time to be conscious of neither fact. He went through his carefully re-hearsed motions, his mind numb and blank. He latched the win-dows of the library and locked each door. This was to be an impos-sible crime, one that could never conceivably be proved on him or on any innocent.

Mr. Partridge stood beside the corpse in the midst of the per-fectly locked room. It was four minutes past five. He screamed twice, very loudly, in an unrecognizably harsh voice. Then he plugged his portable instrument into a floor outlet and turned a switch.

It was four nineteen. Mr. Partridge unplugged his machine. The room was empty and the door open.

Mr. Partridge knew his way reasonably well about his cousin's house. He got out without meeting anyone. He tucked the ma-chine into the rumble seat of his car and drove off to Faith Pres-ton's. Toward the end of his long journey across town he carefully drove through a traffic light and received a citation noting the time as four-fifty. He reached Faith's at four fifty-four, ten minutes be-fore the murder he had just committed.

Simon Ash had been up all Thursday night cataloging Stan-ley Harrison's latest acquisitions. Still he had risen at his usual hour that Friday to get through the morning's mail before his luncheon date with Faith. By four thirty that afternoon he was asleep on his feet.

He knew that his employer would be coming into the library in half an hour. And Stanley Harrison liked solitude for his daily five o'clock gloating and meditation. But the secretary's work desk was hidden around a corner of the library's stacks, and no other physical hunger can be quite so dominantly compelling as the need for sleep.

Simon Ash's shaggy blond head sank onto the desk. His sleep-heavy hand shoved a pile of cards to the floor, and his mind only faintly registered the thought that they would all have to be alphabetized again. He was too sleepy to think of anything but pleasant things, like the sailboat at Balboa which brightened his weekends, or the hiking trip in the Sierras planned for his next vacation, or above all Faith. Faith the fresh and lovely and perfect, who would be his next month—

There was a smile on Simon's rugged face as he slept. But he woke with a harsh scream ringing in his head. He sprang to his feet and looked out from the stacks into the library.

The dead hulk that slumped over the desk with the hilt protruding from its back was unbelievable, but even more incredible was the other spectacle. There was a man. His back was toward Simon, but he seemed faintly familiar. He stood close to a complicated piece of gadgetry. There was the click of a switch.

Then there was nothing.

Nothing in the room at all but Simon Ash and an infinity of books. And their dead owner.

Ash ran to the desk. He tried to lift Stanley Harrison, tried to draw out the knife, then realized how hopeless was any attempt to revive life in that body. He reached for the phone, then stopped as he heard the loud knocking on the door.

Over the raps came the butler's voice. "Mr. Harrison! Are you all right, sir?" A pause, more knocking, and then, "Mr. Harrison! Let me in, sir! Are you all right?"

Simon raced to the door. It was locked, and he wasted almost a minute groping for the key at his feet, while the butler's entreaties became more urgent. At last Simon opened the door.

Bracket stared at him—stared at his sleep-red eyes, his blood-red hands, and beyond him at what sat at the desk. "Mr. Ash, sir," the butler gasped. "What have you done?"

Faith Preston was home, of course. No such essential element of Mr. Partridge's plan could have been left to chance. She worked best in the late afternoons, she said, when she was getting hungry for dinner; and she was working hard this week on some entries for a national contest in soap carving.

The late-afternoon sun was bright in her room, which you might call her studio if you were politely disposed, her garret if you were not. It picked out the few perfect touches of color in the scanty furnishings and converted them into bright aureoles surrounding the perfect form of Faith.

The radio was playing softly. She worked best to music, and that, too, was an integral portion of Mr. Partridge's plan.

Six minutes of unmemorable small talk—What are you working on? How lovely! And what have you been doing lately? Pottering around as usual. And the plans for the wedding?—and then Mr. Partridge held up a pleading hand for silence.

"When you hear the tone," the radio announced, "the time will be exactly five seconds before five o'clock."

"I forgot to wind my watch," Mr. Partridge observed casually. "I've been wondering all day exactly what time it was." He set his perfectly accurate watch.

He took a long breath. And now at last he knew that he was a new man. He was at last the Great Harrison Partridge.

"What's the matter?" Faith asked. "You look funny. Could I make you some tea?"

"No. Nothing. I'm all right." He walked around behind her and looked over her shoulder at the graceful nude emerging from her imprisonment in a cake of soap. "Exquisite, my dear," he observed. "Exquisite."

"I'm glad you like it. I'm never happy with female nudes; I don't think women sculptors ever are. But I wanted to try it."

Mr. Partridge ran a dry hot finger along the front of the soapen nymph. "A delightful texture," he remarked. "Almost as delightful as—" His tongue left the speech unfinished, but his hand rounded out the thought along Faith's cool neck and cheek.

"Why, Mr. Partridge!" She laughed.

The laugh was too much. One does not laugh at the Great Harrison Partridge, time traveler and perfect murderer. There was nothing in his plan that called for what followed. But something outside of any plans brought him to his knees, forced his arms around Faith's lithe body, pressed tumultuous words of incoherent ardor from his unwonted lips.

He saw fear growing in her eyes. He saw her hand dart out in instinctive defense and he wrested the knife from it. Then his own eyes glinted as he looked at the knife. It was little, ridiculously little. You could never plunge it through a man's back. But it was sharp—a throat, the artery of a wrist—

His muscles had relaxed for an instant. In that moment of non-vigilance, Faith had wrested herself free. She did not look backward. He heard the clatter of her steps down the stairs, and for a fraction of time the Great Harrison Partridge vanished and Mr. Partridge knew only fear. If he had aroused her hatred, if she should not swear to his alibi—

The fear was soon over. He knew that no motives of enmity could cause Faith to swear to anything but the truth. She was honest. And the enmity itself would vanish when she realized what manner of man had chosen her for his own.

It was not the butler who opened the door to Faith. It was a uniformed policeman, who said, "Whaddaya want here?"

"I've got to see Simon . . . Mr. Ash," she blurted out.

The officer's expression changed. "C'mon," and he beckoned her down the long hall.

The tall young man in plain clothes said, "My name is Jackson. Won't you sit down? Cigaret?" She waved the pack away nervously. "Hinkle says you wanted to speak to Mr. Ash?"

"Yes, I—"

"Are you Miss Preston? His fiancée?"

"Yes." Her eyes widened. "How did you—Oh, has something happened to Simon?"

The young officer looked unhappy. "I'm afraid something has. Though he's perfectly safe at the moment. You see, he—Damn it all, I never have been able to break such news gracefully."

The uniformed officer broke in. "They took him down to headquarters, miss. You see, it looks like he bumped off his boss."

Faith did not quite faint, but the world was uncertain for a few minutes. She hardly heard Lieutenant Jackson's explanations or the message of comfort that Simon had left for her. She simply held very tight to her chair until the ordinary outlines of things came back and she could swallow again.

"Simon is innocent," she said firmly.

"I hope he is." Jackson sounded sincere. "I've never enjoyed pinning a murder on as decent-seeming a fellow as your fiancé. But the case, I'm afraid, is too clear. If he is innocent, he'll have to tell us a more plausible story than his first one. Murderers that turn a switch and vanish into thin air are not highly regarded by most juries."

Faith rose. The world was firm again, and one fact was clear. "Simon is innocent," she repeated. "And I'm going to prove that. Will you please tell me where I can get a detective?"

The uniformed officer laughed. Jackson started to, but hesitated. "Of course, Miss Preston, the city's paying my salary under the impression that I'm one. But I see what you mean: You want a freer investigator, who won't be hampered by such considerations as the official viewpoint, or even the facts of the case. Well, it's your privilege."

"Thank you. And how do I go about finding out?"

"Acting as an employment agency's a little out of my line. But rather than see you tie up with some shyster shamus, I'll make a recommendation, a man I've worked with, or against, on a half dozen cases. And I think this set-up is just impossible enough to appeal to him. He likes lost causes."

"Lost?" It is a dismal word.

"And in fairness I should add they aren't always lost after he tackles them. The name's O'Breen—Fergus O'Breen."

Mr. Partridge dined out that night. He could not face the harshness of Agatha's tongue. After dinner he made a round of the bars on the Strip and played the pleasant game of "If only they knew who was sitting beside them." He felt like Harun-al-Rashid, and liked the glow of the feeling.

On his way home he bought the next morning's *Times* at an intersection and pulled over to the curb to examine it. He had expected sensational headlines on the mysterious murder which had the police completely baffled. Instead he read:

SECRETARY SLAYS EMPLOYER

After a moment of shock the Great Harrison Partridge was himself again. He had not intended this. He would not willingly cause unnecessary pain to anyone. But lesser individuals who obstruct the plans of the great must take their medicine.

Mr. Partridge drove home, contented. He could spend the night on the cot in his workshop and thus see that much the less of Agatha. He clicked on the workshop light and froze.

There was a man standing by the time machine. The original large machine. Mr. Partridge's feeling of superhuman self-confidence was enormous but easily undermined, like a vast balloon that needs only the smallest pin prick to shatter it. For a moment he envisioned a scientific master mind of the police who had deduced his method, tracked him here, and discovered his invention.

Then the figure turned.

Mr. Partridge's terror was only slightly lessened. For the figure was that of Mr. Partridge. There was a nightmare instant when he thought of Doppelgänger, Poe's William Wilson, of dissociated personalities, of Dr. Jekyll and Mr. Hyde. Then this other Mr. Partridge cried aloud and hurried from the room, and the entering one collapsed.

A trough must follow a crest. And now blackness was the inexorable aftermath of Mr. Partridge's elation. His successful murder, his ardor with Faith, his evening as Harun-al-Rashid, all vanished. He heard horrible noises in the room, and realized only after minutes that they were his own sobs.

Finally he pulled himself to his feet. He bathed his face in cold water from the sink, but still terror gnawed at him. Only one thing could reassure him. Only one thing could still convince him that he was the Great Harrison Partridge. And that was his noble machine. He touched it, caressed it as one might a fine and dearly loved horse.

Mr. Partridge was nervous, and he had been drinking more than his frugal customs allowed. His hand brushed the switch. He looked up and saw himself entering the door. He cried aloud and hurried from the room.

In the cool night air he slowly understood. He had accidentally sent himself back to the time he entered the room, so that upon entering he had seen himself. There was nothing more to it than that. But he made a careful mental note: Always take care, when using the machine, to avoid returning to a time and place where you already are. Never meet yourself. The dangers of psychological shock are too great.

Mr. Partridge felt better now. He had frightened himself, had he? Well, he would not be the last to tremble in fear of the Great Harrison Partridge.

Fergus O'Breen, the detective recommended—if you could call it that—by the police lieutenant, had his office in a ramshackle old building at Second and Spring. There were two, she imagined they were clients, in the waiting room ahead of Faith. One looked like the most sodden type of Skid Row loafer, and the elegant disarray of the other could mean nothing but the lower reaches of the upper layers of Hollywood.

The detective, when Faith finally saw him, inclined in costume toward the latter, but he wore sports clothes as though they were pleasantly comfortable, rather than as the badge of a caste. He was a thin young man, with sharpish features and very red hair. What you noticed most were his eyes—intensely green and alive with a restless curiosity. They made you feel that his work would never end until that curiosity had been satisfied.

He listened in silence to Faith's story, not moving save to make an occasional note. He was attentive and curious, but Faith's spirits sank as she saw the curiosity in the green eyes deaden to hopelessness. When she was through, he rose, lit a cigaret, and began pacing about the narrow inner office.

"I think better this way," he apologized. "I hope you don't

mind. But what have I got to think about? The facts you've told me are better than a signed confession for any jury."

"But Simon is innocent," Faith insisted. "I know him, Mr. O'Breen. It isn't possible that he could have done a thing like that."

"I understand how you feel. But what have we got to go on besides your feelings? I'm not saying they're wrong; I'm trying to show you how the police and the court would look at it."

"But there wasn't any reason for Simon to kill Mr. Harrison. He had a good job. He liked it. We were going to get married. Now he hasn't any job or . . . or anything."

"I know." The detective continued to pace. "That's the one point you've got—absence of motive. But they've convicted without motive before this. And rightly enough. Anything can be a motive. The most outrageous and fascinating French murder since Landru was committed because the electric toaster didn't work right that morning. But let's look at motives. Mr. Harrison was a wealthy man; where does all that money go?"

"Simon helped draft his will. It all goes to libraries and foundations and things. A little to the servants, of course—"

"A little can turn the trick. But no near relatives?"

"His father's still alive. He's terribly old. But he's so rich himself that it'd be silly to leave him anything."

Fergus snapped his fingers. "Max Harrison! Of course. The superannuated robber-baron, to put it politely, who's been due to die any time these past ten years. And leave a mere handful of millions. There's a motive for you."

"How so?"

"The murderer could profit from Stanley Harrison's death, not directly if all his money goes to foundations, but indirectly from his father. Combination of two classic motives—profit and elimination. Who's next in line for old man Harrison's fortune?"

"I'm not sure. But I do know two people who are sort of second cousins or something. I think they're the only living relatives. Agatha and Harrison Partridge."

Fergus' eyes were brightening again. "At least it's a lead. Simon Ash had no motive and one Harrison Partridge had a honey. Which proves nothing, but gives you some place to start."

"Only—" Faith protested. "Only Mr. Partridge couldn't possibly have done it either."

Fergus stopped pacing. "Look, madam. I am willing to grant the unassailable innocence of one suspect on a client's word. Otherwise I'd never get clients. But if every individual who comes up is going to turn out to be someone in whose pureness of soul you have implicit faith and—"

"It isn't that. Not just that. The murder was just after five o'clock, the butler says. And Mr. Partridge was with me then, and I live way across town from Mr. Harrison's."

"You're sure of the time?"

"We heard the five o'clock radio signal and he set his watch." Her voice was troubled and she tried not to remember the awful minutes afterward.

"Did he make a point of it?"

"Well . . . we were talking and he stopped and held up his hand and we listened to the bong."

"Hm-m-m." This statement seemed to strike the detective especially. "Well, there's still the sister. And anyway, the Partridges give me a point of departure, which is what I needed."

Faith looked at him hopefully. "Then you'll take the case?"

"I'll take it. God knows why. I don't want to raise your hopes, because if ever I saw an unpromising set-up it's this. But I'll take it. I think it's because I can't resist the pleasure of having a detective lieutenant shove a case into my lap."

"Bracket, was it usual for that door to be locked when Mr. Harrison was in the library?"

The butler's manner was imperfect; he could not decide whether a hired detective was a gentleman or a servant. "No," he said, politely enough but without a "sir." "No, it was most unusual."

"Did you notice if it was locked earlier?"

"It was not. I showed a visitor in shortly before the . . . before this dreadful thing happened."

"A visitor?" Fergus' eyes glinted. He began to have visions of all the elaborate possibilities of locking doors from the outside so that they seem locked on the inside. "And when was this?"

"Just on five o'clock, I thought. But the gentleman called here today to offer his sympathy, and he remarked, when I mentioned the subject, that he believed it to have been earlier."

"And who was this gentleman?"

"Mr. Harrison Partridge."

Hell, thought Fergus. There goes another possibility. It must have been much earlier if he was at Faith Preston's by five. And you can't tamper with radio time signals as you might with a clock. However—"Notice anything odd about Mr. Partridge? Anything in his manner?"

"Yesterday? No, I did not. He was carrying some curious contraption—I hardly noticed what. I imagine it was some recent invention of his which he wished to show to Mr. Harrison."

"He's an inventor, this Partridge? But you said yesterday. Anything odd about him today?"

"I don't know. It's difficult to describe. But there was something about him as though he had changed—grown, perhaps."

"Grown up?"

"No. Just grown."

"Now, Mr. Ash, this man you claim you saw—"

"Claim! Damn it, O'Breen, don't you believe me either?"

"Easy does it. The main thing for you is that Miss Preston believes you, and I'd say that's a lot. Now this man you saw, if that makes you any happier in this jail, did he remind you of anyone?"

"I don't know. It's bothered me. I didn't get a good look, but there was something familiar—"

"You say he had some sort of machine beside him?"

Simon Ash was suddenly excited. "You've got it. That's it."

"That's what?"

"Who it was. Or who I thought it was. Mr. Partridge. He's some sort of a cousin of Mr. Harrison's. Screwball inventor."

"Miss Preston, I'll have to ask you more questions. Too many sign-posts keep pointing one way, and even if that way's a blind alley I've got to go up it. When Mr. Partridge called on you yesterday afternoon, what did he do to you?"

"Do to me?" Faith's voice wavered. "What on earth do you mean?"

"It was obvious from your manner earlier that there was some-thing about that scene you wanted to forget."

"He—Oh, no, I can't Must I tell you, Mr. O'Breen?"

"Simon Ash says the jail is not bad after what he's heard of jails, but still—"

"All right, I'll tell you. But it was strange. I . . . I suppose I've known for a long time that Mr. Partridge was—well, you might say in love with me. But he's so much older than I am and he's very quiet and never said anything about it and—well, there it was, and I never gave it much thought one way or another. But yesterday— It was as though . . . as though he were possessed. All at once it seemed to burst out and there he was making love to me. Fright-fully, horribly, I couldn't stand it. I ran away. That's all there was to it. But it was terrible."

"You pitched me a honey this time, Andy."

Lieutenant Jackson grinned. "Thought you'd appreciate it, Fergus."

"But look: What have you got against Ash but the physical set-up of a locked room? The oldest cliché in murderous fiction, and not unheard of in fact."

"Show me how to unlock this one and your Mr. Ash is a free man."

"Set that aside for the moment. But look at my suspect, whom we will call, for the sake of novelty, X. X is a mild-mannered, inoffensive man who stands to gain several million by Harrison's death. He shows up at the library just before the murder. He's a crackpot inventor, and he has one of his gadgets with him. He shows an alibi-conscious awareness of time. He tries to get the butler to think he called earlier. He calls a witness' attention ostentatiously to a radio time signal. And most important of all, psychologically, he changes. He stops being mild-mannered and inoffensive. He goes on the make for a girl with physical violence. The butler describes him as a different man; he's grown."

Jackson drew a note pad toward him. "Your X sounds worth questioning, to say the least. But this reticence isn't like you, Fergus. Why all this innuendo? Why aren't you telling me to get out of here and arrest him?"

Fergus was not quite his cocky self. "Because you see, that alibi I mentioned—well, it's good. I can't crack it. It's perfect."

Lieutenant Jackson shoved the pad away. "Run away and play," he said wearily.

"It couldn't be phony at the other end?" Fergus urged. "Some gadget planted to produce those screams at five o'clock to give a fake time for the murder?"

Jackson shook his head. "Harrison finished tea around four thirty. Stomach analysis shows the food had been digested just about a half hour. No, he died at five o'clock, all right."

"X's alibi's perfect, then," Fergus repeated. "Unless . . . unless—" His green eyes blinked with amazed realization. "Oh, my dear God—" he said softly.

Mr. Partridge was finding life pleasant to lead. Of course this was only a transitional stage. At present he was merely the—what was the transitional stage between cocoon and fully developed insect? Larva? Imago? Pupa? Outside of his own electro-inventive field, Mr. Partridge was not a well-informed man. That must be remedied. But let the metaphor go. Say simply that he was now in the transition between the meek worm that had been Mr. Partridge and the Great Harrison Partridge who would emerge triumphant when Great-uncle Max died and Faith forgot that poor foolish doomed young man.

Even Agatha he could tolerate more easily in this pleasant state, although he had nonetheless established permanent living quarters in his workroom. She had felt her own pleasure at the prospect of being an heiress, but had expressed it most properly by buying sumptuous mourning for Cousin Stanley—the most expensive clothes that she had bought in the past decade. And her hard edges were possibly softening a little—or was that the pleasing haze, almost like that of drunkenness, which now tended to soften all hard edges for Mr. Partridge's delighted eyes?

It was in the midst of some such reverie as this that Mr. Partridge, lolling idly in his workshop with an unaccustomed tray of whiskey, ice and siphon beside him, casually overheard the radio announce the result of the fourth race at Hialeah and noted abstractedly that a horse named Karabali had paid forty-eight dollars and sixty cents on a two-dollar ticket He had almost forgotten the only half registered fact when the phone rang.

He answered, and a grudging voice said, "You can sure pick 'em. That's damned near five grand you made on Karabali."

Mr. Partridge fumbled with vocal noises.

The voice went on, "What shall I do with it? Want to pick it up tonight or—"

Mr. Partridge had been making incredibly rapid mental calculations. "Leave it in my account for the moment," he said firmly. "Oh, and—I'm afraid I've mislaid your telephone number."

"Trinity 2897. Got any more hunches now?"

"Not at the moment. I'll let you know."

Mr. Partridge replaced the receiver and poured himself a stiff drink. When he had downed it, he went to the machine and traveled two hours back. He returned to the telephone, dialed TR 2897, and said, "I wish to place a bet on the fourth race at Hialeah."

The same voice said, "And who're you?"

"Partridge. Harrison Partridge."

"Look, brother. I don't take bets by phone unless I see some cash first, see?"

Mr. Partridge hastily recalculated. As a result the next half hour was as packed with action as the final moments of his great plan. He learned about accounts, he ascertained the bookmaker's address, he hurried to his bank and drew out an impressive five hundred dollars which he could ill spare, and he opened his account and placed a two-hundred-dollar bet which excited nothing but a badly concealed derision.

Then he took a long walk and mused over the problem. He recalled happening on a story once in some magazine which proved that you could not use knowledge from the future of the outcome of races to make your fortune, because by interfering with your bet you would change the odds and alter the future. But he was not plucking from the future; he was going back into the past. The odds he had heard were already affected by what he had done. From his subjective point of view, he learned the result of his actions before he performed them. But in the objective physical temporospatial world, he performed those actions quite normally and correctly before their results.

Mr. Partridge stopped dead on the sidewalk and a strolling couple ran headlong into him. He scarcely noticed the collision. He had had a dreadful thought. The sole acknowledged motive for his murder of Cousin Stanley had been to secure money for his researches. Now he learned that his machine, even in its present imperfect form, could provide him with untold money.

He had never needed to murder at all.

"My dearest Maureen," Fergus announced at the breakfast table, "I have discovered the world's first successful time machine."

His sister showed no signs of being impressed. "Have some more tomato juice," she suggested. "Want some tabasco in it? I didn't know that the delusions could survive into the hangover."

"But Macushla," Fergus protested, "you've just listened to an announcement that no woman on earth has ever heard before."

"Fergus O'Breen, Mad Scientist." Maureen shook her head. "It isn't a role I'd cast you for. Sorry."

"If you'd listen before you crack wise, I said 'discovered.' Not 'invented.' It's the damnedest thing that's ever happened to me in business. It hit me in a flash while I was talking to Andy. It's the perfect and only possible solution to a case. And who will ever believe me? Do you wonder that I went out and saturated myself last night?"

Maureen frowned. "You *mean* this?"

"It's the McCoy. Listen." And he briefly outlined the case. "Now what sticks out like a sore thumb is this: Harrison Partridge establishing an alibi. The radio time signal, the talk with the butler—I'll even lay odds that the murderer himself gave those screams so there'd be no question as to time of death. Then you rub up against the fact that the alibi, like the horrendous dream of the young girl from Peru, is perfectly true.

"But what does an alibi mean? It's my own nomination for the most misused word in the language. It's come to mean a disproof, an excuse. But strictly it means nothing but *elsewhere*. You know the classic gag: 'I wasn't there, this isn't the woman, and, anyway, she gave in.' Well, of those three redundant excuses, only the first is an alibi, an *elsewhere* statement. Now Partridge's claim of being elsewhere is true enough. And even if we could remove him from elsewhere and put him literally on the spot, he could say: 'I couldn't have left the room after the murder; the doors were all locked on the inside.' Sure he couldn't—not *at that time*. And his excuse is not an *elsewhere*, but an *elsewhen*."

Maureen refilled his coffee cup and her own. "Hush up a minute and let me think it over." At last she nodded slowly. "And he's an eccentric inventor and when the butler saw him he was carrying one of his gadgets."

"Which he still had when Simon Ash saw him vanish. He committed the murder, locked the doors, went back in time, walked out through them in their unlocked past, and went off to hear the five o'clock radio bong at Faith Preston's."

"But you can't try to sell the police on that. Not even Andy."

"I know. Damn it, I know."

"What are you going to do?"

"I'm going to see Mr. Harrison Partridge. And I'm going to ask for an encore."

"Quite an establishment you've got here," Fergus observed to the plump bald little inventor.

Mr. Partridge smiled courteously. "I amuse myself with my small experiments," he admitted.

"I'm afraid I'm not much aware of the wonders of modern science. I'm looking forward to the more spectacular marvels, spaceships for instance, or time machines. But that wasn't what I came to talk about. Miss Preston tells me you're a friend of hers. I'm sure you're in sympathy with this attempt of hers to free young Ash."

"Oh, naturally. Most naturally. Anything that I can do to be of assistance—"

"It's just the most routine sort of question, but I'm groping for a lead. Now, aside from Ash and the butler, you seem to have been the last person to see Harrison alive. Could you tell me anything about him? How was he?"

"Perfectly normal, so far as I could observe. We talked about a new item which I had unearthed for his bibliography, and he expressed some small dissatisfaction with Ash's cataloging of late. I believe they had had words on the matter earlier."

"Bracket says you had one of your inventions with you?"

"Yes, a new, I thought, and highly improved frame for photostating rare books. My cousin, however, pointed out that the same improvements had recently been made by an Austrian émigré manufacturer. I abandoned the idea and reluctantly took apart my model."

"A shame. But that's part of the inventor's life, isn't it?"

"All too true. Was there anything else you wished to ask me?"

"No. Nothing really." There was an awkward pause. The smell of whiskey was in the air, but Mr. Partridge proffered no hospitality. "Funny the results a murder will have, isn't it? To think how this frightful fact will benefit cancer research."

"Cancer research?" Mr. Partridge wrinkled his brows. "I did not know that that was among Stanley's beneficiaries."

"Not your cousin's, no. But Miss Preston tells me that old Max Harrison has decided that since his only direct descendant is dead, his fortune might as well go to the world. He's planning to set up a medical foundation to rival Rockefeller's, and specializing in cancer. I know his lawyer slightly; he mentioned he's going out there tomorrow."

"Indeed," said Mr. Partridge evenly.

Fergus paced. "If you can think of anything, Mr. Partridge, let me know. This seems like the perfect crime at last. A magnificent piece of work, if you can look at it like that." He looked around the room. "Excellent small workshop you've got here. You can imagine almost anything coming out of it."

"Even," Mr. Partridge ventured, "your spaceships and time machines?"

"Hardly a spaceship," said Fergus.

Mr. Partridge smiled as the young detective departed. He had, he thought, carried off a difficult interview in a masterly fashion.

How neatly he had slipped in that creative bit about Stanley's dissatisfaction with Ash! How brilliantly he had improvised a plausible excuse for the machine he was carrying!

Not that the young man could have suspected anything. It was patently the most routine visit. It was almost a pity that this was the case. How pleasant it would be to fence with a detective—master against master. To have a Javert, a Porfir, a Maigret on his trail and to admire the brilliance with which the Great Harrison Partridge should baffle him.

Perhaps the perfect criminal should be suspected, even known, and yet unattainable—

The pleasure of this parrying encounter confirmed him in the belief that had grown in him overnight. It is true that it was a pity that Stanley Harrison had died needlessly. Mr. Partridge's reasoning had slipped for once; murder for profit had not been an essential part of the plan.

And yet what great work had ever been accomplished without death? Does not the bell ring the truer for the blood of the hapless workmen? Did not the ancients wisely believe that greatness must be founded upon a sacrifice? Not self- sacrifice, in the stupid Christian perversion of that belief, but a true sacrifice of another's flesh and blood.

So Stanley Harrison was the needful sacrifice from which should arise the Great Harrison Partridge. And were its effects not already visible? Would he be what he was today, would he so much as have emerged from the cocoon, purely by virtue of his discovery?

No, it was his great and irretrievable deed, the perfection of his crime, that had molded him. In blood is greatness.

That ridiculous young man, prating of the perfection of the crime and never dreaming that—

Mr. Partridge paused and reviewed the conversation. There had twice been that curious insistence upon time machines. Then he had said—what was it?—"The crime was a magnificent piece of work," and then, "You can imagine almost anything coming out of this workshop." And the surprising news of Great-uncle Max's new will—

Mr. Partridge smiled happily. He had been unpardonably dense. Here was his Javert, his Porfir. The young detective did indeed suspect him. And the reference to Max had been a temptation, a trap. The detective could not know how unnecessary that fortune had now become. He had thought to lure him into giving away his hand by an attempt at another crime.

And yet, was any fortune ever unnecessary? And a challenge like that—so direct a challenge—could one resist it?

Mr. Partridge found himself considering all the difficulties. Great-uncle Max would have to be murdered today, if he planned on seeing his lawyer tomorrow. The sooner the better. Perhaps his habitual after-lunch siesta would be the best time. He was always alone then, dozing in his favorite corner of that large estate in the hills.

Bother! A snag. No electric plugs there. The portable model was out. And yet—

Yes, of course. It could be done the other way. With Stanley, he had committed his crime, then gone back and prepared his alibi. But here he could just as well establish the alibi, then go back and commit the murder, sending himself back by the large machine here with wider range. No need for the locked-room effect. That was pleasing, but not essential.

An alibi for one o'clock in the afternoon. He did not care to use Faith again. He did not want to see her in his larval stage. He might obtain another traffic ticket. Surely the police would be as good as—

The police. But how perfect. Ideal. To go to headquarters and ask to see the detective working on the Harrison case. Tell him, as a remembered afterthought, about Cousin Stanley's supposed quarrel with Ash. Be with him at the time Great-uncle Max is to be murdered.

At twelve thirty Mr. Partridge left his house for the central police station.

Fergus could hear the old man's snores from his coign of vigilance. Getting into Maxwell Harrison's hermitlike retreat had been a simple job. The newspapers had for years so thoroughly covered the old boy's peculiarities that you knew in advance all you needed to know—his daily habits, his loathing for bodyguards, his favorite spot for napping.

The sun was warm and the hills were peaceful. There was a purling stream at the deep bottom of the gully beside Fergus. Old Maxwell Harrison did well to sleep in such perfect solitude.

Fergus was on his third cigarette before he heard a sound. It was a very little sound, the turning of a pebble, perhaps; but here in this loneliness any sound that was not a snore or a stream seemed infinitely loud.

Fergus flipped his cigarette into the depths of the gully and moved, as noiselessly as was possible, toward the sound, screening himself behind scraggly bushes.

The sight, even though expected, was nonetheless startling in this quiet retreat: a plump bald man of middle age advancing on tiptoe with a long knife gleaming in his upraised hand.

Fergus flung himself forward. His left hand caught the knife-brandishing wrist and his right pinioned Mr. Partridge's other arm behind him. The face of Mr. Partridge, that had been so bland a mask of serene exaltation as he advanced to his prey, twisted itself into something between rage and terror.

His body twisted itself, too. It was an instinctive, untrained movement, but timed so nicely by accident that it tore his knife hand free from Fergus' grip and allowed it to plunge downward.

The twist of Fergus' body was deft and conscious, but it was not quite enough to avoid a stinging flesh wound in the shoulder. He felt warm blood trickling down his back. Involuntarily he released his grip on Mr. Partridge's other arm.

Mr. Partridge hesitated for a moment, as though uncertain whether his knife should taste of Great-uncle Max or first dispose of Fergus. The hesitation was understandable, but fatal. Fergus sprang forward in a flying tackle aimed at Mr. Partridge's knees. Mr. Partridge lifted his foot to kick that advancing green-eyed face. He swung and felt his balance going. Then the detective's shoulder struck him. He was toppling, falling over backward, falling, falling—

The old man was still snoring when Fergus returned from his climb down the gully. There was no doubt that Harrison Partridge was dead. No living head could loll so limply on its neck.

And Fergus had killed him. Call it an accident, call it self-defense, call it what you will. Fergus had brought him to a trap, and in that trap he had died.

The brand of Cain may be worn in varying manners. To Mr. Partridge it had assumed the guise of an inspiring panache, a banner with a strange device. But Fergus wore his brand with a difference.

He could not blame himself morally, perhaps, for Mr. Partridge's death. But he could blame himself for professional failure in that death. He had no more proof than before to free Simon Ash, and he had burdened himself with a killing.

For murder can spread in concentric circles, and Fergus O'Breen, who had set out to trap a murderer, now found himself being one.

Fergus hesitated in front of Mr. Partridge's workshop. It was his last chance. There might be evidence here—the machine itself or some document that could prove his theory even to the skeptical eye of Detective Lieutenant A. Jackson. Housebreaking would be a small offense to add to his record now. The window on the left, he thought—

"Hi!" said Lieutenant Jackson cheerfully. "You on his trail, too?"

Fergus tried to seem his usual jaunty self. "Hi, Andy. So you've finally got around to suspecting Partridge?"

"Is he your mysterious X? I thought he might be."

"And that's what brings you out here?"

"No. He roused my professional suspicions all by himself. Came into the office an hour ago with the damnedest cock-and-bull story about some vital evidence he'd forgotten. Stanley Harrison's last words, it seems, were about a quarrel with Simon Ash. It didn't ring good—seemed like a deliberate effort to strengthen the case against Ash. As soon as I could get free, I decided to come out and have a further chat with the lad."

"I doubt if he's home," said Fergus.

"We can try." Jackson rapped on the door of the workshop. It was opened by Mr. Partridge.

Mr. Partridge held in one hand the remains of a large open-face ham sandwich. When he had opened the door, he picked up with the other hand the remains of a large whiskey and soda. He needed sustenance before this bright new adventure.

Fresh light gleamed in his eyes as he saw the two men standing there. His Javert! Two Javerts! The unofficial detective who had so brilliantly challenged him, and the official one who was to provide his alibi.

He hardly heeded the opening words of the official detective nor the look of dazed bewilderment on the face of the other. He opened his lips and the Great Harrison Partridge, shedding the last vestigial vestments of the cocoon, spoke:

"You may know the truth for what good it will do you. The life of the man Ash means nothing to me. I can triumph over him even though he live. I killed Stanley Harrison. Take that statement and do with it what you can. I know that an uncorroborated confession is useless to you. If you can prove it, you may have me. And I shall soon commit another sacrifice, and you are powerless to stop me. Because, you see, you are already too late." He laughed softly.

Mr. Partridge closed the door and locked it. He finished the sandwich and the whiskey, hardly noticing the poundings on the door. He picked up the knife and went to his machine. His face was a bland mask of serene exaltation.

Lieutenant Jackson hurled himself against the door, a second too late. It was a matter of minutes before he and a finally aroused Fergus had broken it down.

"He's gone," Jackson stated puzzledly. "There must be a trick exit somewhere."

"'Locked room,'" Fergus murmured. His shoulder ached, and the charge against the door had set it bleeding again.

"What's that?"

"Nothing. Look, Andy. When do you go off duty?"

"Strictly speaking, I'm off now. I was making this checkup on my own time."

"Then let us, in the name of seventeen assorted demigods of drunkenness, go drown our confusions."

Fergus was still asleep when Lieutenant Jackson's phone call came the next morning. His sister woke him, and watched him come into acute and painful wakefulness as he listened, nodding and muttering, "Yes," or, "I'll be—"

Maureen waited till he had hung up, groped about, and found and lighted a cigarette. Then she said, "Well?"

"Remember that Harrison case I was telling you about yesterday?"

"The time machine stuff? Yes."

"My murderer, Mr. Partridge—they found him in a gully out on his great-uncle's estate. Apparently slipped and killed himself while attempting his second murder—that's the way Andy sees it. Had a knife with him. So, in view of that and a sort of confession he made yesterday, Andy's turning Simon Ash loose. He still doesn't see how Partridge worked the first murder, but he doesn't have to bring it into court now."

"Well? What's the matter? Isn't that fine?"

"Matter? Look, Maureen Macushla. I killed Partridge. I didn't mean to, and maybe you could call it justifiable; but I did. I killed him at one o'clock yesterday afternoon. Andy and I saw him at two; he was then eating a ham sandwich and drinking whiskey. The stomach analysis proves that he died half an hour after that meal, when I was with Andy starting out on a bender of bewilderment. So you see?"

"You mean he went back afterward to kill his uncle and then you . . . you saw him after you'd killed him only before he went back to be killed? Oh, how awful."

"Not just that, my sweeting. This is the humor of it: The time alibi, the elsewhen that gave the perfect cover up for Partridge's murder—it gives exactly the same ideal alibi to his own murderer."

Maureen started to speak and stopped. "Oh!" she gasped.

"What?"

"The time machine. It must still be there—somewhere—mustn't it? Shouldn't you—"

Fergus laughed, and not at comedy. "That's the payoff of perfection on this opus. I gather Partridge and his sister didn't love each other too dearly. You know what her first reaction was to the news of his death? After one official tear and one official sob, she went and smashed the hell out of his workshop."

On a workshop floor lay twisted, shattered coils and busbars. In the morgue lay a plump bald body with a broken neck. These remained of the Great Harrison Partridge.

WHISTLER'S MURDER
Fredric Brown

The prolific Fredric William Brown (1906-1972) is revered both as an author of mystery and science fiction. Born in Cincinnati, Ohio, he attended the University of Cincinnati at night and then spent a year at Hanover College, Indiana. He was an office worker for a dozen years before becoming a proofreader for the *Milwaukee Journal* for a decade. He was not able to devote full time to writing fiction until 1949, although he had for several years been a prolific writer of short stories and in the form that he mastered and for which he is much loved today, the difficult-to-write short-short story, generally one to three pages.

Brown was never financially secure, forcing him to write at a prodigious pace, yet he seemed to be enjoying himself in spite of the work load. Many of his stories and novels are imbued with humor, including a devotion to puns and word play. A "writer's writer," he was highly regarded by his colleagues, including Mickey Spillane, who called him his favorite writer of all time; Robert Heinlein, who made him a dedicatee of *Stranger in a Strange Land*; and Ayn Rand, who in *The Romantic Manifesto* described him as ingenious.

After more than 300 short stories, he wrote his first novel, *The*

Fabulous Clipjoint (1947), for which he won an Edgar. His best-known work probably is *The Screaming Mimi* (1949), which served as the basis for the 1957 Columbia Pictures film of the same title that starred Anita Ekberg, Philip Carey, and Gypsy Rose Lee.

"Whistler's Murder" was first published in the December 1946 issue of *Street & Smith's Story Magazine*; it was first collected in *The Shaggy Dog and Other Murders* (New York, Dutton, 1963). It has been reprinted as "Mr. Smith Protects His Client."

Whistler's Murder
Fredric Brown

THE ANCIENT but immaculate automobile turned in at the driveway of the big country house. It came to a stop exactly opposite the flagged walk that led to the porch of the house.

Mr. Henry Smith stepped from the car. He took a few steps toward the house and then paused at the sight of a wreath on the front door. He murmured something to himself that sounded suspiciously like, "Dear me," and paused for a moment. He took off his gold-rimmed pince-nez glasses and polished them carefully.

He replaced the glasses and looked at the house again. This time his gaze went higher. The house had a flat roof surmounted by a three-foot parapet. Standing on the roof behind the parapet, looking down at Mr. Smith, was a big man in a blue serge suit. A gust of wind blew back the big man's coat and Mr. Smith saw that he wore a revolver in a shoulder holster.

The big man pulled his coat together, butttoned it, and stepped back out of sight. This time, quite unmistakably, Mr. Smith said, "Dear me!"

He squared his gray derby hat, went up onto the porch, and rang the doorbell. After about a minute, the door opened. The big man who had been on the roof opened it, and frowned down at Mr. Smith.

"Yeah?" said the big man.

"My name is Henry Smith," answered Mr. Smith. "I would like to see Mr. Walter Perry. Is be home?"

"No."

"Is he expected back soon?" asked Mr. Smith. "I . . . ah . . . have an appointment with him. That is, not exactly an appointment. I mean, not for a specific hour. But I talked to him on the telephone yesterday and he suggested that I call sometime this afternoon." Mr. Smith's eyes flicked to the funeral wreath on the open door. "He isn't . . . ah—"

"No," said the big man. "His uncle's dead, not him."

"Ah, murdered?"

The big man's eyes opened a little more. "How did you know that? The papers haven't—"

"It was just a guess," Mr. Smith said. "Your coat blew back when you were on the roof and I saw you were wearing a gun. From that and your . . . ah . . . general appearance, I surmise that you are an officer of the law. If my guess of murder is correct, I hope that you are, and not . . . ah—"

The big man chuckled. "I'm Sheriff Osborne, not the murderer." He pushed his hat back farther on his head. "And what was your business with Walter Perry, Mr. . . . uh—"

"Smith," said Mr. Smith. "Henry Smith, of the Phalanx Insurance Co. My business with Walter Perry concerned life insurance. My company, however, also handles fire, theft, and casualty insurance. We're one of the oldest and strongest companies in the country."

"Yeah, I've heard of the Phalanx. Just what did Walter Perry want to see you about? Wait, come on in. No use talking in the doorway. There's nobody inside."

He led the way across the hall into a large, luxuriously furnished room in one corner of which stood a mahogany Steinway grand. He waved Mr. Smith to an overstuffed sofa and perched himself on the bench of the piano.

Mr. Smith sat down on the plush sofa and placed his gray derby carefully beside him. "The crime," he said, "I take it, would have occurred last night. You suspect Walter Perry and are holding him?"

The sheriff's head tilted slightly. "And from what," he wanted to know, "do you take all that?"

"Obviously," said Mr. Smith, "it had not yet occurred when I talked to Walter Perry late yesterday, or he would certainly have mentioned it. Then, if the crime had occurred today, I would expect more activity about—coroner, undertaker, deputies, photographers. The discovery must have occurred no later than early this morning for all that to be over with, and the . . . ah . . . remains taken away. I take it that they are, because of the wreath. That would indicate that a mortician has been here. Did you say we had the house to ourselves? Wouldn't an establishment of this size require servants?"

"Yeah," answered the sheriff. "There's a gardener somewhere around and a groom who takes care of the horses—Carlos Perry's hobby was raising and breeding horses. But they aren't in the house— the gardener and the groom, I mean. There were two inside servants, a housekeeper and a cook. The housekeeper quit two days ago and they hadn't hired a new one yet, and the cook— Say, who's questioning who? How did you guess we were holding Walter on suspicion?"

"A not illogical inference, Sheriff," said Mr. Smith. "His absence, your manner, and your interest in what he wanted to see me about. How and when was Mr. Carlos Perry killed?"

"A little after two o'clock, or a little before, the coroner says. With a knife, while he was in bed asleep. And nobody in the house."

"Except Mr. Walter Perry?"

The sheriff frowned. "Not even him, unless I can figure out how— Say, who's questioning who, Mr. Smith? Just what was your business with Walter Perry?"

"I sold him a policy—not a large one; it was for only three thousand dollars—a few years ago while he was attending college in the city. Yesterday I received a notice from the main office that his current premium had not been paid and that the grace period had expired.

That would mean loss of the policy, except for a cash surrender value—very small, considering that the policy was less than three years old. However, the policy can be reinstated within twenty-four hours after expiration of the grace period, if I can collect his premium and have him sign a statement that he is in good health and has had no serious illness since the policy date. Also, I hoped to get him to increase the amount . . . ah—Sheriff, how can you possibly be certain that there was no one else in the house at the time Mr. Perry was killed?"

"Because," said the big man, "there were two men *on* the house."

"You mean, on the roof?"

The sheriff nodded glumly. "Yeah," he answered. "Two private defectives from the city, and they not only alibi each other—they alibi everybody else." He grunted. "Well, I hoped your reason for seeing Walter would tie in somewhere, but I guess it doesn't. If anything comes up, I can reach you through your company, can't I?"

"Of course," said Mr. Smith. But he made no move to go.

The sheriff had turned around to the keyboard of the Steinway grand. With a morose finger he picked out the notes of "Peter, Peter, Pumpkin Eater."

Mr. Smith waited patiently until the sheriff was finished. Then he asked, "Why were two detectives on the roof, Sheriff? Had there been a warning message or threat of some sort?"

Sheriff Osborne turned around on the piano bench and regarded the little insurance agent glumly.

Mr. Smith smiled deprecatingly. He said, "I hope you don't think I'm interfering, but can't you see that it's part of my job, part of my duty to my company, to solve this crime, if I can?"

"Huh? You didn't have insurance on the old guy, did you?"

"No, just on young Walter, But the question arises—is Walter Perry guilty of murder? If he is, I would be doing my employer a disservice to go out of my way to renew his policy. If he is innocent, and I do not remind him that his policy is about to lapse, I am doing a disservice to a client. So I hope you see that my curiosity is not merely. . . ah . . . curiosity."

The sheriff grunted.

"There was a threat, a warning?" Mr. Smith asked.

The sheriff sighed deeply. "Yeah," he said. "Came in the mail three days ago. Letter saying he'd be murdered unless he made restitution to all the people he'd gyped out of money on songs he'd stolen—pirated, I think they call it in that game—from them. He was a song publisher, you know."

"I recall his nephew having mentioned it. Whistler and Company, isn't it? Who is Mr. Whistler?"

"There ain't any," replied the sheriff. "It's a long— All right, I might as well tell you. Carlos Perry used to be in vaudeville—a solo act, whistling. 'Way back when—when there was vaudeville." The sheriff sighed. 'When he took on a girl assistant, an accompanist, he billed himself as Whistler and Company, instead of using his name. See?"

"And then he got into song publishing, and used the same name for a company name. I see. And did he really cheat his clients?"

The sheriff said, "I guess he did. He wrote a couple of songs himself that went fairly well, and used the money he got from 'em to set himself up in publishing. And I guess his methods were crooked, all right. He was sued about a dozen times, but usually came out on top and kept right on making hay. He had plenty. I wouldn't say he was a millionaire, but he must have been half of one, anyway.

"So three days ago this threatening letter comes in the mail, and he showed it to us and wanted protection. Well, I told him we'd work on finding out who sent the letter, but that the county couldn't afford to assign anybody to permanent protection duty and if he wanted that, he'd have to hire it done. So he went to the city and hired two men from an agency."

"A reputable one?"

"Yeah, the International. They sent Krauss and Roberts, two of their best men."

The sheriff's hand, resting on the keyboard, struck what he probably intended as a chord.

"Last night," the sheriff went on, "as it happened, nobody was in or around the place here except the boss—I mean, Carlos Perry—and the two International ops. Walter was staying overnight in the city—went in to see a show and stayed at a hotel, he says. We've checked. He went to the hotel all right, but we can't prove be stayed in his room, or that he didn't. Checked in at about midnight, and left a call for eight. He could've made it here and back, easy.

"And the servants—well, I'd told you the housekeeper had quit and not been replaced yet. Just coincidence the other three all happened to be away. The cook's mother's critically sick; she's still away. It was the gardener's night off; he spent it with his sister and her husband in Dartown, like he always does. The other guy, the horse trainer or groom or whatever you'd call him went to town to see a doctor about an infected foot he'd got from stepping on a nail. Drove in in Perry's truck and the truck broke down. He phoned and Perry told him to have it fixed at an all-night garage, sleep in town, and bring it back in the morning. So, outside of horses and a couple cats, the only people around last night were Perry and the two private ops."

Mr. Smith nodded gravely. "And the coroner says the murder happened about two o'clock?"

"He says that's fairly close, and he's got something to go by, too. Perry turned in about midnight, and just before he went to his room he ate a snack out of the icebox. One of the ops, Roberts, was with him in the kitchen and can verify what he ate and when. So—you know how a coroner can figure time of death, I guess—how far digestion has proceeded. And—"

"Yes, of course," said Mr. Smith.

"Let's go up on the roof," suggested the sheriff. "I'll show you the rest of it, easier'n I can tell you."

He got up from the piano bench and went toward the stairs, Mr. Smith following him like a small tail on a large comet. The sheriff talked back over his shoulder.

"So at midnight Perry turns in. The two ops search the place thoroughly, inside and out. There ain't nobody around then. They'll swear to that, and like I said, they're good men."

"And," said Mr. Smith cheerfully, "if someone was already hiding on the premises at midnight, it couldn't have been Walter Perry. You verified that he checked in at a hotel at midnight."

"Yeah," the sheriff rumbled. "Only there wasn't nobody around. Roberts and Krauss say they'll turn in their licenses if there was. So they went up, this way, to the roof, because it was a moonlight night and that's the best place to watch from. Up here."

They had climbed the ladder from the back second-floor hallway through the open skylight and now stood on the flat roof. Mr. Smith walked over to the parapet.

Sheriff Osborne waved a huge hand. "Look," he said, "you can see all directions for almost a quarter of a mile—farther than that most ways. There was moonlight—not bright enough to read by, maybe, because the moon was low in the sky—but both the International men were on this roof from around midnight to half past two. And they swear nobody crossed any of those fields or came along the road."

"They were both watching all the time?"

"Yeah," the sheriff answered. "They were gonna take turns, and it was Krauss' time off first, but it was so nice up there on the roof and he wasn't sleepy, so he stuck around talking to Roberts instead of turning in. And while they weren't watching all directions every second—well, it'd take anybody time to cross the area where they could've seen him. They say it couldn't have been done."

"And at two thirty?"

The sheriff frowned. "At two thirty Krauss decided to go downstairs and take a nap. He was just going through the skylight there when the bell started to ring—the telephone bell, I mean. The phone's downstairs, but there's an extension upstairs and it rings in both places.

"Krauss didn't know whether to answer it or not. He knew out in the country here, there are different rings for different phones and he didn't know whether it was Perry's ring or not. He went back up on the roof to ask Roberts if he knew, and Roberts did know, and it was Perry's ring on the phone, so Krauss went down and answered it.

"It wasn't anything important; it was just a misunderstanding. Merkle the horse guy had told the all-night garage he'd phone to find out if the truck was ready; he meant when he woke up in the morning. But the garageman misunderstood and thought he was to call when he'd finished working on the truck. And he didn't know Merkle was staying in the village. He phoned out to the house to tell 'em the truck was ready. He's a kind of dumb guy, the one that works nights in the garage, I mean."

Sheriff Osborne tilted his hat back still farther and then grabbed at it as a vagrant breeze almost removed it entirely. He said, "Then Krauss got to wondering how come the phone hadn't waked Perry because it was right outside his bedroom door and he knew Perry was a light sleeper; Perry'd told him so. So he investigated and found Perry was dead."

Mr. Smith nodded. "Then, I suppose, they searched the place again?"

"Nope. They were smarter'n that. Good men, I told you. Krauss went back up and told Roberts, and Roberts stayed on the roof, watching, figuring maybe the killer was still around and he could see him leaving, see? Krauss went downstairs, phoned me, and while I was getting around here with a couple of the boys, he searched the place again, Roberts watching all the time from the roof. Krauss searched the house and the barns and everywhere, and then when we got here, we helped him and went all over it again. There wasn't nobody here. See?"

Mr. Smith nodded again. He took off his gold-rimmed glasses

and polished them, then walked around the low parapet, studying the landscape.

The sheriff followed him. He said, "Look, the moon was low in the northwest. That meant this house threw a shadow across to the barns. A guy could get that far, easy, but to and from the barns he'd have to cross that big field as far as the clump of trees way down there at the edge of the road. He'd stick out like a sore thumb crossing that field. And outside of the barns that there chunk of woods is the nearest possible cover he could've come from. It'd take him ten minutes to cross the field, and he couldn't have done it."

"I doubt," observed Mr. Smith, "that any man would have been so foolish as to try it. The moonlight works both ways. I mean, he could have seen the men on the roof, easily, unless they were hiding down behind the parapet. Were they?"

"Nope. They weren't trying to trap anybody. They were just watching, most of the time sitting on the parapet, one facing each way while they talked. Like you say, he could've seen them just as easy as they could've seen him."

"Um-m-m," said Mr. Smith. "But you haven't told me why you're holding Walter Perry. I presume he inherits—that would give him a motive. But according to what you tell me about the ethics of Whistler and Company, a lot of other people could have motives."

The sheriff nodded glumly. "Several dozen of 'em. Especially if we could believe that threatening letter."

"And can't you?"

"No, we can't. Walter Perry wrote it and mailed it to his uncle. We traced the typewriter he used, and the stationery. And he admits writing it."

"Dear me," declared Mr. Smith earnestly. "Does he say why?"

"He does, but it's screwy. Look, you want to see him anyway, so why don't you get his story from him?"

"An excellent idea, Sheriff. And thank you very much."

"It's all right. I thought maybe thinking out loud would give me some idea how it was done, but it ain't. Oh, well. Look, tell Mike at the jail I said you could talk to Perry. If Mike don't take your word for it, have him phone me here. I'll be around."

At the open skylight Mr. Henry Smith paused to take a last look at the surrounding country. He saw a tall, thin man wearing denim coveralls ride out into the field from the far side of the barn.

"Is that Merkle, the trainer?" he asked.

"Yep," said the sheriff. "He exercises those horses like they was his own kids. A good guy, if you don't criticize his horses—don't try that."

"I won't," said Mr. Smith.

Mr. Smith took another look around, then went down the ladder and the stairs and got back into his car. He drove slowly and thoughtfully to the county seat.

Mike, at the jail, took Mr. Smith's word that Sheriff Osborne had given permission for him to talk to Walter Perry.

Walter Perry was a slight young man who wore horn-rimmed glasses with thick lenses. He smiled ruefully at Mr. Smith. He said, "It was about renewing my policy that you wanted to see me, wasn't it? But you won't want to now, of course, and I don't blame you."

Mr. Smith studied him a moment. He asked, "You didn't . . . ah . . . kill your uncle, did you?"

"Of course not."

"Then," Mr. Smith told him, "just sign here." He produced a form from his pocket and unscrewed the top of his fountain pen. The young man signed, and Mr. Smith folded the paper and put it back in his pocket.

"But I wonder, Mr. Perry," said Mr. Smith, "if you would mind telling me just why you . . . ah—Shriff Osborne tells me that you admit sending a letter threatening your uncle's life. Is that right?"

Walter Perry sighed. "Yes, I did."

"But wasn't that a very foolish thing to do? I take it you never intended to carry out the threat."

"No, I didn't. Of course, it was foolish. It was crazy. I should have seen that it would never work. Not with my uncle." He sighed again and sat down on the edge of the cot in his cell. "My uncle was a crook, but I guess he wasn't a coward. I don't know whether that's to his credit or not. Now that he's dead, I hate to—"

Mr. Smith nodded sympathetically. "Your uncle had, I understand, cheated a great many songwriters out of royalties from their creations. You thought you might frighten him into making restitution to the ones he had cheated?"

Walter Perry nodded. "It was silly. One of those crazy ideas one gets. It was because he got well."

"Got well? I'm afraid I don't—"

"I'd better tell you from the beginning, Mr. Smith. It was two years ago, about the time I was graduated from college—I worked my way through; my uncle didn't foot the bill—that I first learned what kind of an outfit Whistler and Company was. I happened to meet some former friends of my uncle—old-time vaudeville people who had been on the circuits with him. They were plenty bitter. So I started investigating, and found out about all the lawsuits he'd had to fight and—well, I was convinced.

"I was his only living relative, and I knew I was his heir, but if his money was crooked money—well, I didn't want it. He and I had a quarrel and he disinherited me, and that was that. Until a year ago when I learned—"

He stopped, staring at the barred door of the cell. "You learned what?" Mr. Smith prompted.

"I learned, accidentally, that my uncle had some kind of cardiac trouble and didn't have long to live, according to the doctor. Probably less than a year. And—well, it's probably hard for anybody to believe that my motives were good, but I decided that under those circumstances, I was missing a chance to help the people my uncle had cheated, that if I was still his heir, I could make restitution after his death of the money he had stolen from them. You see?"

Walter Perry looked up at the little insurance agent from his seat on the cot, and Mr. Smith studied the young man's face, then nodded.

"So you effected a reconciliation?" he asked.

"Yes, Mr. Smith. It was hypocritical, in one way, but I thought it would enable me to square off those crimes. I didn't want his money, any of it. But I was sorry for all those poor people he'd cheated and—well, I made myself be hypocritical for their sake."

"You know any of them personally?"

"Not all, but I knew I could find most of the ones I didn't know through the records of the old lawsuits. The ones I met first were an old vaudeville team by the name of Wade and Wheeler. I met a few others through them, and looked up some of the others. Most of them hated him like poison, and I can't say I blame them."

Mr. Smith nodded sympathetically. "But the threatening letter. Where does that fit in?"

"About a week ago I learned that his heart trouble was much better. They'd discovered a new treaunent with one of the new drugs, and while he'd never be in perfect health there was every chance he had another twenty years to live—he was only forty-eight. And, well, that changed things."

The young man laughed ruefully. He went on, "I didn't know if I could stand up under the strain of my hypocrisy that long, and anyway, it didn't look as though restitution would come in time to do any good to a lot of the people he owed money to. Wade and Wheeler, for instance, were older than my uncle—he could easily outlive them, and most of the others. You see?"

"So you decided to write a letter threatening his life, pretending that it came from one of the people he'd cheated, thinking it might scare him into giving them their money now?"

"Decided," said Walter Perry, "is hardly the word. If I'd thought about it, I'd have realized how foolish it was to hope that it would do any good. He just hired detectives. And then he was murdered, and here I am in a beautiful jam. I don't blame Osborne for thinking I must have killed him."

Mr. Smith chuckled. "Fortunately for you, the sheriff can't figure out how anybody could have killed him. Ah . . . did anyone know about your hoax, the threatening letter? That is, of course, before the sheriff traced it to you and you admitted writing and sending it?"

"Why, yes. I was so disappointed in my uncle's reaction to receiving it, that I mentioned it to Mr. Wade and Mr. Wheeler, and to a few of the others my uncle owed royalties to. I hoped they could suggest some other idea that might work better. But they couldn't."

"Wade and Wheeler—they live in the city?"

"Yes, they're out of vaudeville now, of course. They get by doing bit parts on radio and television."

"Um-m-m," said Mr. Smith. "Well, thank you for signing the renewal on your policy. And when you are out of here, I'd like to see you again to discuss the possibility of your taking an additional policy."

"Yes, Mr. Smith, I'll be glad to discuss another policy—if I get out of this mess."

Mr. Smith smiled. "Then it seems even more definitely to the interest of the Phalanx Insurance Company to see that you are free as soon as possible."

Mr. Henry Smith drove back to the Perry house even more slowly and thoughtfully than he had driven away from it. He didn't drive quite all the way. He parked his ancient vehicle almost a quarter of a mile away, at the point where the road curved around the group of trees that gave the nearest cover.

He walked through the trees until he could see the house itself, across the open field. The sheriff was still, or again, on the roof.

Mr. Smith walked out into the open, and the sheriff saw him almost at once. Mr. Smith waved and the sheriff waved back. Mr. Smith walked on across the field to the barn, which stood between the field and the house itself.

The tall, thin man whom he had seen exercising the horse was now engaged in currying a horse.

"Mr. Merkle?" asked Mr. Smith, and the man nodded. "My name is Smith, Henry Smith. I am . . . ah . . . attempting to help the sheriff. A beautiful stallion, that gray. Would I be wrong in guessing that it is a cross between an Arabian and a Kentucky walking horse?"

The thin man's face lighted up. "Right, mister. I see you know horses. I been having fun with those city dicks, kidding 'em. They think, because I told 'em, that this is a Clyde, and that chestnut Arab mare is a Percheron. Found out yet who killed Mr. Perry?"

Mr. Smith stared at him. "It is just possible that we have, Mr. Merkle, It is just barely possible that you have told me how it was done, and if we know that—"

"Huh ?" said the trainer. "I told you?"

"Yes," returned Mr. Smith. "Thank you."

He walked on around the barn and joined the sheriff on the roof.

Oshorne grunted a welcome. He said, "I saw you the minute you came out into the open. Dammit, nobody could have crossed that field last night without being noticed."

"You said the moonlight was rather dim, did you not?"

"Yeah, the moon was low, kind of, and—let's see, was it a half moon?"

"Third quarter." said Mr. Smith. "And the men who crossed that field didn't have to come closer than a hundred yards or more until they were lost in the shadow of the barn."

The sheriff took off his hat and swabbed at his forehead with a handkerchief. He said, "Sure, I ain't saying you could recognize anybody that far, but you could see— Hey, why'd you say the men who crossed that field? You mean, you think—"

"Exactly," cut in Mr. Smith, just a bit smugly. "One man could not have crossed that field last night without being noticed—*but two men could!* It seems quite absurd, I will admit, but by process of elimination, it must have been what happened."

Sheriff Osborne stared blankly.

"The two men," said Mr. Smith, "are named Wade and Wheeler. They live in the city, and you'll have no difficulty finding them because Walter Perry knows where they live. I think you'll have no difficulty proving that they did it, once you know the facts. For one thing, I think you'll find that they probably rented the . . . ah . . . wherewithal. I doubt if they have their own left, after all these years off the stage."

"Wheeler and Wade? I believe Walter mentioned those names."

"Exactly," said Mr. Smith. "They knew the setup here. And they knew that if Walter inherited Whistler and Company, they'd get the money they had coming. So they came here last night and killed Mr. Carlos Perry. They crossed that field last night right under the eyes of your city detectives."

"I'm crazy, or you are," declared Sheriff Osborne. "How?"

Mr. Smith smiled gently. "On my way up through the house just now, I verified a wild guess. I phoned a friend of mine who has been a theatrical agent for many years. He remembered Wade and Wheeler quite well. And it's the only answer—possible because of the dim moonlight, the distance, and the ignorance of city-bred men who would think nothing of seeing a horse in a field at night when the horse should be in the barn. Who wouldn't, in fact, even see a horse, to remember it."

"You mean Wade, Wheeler—"

"Exactly," said Mr. Smith. "Wade and Wheeler, in vaudeville, were the front and back ends of a comedy horse."

THE THIRD BULLET
John Dickson Carr

John Dickson Carr (1906-1977) ranks alone as the greatest creator of locked room mysteries, and he didn't mind showing off about the subject. In *The Three Coffins* (1935; published in England as *The Hollow Man*), Carr stops the action to allow to deliver a monologue on the various methods that a murderer could commit a perfect crime in a locked room or other impossible situation. For twenty pages, he describes the apparent situation and then explains how it could have been done, tossing away dozens of plots for potential stories or novels, then dismissing them all by stating that is not how *this* particular murder was accomplished.

Similarly, in "The Third Bullet," Carr does not offer *a* locked room puzzle, but *three*, which is pretty gaudy when one contemplates how difficult it is to create even a single plausible such scenario.

Although an American (born and raised in Pennsylvania), Carr lived in England for some years before returning to the United States and was described as more English than any English author of his time. Carr's work was so quickly recognized as being superior that he was the first American elected to England's prestigious Detection

Club in 1936 after only a few years in England. He was honored as a Grand Master for lifetime achievement by the Mystery Writers of America in 1963. He wrote so prolifically that he created the pseudonym Carter Dickson (originally Carr Dickson until Harper, his American publisher, objected) for the overflow.

"The Third Bullet" was first published as a separate novella as by Carter Dickson (London, Hodder & Stoughton, 1937). It was first published in the United States (as by Carr) in a shortened form in the January 1948 issue of *Ellery Queen's Mystery Magazine*. It is about twenty percent shorter than the book publication, an abridgement wholly endorsed by Carr. It was first collected in *The Third Bullet and Other Stories* (London, Hamish Hamilton, 1954). Note: The present story follows the text of the *EQMM* appearance.

The Third Bullet
John Dickson Carr

ON THE EDGE of the Assistant Commissioner's desk a folded newspaper lay so as to expose a part of a headline: "Mr. Justice Mortlake Murdered" . . . On top of it was an official report-sheet covered with Inspector Page's trim handwriting. And on top of the report sheet, trigger guard to trigger guard, lay two pistols. One was an Ivor-Johnson .38 revolver. The other was a Browning .32 automatic.

Though it was not yet eleven in the morning, a raw and rainy day looked in at the windows over the Embankment, and the green-shaded lamp was burning above the desk. Colonel Marquis, the Assistant Commissioner of Metropolitan Police, leaned back at ease and smoked a cigarette with an air of doing so cynically. Colonel Marquis was a long, stringy man whose thick and wrinkled eyelids gave him a sardonic look not altogether deserved. Though he was not bald, his white hair had begun to recede from the skull, as though in sympathy with the close cropping of the gray mustache. His bony face was as unmistakably of the Army as it was now unmistakably out of it; and the reason became plain whenever he got up—he limped. But he had a bright little eye, which was amused.

"Yes?" he said.

Inspector Page, though young and not particularly ambitious, was as gloomy as the day outside.

"The Superintendent said he'd warn you, sir," John Page answered. "I'm here with two purposes. First, to offer you my resignation—"

Colonel Marquis snorted.

"—and second," said Page, looking at him, "to ask for it back again."

"Ah, that's better," said the Assistant Commissioner, "why the double offer?"

"Because of this Mortlake case, sir. It doesn't make sense. As you can see by my report. . . ."

"I have not read your report," said the Assistant Commissioner. "God willing, I do not intend to read your report. Inspector Page, I am bored; bloody bored; bored stiff and green. And this Mortlake case does not appear to offer anything very startling. It's unfortunate, of course," he added rather hurriedly. "Yes, yes. But correct me if I am wrong. Mr. Justice Mortlake, recently retired, was a judge of the King's Bench Division, officiating at the Central Criminal Court. He was what they call the 'red judge,' and sat in Courtroom Number One on serious offenses like murder or manslaughter. Some time ago he sentenced a man called White to fifteen strokes of the cat and eighteen months' hard labor for robbery with violence. White made threats against the judge. Which is nothing new; all the old lags do it. The only difference here is that, when White got out of jail, he really did keep his threat. He came back and killed the judge." Colonel Marquis scowled. "Well? Any doubt about that?"

Page shook his head. "No, sir, apparently not," he admitted. "*I* can testify to that. Mortlake was shot through the chest yesterday afternoon at half past five. Sergeant Borden and I practically saw the thing done. Mortlake was alone—with White—in a sort of pavilion on the grounds of his house. It is absolutely impossible for anyone else to have reached him, let alone shot him. So, if White didn't kill him, the case is a monstrosity. But that's just the trouble. For if White did kill him—well, it's still a monstrosity."

Colonel Marquis' rather speckled face was alight with new pleasure. "Go on," he said.

"First of all, to give you the background," said Page. He now uncovered the newspaper on the front page of which was a large photograph of the dead judge in his robes. It showed a little man dwarfed by a great flowing wig. Out of the wig peered a face with a parrot-like curiosity in it, but with a mildness approaching meekness. "I don't know whether you knew him?"

"No. I've heard he was active in the Bar Mess."

"He retired at seventy-two, which is early for a judge. Apparently he was as sharp-witted as ever. But the most important point about him was his leniency on the bench—his extreme leniency. It is known, from a speech I looked up, that he disapproved of using the cat-o'-nine tails even in extreme cases."

"Yet he sentenced this fellow White to fifteen of the best?"

"Yes, sir. That's the other side of the picture, the side nobody can understand." Page hesitated. "Now, take this fellow Gabriel White. He's not an old lag; it was his first offense, mind you. He's young, and handsome as a film-actor, and a cursed sight too artistic to suit me. Also, he's well educated and it seems certain that 'Gabriel White' isn't his real name—though we didn't bother with that beyond making sure he wasn't in the files.

"The robbery-with-violence charge was a pretty ugly business, *if* White was guilty. It was done on an old woman who kept a tobacconist's shop in Poplar, and was reputed to be a very wealthy miser: the old stuff. Well, someone came into her shop on a foggy evening, under pretense of buying cigarettes—bashed up her face pretty badly even after she was unconscious—and got away with only two pound-notes and some loose silver out of the till. Gabriel White was caught running away from the place. In his pocket was found one of the stolen notes, identified by the number; and an unopened packet of cigarettes, although it was shown he did not smoke. His story was that, as he was walking along, somebody cannoned into him in the fog, stuck a hand into his pocket, and ran. He thought he was the victim of a running pickpocket. He automatically started to run after the man, until he felt in his pocket and found something had been *put* there. This was just before a constable stopped him."

Again Page hesitated.

"You see, sir, there were several weak points in the prosecution. For one thing, the old woman couldn't identify him beyond doubt as the right man. If he'd had competent counsel, and if it hadn't been for the judge, I don't think there's much doubt that he'd have been acquitted. But, instead of taking any one of the good men the court was willing to appoint to defend him, the fool insisted on defending himself. Also, his manner in court wasn't liked. And the judge turned dead against him. Old Mortlake made out a devilish case against him in his charge to the jury, and practically directed them to find him guilty. When he was asked whether he had anything to say why sentence should not be passed against him, he said just this: '*You are a fool, and I will see you presently.*' I suppose that could be taken as a threat. All the same, he nearly fainted when Mortlake calmly gave him fifteen strokes of the cat."

The Assistant Commissioner said: "Look here, Page, I don't like this. Weren't there grounds for an appeal?"

"White didn't appeal. He said nothing more, though they tell me he didn't stand the flogging at all well. But the trouble is, sir, that all opinions about White are conflicting. People are either dead in his favor, or dead against him. They think he's a thoroughly wronged man, or else a thorough wrong 'un. He served his time at Wormwood Scrubs. Now, the governor of the prison and the prison doctor both think he's a fine type, and would back him anywhere. But the chaplain of the prison, and Sergeant Borden (the officer who arrested him) both think he's a complete rotter. Anyway, he was a model prisoner. He got the customary one-sixth of his sentence remitted for good behavior, and he was released six weeks ago—on September 24th."

"Still threatening?"

Page was positive of this. "No, sir. Of course, he was on ticket-of-leave and we kept an eye on him. But everything seemed to be going well until yesterday afternoon. At just four o'clock we got a phone message from a pawnbroker that Gabriel White had just bought a gun in his place. This gun."

Across the table Page pushed the Ivor-Johnson .38 revolver. With a glance of curiosity at the little automatic beside it, Colonel Marquis picked up the revolver. One shot had been fired from an otherwise fully loaded magazine.

"So," Page went on, "we sent out orders to pick him up—just in case. But that was no sooner done than we got another message by phone. It was from a woman, and it was pretty hysterical. It said that Gabriel White was going to kill old Mortlake, and couldn't we do anything about it? It was from Miss Ida Mortlake, the judge's daughter."

"H'm. I do not wish," observed the other, with a sour and sardonic inflection, "to jump to conclusions. But are you going to tell me that Miss Ida Mortlake is young and charming; that our Adonis with the painful name, Gabriel White, is well acquainted with her; and that the judge knew it when he issued that whacking sentence?"

"Yes, sir. But I'll come to that in a moment. As soon as that message came in, the Superintendent thought I had better get out to

Hampstead at once—that's where the Mortlakes live. I took along Sergeant Borden because he had handled White before. We hopped into a police car and got out there in double time.

"Now, the lay of the land is important. The house has fairly extensive grounds around it. But the suburbs round Hampstead Heath have grown in such a way that houses and villas crowd right up against the grounds; and there's a stone wall, all of fifteen feet high, round the judge's property.

"And there are only two entrances: a main carriage-drive, and a tradesman's entrance. The first is presided over by an old retainer, named Robinson, who lives at a lodge just inside. He opened the gates for us. It was nearly half past five when we got there, and almost dark. Also, it was raining and blowing in full November style.

"Robinson, the caretaker, told us where the judge was. He was in a pavilion, a kind of glorified outbuilding, in a clump of trees about two hundred yards from the house. It's a small place: there are only two rooms, with a hallway dividing them. The judge used one of the rooms as a study. Robinson was sure he was there. It seems that the judge was expecting an old crony of his to tea; and so, about half past three, he had phoned Robinson at the lodge-gates. He said that he was going from the house across to the pavilion; and when the crony showed up, Robinson was to direct the visitor straight across to the pavilion.

"Borden and I went up a path to the left. We could see the pavilion straight ahead. Though there were trees round it, none of the trees came within a dozen feet of the pavilion, and we had a good view of the place. There was a door in the middle, with a fanlight up over it; and on each side of the door there were two windows. The two windows to the right of the door were dark. The two windows of the room to the left, though they had heavy curtains drawn over them, showed chinks of light. Also, there was a light in the hall; you could see it in that glass pane up over the top of the door. And that was how we saw a tall man duck out of the belt of trees towards the right, and run straight for the front door.

"But it wasn't all. The rain was blowing straight down the back of our necks, and there was a good deal of thunder. The lightning came just before that man got his hand on the front door. It was a real blaze, too. For a couple of seconds the whole place was as dead-bright as a photographer's studio. As soon as we had seen the man duck out from the trees, Borden let out a bellow. The man heard us, and he turned round.

"It was Gabriel White, right enough; the lightning made no doubt of that. And when he saw us, he took that revolver out of his pocket. But he didn't go for us. He opened the door of the pavilion, and now we could see him fully. From where we were standing (or running, now) we could see straight down the little hall inside; he was making for the door to the judge's study on the left.

"We started running—Borden was well ahead of me—and Borden let out another bellow as loud as Doomsday.

"That was what brought the judge to the window. In the room on the left-hand side Mr. Justice Mortlake drew back the curtains of the window nearest the front door and looked out. I want to emphasize this to show there had been no funny business or hocus-pocus. It was old Mortlake: I've seen him too many times in court, and at this time he was alive and well. He pushed up the window a little way and looked out; I saw his bald head shine. He called out, 'Who's there?' Then something else took his attention away from the window. He turned back into the room.

"What took his attention was the fact that Gabriel White had opened the hall door to his study, had run into the study, and had turned the key in the lock as he went through. Sergeant Borden was on White's tail, but a few seconds too late to get him before he locked the door. I saw that *my* quickest way into the study, if I wanted to head off anything, would be through that window—now partly open. Then I heard the first shot.

"Yes, sir: I said the *first* shot. I heard it when I was about twenty running paces away from the window. Then, when I was ten paces from the window, I heard the second shot. The black curtains were only partly drawn and I couldn't see inside until I had drawn level with the window.

"Inside, a little way out and to my left, old Mortlake was lying forward on his face across a flat-topped desk. In the middle of the room Gabriel White stood holding the Ivor-Johnson revolver out stiffly in front of him, and looking stupid. He wasn't savage, or defiant, or even weepy; he'd only got a silly sort of look on his face. Well, sir, the only thing for me to do was to climb through the window. There wasn't much danger in it. White paid no attention to me and I doubt if he even saw me. The first thing I did was to go over and take the gun out of White's hand. He didn't resist. The next thing I did was to unlock the door leading into the hallway—Borden was still hammering at it outside—so that Borden could get in.

"Then I went to the body of Mr. Justice Mortlake.

"He was lying on his face across a big writing table. From the ceiling over the desk hung a big brass lamp shaped like a Chinese dragon, with a powerful electric bulb inside. It poured down a flood of light on the writing desk, and it was the only light in the room. At the judge's left hand was a standing dictaphone, with its rubber cover off. And the judge was dead, right enough. He had been shot through the heart at fairly close range, and death had been almost instantaneous. There had been two shots. One of the bullets had killed him. The other bullet had smashed the glass mouth of the speaking tube hung on the dictaphone, and was embedded in the wall behind him. I dug it out later.

PLAN OF STUDY IN PAVILION

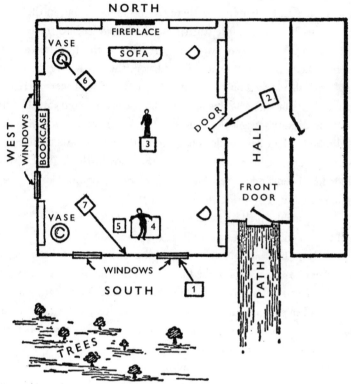

1. Window by which Inspector Page entered.
2. Door outside which Sergeant Borden stood.
3. Where White was standing when police entered.
4. Position of body across writing table.
5. Dictaphone.
6. Vase in which Browning .32 automatic was found.
7. Arrow shows position in wall where bullet from Ivor-Johnson .38 revolver lodged.

"If you look at the plan I've drawn, you will get a good general idea of the room. It was a large, square room, furnished chiefly with bookcases and leather chairs. There was no fireplace, but in the north wall a two-bar electric fire (turned on) had been let into the wall. In the west wall there were two windows. (But both of these windows were locked on the inside; and in addition, their heavy wooden shutters were also locked on the inside.) In the south wall there were two windows. (But this was the side by which I had entered myself. One of these windows was locked and shuttered; the other, through which I climbed, I had kept under observation the whole time.) There was only one other exit from the room—the door to the hall. (But this door had been under the observation of Sergeant Borden from the moment White ran inside and locked it.)

"Of course, sir, all this was routine. We knew the answer. We had White in a closed circle with his victim. Nobody else could have escaped from that room. Nobody was hiding there when we entered; as a matter of routine, we searched that room thoroughly. Gabriel White had fired two bullets, one of which had killed the old man, and the other had missed him and stuck in the wall. It was all smooth, easy sailing—until it occurred to me, purely as routine, to break open the Ivor-Johnson revolver and look at the magazine."

"Well?" inquired Colonel Marquis.

"Well," Inspector Page said grimly, *"only one bullet had been fired from White's gun."*

That his chief was enjoying this, Page had no doubt. Colonel Marquis had sat up straighter; and his speckled shiny face had grown less sardonic.

"Admirable," he said, lighting another cigarette. "What I like, inspector, is your informal style of making a report."

Page was never certain how to take the man, but he went at it with a grin.

"Frankly, sir, we couldn't believe our eyes. The gun was just as you

see it now: fully loaded except for one exploded cartridge case. Theo-
retically, of course, he *might* have walked into that room and fired one
bullet; then he might have carefully opened the magazine, extracted
the spent cartridge case, put in another bullet in its place, and fired
that—leaving the magazine as we found it."

"Rubbish," said Colonel Marquis.

"Yes, sir. Why should anybody have done such a crazy trick as
that, when the magazine was full to begin with? Besides, he couldn't
have done it. In that case, there'd have been an extra shell to account
for—the cartridge case of the first bullet—and it wasn't anywhere in
the room or on his person. We made sure of that."

"What did the accused say?"

Page took a notebook out of his pocket and got the right place.

"I'll read you his testimony verbatim," Page said, "although he was
in pretty bad shape and what he said wasn't any more coherent than
the rest of this business. First, I warned him that anything he said
would be taken down and might be used in evidence. And here it is:

Q. So you shot him after all?

A. I don't know.

Q. What do you mean, you don't know? You don't deny you
shot him?

A. I shot at him. Then things all went queer. I don't know.

Q. And you shot at him twice?

A. No, I didn't. So help me God, I didn't. I only shot at him
once. I don't know whether I hit him; but he didn't fall or anything.

Q. Are you trying to tell me there was only one shot?

A. No, no, there were two shots right enough. I heard them.

Q. Which one of them did you fire?

A. The first one. I shot at the old swine as soon as I got in here.
He was just turning round from that window and he put out
his hands towards me and I shot at him.

Q. Do you mean that there was somebody in here who fired a second shot?

A. I don't know.

Q. Well, did you see anybody else in here?

A. No. There isn't any light except that one directly over the desk, and I couldn't see.

Q. Do you mean to say that if somebody let off a gun in this room right under your nose, you wouldn't see the man or the gun or anything else?

A. I don't know. I'm just telling you. I shot at the old swine and he didn't fall. He started to run over to the other window to get away from me, and shouted at me. Then I heard another shot. He stopped, and put his hands up to his chest, and took a couple of steps forward again, and fell over, on his face across that table.

Q. What direction did this shot come from?

A. I don't know.

"I had just asked him this question when Sergeant Borden made a discovery. Borden had been prowling over along the west wall, near those two enormous yellow porcelain vases. They were standing in the two corners of the room along that wall *(see the plan)*. Borden bent over beside one of them, in the northwest angle of the wall. And he picked up a spent cartridge case.

"At first, of course, Borden thought it was the shell we were looking for out of the Ivor-Johnson revolver. But as soon as I glanced at it I saw it wasn't. It was a shell ejected from a .32 automatic. And then we looked inside that vase and we found this."

Again grinning wryly, Page pushed across the table the Browning .32 automatic.

"This pistol was lying at the bottom of the vase, where somebody had dropped it. The vase was too high to reach down inside with an arm. But the judge had brought an umbrella to the pavilion; we found it leaning up against the wall in the hall, so we reached down and fished out the gun with the crook of the umbrella.

"By the smell of the barrel I could tell that the Browning .32 had been fired within the last few minutes. One bullet was missing from the clip. The cartridge case from that bullet (our firearms expert swears to this) was the one we found lying beside the vase. The cartridge case, when I touched it, was still very faintly warm: in other words, sir, it had been fired within the last few seconds."

Page tapped one finger on the edge of the desk.

"Consequently, sir," he said, "there is absolutely no doubt that a second shot was fired from that Browning automatic; that it was fired by somebody *inside the room;* and that afterwards somebody dropped the gun into that vase."

"Which bullet killed him?"

"That's the point, sir; we don't know."

"You don't know?" repeated the other sharply. "I should think it would be fairly easy. There were two bullets, a .38 revolver and a .32 automatic. One of them was, to put it in an undignified way, in the judge; the other was in the wall. You tell me you dug out the one in the wall. Which was it?"

From his pocket Page took a labeled envelope and shook out of it a lead pellet which had been flattened and partly chipped.

"This was in the wall," he said. "It's a brick wall and the bullet's been splintered a little. So we can't go entirely by weight—that is, not beyond any doubt. I'm almost certain this is the .38 bullet from White's revolver. But it can't be put into record until I get the post-mortem report from Dr. Blaine and get my claws on the one in the judge's body. Dr. Blaine is doing the post-mortem this morning."

Colonel Marquis' expression became a broad grin, changing to extreme gravity.

"You are thorough, Inspector," he said. "All the same, where do you think we stand? If that bullet turns out to be the .38 revolver, then Gabriel White fired and missed. So far, so good. But what happened afterwards? Not more than a few seconds afterwards, according to your story, someone blazed away with the Browning automatic and killed Mr. Justice Mortlake. By the way, were there fingerprints on the Browning?"

"No, sir. But then White was wearing gloves."

Colonel Marquis raised his eyebrows. "I see. You think White may have fired both shots after all?"

"I think it's a possibility. He may have come to the pavilion equipped with two guns and done all that funny business as a deliberate blind, to make us think that the second shot which really killed the judge was fired by somebody else. And yet—"

"It's a very large 'and yet,'" grunted the other. "I agree. If he had indulged in any such elaborate hocus-pocus as that, he would have taken good care to see that the room wasn't sealed up like a box; he wouldn't have taken such precautions to prove that nobody else *could* have fired the shot. His actions, in blazing away directly under the noses of the police, sound more like a deliberate bid for martyrdom. That's reasonable enough; there are plenty of cranks. But the use of two pistols, under such circumstances, would be rank insanity. Whether Gabriel White is a crank or whether he isn't, I presume you don't think he is three times madder than a March hare."

Page was disturbed. "I know, sir. Also, they talk about 'acting,' but I would be willing to swear that the expression on White's face— when I looked through that window—was absolutely genuine. There isn't an actor alive who could have managed it. The man was staggered with surprise—half out of his wits at what he saw. But there it is! What else can we believe? The room was, as you say, sealed up like a box. So White must have fired both shots. Nobody else could have done it."

"You don't see any alternative?"

"Yes, sir," said Page. "I do."

"Ah, I hoped you would," said Colonel Marquis. "Well?"

"There's the possibility that White might be shielding somebody.

For instance, suppose somebody else had been in that room, armed with the Browning. White fires, and misses. X, the unknown, fires and rings the bell. Whereupon—the police being at the door—X hops out one of the windows in the west wall, and White locks the windows and the shutters after X has gone."

He raised his eyes and the other nodded.

"Yes. Let's suppose, just for the sake of argument," said Colonel Marquis, "that White didn't kill the judge after all. Let's have a little personal information. Was anyone else interested in killing him? What about his household or his friends?"

"His household is small. He's a widower; he married rather late in life and his wife died about five years ago. He leaves two daughters— Carolyn, the elder (twenty-eight), and Ida, the younger (twenty-five). Aside from servants, the only other member of the household is an old man by the name of Penney: he's been the judge's legal clerk for years, and was taken into the house after the judge's retirement to help Mortlake on his book about 'Fifty Years at Bench and Bar,' or some such thing—"

"Inevitable, of course," said the colonel. "What about friends?"

"He's got only one close friend. You remember my telling you, sir, that a crony of the judge was expected to come to tea yesterday afternoon and the judge sent word that he should come over to the pavilion as soon as he arrived? That's the man. He's a good deal younger than Mortlake. You may be interested to know that he's Sir Andrew Travers—the greatest criminal lawyer of 'em all. He's upset more than one of our best-prepared cases."

The Assistant Commissioner stared.

"I *am* interested," he said. "Travers. Yes. I don't know him personally, but I know a good deal about him. So Travers was invited to tea yesterday. Did he get there?"

"No. He was delayed; he phoned afterwards, I understand."

Colonel Marquis reflected. "What about this household? I don't suppose you've had a chance to interview all of them; but one lead stands and shines. You say that the younger daughter, Ida, got in touch with you and told you Gabriel White was going to kill her father; you also think she knew White personally?"

"Yes, sir. I've seen Miss Ida Mortlake. She's the only one of the household I have seen, because both Miss Carolyn Mortlake and Penney, the clerk, were out yesterday afternoon. You want my honest opinion of her? Well, she's grand," said Page, dropping into humanity with such violence that Marquis blinked.

"Do you mean," asked the other, "that she has the grand manner, or merely what I think you mean?"

"Grand manner? Far from it. I mean I'd back her against any field," replied Page. He could admit how much he had been impressed. He remembered the big house in the park, a sort of larger and more ornate version of the pavilion itself; and Ida Mortlake, white-faced, coming down the stairs to meet him. "Whatever happened at the pavilion," he went on, "it's certain she had nothing to do with it. There's nothing hardboiled or modern about her. She's fine."

"I see. Anyhow, I take it you questioned her? You asked her about her association with White, if there was any association?"

"The fact is, sir, I didn't question her too closely. She was rather upset, as you can imagine, and she promised to tell me the whole story today. She admitted that she knew White, but she knows him only slightly and acknowledges that she doesn't particularly like him. I gather that he'd been attentive. She met him at a studio party in Chelsea. Studio parties seem to be a craze of the elder daughter, who appears to be along the hardboiled line. On this occasion Ida Mortlake went along and met—"

Whenever there appeared on Colonel Marquis' face a wolfish grin, as happened now, it seemed to crackle the face like the skin of a roast pig. He remained sitting bolt upright, studying Page with a bleak eye.

"Inspector," he said, "your record has been good and I will refrain from comment. I say nothing against the young lady. All I should like to know is, why are you so certain she couldn't have had anything to do with this? You yourself admitted the possibility that White might be shielding somebody. You yourself admitted that there might have been somebody else in the room who got out of a window after the shot was fired, and that White might have locked the window afterwards."

"Did I?" said Page, glad to hit back at the old so-and-so. "I don't think I said that, Colonel. I considered it. I also found, later, that it wouldn't work."

"Why?"

"Before and after the shots I had the two south windows under my eye. Nobody came out of either window at any time. Borden was watching the door. The only remaining way out would be one of the west windows. But we learned from Robinson, the gatekeeper, that neither of the west windows had been touched for over a year. It seems that those two windows were loose in the frame and let in bad draughts. The judge used that pavilion, as a rule, only in the evening; and he was afraid of draughts. So the windows were always locked and the shutters always bolted into place outside them. You see, when Borden and I came to examine them, the locks were so rusted that it took our combined strength to budge them. The shutters outside the windows had their bolts so rusted from exposure that we couldn't move them at all. So that's definitely o-u-t."

Colonel Marquis used an unofficial word. "So we come directly round in a circle again?"

"I'm afraid so, sir. It really does seal the room up. Out of four sides of a square, one was a blank wall, one was impregnable with rusted bolts, and the other two were watched. We have got to believe Gabriel White fired both those shots—or go crazy."

The telephone on the Assistant Commissioner's desk rang sharply. Colonel Marquis, evidently about to hold forth on his refusal to go crazy, answered it with some annoyance; but his expression changed. He put a hand over the mouthpiece of the phone.

"Where is White now? You're holding him, naturally?"

"Naturally, sir. He's downstairs now. I thought you might like to have a talk with him."

"Send them both in," Marquis said to the telephone, and hung up in some satisfaction. "I think," he went on to Page, "it will be a good idea, presently, to confront everybody with everybody else. And I am very curious to form my own opinion of this saint-martyr, or rotter-murderer, Mr. Gabriel White. But at the moment we have visitors. No, don't get up. Miss Ida Mortlake and Sir Andrew Travers are on their way in."

Though Page was afraid he might have pitched it too strongly in his description of Ida Mortlake, her appearance reassured him. Seen now for the second time, she was a slender girl with a coolness and delicacy like Dresden china. Though she was rather tall, she did not seem tall. Her skin was very fair, her hair clear yellow under a black close-fitting hat with a short veil, her eyes blue; and she had a smile capable of loosening Page's judgment. She wore a mink coat which Page—who had been out after fur-thieves in the West India Dock Road the week before—valued at fifteen hundred guineas.

This depressed him. For the first time it occurred to him that, with the old judge out of the way, Ida Mortlake would be a very rich woman.

"Colonel Marquis?" she said, her color rising. "I thought—"

A clearing of the throat behind her interrupted the speech, for someone towered there. Page had never seen Sir Andrew Travers without his barrister's wig and gown; yet he had the same mannerisms in private life as in a courtroom. They had become, evidently, a part of him. Sir Andrew Travers had a massive head, a massive chest, a blue jowl, and an inscrutable eye. His wiry black hair was so thick that you expected it to be long, but it was cropped off just above the ears. He was formidable, but he was also affable. He wore a dark overcoat, through which showed a gray cravat; and he formally carried top hat and gloves. His full, rich voice compassed the room.

"In such a shocking affair, Colonel Marquis," he said, "you will readily understand Miss Mortlake's feelings. As a personal friend of poor Mortlake's, I asked the liberty of accompanying her here—"

Page had got up hastily to stand at attention against the wall, while Marquis indicated chairs. Ida recognized him and gave him a smile. As Sir Andrew Travers lowered himself into a chair, Page seemed to see a manservant at work brushing him to give him that gloss. Sir Andrew assumed his most winning air.

"Frankly, Colonel Marquis, we are here to ask for information—"

"Oh, *no*," said Ida. She flushed again and her eyes were bright. "It isn't that. But I do want to tell you that I can't believe Gabriel White killed father."

Travers looked slightly annoyed and Colonel Marquis was very bland. He addressed himself to Travers.

"You are familiar with the details?" he asked.

"Only, I regret to say, what I have read here," said Travers. He reached out and touched the newspaper. "You can understand," Travers went on, "that I am in a position of some delicacy. I am a barrister, not a solicitor. At the moment I am here only as a friend of Miss Mortlake. Frankly, is there some doubt of this unfortunate young man's guilt?"

The Assistant Commissioner considered. "There is," he said, "what I can only call—an *un*reasonable doubt. And therefore," Colonel Marquis went on, "would Miss Mortlake mind answering a few questions?"

"Of course not," the girl replied promptly. "That's why I'm here, although Andrew advised me not to. I tell you, I *know* Gabriel White couldn't have done it."

"Forgive the question, but are you interested in him?"

Her face became still more pink and she spoke with eagerness.

"No! No, honestly I'm not: not in the way you mean, that is. In the way you mean, I think I rather dislike him, though he's been very nice to me."

"Yet you knew that he was sentenced to flogging and imprisonment for a particularly brutal case of robbery with violence."

"Yes, I knew it," she said calmly. "I know all about that. He told me. He was innocent, of course. You see, it's not in Gabriel's nature; he's too much of an idealist; a thing like that is directly opposed to all he believes in most strongly. He hates war and he hates violence of all kinds. He's a member of all kinds of societies opposed to war and violence and capital punishment. There's one political society, called the Utopians—he says it's the political science of the future—and he's the leading member of that. You remember when he was tried, the prosecution asked what a respectable citizen was *doing* in a slum district like Poplar on the night that poor old woman was robbed? And he refused to answer. And they made quite a lot of that." She was speaking in a somewhat breathless rush. "Actually, he was going to a meeting of the Utopians. But most of their members are very poor, and a lot of them are foreigners. Gabriel said that, if he had answered, the jury would merely have thought they were a lot of anarchists. And it would only have prejudiced the case still more against him."

"H'm," said Colonel Marquis, after a pause. "How long have you known him, Miss Mortlake?"

"Oh, nearly three years, I should think. I mean, I knew him about a year before he—before they put him in prison."

"What do you know about him?"

"He's an artist."

"There is just one thing," pursued Colonel Marquis, examining his hands, "which does not seem to square with this. You are willing to swear, Miss Mortlake, that White could not have killed your father. And yet, if I understand correctly, you were the one who rang up here yesterday afternoon at four thirty o'clock and begged for men to protect your father because White had threatened to kill him. Is that true?"

"I know I said so," answered the girl, with a sort of astounding simplicity which never turned a hair; "but, of course, I never thought he would really. I was panicky, horribly panicky. The more I thought of it, the worse it seemed—You see, I met Gabriel yesterday afternoon between three thirty and four o'clock, I think it was. If you remember, it started to rain about four or a little past. I wasn't very far down North End Road when I saw Gabriel. He was walking along with his head down, looking like thunder. I stopped the car. At first he didn't want to speak to me. But the car was right outside a Lyons', and he said in that curt way of his, 'Oh, come in and have some tea.' We did. At first he wouldn't talk much, but at last he broke out raving against my father. He said he was going to kill him—"

"And you weren't impressed?"

"Gabriel always talks like that," she answered. She made a slight, sharp gesture of her gloved hand. "But I didn't want a row in a public place like that. At last I said, 'Well, if you can't behave any better than this, perhaps I'd better go.' I left him sitting there with his elbows stuck out on the table. By that time it had begun to rain and lightning, and I'm frightened of storms. So I drove straight back home as soon as I'd got a book from the lending library."

"Yes?" he prompted, as she hesitated.

"Well, I warned Robinson—the gatekeeper—not to let anybody in, anybody at all, even by the tradesman's entrance. There's a big wall all around, with jagged glass on the top. As a matter of fact, I still don't see how Gabriel got in. I went up to the house. I suppose it was the fact that there was nobody in the house, and there was a storm outside that made me get panicky and still more panicky. At last I simply grabbed the phone, and—" She sat back, breathing hard. "I lost my silly head, that was all."

"Did your father know White, Miss Mortlake?" asked Marquis.

She was troubled. "Yes, I'm pretty sure he did. At least, he knew I had been—seeing Gabriel."

"And he didn't approve?"

"No; I'm sure I don't know why. He certainly never saw Gabriel in my presence."

"So you think there might have been a personal reason why he ordered a flogging? I am aware," Marquis snapped quickly, as Travers opened his mouth, "that you don't have to answer that, Miss Mortlake. Sir Andrew was going to advise you not to answer. But it strikes me the defense will need all the help it can get. In spite of your gallant words in White's favor he admits firing one of the shots. You knew that?"

The girl's blue eyes widened and the color went out of her face, leaving it soft-looking and (for a second) curiously ineffectual. She glanced at Page. "No, I didn't," she said. "But this is horrible. If he really admits doing it after all—"

"No, he doesn't admit firing the shot that actually killed your father. That's the trouble." Colonel Marquis very rapidly gave a summary of the case. "So, you see, it seems we shall have to prosecute White or, as the inspector says, go crazy. Do you know of anyone else who might have wished to kill your father?"

"Nobody in the world," she admitted. "Quite to the contrary, everybody in public life loved him. You've heard how lenient he was. He never had any animosity from any of the people he sentenced."

"And in private life?"

This evidently surprised her. "Private life? What on earth? Certainly not! Of course," she hesitated, "sometimes—there's no harm in my saying it, is there?—sometimes he was difficult. I mean, he had splendid humanitarian principles and he was always trying to make the world better, but I did wish sometimes he would be less gentle in court and at banquets and a little more humanitarian at home. Please don't misunderstand me! He was a wonderful man and I don't think he ever spoke an unkind word to us in his life. But he loved to lecture, on and on in that smooth, easy voice of his. I—I suppose it was for our own good, though."

For the first time, and with a sort of shock, it occurred to Page that the liberal and lenient Mr. Justice Charles Mortlake might have been a holy terror to live with. Colonel Marquis looked at Travers. "You agree with that, Sir Andrew?"

Travers clearly had to draw back his attention from other matters. He had picked up the little Browning automatic from the desk and was turning it over in his fingers.

"Agree? About Mortlake having any enemies? Oh, emphatically."

"You have nothing to add to that?"

"I have a great deal to add to it," said Travers with sharpness. He seemed to have developed a number of little wheezes in his throat. "So the second shot was fired from this? Well, it alters matters. I don't know whether or not White is guilty. But I know that now I can't undertake his defense . . . you see, *this Browning automatic belongs to me.*"

Ida Mortlake let out an exclamation. With great urbanity Travers reached into his breast pocket, drew out a wallet, and showed the card of a firearms license. "If you will compare the serial numbers," he said, "you will see that they agree."

"H'm," said Marquis, "are you going to confess to the murder, then?"

Travers' smile grew broader and more human. "God love us, I didn't kill him, if that's what you think. I liked him too well. But this is an unusual position for me, and I can't say it's a pleasant one. I thought I recognized this little weapon as soon as I came in here, although I thought it couldn't possibly be the same one. The last time I saw it, it was in my chambers at the Inner Temple. To be exact, it was in the lowest left-hand drawer of the desk in my study."

"Could White have stolen it from there?"

Travers shook his head.

"I don't think so. I should regard it as extremely unlikely. I don't know White; to my knowledge, I've never even seen him. And he's never been in my chambers, unless it was burglary."

"When did you last see the gun?"

"I'm afraid I can't answer that," said Travers. He was now at his ease, studying the matter as though in luxurious debate. But Page thought he was watchful. "The pistol was too much part of—the domestic furniture, so to speak. I think I can say I haven't taken it out of the drawer for over a year; I had no use for it. It may have been gone for a year. It may have been gone for no longer than a few days."

"Who could have stolen it?"

There was a heavy cloud on Travers' face. "I can hardly answer that, can I? Anyone with free access to my rooms might have done it."

"A member of Mr. Justice Mortlake's household, for instance?"

"Oh, yes, it's possible," replied Travers.

"Very well," said the Assistant Commissioner. "Would you mind, Sir Andrew, giving an account of your movements yesterday afternoon?"

The barrister reflected. "I was in court until about half past three in the afternoon. Afterwards I walked across the street to the Temple. Let me see. When I passed through Fountain Court, I remember noticing by the sun-dial on the wall that it was twenty minutes to four. I had promised to be at Hampstead, for tea with Mortlake, by four thirty at the latest. Unfortunately, my clerk told me that Gordon Bates had gone on the sick-list and had insisted on turning the brief in the Lake case over to me. The Lake case comes up for trial today, and it's rather a complicated business. I knew that I should have to swot up on it all yesterday afternoon and probably all night, to be in shape to argue it today. Which killed any possibility of my going to Hampstead for tea. So I stayed in my chambers with the brief. It was twenty minutes to six when I suddenly realized I hadn't made any excuses over the phone. But by that time—well, poor Mortlake was dead. I understand he was shot about half past five."

"And all this time you were in your chambers? Have you any confirmation of this?"

"I believe I have," the other affirmed with grave attention. "My clerk should confirm it. He was in the outer room until nearly six o'clock. I was in the inner part of the chambers: my living quarters. There is only one way out of the chambers; and to leave them, I should have had to pass through the room where my clerk was. I believe he will give me an alibi."

Supporting himself on his cane, Colonel Marquis got up with great formality and nodded.

"Right," he said. "I have just one request. I wonder whether I can trespass on your time by asking you to wait in another room for about ten minutes? There is something I must do, and then I should like to speak with both of you again."

He pressed a buzzer on his desk. He swept them out of the room with such effortless smoothness that even Travers had scarcely time to protest.

"Remarkable! Excellent!" said Colonel Marquis, who was rubbing his hands with fiendish glee. Page felt that if his chief had not been lame, he would have danced. Marquis pointed a long forefinger at his subordinate. "You are shocked," he went on. "In the depths of your soul you are shocked at my lack of dignity. Wait until you are my age. Then you will realize that the greatest joy of passing sixty is being able to act as you jolly well please. Inspector, this case is a sizzler; it has possibilities; and doubtless you see them?"

Page considered. "As for the possibilities, sir, there seems to be something very fishy about that theft of Sir Andrew Travers' gun. If White couldn't have done it—"

"Ah, White. Yes. That's why I wanted our friends out of the room; I should like to have a little talk with White, alone."

He got on the telephone again and gave orders for White to be brough up.

There was little change in the young man's appearance since last night, Page noticed, except that he was now dry and brushed. Two constables brought him in: a tall, rather lanky figure still wearing his shabby topcoat. His darkish fair hair was worn rather long, brushed back from the forehead, and he smoothed at it nervously. His face was strong, with a delicate nose but a strong jaw; and he had good gray eyes under pinched brows. The face was slightly hollow, his movements jerky. At the moment he seemed half belligerent, half despairing.

"Why don't you tell us what really happened at that pavilion?" Marquis began.

"I wish you'd tell *me*," the other said simply. "Do you think I've been pounding my head about anything else since they nabbed me? Whatever happens, I'm due for a long stretch at the Moor, because I really did take a crack at the old swine. But, believe it or not, I—*did—not—kill—him.*"

"Well, that's what we're here to discover," Marquis said comfortably. "You are an artist, I've heard?"

"I am a painter," said White, still shortly. "Whether or not I am an artist remains to be seen." The light of the fanatic came into his eyes. "By heaven, I wish Philistines would not persist in misusing terms they do not understand! I wish—"

"We are coming to that. I understand you've got some strong political views. What do you believe in?"

"So you want to know what I believe in?" he demanded. "I believe in a new world, an enlightened world, a world free from the muddle we have made of this. I want a world of light and progress, that a man can breathe decently in; a world without violence of war; a world, in that fine phrase of Wells's, 'waste, austere and wonderful.' That's all I want, and it's little enough."

"And how would you bring this about?"

"First," said White, "all capitalists would be taken out and hanged. Those who opposed us, of course, would merely be shot. But capitalists would be hanged, because they have brought about this muddle and made us their tools. I say it again: we are tools, tools, tools, TOOLS."

Page thought: The fellow's off his onion. But there was about Gabriel White such a complete and flaming earnestness that it carried conviction. White stopped, breathing so hard that it choked him.

"And you think Mr. Justice Mortlake deserved death?"

"He was a swine," answered White calmly. "You don't need political science to tell you that."

"Did you know him personally?"

"No," said White, after a hesitation.

"But you know Miss Ida Mortlake?"

"I know her slightly." He was still inscrutable. "Not that it matters. There is no need to drag her into this; she knows nothing of it."

"Naturally not. Well, suppose you tell us exactly what happened yesterday afternoon. To begin with, how did you get inside the grounds?"

White looked dogged. "I'd better tell you about that, yes, because it's the one thing I'm ashamed of. You see, I met Ida yesterday afternoon. We were at a Lyons' in Hampstead. Naturally I didn't want to meet her just then; but I felt bound to warn her I was going to kill the old man if I could." There was a dull flush under his cheek bones. His fine, rather large-knuckled hands were fidgeting on his knees. "The fact is, I hid in the back of her car. She didn't know it. After she'd left the tea shop, she was going to a lending library just down the road. I knew that. So I followed. While she was in the library, I nipped into the back of the car and got down under a rug. It was a very dark day and raining hard, so I knew she wouldn't notice me. Otherwise I couldn't have got inside the grounds at all. The gatekeeper keeps a sharp lookout.

"She drove through the gates and up to the house. When she put the car in the garage, I sneaked out. The trouble was I didn't know *where* the old swine was. How was I to know he was at the pavilion? I thought I should find him in the house.

"I wasted nearly an hour trying to get into that house. There seemed to be servants all over the place. Finally I did get in—through a side window. And I nearly walked into the butler. He was just going into a front room, drawing room or the like, where Ida Mortlake was sitting. He said it was getting very late, and asked whether she wanted tea served? She said yes; she said to go ahead and serve it, because her father was at the pavilion and probably wouldn't be up for tea. That was how I knew, you see. So I hopped out the side window again."

"What time was this?"

"God knows; I wasn't paying any attention to that. Stop a bit, though." White reflected. "You can easily enough find out. I ran straight down to the pavilion, as hard as I could pelt. There I ran into your police officers—I supposed they were police officers—and by that time I was determined to kill the old devil if it was the last thing I ever did."

The breath whistled out of his nostrils. Colonel Marquis asked:

"We can put it, then at half past five? Good. Go on. Everything!"

"I've gone over it a hundred times since then," said White. He shut his eyes, and spoke slowly. "I ran to the door of the study. I ran inside and locked the door. Mortlake had been standing at the window, shouting something to the police officer outside. When he heard me come in, he turned round from the window. . . ."

"Did he say anything?"

"Yes. He said, 'What is the meaning of this?' or 'What do you want here?' or something of that sort. I can't remember the exact words. Then he put his hand up in front of him, as though I were going to hit him, when he saw the gun in my hand. Then I fired. With that pistol," said White, touching the Ivor-Johnson .38.

"H'm, yes. D'you hit him?"

"Sir, I'm practically certain I didn't," declared the other, bringing down his fist on the edge of the desk. "Look here: there was a very bright light up over the desk. It was in a brass holder of some kind, and it left most of the room pretty dark because it was concentrated.

But it lit up the desk and the space between the windows. Just as I pulled the trigger, I saw the bullet hole jump up black in the wall behind him. And he was still moving and running. Besides . . ."

"Well?"

"It isn't as easy," said White, suddenly looking like an old man, "to kill a man as you might think. It's all right until your hand is actually on the trigger. Then something seems to wash all out of you. It seems as though you can't, physically can't, do it. It's like hitting a man when he's down. And it's a queer thing—just at that second, I almost pitied the old beggar. He looked so *scared*, flapping away from my gun like a bat trying to get out."

"Just a moment," interposed Marquis. "Are you accustomed to use firearms?"

White was puzzled. "No. I don't suppose I've ever handled anything more deadly than an air rifle when I was a boy. But I thought, shut up in a room, I couldn't very well miss. Then—I did miss. Do you want me to go on? He started to run away from me, along the back wall. He was alive then, all right. I want you to understand that the whole thing was such a brief matter of seconds, all compressed, that it's a bit confused. At this time he was facing, slightly sideways, the wall behind me on my right . . ."

"Facing, then, the corner where the yellow vase stood? The vase where the automatic was later found?"

"Yes. It seemed as though he'd turned round to swing out into the room. Then I heard another shot. It seemed to come from behind me and to my right. I felt—a kind of wind, if you know what I mean.

"After this he put his hands up to his chest. He turned round and took a few steps back the way he'd come, and swung a little back again, and then fell headfirst across the desk. Just as he fell, your police officer"—White nodded towards Page—"came in through the window. And that's the best I can do."

"Did you see anybody else in the room, either before or after this shot?"

"No."

The Assistant Commissioner's sombre eyes wandered over to Page. "A question for you, Inspector. Would it be possible for there to have been any mechanical device in that room, hidden somewhere, which could have fired a shot and concealed the pistol without anyone else being there?"

Page was prompt. He and Borden had searched that room too well.

"It's absolutely impossible, sir," he answered. "We nearly took that pavilion to pieces. Also," he smiled a little, "you can rule out any idea of a secret passage or a trap-door. There wasn't so much as a mouse hole. . . . Besides, there's the gun in the yellow vase, which really was fired inside that room."

Colonel Marquis nodded dully. He said:

"Yes, I think we have got to acknowledge that the second shot was fired by somebody inside the room. Look here, White: how far were you away from the judge when you shot at him?"

"About fifteen feet, I should think."

"H'm, yes. Very well. We assume somebody dropped that pistol into the vase. You say the vase was much too high for anybody's arm to reach down inside and deposit the gun there. So it must have made some noise when it fell." He looked at White. "Did you hear any noise?"

White was troubled. "I don't know. I honestly don't know. I can't remember—"

"You realize," said Marquis, with sudden harshness, "that you are telling us an absolutely impossible thing? You are saying that somebody must have escaped from a room which was locked and guarded on all sides? *How?* . . . Yes, yes, what is it?"

He broke off as his secretary came into the room and spoke in a low tone. Colonel Marquis nodded, becoming affable again.

"It's the police surgeon," he said to Page. "He's performed the postmortem. And the results seem to be so interesting that he wants to see me directly. Most unusual. Send him in."

There was a silence. White sat quietly in his chair; but he had braced his elbows against the back of the chair and his heavy handsome face had a blankness of waiting. Page knew what goblins had come into the room to surround the prisoner. If the bullet in the judge's body turned out to be a .38 after all, it meant the end of him. Dr. Gallatin, the police surgeon, a worried bustling man, came into the room with a briefcase in his hand.

"Good morning, doctor," said Colonel Marquis. "We were waiting for you. We can't go any further until we know. What's the verdict?" He pushed the two pistols across the desk. "Public opinion is divided. One branch thinks Mr. Justice Mortlake was killed by a bullet from an Ivor-Johnson .38 revolver, fired from a distance of about fifteen feet. The other branch denies this and says he was killed by a bullet from a Browning .32 automatic, fired from a distance of about twenty-five feet. Which side is right?"

"Neither," said the doctor.

Colonel Marquis sat up very slowly. "What the devil do you mean, neither?"

"I said neither," replied the doctor, "because both sides are wrong, sir. As a matter of fact, he was killed by a bullet from an Erckmann air pistol, roughly corresponding to a .22 caliber, fired from a distance of about ten feet."

Although Marquis did not bat an eyelid, Page felt that the old so-and-so had seldom in his life received so unexpected an announcement. He remained sitting bolt upright, looking coldly at the doctor.

"I trust, Dr. Gallatin," he said, "that you are sober?"

"Quite sober, worse luck," agreed the doctor.

"And you are seriously trying to tell me that there was still a THIRD shot fired in that room?"

"I don't know anything about the case, sir. All I know is that he was plugged at fairly short range"—Gallatin opened the little cardboard box and took out a flattish lump of lead—"by this bullet from an Erckmann air pistol. As a rule you see the Erckmann army pistol, which is a lot heavier than this. But this one is a dangerous job, because it's got much more power than an ordinary firearm, and it's almost noiseless."

Colonel Marquis turned to White. "What have *you* got to say to this?"

White was evidently so strung up that he had forgotten his rôle as light-bringer and social reformer; he spoke like a schoolboy, with sullen petulance. "Here, I say! Fair play! I don't know any more about it than you do."

"Did you hear or see *another* shot fired in that room?"

"No, I did not."

"Inspector Page: you searched the room immediately after you went in. Did you find any air pistol?"

"No, sir," said Page firmly. "If there had been one, I'm certain we should have found it."

"And you also searched the prisoner. Did he have any such pistol on him, or could he have disposed of it."

"He did not and he could not," replied Page. "Besides, three pistols carried by one man would be coming it a little too strong. In a case like that, I should think it would have been simpler to have used a machine gun." He saw the Colonel's eye grow dangerous, and added: "May I ask a question? Doctor, would it have been possible for that air pistol bullet to have been fired either from a Browning .32 or an Ivor-Johnson .38? A sort of fraud to make us think a third gun had been used?"

Dr. Gallatin grinned. "You don't know much about ballistics, do you?" he asked. "It's not only impossible, it's mad. Ask your firearms man. This little pellet had to be fired, and was fired, from an Erckmann air pistol."

Now that the reaction had set in, White was deadly pale. He looked from one to the other of them.

"Excuse me," he said, with the first trace of humility he had shown, "but does this mean I'm cleared of the actual—murder?"

"Yes," said Colonel Marquis. "Brace up, man! Here, pull yourself together. I'm sending you downstairs for a while. This alters matters considerably."

He pressed the buzzer on his desk. White was escorted out, talking volubly but incomprehensibly about nothing at all. The Assistant Commissioner remained staring after him with sombre concentration, and knocking his knuckles against his desk.

Page and the doctor watched him.

"This is insanity," he went on. "Let us see where we stand: There is now no doubt that three shots were fired: from the Ivor-Johnson, *and* the Browning, *and* the missing Erckmann. The trouble is that we lack a bullet, for only two of the three bullets have been found. By the way, Inspector, pass me over that pellet you found stuck in the wall." Page gave it to him and Colonel Marquis weighed it in his hand. "You say this is from the Ivor-Johnson .38. I agree, decidedly. We'll get a third opinion; what's your guess, doctor?"

Gallatin took the bullet and studied it.

"It's a .38, all right," he agreed. "No doubt of it. I've handled too many of them. This has been chipped a bit, that's all."

"Right, then. This is the one White admits having fired at the judge, as soon as he walked into the judge's study. So far, so good. But what about afterwards? What sort of witchcraft or hocus-pocus happened in the next two or three seconds?—By the way, doctor, you said an Erckmann air pistol is almost noiseless. *How* noiseless?"

Gallatin was cautious. "That's out of my department, you know. But I think I can give you an idea. It isn't a great deal louder than the noise you make when you press the catch of an electric-light switch."

"Then, sir," interposed Page slowly, "you mean the Erckmann might have been fired in that room almost under White's nose, and (especially with a storm going on outside) he mightn't have heard it at all?"

Marquis nodded. "But take it in order," he said. "After White fires his revolver, the judge starts to run away. Then someone else—standing behind and to the right of White, over in the corner by the yellow vase—fires a shot with the Browning automatic. This shot is heard by Inspector Page, who is within ten steps of the window. But the *bullet* from the Browning disappears. If it didn't kill the judge, where did it go? Where did it lodge? Where is it now?

"Finally, someone cuts loose with an Erckmann air pistol and fires the shot which really does kill Mortlake. But this time the *gun* disappears. Whoosh!" said Colonel Marquis, with an imaginative flourish. "Just as Mortlake falls forward dead across the writing table, Inspector Page arrives at the window, in time to find the room sealed up impregnably from every side—the only point being that the *murderer* has disappeared."

He paused, letting them picture the scene for themselves.

"Gentlemen, I don't believe it. But there it is. Have you any suggestions?"

"Only questions," Page said gloomily. "I take it we agree, sir, that White can't be the murderer?"

"Yes, we can safely say that."

Page took out his notebook and wrote: "Three questions seem to be indicated, all tied up with each other. (1) Did the same person who fired the Browning automatic also fire the Erckmann air pistol? And, if not, were there two people in the room besides White? (2) Was the fatal shot fired immediately before, or immediately after, the shot from the Browning? (3) In either case, where was the actual murderer standing?"

He looked up from his notebook, and Marquis nodded.

"Yes, I see the point. Number three is the hardest question of the lot," the Assistant Commissioner said. "According to the doctor here, Mortlake was shot through the heart at a distance of about ten feet. White, by his own confession, was standing fifteen feet away from Mortlake. How the devil does it happen, then, that White didn't see the murderer? Gentlemen, there is something so internally fishy about this case."

"You mean," Page volunteered, "you mean the old idea that White might be shielding somebody?"

"But that's the trouble. Even if White is shielding anybody, how did anybody get out of the room? There was certainly one other person in there, and possibly two. Suppose one, or two, or six people took a shot at the judge: where did the whole procession vanish to—in the course of about eight or ten seconds?" He shook his head. "I say, doctor, is there anything in the medical evidence that would help us?"

"Not about the vanishing, certainly," said Gallatin. "And not much about anything. Death was almost instantaneous. He might have taken a step or two afterwards, or made a movement; but not much more."

"In that case," said the colonel, "*I* am going to find out. Let's have a car round here, Page, and run out to Hampstead. This interests me."

He limped across after his hat and coat. In his dark blue overcoat and soft gray hat, Colonel Marquis presented a figure of great sartorial elegance, except for the fact that he jammed on the hat so malevolently as to give it a high crown like Guy Fawkes's. First, Page had to issue instructions: a man must be sent to verify Travers' alibi, and the files of the firearms department ransacked to find any record of who might own an Erckmann air pistol. Then Colonel Marquis went limping out, towering over nearly everyone in the office. When Page protested that Ida Mortlake and Sir Andrew Travers were still waiting, he grunted.

"Let 'em wait," he said impolitely. "The case has taken such a turn that they will only confuse matters. Between ourselves, inspector, I don't care to have Travers about when I examine the scene. Travers is a trifle too shrewd." He said little more while the police car moved through wet and gusty streets towards Hampstead. Page prompted him.

"It seems," the inspector said, "that we've now got a very restricted circle."

"Restricted circle?"

"Like this, sir. There seems no reason why Travers should have killed the judge; and, on top of it, he's got a sound alibi. Next, Ida Mortlake has an alibi—an unintentional alibi—"

"Ah; you noticed that," observed Colonel Marquis, looking at him.

"Provided, unintentionally, by White himself. You remember what White said. He got through a window into the judge's house, not knowing the judge was at the pavilion. And he didn't learn the truth until he heard the butler asking Ida whether tea should be served. As soon as he heard this, he nipped out of the window and ran straight to the pavilion. This was at five thirty, for he met Borden and myself on the way. Consequently, Ida must still have been at the house; and we can probably get the butler's corroboration. That's a sound alibi."

"Quite. Anything else?"

"If," answered Page thoughtfully, "if, as seems likely, no outsider could have got into the grounds—well, it looks as though he must have been killed either by one of the servants or by Miss Carolyn Mortlake or by old Penney, the clerk."

Colonel Marquis grunted out something which might have been assent or disagreement and pointed out that they would soon know. The car had swung into the broad suburban thoroughfare along one side of which ran the high wall of the judge's house. It was a busy street, where a tramline and a bus route crossed. Along one side were several shops, contrasting with the lonely stone wall across the street, beyond which elms showed tattered against a drizzling sky. They stopped before iron-grilled gates; and old Robinson, recognizing the police car, hastened to open.

"Anything new?" Page asked.

Robinson, the gatekeeper, a little man with a veined forehead and a dogged eye, thrust his head into the back of the car.

"Nossir," he said. "Except your sergeant is still dead-set trying to find out whether anybody could have sneaked in here yesterday afternoon without my knowing—"

"And could anybody have done that?" asked Colonel Marquis.

Robinson studied him, wondering. "Well, sir, they told me to keep people out—or Miss Ida did, yesterday—and I *did* keep people out. That's my job. You just take a look at them walls. Anybody'd need a ladder to get over 'em, and there's no side of the walls where you could prop up a ladder without being seen by half the people in Hampstead. There's a main road in front and there's people's back gardens coming up against the walls on every other side." He cleared his throat, like a man about to spit, and grew more dogged. "There's only two gates, as you can see for yourself, and I was sitting right by one of them!"

"What about the other gate—the tradesmen's entrance?"

"Locked," said Robinson promptly. "When Miss Ida come back from her drive yesterday, about four twenty, no more, she told me to lock it and I did. There's only one other key besides mine, and Miss Ida's got that."

"You said that both Miss Carolyn Mortlake and Mr. Penney weren't here yesterday afternoon?"

"I don't remember whether I said so to you. But it's true."

"What time did they go?"

"Miss Carolyn—'bout quarter to four. Yes. Becos she'd wanted the car. And Miss Ida had already taken the car and gone out a quarter of an hour before that. Miss Carolyn, she was pretty mad; she was going to a cocktail party (people name o' Fischer at Golder's Green); and she wanted that car. As for Alfred Eric Penney, don't ask me when *he* went out. About ten minutes past four, I think."

Colonel Marquis was bland. "For the sake of clearness, we had better make this a timetable. The judge went from his house across to the pavilion—when?"

"Half past three," answered Robinson firmly. "That's certain."

"Good. Ida Mortlake leaves here in the car about the same time. Correct? Good. Carolyn Mortlake leaves for a cocktail party at fifteen minutes to four. At ten minutes past four, Penney also leaves. At twenty minutes past four, the rain having then begun, Ida Mortlake returns in the car. They all seem to have missed each other most conveniently; but that, I take it, is the timetable."

"I suppose it is; yes, sir," Robinson admitted.

"Drive on," said Colonel Marquis.

The car sped up a gravel drive between doleful elms. Page indicated where a branch of this path turned towards the pavilion, but the pavilion was some distance away, hidden in an ornamental clump of trees, and Marquis could not see it. The house itself would not have pleased an architect. It was of three stories, stuccoed, and built in that bastard style of Gothic architecture first seen at Strawberry Hill, but revived with gusto by designers during the middle of the nineteenth century. Its discolored pinnacles huddled together under the rain. Most of the long windows were shuttered, but smoke drooped down from all the chimneys. Though it was a landmark of solid Victorian respectability and prosperity there was about it something close-lipped and definitely evil.

The height of respectability also was the grizzled, heavy-headed manservant who admitted them. He fitted; you would have expected him. Page had seen him yesterday, although he had taken no statement. They now learned his name, which was Davies.

"If you don't mind, sir," he said, "I'll call Miss Carolyn. As a matter of fact, Miss Carolyn was just about to set out to see you. She—"

"And if *you* don't mind," said a new voice, "I should prefer to handle this myself, please."

The hall was shadowed by a window of red glass at the back. A woman came out between the bead curtains (which still exist) of an archway to the right. Carolyn Mortlake was one of those startling family contrasts (which, also, still exist). Where Ida was rather tall and soft, Carolyn was short, stocky, and hard. Where Ida was fair, Carolyn was dark. She had a square, very good-looking but very hard face; with black eyes of a snapping luminousness and a mouth painted dark red. They could see her jaw muscles. She came forward at a free stride, wearing a tilted hat and a plain dark coat with a fur collar. But

Page noticed, curiously enough, that her eyelids were puffy and reddish. She appraised them coolly, a heavy handbag under her arm.

"You are—?" she said.

Colonel Marquis made the introductions, and in his politeness the girl seemed to find something suspicious.

"We are honored," she told him, "to have the Assistant Commissioner visit us in person. Perhaps I had better give you this."

With a decisive snap she opened the catch of her handbag, and took out a nickeled pistol with a rather long and top-heavy barrel.

"It is an Erckmann air pistol," she said.

"So it is, Miss Mortlake. Where did you get it?"

"From the bottom drawer of the bureau in my bedroom," replied Carolyn Mortlake, and lifted her head to stare at him defiantly.

"Perhaps," she said after a pause, "you had better come this way." In spite of her defiance, it was clear that she was shaking with some strong inner strain. But she was as cool as ever when she led them through the bead curtains into a thick-cluttered drawing room.

"I don't know quite what the game is," she went on. "I can't see why anybody should want to do it, because obviously my father wasn't killed with that gun. . . . But I think I know what I was intended to do when I found it. I was supposed to become panicky, and hide the gun away again in case I should be suspected of something, and generally behave like a silly ass. Well, you jolly well won't find *me* doing things like that; I'm not such a fool." She smiled, without humor, and reached for a cigarette box. "There's the gun and you may take it or leave it."

Colonel Marquis turned the pistol over in his fingers. "You think, then," he said, "that somebody deliberately hid this in your room? You have probably observed that one bullet has been fired from it."

"I am not going to pretend to misunderstand when I understand perfectly well what you mean. Or what I think you mean. Yes, I thought of that too. But it's absolutely impossible. There were only two guns, a .32 and a .38; and this isn't either."

"Well . . . waiving that for a moment: you don't happen to know who owns this gun? You've never seen it before?"

"Of course I've seen it before—dozens of times. It belonged to Father."

Page stared at this extraordinary witness who spoke with such a contempt in amazement. But the Assistant Commissioner only nodded, with an appreciative smile.

"Ah, yes. Where did your father keep it?"

"In the drawer of his writing table at the pavilion."

"And when did you see it last, if you can remember?"

"I saw it yesterday afternoon, in the writing table drawer as usual."

"You will perceive, by the haste with which Inspector Page goes after his notebook," Marquis told her suavely, "that these discoveries are coming fast. Suppose, Miss Mortlake, we keep from going too fast, and get these things in order? First of all, naturally, I should like to convey my sympathies in the death of your father . . ."

"Thank you," she said.

"Can you give any reason, Miss Mortlake, why your father seems to have been disliked in his own house? Neither you nor your sister seems to show any great grief at his death."

"Whether I felt any grief or whether I didn't," said Carolyn dispassionately, "I should not be inclined to discuss it with someone I had just met. But didn't you know? He is not our father, really. We were very young when he married our mother; but our real father is dead. I do not see that it matters, but you had better have the facts straight."

This was news both to Page and Marquis, who looked at each other. The Assistant Commissioner ignored the justifiable thrust in reply to his question.

"I have no intention, Miss Mortlake, of trying to trap you or hide things from you. Your father—we'll call him that—really was shot with the air pistol." He gave a very terse but very clever account of the affair, up to the point they had reached. "That," he added, "is why I need your help."

She had been staring at him, her face dark and rather terrible. But she spoke calmly enough. "So someone really was trying to throw suspicion on me?"

"It would seem so. Again, while it's *possible* that an outsider could have committed the crime, still you'll agree with me that it's very improbable. It would appear to be somebody in this house. Is there anybody here who has a grudge against you?"

"No, certainly not!"

"Tell me frankly, then: how did you get on with your father?"

"As well as people do in most families, I dare say." For the first time she looked troubled.

"You and your sister, I take it, are your father's heirs?"

She tried to force a hard smile. "The old problem of the will, eh?" she inquired, with a mocking ghastliness of waggery. "Yes, so far as I know we were. He made no secret of that. There are small legacies for the servants and a substantial one for Penney, but Ida and I inherit jointly. That's how it used to be, anyhow. He made a will when my mother died. Of course, he may have changed it since, but I don't think so."

Colonel Marquis nodded, and held up the air pistol. "This pistol, Miss Mortlake . . . you say your father kept it constantly by him?"

"Good Lord, no! I didn't say that. No; or he wouldn't have kept it at the pavilion. He kept it as a kind of curio. You see, a friend of his was in the Secret Service during the war, and made him a present of it; I believe those air-guns are a rarity."

"Yes. What I meant was, he didn't keep the gun by him because he feared an attack?"

"No, I'm positive he didn't."

"What about the threats made by Gabriel White?"

"Oh, Gabriel!—" she said. Her gestures seemed to sum up a great deal; then she considered. "Besides, until I saw Ida last night and read the newspapers this morning, I didn't know Gabriel *had* made any threats. Not that he would not have had reason to. My father knew

Gabriel—or, at least he knew of him. I don't know how. He never spoke much about it. But he never troubled to conceal his belief that Gabriel was a swine."

"You liked White?"

"Yes. No. I don't know." She paused, and her square handsome face had an expression of cynicism so deep that it seemed to have been put there with a stamp. "My opinion! You flatter me, Colonel. I have been asked my opinion more times in the last ten minutes than I have been asked for it in the last ten months. I rather like Gabriel, to tell you the truth; and I think he's quite straight. But, my God, I hate lame ducks!"

"I see. Now, for the benefit of Inspector Page's notebook, how did you spend yesterday afternoon?"

"Ah, the alibi," murmured Carolyn, slightly showing her teeth. "Well, let's see. The earlier part of the afternoon I spent interviewing a horde of prospective servants. Our maid—we boast only one—is leaving us next month to get married. Ah, romance! So we've got to replace her."

Inspector Page interposed.

"There seem to be a lot of things we haven't heard of, Miss Mortlake," he said. "You mean there were a number of outsiders here in the grounds yesterday afternoon?"

She studied him and at length decided to be civil. "You may set your mind and notebook at rest, Inspector," she informed him. "All of the lot were out of the house and out of the grounds at least two hours before my father was shot. Robinson at the gate can tell you that, if he overcomes his usual closed-mouth tactics. He let 'em in, and counted 'em, and let 'em out.

"The last of them left between half past three and a quarter to four. I know that, because I was anxious to get out of the house myself. Then I discovered that Ida had gone out and taken the car. That was a bloody bore because I had been rather under the impression it was promised to me. But there it was. I could get a taxi, anyhow. First, however, I went down to the pavilion. . . ."

"Why did you go to the pavilion, Miss Mortlake?"

She flushed a little. "I wanted some pocket-money. Besides, I wanted to tell him, in a dutiful way, that I had engaged a new maid."

"Go on, please."

"He had only been at the pavilion five minutes or so when I got there; he went down about half past three. You may be interested to know that I got the money. That, incidentally, is how I happen to know the air pistol was in the drawer of his writing table at that time. He opened the drawer to get his check book. It was too late for the bank, but I knew where I could get the check cashed. When he opened the drawer I saw the gun."

"Was the drawer locked or unlocked?"

She reflected, her hand shading her eyes. "It was locked. I remember: he got a bunch of keys out of his pocket and opened it."

"Did he lock it afterwards?"

"I'm not sure. I didn't notice—after I'd got the check. But I rather think he did. His precious manuscript was there."

"I see. Did he do or say anything notable that you remember?"

"Notable is good. No, not that I remember. He was a little short, because he doesn't like being interrrupted when he's down there reciting chapters of his book to that dictaphone. He wrote down the name of the maid I was going to engage: he wanted to check her credentials before she came here next month. . . . Oh, yes; and he mentioned that Sir Andrew Travers was coming there to tea. They were going to have tea at the pavilion. In the other room at the pavilion—the one across the hall from the study—he has an electric kettle and all the doings. I suggested that he'd better switch on the electric fire in the room across the hall or it would be freezing cold when Andrew got there."

"And did he switch it on?"

She was puzzled. "Yes. Or, rather, I did it for him."

"Inspector, when you and Sergeant Borden searched the pavilion, I suppose you looked into this other room across the hall? Was the electric fire burning in that room?"

Page saw an angry flush come into Carolyn Mortlake's face, but he checked her outburst.

"Yes, sir, the fire was on."

"Thank you," snapped Carolyn Mortlake.

"I don't think you quite understand the meaning of the last question," the Colonel told her calmly. "Now, will you go on with your story, please?"

"I left the pavilion, and the grounds; that was about a quarter to four."

"Yes; and afterwards?"

She folded her hands in her lap with great nicety. Taking a deep breath, she lifted her head and looked him in the eye. Something had blazed and hardened, like the effect of a fire.

"I'm sorry," she said; "but that's where the story stops. That's all I have to say."

"I don't understand this," said Colonel Marquis sharply. "You mean you won't tell us what you did after you left the house?"

"Yes."

"But that's absurd. Don't be a young fool! Your gatekeeper himself told us you were going to a cocktail party at Golder's Green."

"He had no right to tell you any such thing," she flared. "You'll only waste your time inquiring after me at the Fischers'. I didn't go. I intended to go, but an hour or so before I left the house I got a telephone message which made me change my mind. That's all I can tell you."

"But why shouldn't you tell us?"

"In the first place, because you wouldn't believe me. In the second place, because I can't prove where I was during the afternoon, so it's no good as an alibi. In the third place—well, that's what I prefer to keep to myself. It's no good coming the high official over me. I've said I won't tell you, and I mean it."

"You realize, Miss Mortlake, that this puts you under suspicion for murder?"

"Yes."

Page felt that she was about to add something else; but at that moment all emotion, protest, or explanation was washed out of her. She became again a person of shuttered defiance. For someone had come into the room—they heard hesitant footsteps, and the faint clicking of the bead curtains at the door.

The newcomer was a little, deprecating man with a stoop and a nervously complaisant manner. They felt that it must be Alfred Penney, the clerk. Penney's feet were enormous and his hands seemed all knuckles. He had a few strands of iron-gray hair brushed across his skull like the skeleton of a fish, and something suspiciously like side whiskers. But he had a faithful eye, blinking at them while he dabbed his hand at it.

"I beg your pardon," he said, wheeling round quickly.

Carolyn Mortlake rose. "Alfred, this is Colonel Marquis, the Assistant Commissioner of Police, and Inspector Page. Tell them what you can. For the moment, I think they will excuse *me*."

While Penney blinked at them, his mouth a little open, she strode past out of the room. Then his face assumed his legal manner. "I really beg your pardon," he repeated. "I should not have intruded, but I saw Davies, the butler, in the hall intently listening to what was going on in here, and—no matter. You are the police? Yes; of course."

"Sit down, Mr. Penney," said Colonel Marquis.

"This is a terrible thing, gentlemen. Terrible," said Penney, balancing himself gingerly on the edge of a chair. "You cannot realize what a shock it has been to me. I have been associated with him for thirty years. Twenty-nine and a half, to be exact." His voice grew even more mild. "I trust you will not think me vindictive, gentlemen, if I ask you whether you have taken any steps with regard to this young hound who killed him?"

"Gabriel White?"

"If you prefer to call him that."

"So?" prompted Marquis, with a gleam of interest. He lifted his eyebrows. "It has been suggested, Mr. Penney, that 'Gabriel White' is not the man's real name. The judge knew him?"

The little man nodded. "I am not ashamed to tell you," he replied, tilting up his chin, "that he did. If he condemned him, he dealt out moral justice; and moral justice was always Charles Mortlake's aim. Charles Mortlake knew the young man's father very well and has been acquainted with the young man since he was a boy. 'Gabriel White' is really Lord Edward Whiteford, a son of the Earl of Cray."

There was a pause, while Penney stared sideways at the fire. "Fortunately," he went on, knitting the baggy skin of his forehead, "the Earl of Cray does not know where his son is, or how he has sunk; and Charles Mortlake was not so inhumane as to enlighten him. . . . Gabriel White, since he prefers to call himself that, started in the world with every advantage. At Oxford he had a distinguished career. He was a leading member of the Union and great things were predicted for him. Also, he was a popular athlete. I believe he holds the university record for the broad jump; and he was also an expert swordsman and pistol shot. But, like so many who start with advantages—"

"Hold on," interrupted Marquis in a voice so sharp and official that Penney jumped a little. "I want to get this straight. You say he was an expert pistol shot? In my office this morning he told us that he had never handled a gun in his life."

"I am afraid he lied, then," Penney said without rancor. "Lying is a habit of his."

Marquis took the air pistol from the chair and held it up.

"Ever see this before?"

"Yes, sir. Often," said Penney, taken aback. "It belonged to Charles Mortlake. May I ask why—"

"When did you last see it?"

"A few days ago, I think; but I am afraid I cannot swear to the exact time. He kept it in the drawer of his writing table at the pavilion."

"Were you at the pavilion yesterday afternoon?"

"Yes, I was at the pavilion yesterday afternoon—for a very brief time. Five minutes, perhaps. Yesterday afternoon I was going to the Guildhall Library to verify a series of references for the book he was writing. I left the house at shortly after four o'clock—it had begun to rain, I may remark—and on my way down to the gate it occurred to me that I had better go to the pavilion and inquire whether there were any additional material he wished me to consult.

"I found him alone at the pavilion, speaking to the dictaphone." The clerk paused and something like the edge of a tear appeared in the corner of each eye. "He said there was nothing further he wished me to do at the library. So I left the grounds about ten minutes past four. It was the last time I ever saw him alive. But . . ."

"But?"

"I should have been warned," said Penney, fixing his questioner with grave attention. "There was somebody prowling round the pavilion even then. While we were speaking together, I distinctly heard footsteps approaching the windows."

"Which windows?"

"The west windows, sir. The windows whose locks and shutters are so rusted it is impossible to open them."

"Go on."

"Immediately after that, I was under the impression that I heard a sound of someone softly pulling or rattling at one of the west windows, as though trying to open it. But the rain was making some noise then, and I am not certain of this."

"The judge heard it as well?"

"Yes. I am afraid he regarded it as imagination. But only a few seconds afterwards something struck the outer shutter of one of the *other* windows. I am under the impression that it was a pebble, or light stone of some kind, which had been thrown. This window was one of those in the south wall. . . . Judging from accounts I have heard," he turned mildly to Page, "it was the window through which you, Inspector, were obliged to climb nearly an hour and a half afterwards. When Charles Mortlake heard this noise, he pushed back the curtains, pushed up the window, unlocked the shutters, and looked out. There was nothing to be seen."

"What did he do then?"

"He closed and relocked the window, although he did not relock the shutters. He left them open against the wall. He was . . . I fear he was somewhat annoyed. He accused me of entertaining fancies. There is a tree some dozen or so feet away from the window; and he declared that a twig or the like had probably come loose in the storm, and had blown against the shutter. It is true that there was a strong wind, but I could not credit this explanation."

"Do you know whether this air pistol was then in the table drawer?"

"I don't know; I should suppose so. He had no occasion to open the drawer. But my thoughts did not go—well, quite to the edge of violence in that line." His eyes did not fall before Marquis' steady stare; and presently he went on: "You will wish to know what I did afterwards. I went from here, by Underground, to Mansion House station, and thence to the Guildhall Library on foot. I arrived there at 4:35, since I happened to notice the clock. I left the library at just 5:00. In coming home I experienced some delay and did not arrive here until 5:40, when I heard Charles Mortlake was dead. I am afraid that is all I have to say. . . . And now may I ask why are you concerned with that air pistol?"

Again Colonel Marquis told the familiar story. As he did so, Penney did not look startled; he only looked witless. He remained sitting by the fire, a gnome with veined hands, and he hardly seemed to breathe. Marquis concluded:

"You see, we are compelled to accept White's innocence. Even if you argue that the air pistol was in the table drawer and White might have used it himself, still he would not have had the time to fire *three* shots. Next, though he was seized by police officers instantly, the air pistol had completely vanished; and he could not have concealed it. Finally, he was at once taken to the police station; so that he could not have conveyed the air pistol to this house. But it was actually found here this morning."

Penney said, "Good heaven!—" and somehow the expletive seemed as weak and ineffectual as himself. "But this is surely the most preposterous thing I have heard of," he stammered. "I cannot imagine you are serious. You are? But there is no reason in it! Life works by reason and system. You cannot believe that there were three prospective murderers shut up in that room?"

At this point Page had the impression that Marquis was playing with his witness; that he was juggling facts for his own amusement, or to show his skill; and that the colonel had an excellent idea of what really happened in the locked room. Marquis remained urbane.

"Will you argue theories, Mr. Penney? Not necessarily *three*, but certainly two. Has it occurred to you, for example, that the same person who fired the Browning may also have fired the Erckmann air pistol?"

"I do not know what has occurred to me," Penney retorted simply. He lifted up his arms and dropped them with an oddly flapping gesture. "I only know that, however my poor friend was killed, Lord Edward Whiteford—or Gabriel White, if you prefer—killed him. Sir, you do not know that young man. I do. It sounds exactly like him. He would, and he could, deceive the devil himself! I cannot tell you how strongly I feel about this, or how clever that young hound is. With him it is always the twisted way, the ingenious way."

"Still, you don't maintain he can perform miracles?"

"Apparent miracles, yes," Penney replied quite seriously. "You don't know his cleverness, I repeat; and you won't know it until he somehow hoodwinks and humiliates you as well. For instance, how did he get into the grounds at all?"

"He has already answered that himself. While Miss Ida Mortlake was getting a book at a lending library, he got into her car and crouched down under a rug in the tonneau. When she drove up to the garage, he waited until she had gone and then got out. The day was too dark for her to notice him."

At the doorway someone coughed. It was hardly a cough at all, so modest and self-effacing was the sound. They looked up to see the grizzled and heavy-faced Davies, the butler.

"May I say a word, sir?" he inquired.

"Eh?" said Colonel Marquis irritably. "All right: what is it?"

"Well, sir, under the circumstances I'll make no bones about saying I overheard what was being said. I mean about the man White, sir, and how he got in by hiding under the rug in Miss Ida's car. However he got into the grounds, it certainly wasn't that way. *He wasn't hiding in the back of the car*—and I can prove it!"

As Davies came into the room, his hands folded in front of him, Penney gave a mutter of petulant protest which changed to interest as soon as he appeared to understand what Davies was talking about. Beyond any doubt Davies looked competent; he was bulbous-nosed and bulbous-eyed, but he had a strong jaw.

"Yes, sir, I admit I listened," he said. "But I look at it like this. We're all shut up in here. Like a ship, as it were. It's to our advantage, servants most of all, to show we didn't have anything to do with killing the poor judge. If you see what I mean, sir. We've got to do it. Besides, it isn't as though I was a proper *butler*. I'm not even allowed to engage a maid, as a proper butler would. Fact is, sir, I was a court crier down on my luck (the drink did it, in Leeds) when the judge picked me up and gave me this job to make good. And I think I did make good, though all I ever knew about being a butler I got from the judge and out of a book. Now that he's dead, my lady friend and I are going to marry and settle down. But, just because he is dead, it doesn't mean we don't care who killed him and that we don't appreciate what he's done for us. So—I listened."

Penney almost sputtered. He acted as though a picture on the wall had suddenly made a face at him.

"You never acted like this before. You never talked like this before—"

"No, sir," said Davies. "But I never had occasion to talk like this before. The judge would've sacked me." He looked at Marquis steadily. "But I think I can do a bit of good."

Colonel Marquis was interested. "A court crier turned butler, eh?" he said, turning the idea over in his mind. "Been with the judge long?"

"Eleven years, sir."

"Benefit under the judge's will?"

"Yes, sir: five hundred pounds. He showed me the will. And I've got a bit saved as well."

"All right. Let's hear about this business of White, or Lord Edward Whiteford; and how he didn't get in here by hiding in Miss Mortlake's car, and how you knew about it."

Davies nodded, not relaxing his butleresque stance. "The thing is sir, she went out in the car yesterday afternoon. It started to rain, and I knew she hadn't an umbrella with her. Now, the garage is twenty yards or so from the house. At near on half past four—maybe twenty or twenty-five minutes past—I saw her drive back. I was in the kitchen, looking out of the window, when I saw the car swing round the drive. So I got an umbrella and went out to the garage and held it over her coming back to the house so she shouldn't get wet."

"Yes; go on."

"Now, I was out to the garage before she'd even got out of the car. I did what you naturally do; as soon as Miss Ida got out, I opened the door of the back and looked to see whether she'd brought any parcels.

There was nobody in the back of that car. And nobody could have nipped out before I looked in, because there was nowhere to go."

"Would it have been possible," Page asked, "for him to have slipped out of the car as it came through the gates, or somewhere on the drive before Miss Mortlake reached the garage?"

"I can't tell you that, sir. You'd better ask Robinson or Miss Ida. But if he *said* he didn't slip out until the car came to the garage—?"

Colonel Marquis did not comment. For a brief time he stared across the room. "Anything else?" he prompted.

"Yes, sir. A bit of exoneration," replied Davies promptly. "Even though I'm not a proper butler, still I feel responsible for the other servants. If you see what I mean. Now, sir, there's only three of us, excluding Robinson, of course, but then he rarely comes to the house. There used to be four, when the judge kept a chauffeur; but he let the chauffeur go and pensioned him handsome. At present, then, there's the cook, the maid, and me. Can I take it for granted that the judge was killed between, say, twenty minutes past five and twenty minutes to six?"

"You can," Colonel Marquis agreed, and glanced at Page. "Did you note, inspector, the exact time to the minute or second when all the shots were being fired?"

Page nodded. "I looked at my watch as soon as I got into the pavilion and took the gun out of White's hand. It was half past five, almost to the second."

"Thank you, sir," said Davies, with heartiness and almost with a smile. "Because all three of us, cook, maid, and me, happened to be in the kitchen at that time. We were together until a quarter to six, as a matter of fact. I know that, because it's the time the evening post arrives, and I went to the door to see whether there were any letters. So we can produce a corporate alibi, if you see what I mean."

Marquis spoke musingly, his fingertips together and his cane propped against his leg. "By the way, we might check up on another part of White's story and see whether it tallies. He admits that he came here in order to kill the judge—"

"Ah," said Penney softly.

"—and thinking the judge was here in the house, he prowled round until he got through a side window. He says that at close to half past five he was here in hiding, and heard you ask Miss Ida Mortlake whether tea should be served at last. Is that true?"

"So that's why the window was unfastened," muttered Davies, and pulled himself up. "Yes, sir: quite true. It was at twenty minutes past five. Just after I asked her that, I went out to the kitchen; that's how I know all the servants were together. She also told me she had telephoned the police about this man White—or whoever he is—and the cook was in a considerable flutter."

"There's something on your mind," Marquis said quietly. "Better speak up. What is it?"

For the first time Davies was showing signs of discomfort. He started to glance over his shoulder; but, evidently thinking that would be unbecoming, he assumed a stolid expression.

"Yes, sir, I know I've got to speak up. It's about Miss Carolyn. I think I can tell you where she went yesterday.

"As you heard, sir, the maid is leaving next month to get married. Yesterday Miss Carolyn was interviewing a lot of applicants. Now, it happens that the maid's got a cousin—a nice girl—and she was anxious for her cousin to get the place. But Miss Carolyn said sentiment has no business in a thing like that. Well, Millie Reilly (that's the maid) wasn't afraid of her cousin being beat out of it by casual applicants who might come here, but she *was* afraid the Agency might dig up somebody with references a yard long. And the Agency has been 'phoning here several times. So the long and short of it is," Davies squirmed a little but spoke in his best court voice, "that Millie's got into the habit of listening in to all the phone conversations, in case it should be the Agency. There's a phone extension upstairs."

Colonel Marquis leaned forward.

"Good," he said. "I was hoping we should come across something like that. Don't apologize for the delinquencies. Miss Mortlake told us that she intended to go to a cocktail party, but that she received a phone message which caused her to change her mind. Did Millie hear that message?"

"Yes, sir." Davies' discomfort had grown acute, and he fiddled with his cuffs; he spoke almost violently: "She listened. A man's voice said, 'If you want to know something that vitally concerns you and Ralph Stratfield, go to the stationer's shop at 66 Hastings Street, W.C.1, and ask for a letter written to you under the name of Carolyn Baer. Don't fail, or it may be the worse for you.'"

Colonel Marquis sat up and Page almost whistled. Unless there was a coincidence of names, here was again a crossing of the ways with the C.I.D. The Ralph Stratfield he knew was well known to Scotland Yard, although they had never been able to obtain a conviction and Stratfield swanked it in the West End with his thumb to his nose. Ralph Stratfield was a super-gigolo who lived off women. Several times he had skirted the line of blackmail and once he had been brought to court for it. But he had been ably defended—by Sir Andrew Travers, Page now remembered—and had come off scot-free. Also, Page realized why Carolyn Mortlake might have been so determined to keep her mouth shut, even under bad risks.

The bead curtains were swept aside. Carolyn Mortlake came into the room with short, quick steps. Her face was sallow with rage and the eyes so dead that they looked like currants in dough. She stood trying to control her voice, but behind this shaking there was an inner emotion; and that inner emotion was shame.

"You may go, Davies," she said, calmly enough. "I will speak to you later. But I should advise you to begin packing at once. You will have to accept a month's wages in place of notice."

"Stay here, Davies," said Colonel Marquis.

He hoisted himself to his feet, supporting himself on his cane. He towered over her in the firelight.

"I'm afraid the police have first claim, Miss Mortlake," he went on, after an explosive pause. "You can't order the witnesses about like that, you know, when they have something to tell us. You are at liberty to discharge him, naturally; but I should be sorry to see you do it. He was only trying to protect you."

"You—," said the girl. It was an ugly word, and it had even more startling a quality in this sheltered Victorian room.

"Ralph Stratfield is poor company, Miss Mortlake."

"I think," she said with sudden politeness, "it is none of your damned business with whom I choose to go, or whom I see. Or is it?"

"Under the circumstances, yes. Look here, you know how you're feeling as well as I do. Now that it's said and done, there's no reason why it should come out. All we care about is where you happened to be yesterday afternoon. Will it do any great harm to tell us whether you really went there?"

She had herself well in hand now. "I'm sure I don't know. I'm sure it won't do any particular good. You needn't preach about Ralph Stratfield: Ralph had nothing to do with that message. It was a fake. In other words, Mr. Clever, I was got out of the way by one of the oldest, most bewhiskered tricks ever used in shilling shockers. There is no such address as 66 Hastings Street. There is only one stationer's in the street and that wasn't the place. It took me quite a time to tumble to it, unfortunately, and it succeeded. For, you see, I can't prove where I was yesterday and I'm in exactly the same situation I was before. Why anyone should—"

She stopped, and for a moment Page had an uncomfortable feeling that this hard-headed, savage young lady was going to collapse in tears. She almost ran out of the room. Penney, muttering inarticulately, followed her. When they had gone the force of her emotion surcharged the room still. Davies made a feint of mopping his forehead.

"It's a good thing I've got a bit of money saved," he said.

"It would appear," mused Colonel Marquis, "that neither of Mr. Justice Mortlake's daughters selected the company he would have chosen for them. By the way, did you ever see Gabriel White?"

"No, sir. He never came here. The only time I ever saw him was yesterday afternoon, between two police officers. Mr. Penney says he's a lord?"

Marquis smiled with tight-lipped amusement. "No, my lad. No: you're not supposed to question me. I'm supposed to question you. And I dare say you've kept your ears and eyes open. Who do you think killed the judge?"

"The only thing I've got, I admit, is a germ of an idea, and it may not be worth much. But if I were you, sir, I should keep a sharp eye out for Sir Andrew Travers."

"So? You think he's the murderer?"

"N-no, no, I don't mean that, exactly." Davies seemed a trifle hurried, and he was certainly not anxious to commit himself. "I only said, keep a sharp eye out. From what I heard it struck me that there's one thing that doesn't seem to fit anywhere. It's this: it's one of them shots, *and* Sir Andrew's gun. That's what's throwing you all skew-wiff. It's that one shot, from the Browning automatic, which won't fit in anywhere no matter how you explain the case. It's a kind of excrescence, if I've got the right word. Incidentally, sir, everybody seems all hot and bothered about one thing which seems fairly simple to me."

"I'm glad to hear it. What is that?"

"Well, you're wondering what happened to the bullet out of the Browning. Everything seems to have vanished, and that bullet vanished with it. But common sense must tell you where it went."

"Yes?"

"It went out the window," returned Davies promptly. "You didn't find it in the room and it can't have melted or anything. After the judge had opened the window, he turned back to see White, and White shot at him, and then everybody started firing all over the room. But the window was up a little way—with the inspector here running towards it."

Colonel Marquis seemed genuinely delighted. He rubbed his hands, he jabbed the ferrule of his cane against the floor; and at length he consulted Page.

"What do you think of that suggestion, Inspector? Is it possible?"

Page felt a retrospective shiver. "*If* it happened," he said, "all I've got to say is, it's a wonder I'm not a dead man now. I don't see how it could have missed me. I was running in a dead-straight line for that window. And as I told you, when I heard that shot I wasn't ten steps away from the window. Of course, it may have gone in a diagonal line. It probably did, being fired from the corner where the vase stands. But it's odd that I didn't hear it, or any sound to indicate it, if it came so close to me as that. I didn't notice anything."

Somewhere in the depths of the house a doorbell began to ring. It was a discreet, muffled doorbell, like the house and like the judge. When he heard it, Davies' big body stiffened back into its official posture, as though by an effect of magic or plaster-of-paris. Though he had been about to speak, he went gravely to answer the bell. And then Sergeant Borden burst into the room.

"Robinson told me you were here, sir," he said. "I wish you would come down to the pavilion. I've found something that changes the whole case."

"Well?"

"First, there're some footprints. Pretty good footprints. But that's not the main thing. I've found a bullet fired from a .32 automatic, and probably the Browning."

"Where did you find it, sergeant?" asked Colonel Marquis.

"Stuck in a tree some distance away from the window where you"—he nodded towards Page—"climbed through, sir." After a pause (while Davies, in the background, grinned broadly) Borden continued: "But some of the footprints don't make sense either, sir. It looks as though the murderer must have got in and out through one of the west windows—the ones that are so locked and rusted that you can't open them even now."

They walked down to the pavilion, taking a branch of the gravel path which led them to the back of it. Though the rain had cleared, the sky was still gray and heavy-looking, and what wet foliage still remained clinging to the trees hung down dispirited.

Rounding the side of the pavilion, they came on Robinson, in a cap and a big sou'wester, morosely regarding the ground. Under the west window nearest the northern end—just inside was the vase in which the Browning had been found—a few wooden boxes had been upended in a line to protect the exhibits from rain. Borden lifted the boxes almost reverently. Along the side of the wall ran what in summer must have been a flower bed, terminating in a brick border below the window. The flower bed was a big one, running out ten feet from the window. Five footprints were visible in the uneven soil, though they were so churned and blurred by the rain that they could be distinguished as little more than outlines of feet. But the toes were all pointing *away* from the pavilion, and all were made by the same pair of shoes.

Borden snapped on a flashlight, following the ragged line across the ten-foot expanse of flower-bed, and Colonel Marquis studied it.

"Were those tracks here yesterday afternoon, sergeant?"

The sergeant hesitated and looked at Page, who undertook the responsibility. "I don't know, sir," Page answered. "I imagine they must have been, but we didn't go outside the pavilion once we found it was locked up from the inside. It's another oversight, but there it is. Anyhow, it seems to corroborate one thing Penney said, if you remember. He said that when he was talking to the judge yesterday a few minutes past four, he heard somebody prowling round the house; also, that he thought he heard the prowler testing the shutters on one of the west windows." Then Page stopped and looked at the tracks. "Hold on, though! That won't do. Because—"

"Exactly," said Marquis, with dry politeness. "Every one of these tracks comes *away* from the window, as though somebody got out the window and slogged back. Well, how did the prowler get *to* the window?" He turned round almost savagely. "Let's understand things. Inspector, are you certain beyond any doubt that those windows haven't been tampered with?"

"Beyond any doubt," said Page, and Borden agreed with him.

"Robinson, do you agree with that?"

"I do," said the man. He pondered. "Here! Point o' fact, there was trouble about those same windows only a few days ago. Miss Ida, she wanted the judge to get new frames put in 'em, because the old ones are bad and that's why the shutters have to be kept up. She said it was sense, because then the judge could have light instead of being in the half dark all the time. I was going to do it, but the judge wouldn't hear of it."

In the gloom Page could see that a slight transformation had gone over the Assistant Commissioner's face: an expression as though he were blinking or making a face—or seeing light. He turned away, poking at the ground with his cane. When he turned back again, he was calm and almost brisk.

"Put your light on those tracks again," he ordered. "What do you. make of them, Inspector?"

"It's a big shoe," said Page. "A number ten at the smallest. The trouble is that you can't make any clear estimate about the weight of the man who wore it, because tracks are flooded and there's no indication of what their depth was."

"Does anyone we know wear a number ten?"

"White doesn't: I can tell you that. He's tall, but he doesn't wear more than a number seven or eight."

"Very well. For the moment . . . what other exhibits have you to show us, sergeant?"

"Round to the front, now, sir," said Borden. "There's that bullet in the tree; and to round it off, there's more footprints. And a woman's this time."

Colonel Marquis did not seem so surprised as Page would have expected. "Ah, I rather thought we should come to that," he remarked, with almost a comfortable air.

The front of the pavilion was unchanged, except that now the shutters on both windows of the study were folded back against the wall. Page tried to visualize the scene as it had been yesterday. But he was astonished at the tree to which Borden led them. This was a thick-waisted elm some fifteen feet away from the window in a direct line. Page remembered the tree well enough. When he had been running for the window, he had passed that tree so closely as to brush it; and retracing every step in his mind, he realized that he had been passing the tree at just about the time the second shot had been fired.

Sergeant Borden pointed with a pardonable air of triumph and directed the beam of his flashlight at the bole of the tree. "Now look sharp, sir—some little distance up. If you reach up you can touch it. That makes about the right height if it came out through the window. That's a bullet hole, and it's pretty sure to be a .32 Browning bullet embedded in there."

Colonel Marquis studied the crumbled and sodden little hole, and then looked back towards the window. "Dig it out," he said.

When Borden's penknife had produced another lead pellet, not quite so flattened by the soft wood in which it had been buried, it was passed from hand to hand and weighed. Page now had no doubt. "Subject to examination," he said cautiously, "I'd say that's certainly the .32 Browning bullet. But," he added with some explosiveness, "how in the name of God—?"

"You have doubts? H'm, yes," grinned the colonel. "But wait until we have finished. Borden, as soon as you've shown us the footprints, get on the phone to the Yard and have the photographer out here. I want photographs and measurements of that bullet hole. You see the queer thing about it? The bullet went in an almost direct line."

"Photographer's coming, sir," Borden told him. "And here are the other footprints." Moving his companions back a little, Borden threw his light to indicate a spot some distance behind and to the right of the tree as you faced the pavilion. The grass under the tree was soft and sparse, well protected by the branches above. Impressed in the soil was the clear print of a woman's shoe, narrow, pointed, and high-heeled. It was the right shoe, a smudged toe print of the left one being about six inches away from it. It looked as though someone had been hiding behind the tree and peering round it. But—the moment Page saw that print—his scepticism increased to complete unbelief.

"We'd better go easy, sir," he said calmly. "This thing's fake."

Sergeant Borden made a protesting noise, but Marquis regarded him with bright and steady eyes of interest.

"Exactly what do you mean by that, Inspector?"

"I mean that somebody's been manufacturing evidence since yesterday afternoon. I'll take my oath there was nobody standing behind that tree. I know, because I passed within a couple of inches of it, and I should have seen anybody in that whole vicinity." He knelt beside the two prints and studied them. "Besides, take a look at the marks. (Got a tape measure, Borden?) They're much too deep. If a woman made that right-hand one, the woman must have been an Amazon or a fat lady out of a circus; whoever made those prints weighed twelve or thirteen stone. Or else—"

Marquis, who had been beating his hands together softly and peering round him, nodded. "Yes; I don't think there's much doubt of that. The person who made the marks was either a man, or else a woman who stamped violently on the ground with the right foot in order to leave a sharp, unmistakable impression. . . . It's manufactured evidence, right enough. So, I am inclined to think, are those other number-ten footprints on the far side of the pavilion. We were intended to find both sets of prints. But there's one thing which doesn't seem to fit in. What about the .32 bullet in the tree? Is that manufactured evidence too?—and if so, why?"

Page contemplated Old Man River, wondering whether this was a catechism or whether Old Man River really did not know the answer.

"I'll admit, sir," he said, "that Davies' deductions seem to have been right. He said we'd find a bullet out side somewhere and here it is. But it's very fishy all the same. I was passing that tree when the shot was fired. How is it I didn't hear anything: the vibration of it or the sound of the bullet hitting the tree? It *might* have been done without my knowing it. It's possible. But there's one thing that's not possible at all . . ."

"The line of the bullet?"

"The line of the bullet. As you say, it's gone into the tree on a dead straight line from that window. Well, the Browning was fired from the far corner of the room. As we stand here facing the pavilion, that corner is on our left. In order to get into the tree in this position, that bullet must have curved in the air like a boomerang—a kind of parabola, or whatever they call it. Which is nonsense."

"Yes," said Colonel Marquis. "Into the pavilion, now."

They tramped in during a gloomy silence. Page switched up the lights in the little central hall, and opened the door of the study on the left. Nothing had been altered. The big room smelt close and stuffy. When Page touched another switch, a flood of light poured down from the dragon lamp hanging above the judge's writing table. It was true that little could be seen beyond the immediate neighborhood of the table; the opaque sides of the lamp gave it the effect of a spotlight, and the room became a masked shadow of bookshelves from which the big yellow vases gleamed faintly.

First Colonel Marquis went across to the west windows and satisfied himself that these were impregnable. "Yes," he growled. "Unless the murderer made himself as thin as a picture postcard, he didn't go out there. Also, this room is genuinely dark. We'll try a little experiment. I was careful to bring this along." With sour suavity he produced Sir Andrew Travers' Browning from his coat pocket. "But before we do . . ."

He juggled the pistol in one hand, his eye measuring distances. He then walked slowly round the room, examining each window. At the writing table he paused, and the other two followed him there.

The drawer of the writing table was unlocked. He pulled it out, exposing neat sheets of typewritten manuscript. On top of them lay a memorandum pad and a check-book on the Whitehall Bank. On the memorandum pad were a few lines of small, precise handwriting:

> Sara Samuels,
>> 36d, Hare Road, Putney.
> Refs.: Lady Emma Markleton, "Flowerdene," 18, Sheffield Terrace, Kensington, W.8. (Have Penney write).

"The new maid and her references," said Colonel Marquis. "Not much there. As a last hope let's try our reconstruction."

The other limped across the room to the corner by the yellow vase in the far corner, and again he juggled Sir Andrew Travers' Browning.

"I am going to stand here and fire a shot in the general direction of where the judge was standing. Afterwards I will drop the pistol into the vase. Inspector, you will represent White. Stand where White was standing, about the middle of the room. When you hear the shot, whirl around—and tell me whether you can see me."

Page took up his position. He had expected the shot immediately, but no shot came. Colonel Marquis was playing for time so as to take him off guard; so much he realized while he waited.

The shot was so loud that it seemed to make the room shake like a cabin at sea. Startled in spite of himself, he swung round against the vibrations. He had been looking at the brilliant beam of light from the dragon lamp, and he was a quarter blind when he stared into the corner. He could see absolutely nothing, for the darkness appeared to have speckles in it; but he heard a faint noise as of someone putting an umbrella into a porcelain umbrella stand.

"Well, can you see me?" rumbled a drawling voice out of the darkness.

Page's eyes were growing accustomed to the dark. "No, sir," he answered. "By this time I can only see a kind of shadow along the vase."

Colonel Marquis limped forward, twirling the pistol with his finger through the trigger guard. He put out a long arm and pointed. "You observe, Inspector, that the bullet did not go out of the window."

A much-annoyed Sergeant Borden was already examining the fresh scar. In the yellow-papered wall between the south windows there were now two bullet holes. The bullet fired by Colonel Marquis was close to the left-hand window, it is true; but it had not come within a foot of going out the open space.

"Yes, but if it didn't go there," insisted Borden doggedly; "now, I ask you, sir, where did the other one go? I'm fair sick of bullets. It's raining bullets. And there's no sense in any of 'em."

At half past five that afternoon Inspector Page emerged from the Underground at Westminster Station and tramped wearily up the Embankment to New Scotland Yard. He had made undeniable progress; his notebook contained evidence of both acquittal and accusation. But he had got no lunch and no beer.

Not more than a popgun's shot away from Scotland Yard there is a public house, tucked away in such fashion that it is not generally noticed; and, in fact, there is a pretense that it does not exist at all. But it is much patronized by members of the Force. Pushing up through the chilly dampness which was bringing fog off the river, Page found that the pub had just opened its doors. He did not go into the public bar. Moving on to a private room, where a bright fire burned, he was surprised to find it occupied. A figure sat with its long legs stretched out to the fire, showing a head with sparse white hair over the back of the chair, a pint tankard in a speckled hand, and a cloud of cigarette smoke over all. Then the figure craned round, revealing the grinning face of Colonel Marquis.

Now this was unheard of. If Assistant Commissioners go into pubs, they do not go into pubs patronized by their subordinates; and it would cause surprise to see them drinking with anybody less than a chief inspector. But Colonel Marquis enjoyed above all things to break rules.

"Ah, Inspector," he said. "Come in. Yes, it is the old man in the flesh; don't stare. I had been rather expecting you." He took charge of matters. "Beer," he went on. "And take a long pull before you start to talk." When the beer was brought, he smoked thoughtfully while Page attacked it. "Now then. What luck?"

"Aaah," said Page, relaxing. "I don't know about luck, but there have certainly been plenty of developments. The case has gone pfft."

"What the devil do you mean, 'pfft'?" inquired Marquis with austerity. "Kindly stop making strange noises and answer my question. It is a regrettable thing if an inspector of Metropolitan Police—"

"Sorry, sir. I mean that two of our calculations have been upset. The person who looked most suspicious, and didn't have an alibi, is pretty well exonerated entirely. The person we regarded as being more or less above suspicion is—well, not above suspicion now."

Marquis opened his eyes. "H'm. I'm not surprised. Who is exonerated?"

"Carolyn Mortlake," Page answered wearily. "I wish she hadn't given us all that trouble. Maybe she doesn't know it herself, but she's got a cast-iron alibi. . . . She really did go to Hastings Street. I went there myself this afternoon to see whether I could pick up any trace of her. I was equipped with a photograph. There's no stationer's at number 66, but there is a newsagent's at number 32: which is the closest anybody could find to it. And she tried that as a last resort. The woman who keeps the shop had noticed a woman prowling up and down the street, looking at numbers and acting queerly. Finally this stranger made a dash, came into the newsagent's, and asked for a letter in the name of Carolyn Baer. I got out my photograph. There's no doubt of it; the proprietress of the shop identifies her as Carolyn Mortlake. . . . There was no letter, of course. The thing was a trumped-up job. But she was in that shop at twenty minutes past five yesterday, a shop in Bloomsbury. Not even if she had flown or used seven-leagued boots could she have got to Hampstead by five thirty. And she's out of it."

Colonel Marquis drew a deep breath. For a brief time he remained staring at the fire, and then he nodded. "It clears the air, anyhow," he said. "What's next? If one person is exonerated, who's the one to go back under suspicion?"

"Sir Andrew Travers."

"Good God!" said Marquis.

He had clearly not expected this. He got up out of his chair and limped up and down the room with angry bumps of his cane.

"I see, sir," remarked Page, with a broad smile. "I'll lay you a small bet. I'll bet you thought I was going to say Miss Ida Mortlake."

"Shrewd lad," said Marquis, looking at him. "You're not a fool, then?"

"Not altogether," said Page, considering this. "I know you've been thinking that I've rather too pointedly overlooked her. You'll adduce evidence—of contradictory times. White says she was in the house, talking to the butler, at close on five thirty; just before White himself rushed down to the pavilion. Result: alibi. Davies says she was talking to him at twenty minutes past five, and after that Davies left her. Result: no alibi."

"Yes, I'd thought of it," agreed the other shortly. "Waiter! More beer!"

"You could even say that there seems to be a woman's touch about this crime. And it's certain there was a strong effort to throw suspicion on Carolyn Mortlake. But my early opinion of Ida holds. And I'll tell you something more," continued Page with fierce earnestness, and tapped the table. "The brain behind this business is a man's."

"I agree, yes. But go on about Travers. Why is he back under suspicion?"

"Maybe that's too strong a statement. Sir Andrew stated that he was in his chambers all yesterday afternoon; and that there is no way out of the chambers except through the clerk's room. . . . Well, sir, that's a plain, flat, thundering lie. There is another way out. There's a fire escape at the back of the building and it runs past the window of Travers' study. Sir Andrew Travers could have gone down that. I don't say he *did*, you understand.

"H'm," said Marquis. He sat down again and eyed the overmantel dreamily. "There is a hive of offices thereabouts," he added. "Somehow, I can't help feeling that the spectacle of a portly and dignified barrister in a top hat climbing down a fire escape in the middle of the afternoon would be bound to excite some comment, not to say mirth. Damn it, Page, the picture is all wrong. In this case Sir Andrew Travers is like Sir Andrew Travers' own pistol: he's an excrescence. How does he fit in? Where is his motive for murdering his friend? How could he have got inside the grounds of the house under Robinson's watchful eye? No, I don't see that stately top hat involved in any such business as this."

"I thought you had some idea of the truth, sir?" Page suggested. He was not without malice in saying it, and he stung Marquis.

"You are quite right, young man. I know the murderer and I know how the crime was committed. But I need facts and I need proof; in addition to which, I have sufficient humility to think I may be wrong, though the possibility is so slight that it needn't bother us. Hum. Let's have facts. Did you dig up anything more today?"

"No more that concerns alibis. For instance, there's Davies." He looked sharply at the other, but Colonel Marquis was very bland. "His alibi—the story that he was in the kitchen with the cook and the maid between twenty minutes past five and a quarter to six—is more or less substantiated. I say 'more or less' because the cook says he was down in the cellar, fetching beer, for some three minutes round about five thirty. The question is whether he would have had time to nip down to the pavilion, vanish, and nip back again.

"There's only one other person associated with the case—old Alfred Penney. He hasn't got an alibi, in the sense that it's impossible to check it. He says he left the Guildhall Library at five o'clock and came home by Underground; but due to missing trains at a couple of changes and being held up generally, he didn't arrive home until five-forty. The last man in the world whose movements you can ever prove is someone traveling by Underground. Personally, I think he's telling the truth."

Page closed his notebook with a snap. "And that's the lot, sir," he concluded. "That's *everybody* connected with the case. It's got to be one of those. I have two pieces of evidence which round out my report, and I'll repeat them if you like; but they only go to show how narrow the circle has become."

"We'd better have everything."

"Yes, sir. I tried to find out who had faked those number ten shoe-prints and also the woman's tracks. I had no difficulty getting permission to go through any wardrobe in the house I liked. That print of a woman's right slipper was a number four. Both Ida and Carolyn wear number fours. But there was no sign of mud on any of the shoes in the house, aside from the ordinary rain splashes you'd get walking about in the street. That's point number one. Point number two concerns the men's shoes. Only one person in that house wears number tens—"

"Who's that?" demanded Colonel Marquis sharply.

"Penney."

From the other's expression, Page could not tell whether he was stimulated or disappointed; but there was undoubtedly a reaction of some kind. He sat forward in the firelight, snapping his long fingers, and his eyes were shining. But since he did not comment, Page went on:

"Penney owns two pairs of shoes; no more. That's established. There's a brown pair and a black pair. The black pair he wore yesterday, and were wet. But neither pair had any mud stains; and mud is devilish difficult to clear off completely so that you leave *no* traces."

He stopped, because he noticed that the waiter who had served them was now poking his head cautiously round the door of the room and looking mysterious. The waiter approached.

"Excuse me," he said, "but are you Colonel Marquis? Yes. I think," he added in the manner of one making a deduction, "you're wanted on the telephone."

The Assistant Commissioner got up sharply and Page observed that for the first time he looked uneasy. "All right," he said, and added to Page: "Look here, this is bad. Only my secretary knows where I am. I told him he wasn't to get in touch with me unless . . . you'd better come along, Inspector."

The telephone was in a narrow hallway, smelling of old wood and beer, at the back of the house. A crooked light hung over it; Page could see the expression on his superior's face and the same uneasiness began to pluck at his own nerves. A heavy voice popped out of the telephone receiver, speaking so loudly and squeakily that Colonel Marquis had to hold the receiver away from his ear. Page heard every word. It was a man's voice and the man was badly rattled.

"Is that you?" said the voice. "Andrew Travers speaking." It cleared its throat, wavered, and became loud again. "I'm at Mortlake's place," the voice added.

"Anything wrong?"

"Yes. Do you know anything about a girl—named Sara Samuels, I think—who's just been engaged as a maid here, and who was to come next month to replace Millie Reilly? You do. Well, you know she was in the grounds here yesterday afternoon and was the last of the maid contingent to leave. She phoned here about an hour ago. She asked to speak to Carolyn; she said she had something vitally important to tell her, and was afraid to tell it to anybody else; Carolyn engaged her, you see, and she doesn't seem to trust anybody else. But Carolyn's out, seeing to the funeral arrangements. I said I was the—legal representative. I asked whether she couldn't tell me. She hemm'd and haw'd, but finally she said she would come round to the house as soon as she could."

"Well?"

Now Page could imagine Sir Andrew Travers' large white face, its chin showing more blue against the pallor, almost shouting to the telephone. "She never got to the house, Marquis," he said. "She's lying out in the driveway here, dead, with the knife out of a carving set run through her back."

Very slowly Colonel Marquis replaced the receiver, contemplated the telephone, and turned away. "I might have expected that," he said. "My God, Inspector, I might have foreseen it. But I never saw the explanation of one thing until just that second when Travers spoke . . . Evidently someone at Mortlake's was listening in on that telephone extension again."

"You mean she was killed to shut her mouth about something?" Page rubbed his forehead. "But I don't understand what it was she could have seen or heard. Even if she stayed a bit behind the others and went out after them, she must have gone before four o'clock. At that time the judge was alive and well."

His companion did not seem to hear him. Colonel Marquis had almost reached a point of biting his nails. "But that's not what is bothering me, Inspector. I might have assumed the murderer would have killed Sara, Samuels. But in that way? No, no. That was a bad blunder, a fatal blunder. You can see that I've got my evidence now; one more thing to do and I can make an arrest. Yes, I can't understand why the murderer killed her in that particular way, and inside the grounds of the place; unless it was blind panic, of course, or unless—"

He swept his worry aside; he became brisk.

"You are in charge, Inspector. Hop into a squad car and get out there as fast as you can. Carry the usual routine until I get there. I'll follow in a very short time. I am going to bring two people along with me when I follow you. Both are very important witnesses. One is—you will see. But the other is Gabriel White."

Page stared at him. "I suppose you know what you're doing, sir. Do you think Gabriel White was guilty after all?"

"No, White didn't kill the judge. And it isn't likely he killed the Samuels girl while he was sitting under our eye at Scotland Yard. But he will be very useful in the reconstruction," said Colonel Marquis, with slow and terrifying pleasantry, "when I demonstrate, in about an hour's time, *how the murderer got out of the locked room!*"

The lights of the Scotland Yard car were turned almost diagonally across the drive in the darkness. Ahead the broad gravel driveway curved up a slight incline towards the house; there were elm trees on either side, and due to the ornamental curves of the drive, this point was visible neither from the house nor from the lodge gates. Outlines were still more blurred by a smoky white vapor, not light enough to be called mist or thick enough to be called fog, which clung to the ground like a facecloth and moved in gentle billows.

In the front of the police car Page stood up and looked over the windscreen. The headlights played directly across on a body lying some two or three feet off the drive to the left, near the base of an elm. It was that of a woman, lying partly on her back and partly on her right side.

Page got out of the car, taking his flashlight. There were other figures, shrinking or motionless, drawn some distance away from the body. Sir Andrew Travers was there; hatless, and with the collar of his blue overcoat drawn up, he looked somewhat less impressive. Ida Mortlake was there, looking round the edge of a tree. Finally, Robinson the gatekeeper stood guard like a gnome in a sou'wester, holding a lantern.

The dead woman lay on a carpet of fallen leaves which, Page realized, would make it impossible to trace any footprints. By the condition of the leaves it was clear that she had been struck down in the driveway and then had been dragged over to where she lay. Without moving the body, he could see by stooping down the handle of the knife protruding from her back just under the left shoulder blade. His light showed that it was an ordinary carving knife, such as may be seen on any dinner table, with a black bone handle of fluted design. There was a good deal of blood.

She was a woman in the late twenties, short, rather plump, and quietly dressed. No good idea could be gained of the face under the tipsy hat, for the face was grimy with mud and cut with gravel. When the murderer took her from behind, she had evidently been flung forward on her face in the drive; and afterwards she had been turned on her back and dragged to where she lay.

Page's light roamed round the spot, in and out of the trees, and across in the direction of the pavilion. "Damn," he said; and focused the beam. Some three or four feet away from the body therelay in the leaves a heavy hammer.

"Right," said Page, straightening up towards the police car. "Crosby, photographs first. Laine, fingerprints. The rest of you over here a little way, please. Who found the body?"

Robinson, defiantly, held up the lantern so as to illumine his swollen-veined face and telescopic neck.

"Me," he said. "'bout half an hour ago. Maybe. I dunno. Sir Andrew," he nodded. "'phoned down and said to expect a woman name of Samuels, and to let her in. She got here and I did. When she went up the drive, I stuck my head out the door of the lodge and looked up after her. I couldn't see her, becos the drive turns so much. Like it is here. I was going to shut the door, but I heard a queer sort of noise."

"What sort of noise? A cry? A scream?"

Robinson jumped a little. "I dunno. More like a gurgle. Only loud. I didn't like it, but there wasn't nothing else to do. I got my lantern and started running up the drive. Just as I turned round the corner—right here—I see something like someone dropping something and running away. I didn't *see* much. Kind of a rustle, like, and something like a coat. It run away in the trees. It dropped something. If you want to know what I think it dropped, it was that." He pointed unsteadily towards the hammer lying among the leaves. "I'd got a bit of an idea that someone turned the poor damn woman over on her back and was going to bash in 'er face with that hammer. Only I got here too quick. Then I hopped it up to the house and told Sir Andrew."

At this point Page became conscious that the group was growing; that other people were silently drawn to the magnet of a dead body and the dull lights. A rich, husky, old-port voice, the voice of Davies, spoke up.

"If you'll let me get a better look, sir," said Davies grimly, "I think I can identify both the knife and the hammer. I think that's the carving knife out of the ordinary set in our dining room. The hammer looks like one that's kept at a work bench in the cellar."

"Sir Andrew Travers—?" said Page.

Travers, though a trifle hoarse, was master of himself again, as his courtroom manner showed. "At your service, Inspector," he intoned, in a vein of attentive irony.

"Were you here at the house all afternoon, Sir Andrew?" Page asked.

"All afternoon, since about three o'clock. I believe I reached here just as you, Inspector, were leaving. When Robinson brought the news to the house, I was playing backgammon with Miss Mortlake here. We have been in each other's company all afternoon. That's true, isn't it, Ida?"

Ida Mortlake opened her mouth and shut it again. "Yes, of course," she answered. "Why, certainly it's true. They don't think any differently, do they, Andrew? Oh, this is *horrible!* Mr. Page—?"

"Just a minute, miss," said Page, and swung round as he heard a step on gravel. "Who's there?"

Out of the dimness of flickering lights swam the white, square, pale face of Carolyn Mortlake; and it had a startled expression which vanished instantly. What caused that startled expression Page could not see, but it became again the old cynical mockery which could not quite keep back fear. She cradled her arms in her sleeves and jeered.

"It's only the black sheep," she said. "Only the poor so-and-so, I mean, who runs around with blackmailers, turning up again like a bad pen—" She stopped. "I say, that reminds me. Where is Penney?"

"Mr. Penney's at the pavilion," Ida replied. "He went there an hour or so ago to straighten up some of father's papers."

Page interposed, "You say Mr. Penney is still at the pavilion? Hasn't anyone told him?"

"I'm afraid not," said Ida. "I—I'm afraid I never thought of it. And he probably hasn't heard anything—"

"Look out!" cried Carolyn Mortlake suddenly.

With a roar, a flourish, and a glare of headlamps, another police car had swung through the lodge gates a little way down the slope, and it came bucketing round the curve towards them in a way that made Page jump back. When it was almost on the group, the driver jammed on his brakes as though at a signal. The black bulk ground to a dead stop. Then, behind a faintly luminous windscreen in the front seat, a tall figure rose with great politeness and lifted its hat.

"Good evening, ladies and gentlemen," said Colonel Marquis, like a B.B.C. announcer.

There was a silence. Page was well enough acquainted with his chief to be aware of the latter's deplorable fondness for flourish and gesture. Yet, as Colonel Marquis leaned his elbows on the windscreen and peered out over the group with an air of refreshed interest, there was a curious grimness of certainty about him. In the rear of the car Page could see that three persons were sitting, but he could not tell who they were.

"Most of you are here, I notice," Colonel Marquis went on. "Good! I should be obliged if you would all come over to the pavilion with me. Yes, all of you. I have one other guest to increase our number. He

calls himself Gabriel White, though some of you know him under another name." He made a gesture. One of the dark figures in the back
of the car stirred and climbed out. In the group before the headlights
there was silence; Page could read no expressions. But Gabriel White
himself seemed drawn and nervous.

They walked in a sort of Indian file to the pavilion, choosing the
path so that they might not interfere with any traces round the body.
All of them were aware that this was the end, although few of them
knew what end.

The pavilion was illuminated in all its rooms, the curtains drawn
across the windows. When that tramping procession went down to
the study a somewhat frightened Mr. Alfred Penney—with a pair of
spectacles down his nose—started up from behind the judge's desk.

"Join the group, Mr. Penney," said Colonel Marquis. "You will be
interested in this."

Again from various pockets he produced his arsenal of three pistols
and arranged them in a line on the writing table, from which Penney
had moved back. Page noticed the positions of the various people. Ida
Mortlake stood very far back from the table, in shadow, with Travers
beside her. Carolyn Mortlake, her arms folded with a swaggering gesture, leaned against the east wall. Davies, imperturbable, but clearly
enjoying this, was at Colonel Marquis' elbow as though to anticipate
any want. Penney hovered in the background. The defiant Robinson
(still refusing to remove his cap) was by the window. Gabriel White—
who suddenly seemed on the verge of crumbling to pieces—stood in
the middle of the room with his hands in his pockets.

And Colonel Marquis took up a position behind the table under
the lamp, smiling at them, with the three pistols ranged before him.
"At this moment, ladies and gentlemen, Sergeant Borden is showing
the body of Sara Samuels to someone who may make a strange identification. But in the meantime, in order to round out my evidence, I
should like to ask two questions . . . of Miss Ida Mortlake."

Ida took a step forward, more vigorous than Page had ever seen her. Her lovely face had little color; but it looked much less soft. "Whatever you wish to know," she said.

"Good! At the beginning of this investigation, Miss Mortlake, we heard that there were two keys to the tradesmen's entrance in the wall round these grounds. Robinson had one; you, in your nominal capacity as housekeeper, had the other. They were of value only yesterday afternoon, when you asked for that gate to be locked. Robinson locked the gate with his key. Where was, and is, yours?"

She looked at him calmly. "It was in the drawer of the butler's pantry, along with the other keys. And it's still there."

"But—a corollary to the first question—the key could be taken out, a copy made, and put back again, without anyone being the wiser?"

"Well . . . yes, I should think so. It was never used. But why?"

"Good. My last question, then. Today our friend Robinson told us a significant thing. He said that a short time ago a great rumpus was being cut up about these east windows in here: the ones with the loose frames on which the judge kept the shutters closed at all times. He said that you suggested getting new frames put into the windows, so that there could be more light in the room. I want you to think carefully before you answer. Was what Robinson said true?"

Her eyes widened. "Well . . . yes in a way. That is, I was the one who actually *spoke* about it to father. But he wouldn't hear of it; there was a most awful argument, and I let it drop. But it wasn't my idea, really."

"Then who suggested it to you? Can you remember?"

"Yes, of course. It—"

There was a clumping of feet outside in the hall and the door opened. Sergeant Borden appeared, saluting, his shining face well satisfied. "All set, sir," he reported. "It took a few minutes longer than we thought, because this Samuels girl's face was dirty and we had to wash it before the lady could be sure. But here she is and she's ready to testify any time you like."

He stood aside, to show a flustered, dumpy little woman, with a glassy eye and gray hair. She wore black; she took protection behind an umbrella; and at first glance Page thought he had never seen her before. Then he realized with a shock who she was. Colonel Marquis nodded to her. "That's settled, then," he said. "Your name, madam?"

"Clara McCann," replied the woman; getting her breath. "Mrs." she added.

"What is your occupation, Mrs. McCann?"

"*You* know what it is, sir. I keep a newsagent's shop at number 32 Hastings Street, Bloomsbury."

"You have just looked at the body of Sara Samuels, Mrs. McCann. Did you ever see her before?"

Mrs. McCann took a grip of her umbrella and spoke in a rush: "Yes, sir, I did. There's no mistake about it now, like there was when I only saw the photograph. She was the lady who came into my shop yesterday afternoon at twenty minutes past five and asked if I had a letter for her in the name of Carolyn Baer."

At the end of a dead silence, which sounded in Page's ears like a sort of roar, one face in the room shifted and changed. Colonel Marquis lifted his hand.

"Your warning, Inspector," he said. "It's not my duty to give it. But there's your prisoner."

Page said: "Carolyn Mortlake, I arrest you for the murder of Charles Mortlake and Sara Samuels. I have to warn you that anything you say will be taken down in writing and may be used as evidence."

For a space of time in which you might have counted five slowly, no one moved or spoke. Carolyn Mortlake remained leaning against the wall, her arms folded; the only change about her was that her eyes had acquired a steady, hard shine, and her dark-painted mouth stood out against her face.

"Don't—don't be an ass," she said harshly. "You can't prove that." Then she screamed one word at him, and was calm again.

"I can prove it, my young lady," said Colonel Marquis. "I'll show you just how far I can prove it by giving you time to think of an answer and a defense. I'll leave you alone with your thoughts for a few minutes, while I speak of somebody else."

He swung round abruptly, the light making harsh shadows on his face. There was a queer sucking sort of noise: the noise of Gabriel White trying to moisten his lips. White was not standing quite so erect. It was his face which had shifted and changed, not Caroline Mortlake's.

"Yes, I mean you," said Colonel Marquis. "I mean Carolyn Mortlake's lover. I mean Gabriel White, or Lord Edward Whiteford, or whatever you care to call yourself. God's death, you're a pretty pair, you are!"

"You haven't got anything on me," said White. "*I* didn't kill him."

"I know you didn't," agreed the other. "But all the same, I can send you to the gallows as accessory before and after the fact."

White took a step forward. But Sergeant Borden put a hand on his shoulder. "Watch him, Borden," ordered Colonel Marquis. "I don't think he's got the nerve for anything now, but he's a dead shot—and he once beat a woman half to death in a tobacconist's shop merely because she had only a pound or two in the till when he needed a little spending money. The old judge was right. There seems to have been some doubt as to whether Friend White is a saint or a well-defined swine; but the old judge knew long before we did."

Marquis looked at the rest of them. "I owe some of you an explanation, I think," he went on; "and the shortest way will be to show you how I knew that White was lying from the very first—lying through and through—lying about even the things he *admitted* having done. That was (as he believed) the cleverness of his whole plan. Oh, yes: he was going to kill the judge. He would have killed the judge, if his sweetheart hadn't interfered. But he was never going to hang for it.

"Stand back, now, and look at certain bullet holes. There has been one basis in this case, one starting point for all investigation, one solid background which we all believed from the outset. We took it for granted. It concerns the two shots which were fired in here—the shots from the .38 Ivor-Johnson revolver and the .32 Browning automatic—the two shots which did *not* kill the judge. We accepted, on White's word, the statement that the first shot was from the .38 revolver and the second shot from the .32 automatic. We were meant to accept that statement. White's defense was based on it. And that statement was a lie.

"But even at first glance, if you look at the physical evidence, White's story seemed wildly improbable on the very points of guilt that he admitted. Look at this room. Look at your plan of it. What was his story? He said that he rushed into the room, flourishing the .38 revolver; that the judge was then at the open window; that the judge turned round, shouting something; and at this moment, while the judge was still in front of the window, he fired.

"Yes; but what happened to that .38 bullet? That bullet, which White said he fired as soon as he got in here smashed the tube of the dictaphon and crashed into the wall *more than full six feet away from the window where the judge was standing.* Now this is incredible. It cannot be believed that even the worst revolver shot, even one who did not know a pistol from a cabbage, could stand only fifteen feet away from the target and yet miss the target by six feet.

"And what follows? Outside the window—on a direct line with the window—there is a tree; and in this tree—also in a direct line with the window—we find embedded a bullet from the .32 Browning automatic. In other words, this Browning bullet is in precisely the position we should have expected if White, coming into the room, had fired his first shot from the Browning .32. He missed the judge, though he came close; the bullet went through the open window and struck the tree.

"It is therefore plain that his first shot must have been fired from the Browning. As a clinching proof, we note that his story about the mysterious shot from the Browning—the second shot, fired from behind him and to the right, over in the corner by the yellow vase—is a manifest lie. The bullet could not have first described a curve, then gone out the window, and then entered the tree in a straight line. More! Not only was it a lie, but obviously he knew it was a lie.

"So the course of events was like this. He entered this room, he fired with the Browning .32, and he missed. (I will presently show you why he missed.) White then ran across the room, dropped the Browning into the vase, ran back, and *then* he fired the second shot with the Ivor-Johnson .38. Do you care for proof? My own officers can supply it. This morning I conducted a little experiment here. I stood over there in the corner by the vase and I myself fired a shot. I was not aiming at anything in particular, except in the direction of the wall between the windows. It struck the wall between the windows, a foot to the right of the open one. Had I been farther out into the room, more on a line with the table, my bullet would have struck exactly the spot where the Ivor-Johnson .38 shot went into the wall. In other words, where White was standing when he pulled a trigger for the second time."

Sir Andrew Travers pushed to the forefront.

"Are you saying that White fired both the shots after all? But that's insane! You said so yourself. Why did he do it in a room that was sealed up? What was the sense of it?"

"I will try to show you," said Colonel Marquis; "for it was one of the most ingenious tricks I know of. But it went wrong . . .

"The next bit of evidence to claim our attention is a set of well-stamped footprints, made by a man's number-ten shoe, crossing a ten-foot flowerbed outside the west windows. All these tracks led away from the window. We were meant to believe that someone in a number-ten shoe (which was larger than White's) had got out of that window and run away. But it was impossible for anybody to have got out there, due to the condition of the window sashes. So the footprints were obviously faked. Yet, if they were faked, how did the person who made them get *across* that big stretch of flower bed in order to make a line of tracks coming away from the window? It was even asked whether he flew. And the person must have done just that. In other words, he jumped. He jumped across, and walked back, thus faking his evidence an hour or so before the judge was actually killed. There is only one person in the case who is capable of making a leap like that: Gabriel White, who, as Mr. Penney told us this afternoon, holds an unbeaten record for the broad jump at Oxford. . . .

"And next? Next we hear from Robinson of a sudden and energetic plan, originating in the judge's household not long ago, to open up those windows so that they shall be like ordinary windows. All things—you begin to see—center round a phantom murderer who shall kill the judge and escape from that window, leaving his tracks and his gun behind.

"White's plan was just this. He meant to kill Mr. Justice Mortlake, but he is clever enough—kindly look at him now—to know that, no matter how the judge died, he is bound to be suspected. I do not need to review the case to convince you of that. He cannot possibly commit a murder where *no* suspicion will attach to him. If he tries some subtle trick to keep out of the limelight and the public eye, they will nail him. But he can commit a murder for which there will not be enough evidence to convict him, and of which most people will believe him innocent.

"He can—with the assistance of an accomplice in Mortlake's household—obtain possession of a Browning pistol belonging to some friend of the family. It does not really matter what pistol, so Jong as it can be shown that *White* could not have stolen it. Very well. He can make wild threats against the judge in the hearing of anyone. He can with blatant swagger and obviousness purchase a .38 caliber gun from a pawnbroker whom he knows to be a copper's nark—and who, he also knows quite well, will immediately report it. He can also procure, from any source you like, a pair of number-ten shoes which are nothing like his own shoes. He can get, from his accomplice, a duplicate key to the tradesmen's entrance which will enable him to enter the grounds when he likes. Finally, he can get his accomplice's word that the rusted windows and shutters are now in ordinary working order."

"Then he is ready. On any given afternoon, when the judge is alone in the pavilion, he can get into the grounds an hour or so before he means to make his attack. He can implant his footprints. He can give the shutters a pull to make sure they are in order. Then he can alarm the household—get them to chase him—get any convenient witnesses on his trail. He can rush into the pavilion, as though wildly, a long distance ahead of them. The shoes in which he made the tracks are now buried somewhere in the grounds; he wears his own shoes. He can lock the door. He can fire two shots; one a miss, one killing his victim. He can fling up one of the west windows and toss the Browning outside. When the pursuers arrive, there he is: a man who has tried to murder—*and failed*. A real murder, instead, has been done by someone who fired from a window, and jumped out; someone who wore shoes that are not White's shoes and carried a gun White could not have carried. In short, White was blackening his character in order to whitewash it. He was admitting he intended murder; at the same time he was showing he could not have done it. He was creating a phantom. He would not get off scot-free; he was in danger; but he could not possibly be convicted, because in any court there would loom large that horned and devilish discomfort known as the Reasonable Doubt. His deliberate walking into the hangman's noose was the only sure way of making certain it never tightened round his neck."

Page turned round towards White; and again there was a subtle alteration on the young man's face. Though the same ugliness still moved behind the eyes, his handsome face has almost a smile of urbanity and charm. He had drawn himself upright.

"There is still a reasonable doubt, my dear old chap," said Lord Edward Whiteford lightly. "I didn't kill him, you know."

"Look here, Marquis, I am trying to keep my head," thundered Travers. "But I don't see this. Even if this is true, *how did the real murderer get out of the room?* We're as badly off as we were before. And why was White such an ass, or his accomplice such an ass, as to go through with the old scheme when the windows *hadn't* been altered? You say Carolyn is the murderer. I can't believe that—"

"Many thanks, Andrew," interrupted Carolyn mockingly. She shifted her position and walked forward with quick jerky steps. It was clear that she had not got herself completely under control: she could master her intellect, but she could not master her rage, which was a rage at all the world.

"Don't let them force you into admitting anything, Gabriel," she went on almost sweetly. "They are bluffing, you know. They haven't a scrap of real evidence against me. They accuse me of killing father, but they don't seem to realize that in order to do it I must have made myself invisible; and they won't dare go to a jury unless they can show how father really was killed. Besides, they'll make fools of themselves as it is. You spotted it, Andrew. If Gabriel and I were concerned in any such wild scheme, we should have known the windows were sealed up—"

A hoarse voice said: "Miss Carolyn, I lied to you."

Robinson had taken off his hat at last and he was kneading it in his hands. He continued: "I lied to you. I been on hot bricks all day; I been nearly crazy; but, so help me, I'm glad now I lied to you. You— the tall gent—you, sir: a couple of nights ago she gave me a five-pun note if I would sneak down here and put one of them windows right, so it could be opened, anyhow. And I went. But the judge caught me. And he said he'd skin me. And I went back to you; and I wanted that five-pun note; so I lied and said I'd fixed the window. I know I swore on the Bible to you I'd never mention it to anybody, and you said I wouldn't be believed if I told it, but I ain't going to be hanged for anybody. . . ."

"*Catch her, Page,*" snapped Marquis.

But it was not necessary to restrain her. She turned round to face them with a smiling calmness.

"Go on," she said.

"You and White planned this together, then," said Colonel Marquis. "I think you hated the judge almost as much as he did: his every mannerism, his very mildness. Also, I am inclined to believe you were getting into desperate straits over your earlier affair with Ralph Stratfield the blackmailer. If your father ever heard of that, you would be unlikely to get a penny under the will. And you needed money for your various fancy men like Stratfield—and Gabriel White.

"Of course, it was plain from the start that White had an accomplice here in the house. He could not have known so much, got so much, unless that were so. It was also clear that his accomplice was a woman. The case had what Inspector Page described as a woman's touch in it; and no other possible accomplice in the house had any adequate motive except yourself—and your sister. That, I admit, bothered me. I did not know which of you it was. I was inclined to suspect Ida, until it became obvious that all these apparent attempts to throw suspicion on you were really intended against her and one other. . . . What size shoes do you wear, Travers?"

"Tens," said Sir Andrew grimly. "I'm rather bulky, as you've noticed."

"Yes. And it was your pistol; above all, it was your known afternoon to visit the judge. That was why White delayed so long, hoping you would appear. You are—um—associated with Ida Mortlake. Yes; you were the combination intended to bear the suspicion, you two.

"In the scheme as planned, Carolyn Mortlake was to have no hand in the actual murder. But she must have an alibi. For they were going to create a mystery, you see. Anybody might be suspected in addition to Travers and they must keep their own skirts absolutely clean. Hence the trick: 'Ralph Stratfield' was to be used as a blind, in a brilliant alibi which was all the more strong for being a discreditable alibi. Gabriel White should put through a phone call to the house, saying to go to such-and-such an (imaginary) address and ask for a letter. You, Carolyn Mortlake, *were really intended to go.* It was an ingenious sham-plot: there was no such address and you and White knew it; but it would serve more strikingly to call attention to you later, when you wandered up and down a street for the inspection of later witnesses, and had an alibi for half an hour in *any* direction, no matter what time White should kill the judge. It would, in other words, give you an excuse for wandering all over the place under the eyes of certain witnesses. Also, you were to refuse to answer any questions about it: knowing quite well that the police would find it and that the invaluable Millie Reilly, the maid, was listening in to all phone conversations. She would report it. You could afford to have the apparent truth, the 'alibi,' dragged out of you. It was exactly like White's plan: you too were blackening your character in order to whitewash it.

"But you did not go to Hastings Street after all." Marquis stopped. He looked at her curiously, almost gently; then he nodded towards White. "You are very much in love with him, aren't you?"

"Whether I am or not," she told him, "is none of your business and has no connection with this case."

She was pale nevertheless. What puzzled Page throughout this was the gentle, aloof, almost indifferent air of Gabriel White himself, who had none of the bounce or fire which had characterized him in the morning. He stood far away on a polar star.

"Yes," Colonel Marquis said sharply, "it has a great deal of connection with the matter. You were afraid for him. You thought him, and you think him, weak. You were afraid he would lose his nerve; or that he would grow flurried and bungle the business. And above all you were afraid—fiercely afraid—*for* him, because you love him. You wished to remain behind here. Yet you are, I venture to think, a cold-hearted young devil, almost as cold-hearted as that smirking Adonis there. And yet you wanted that alibi. Opportunity knocked at your door yesterday afternoon: you interviewed a batch of applicants for the maid's position—?"

"Well?"

"And one of them looked like you," said the Assistant Commissioner. He glanced at Page. "Surely you noticed it, Inspector, in Sara Samuels? The short, plump figure; the dark good looks? She wasn't by any means a double, but she was near enough for the purpose. Suppose the Samuels girl were sent to Hastings Street? It was a dark, rainy day; the girl could put her coat collar up, as she was instructed; and to a casual witness she would later appear to *be* Carolyn Mortlake. It might be a case of 'Oh, you badly want a job, do you? Then I'll test you. Go to Hastings Street—' and the rest of it—'otherwise you get no job.' The girl would agree.

"If later the Samuels girl came to suspect something . . . well, you weren't much afraid: you have great faith in the power of blackmail and of saying 'You daren't speak now; they'd arrest you.' But it was unlikely the Samuels girl ever would come into it. She was not to take over her job until next month. There was absolutely no reason why the police should think of her at all.

"And there was your plot, all cooked up in ten minutes. You could remain behind now—and even kill the old man yourself if White wavered.

"That, I think, was why you went down to the pavilion before you ostensibly 'left' the grounds. It wasn't that you wanted money. But you did want the gun in your father's desk. To get it without his knowing might have been difficult. But you yourself, unfortunately, gave a clue as to how you might have stolen it, when you were so eager to throw suspicion towards Sir Andrew Travers by stressing the point of his being expected there. You mentioned to your father that the electric fire wasn't turned on in the living room; and that it would be freezing cold, and that the tea things were not set out. We have heard from others about his extremely finicky nature and how he would not allow others to touch things he manipulated himself. He would, to prevent your doing it, go into the living room, turn on the fire, and set out the kettle. In his absence you, in this room, would steal the Erckmann air pistol out of the drawer.

"I don't know whether it occurred to you to shoot him through the heart then and there, and so prevent White's bungling. But you realized the chances against you and you were wise enough not to do it. In one place you erred: you forgot to look closely at the west window, to make sure Robinson had repaired it as he had sworn. Well, you left the grounds after that.

"Meantime, White is talking to your sister at a teashop. He didn't want to see her, really; it was a bad chance meeting; but since it couldn't be avoided, he tried to pile it on thickly by raving out threats against your father so as to strengthen his position. But, unfortunately, he went too far. He scared her. He scared her to such an extent that when she went home, she phoned the police. You two conspirators did not want the police—emphatically not; it was too dangerous. White wanted to run into that pavilion pursued by a servant, or seen by a few servants; no more.

"When Ida had gone home, White followed and let himself in through the tradesmen's entrance with the duplicate key. It was foresight to have had that key, for he couldn't have known in the ordinary way that Ida would order the gate locked. By the way, my friend White: you told a foolish lie when you said you got into the grounds in her car. That was not only foolish, it was unnecessary. And I am tolerably sure it was done to direct attention towards her, making us wonder just how innocent she might have been in the rest of it.

"For consider—I am still following you, White—what you did then. Once in the grounds you set about prowling round the pavilion. You made your tracks. When you touched the shutters of the west window they still seemed tolerably solid: which bothered you. You went round and threw a pebble at one of the front windows, so as to draw the judge and Penney (who was with him then) to the front of the pavilion. And then you would be able to get a closer look at the shutters on the west window. Unfortunately, the judge only opened the front window and looked out; you didn't draw him away at all. But you thought, as Carolyn had assured you on Robinson's word, that the west window would open easily from inside.

"Presently you went to the house. In the yarn you told us there was one truth: you did get into the house through a side window, after a long failure to penetrate anywhere else. The purpose was to appear suddenly in the house before the servants; to run out pursued by the redoubtable Davies; to be seen lurking and dashing, and leave a trail to the pavilion. But—when you got through a window at twenty minutes past five—you heard a terrible thing. You heard Ida Mortlake talking to the butler. I say, Davies: in that conversation did Miss Mortlake tell you anything else besides the fact that the judge was taking tea at the pavilion?"

Davies nodded glumly.

"Yes, sir. She said not to be alarmed if I saw any policemen on the grounds. She said she had telephoned for them. I already knew it, as a matter of fact. Millie heard her on the phone extension."

Colonel Marquis snapped his fingers. "Good! Now see White's position. He is up in the air. He is wild. He doesn't want the police or he may lose his nerve. Or will he? He climbs out of the window and stands in the rain wondering like hell. And White omitted to tell us about that hiatus of ten minutes next day; he placed the conversation at close on half past five, thereby neatly throwing suspicion on Ida Mortlake when we learned the real time of it. Thus he stands in the rain, and finally he goes to the pavilion, still wild and weak and undecided. But thunder and lightning inspired him and he makes up his mind to be a god. He makes up his mind to kill the judge in front of all the police in the world . . . just as lightning shows him two policemen in the path. . . .

"But," snapped Marquis grimly, "let's not forget Miss Carolyn Mortlake, for hers is now the most important part in the story.

"She has come back into the grounds, unknown to White. (She was almost locked out unexpectedly; and, if White hadn't conveniently left the tradesmen's entrance unlocked when *he* went through, she wouldn't have been able to get in at all.) She is watching, and I am inclined to think she is praying a little. And what does she hear? At close on half past five, near the lodge gates, she hears Robinson arguing with a couple of police officers who have just arrived.

"This must seem like the end. She runs back towards the pavilion before they can get there. There are trees round that pavilion. There is one particular tree, a dozen or more feet out from one of the front windows, and she hides behind that. And she sees two things in the lightning—the policemen running for the pavilion and a distracted Gabriel White running for it ahead of them.

"There is now no question about worrying whether he might lose his nerve; she KNOWS he has lost his nerve and will smash all their plans like china, if he goes ahead now. The worst of it is that she cannot stop him. He will be caught and hanged for a certainty. Is there any way she can keep him from being caught for a murder which has now become a foolery? There is none . . . but she is given one.

"She is now in front of the tree, between it and the pavilion, hidden from Page's view by the bole of the tree. But at Sergeant Borden's yell the providential occurs. The curtains are pushed back. Mr. Justice Mortlake opens the window halfway, thrusts out his head, and shouts. There is her stepfather, facing her ten feet away, illuminated like a target in the window. There is one thing, my lads, you have forgotten. If a Browning .32 bullet can fly out of an open window, *an Erckmann air pistol bullet can fly in!*

"She lifts the Erckmann and fires. There is no flash. There is no noise, nothing which would not be drowned out easily by the storm. The Erckmann bullet was in Mr. Justice Mortlake's chest about one second before Gabriel White threw open the door of the study. She has only to draw to the other side of the tree and the inspector will not see her as he runs past."

Sir Andrew Travers put out his hand like a man signaling a bus.

"You mean that it was the *first* shot? That both the other two were fired afterwards?"

"Of course I do. And now you will understand. Struck in the chest, he barely knows what has happened when White bursts into the room. Remember, the doctor told us that death was not instantaneous; that Mortlake could have taken several steps, or spoken, before he collapsed. He turned round when he heard White enter. And then . . .

"You will be able to see what turned our friend White witless and inhuman, and why he had on his face an expression of bewilderment which no actor could produce. White lifted the Browning and fired; but on the instant he fired or even before, his victim took a few sideways steps and fell across the writing table. Well, has he shot the judge or hasn't he? What is more, he has no time to find out. He has forgotten that window. He has bolted the door, but now they may be in and catch him before he can make his second-to-second plans. He runs to the window to throw out the Browning. And the universe collapses, for the window will not budge. There is only one thing he can do; he simply drops the Browning, and it goes into the vase. Now all he wants to do is strike back, for he hears Page's footsteps within ten paces of the window. He swings round with the .38 revolver and fires blindly again. Was it with the intention of completing his story and his plan somehow? Yes. For, whatever happens, he has got to stick to his story. The worst and most devilish point is this: he does not really know whether he has killed the judge. He does not know it until this morning.

"But now you will be able to see why Inspector Page, running for that window, swore no bullet could have been fired past him into the tree, or he would have heard signs of it. It was because the bullet which struck the tree was the first of the two fired by White, and was fired when the inspector was seventy feet away from the tree. You also see why Page saw no women or no footprints. She had already run away. But she came back, after he had climbed through the window. She hid behind the tree and peered round it, in order to get a direct view into the room. That was how she slipped—you noticed the blurred toe-print on one shoe—and planted that smashing heavy footprint (all unknowingly) in the soft soil. It is a great irony, gentlemen. For that was a perfectly genuine footprint. We must assume that she remembered it and destroyed the slippers afterwards.

"We must assume many things, I think, until I prove them in the case of Sara Samuels. When you went out this afternoon, Miss Mortlake, did you see the Samuels girl on her way here? Did you realize that she knew the trap alibi she had fallen into and that she was coming here to betray you? Did you dodge here ahead of her, through that invaluable tradesmen's entrance now unlocked? Did you get into the house unobserved and find the knife and the hammer? Did you wish to make her unrecognizable, so that it should never be observed that she looked like you and thus betray the alibi? Only you had interviewed her, you know, and Robinson had no good description. It was blind panic. You little devil, it was murderous panic. But at least you did not err on the side of over-subtlety— as you have done ever since you planted that air pistol in your own bureau drawer, and so conveniently made out that your sister was trying to throw suspicion on you."

Carolyn Mortlake opened and shut her hands. She remained under the brilliant light by the table; but abruptly she flung round towards White. She did not scream, because her voice was very low, but her words had the effect of a scream of panic.

"Aren't you going to do anything?" she cried to White. "Aren't you going to say anything? Deny it? Do something? Are you a man? Don't stand there like a dummy. For God's sake don't stand there smirking. They haven't got any evidence. They're bluffing. There's not one piece of real evidence in anything he's said."

White spoke in such a cool, detached voice that it was like a physical chill on the rest of them.

"Terribly sorry, old girl," he said, with a grotesque return of the old school tie; "but there really isn't much I can say, is there?"

She stared at him.

"After all, you know, that attack on the girl—that was a nasty bit of work," he went on, frowning. "I couldn't be expected to support that. It's like this. Rotten bad luck for you, but I'm afraid I shall have to save my own skin. *Sauve qui peut*, you know. I didn't commit the murder. Under the circumstances I'm afraid I shall have to turn King's evidence. I must tell them I saw you shoot the old boy through the window; it can't hurt you any more than their own evidence, now that the murder's out, and it may do me a bit of good. Sorry, old girl; there it is."

He adjusted his shabby coat, looked at her with great charm, and was agreeable. Page was so staggered that he could not speak or even think. Carolyn Mortlake did not speak. She remained looking at him curiously. It was only when they took her away that she began to sob.

"So," said Colonel Marquis formally, "you saw her fire the shot I take it?"

"I did. No doubt about that."

"You make that statement of your own free will, knowing that it will be taken down in writing and may be used as evidence?"

"I do," said White with the air of a martyr. "Rotten bad luck for her, but what can I do? How does one go about turning King's evidence?"

"I am happy to say," roared Colonel Marquis, suddenly rising to his full height, "that you can't. Making a statement like that will no more save your neck than it saved William Henry Kennedy's in 1928. You'll hang, my lad, you'll hang by the neck until you are dead; and if the hangman kicks your behind all the way to the gallows, I can't say it will ever weigh very heavily on my conscience."

Colonel Marquis sat at the writing table under the dragon lamp.

He looked pale and tired and he smoked a cigarette as though it were tasteless. In the room now there were left only Ida Mortlake, Sir Andrew Travers, and Page busy at his notebook.

"Sir," said Travers in his most formal fashion, "my congratulations."

Marquis gave him a crooked grin. "There is one thing," he said, "on which you can enlighten me. Look here, Travers: why did you tell that idiotic lie about there being no way out of your rooms at the Temple except through the front? No, I'll change the question: what were you really doing at five thirty yesterday afternoon?"

"At five thirty yesterday afternoon," Travers replied gravely, "I was talking on the telephone with the Director of Public Prosecutions."

"Telephones!" said Marquis bitterly, striking the desk. Then he looked up with an air of inspiration. "Ha! I see. Yes, of course. You had an absolutely water-tight alibi, but you didn't care to use it. You spun out all that cloud of rubbish because—"

"Because I was afraid you suspected Miss Ida Mortlake," said Travers. Page, glancing up, thought that he looked rather a stuffed shirt. "I—hum—there were times when I was afraid she might have been—" He grew honest. "Fair is fair, Marquis. She might have done it, especially as I thought she might have stolen my gun. So I directed your attention towards me. I thought if the hounds kept on my trail for a while, I could devise something for her whether she were guilty or whether she were innocent. I had a sound alibi, in case you ever arrested me. You see, I happen to be rather fond of Miss Mortlake."

Ida Mortlake turned up a radiant and lovely face.

"*Oh, Andrew*," she said—and simpered.

If a hand-grenade had come through the window and burst under his chair, Page could not have been more astounded. He looked up from his notebook and stared. The sudden gush of those words, no less than the simper, caused a sudden revulsion of feeling to go through him. And it was as though, in his sight, a blurred lens came into focus. He saw Ida Mortlake differently. He compared her with Mary O'Dennistoun of Loughborough Road, Brixton. He thought again. He was glad. He fell to writing busily, and thinking of Mary O'Dennistoun. . . .

"In one way this has been a very remarkable case," said Colonel Marquis. "I do not mean that it was exceptionally ingenious in the way of murders, or (heaven knows) that it was exceptionally ingenious in the way of detection. But it has just this point: it upsets a long-established and domineering canon of fiction. Thus. In a story of violence there are two girls. One of these girls seems dark-browed, sour, cold-hearted, and vindictive, with hell in her heart. The other is pink-and-white, golden of hair, innocent of intent, sweet of disposition, and (ahem) vacant of head. Now by the rules of sensational fiction there is only one thing that can happen. At the end of the story it is proved that the sullen brunette, who snarls all the way through, is really a misjudged innocent who wants a lot of children and whose hard boiled worldly airs are a cloak for a modern girl's sweet nature. The baby-faced blonde, on the other hand, will prove to be a raging, spitting demon who has murdered half the community and is only prevented by arrest from murdering the other half. I glorify the high fates, we have here broken that tradition! We have here a dark-browed, sour, cold-hearted girl who really *is* a murderess. We have a rose-leaf, injured, generous innocent who really *is* innocent. Play up, you cads! *Vive le roman policier! Ave Virgo!* Inspector Page, gimme my hat and coat. I want a pint of beer."

FINGERPRINT GHOST
Joseph Commings

The series character in the stories of Joseph Commings (1913-1992) was Senator Brooks U. Banner, the giant (6'3," 270-pound) accomplished magician and adventurer. The adventures of the elephantine detective were developed when Commings made up stories to entertain his fellow soldiers in Sardinia during World War II. With some rewriting after the war, he found a ready market for them in the pulps *10-Story Detective* and *Ten Detective Aces* (whose editor changed the character's name to Mayor Tom Landin; when later reprinted, the name was changed back to Banner).

The pulps were dying in the late 1940s, but new digest-sized magazines came to life and Commings sold stories to *Mystery Digest*, *The Saint Mystery Magazine*, and *Mike Shayne Mystery Magazine*. Although he wrote several full-length mystery novels, none ever was published, in spite of the encouragement of his friend John Dickson Carr. The only Commings novels to see print were paperback original softcore porn novels. The only book edition of his stories was published posthumously in 2004 in *Banner Headlines: The Impossible Files of Senator Brooks U. Banner*.

It should be no surprise that Commings, one of the masters of the locked room mystery, enjoyed the friendship of Edward D. Hoch, one of the greatest and most prolific writers in that challenging sub-genre, and Robert Adey, one of the foremost experts of detective fiction generally and impossible crimes specifically. Born in New York City, Commings lived there most of his life and met Hoch when the latter was stationed there for his army service in 1952 and 1953. They began a weekly correspondence that lasted until Commings had a stroke in 1971, continuing sporadically until his death.

"Fingerprints Ghost" was originally published in the May 1947 issue of *10-Story Detective Magazine*; its first appearance in book form was in *Banner Headlines: The Impossible Files of Senator Brooks U. Banner* (Norfolk, Virginia, Crippen & Landru, 2004).

Fingerprint Ghost
Joseph Commings

SENATOR BROOKS U. Banner, sitting huge and untidy in the glass telephone booth, was unable to get his own number. It was Halloween, but in the old and ornate Sphinx Club on Murray Hill the ghosts of the dead magicians were still slumbering. In the quiet, Banner couldn't help but overhear the angry voice of the man two booths away.

"There's no use talking," Drollen was saying into his phone. "We were washed up long ago. You decided that for yourself. I'm through with it." Larry Drollen, rangy and angular, was billed at the Lyceum Theater as Drollen, Master of Magic.

Something like a voice from another world filtered out of the receiver.

Drollen said loud and plain, "This's final. I could spill plenty. I'm having nothing more to do with you, you're no good!" The receiver clashed against the hook and the coin box jangled.

He rose up from the booth.

Banner gave up trying to get his own number. He winked at Drollen.

Drollen returned a Cheshire Cat smile. He was wearing his working clothes, white tie and tails. He looked at his pocket watch with the skeleton numerals. It was almost showtime. He turned the watch over in his long, loose-jointed fingers and made it vanish.

"Murder," he said.

"Murder?" Heavy and restless, Banner stirred with attention in his booth and got up. "Gimme the gory details, slim. I beat a hasty retreat from the Potomac this afternoon. I'm behind on my scare headlines. Who's been cutting up whom?"

Drollen's smile broadened at Banner. "I thought that would get a rise out of you, Banner. But this murder has you outclassed. True, you've solved some unholy terrors in your day, but the solution of this one is for the occult."

Banner lowered his furry charcoal eyebrows. "I'm an occult," he said. He peered down the long hall with its Flemish tapestry wall panels. His mat of white hair was thick, his frock coat seedy, and his gray breeches hung on him in creases and bags like an old elephant's hide. "I had to perform a feat of magic during my initiation into the club, didn't I?"

Drollen laughed. "Yes, you showed us how to take off a man's vest without removing his coat." He grew serious. "The murdered man was a doctor named Gabriel Garrett. He had a house and office on 104th Street. A little over two weeks ago he was murdered in his office, stabbed with a silver-handled knife. His knife."

"Any fingerprints on it?" said Banner.

"No. The office itself was full of the fingerprints of his patients. The police claimed they found no clues, had no lead. The two people most personally interested in the outcome of the case are Garrett's fairly new wife, Ivy, and his old aunt, Letitia Cody. The aunt lived with them. Last week a spirit medium named Ted Wesley claimed that for a large fee he'd return Garrett's spirit to earth and have him name his killer. So Wesley, Mrs. Garrett, and Miss Cody held a séance.

"I read a detailed account of it. It was the usual fakery: voices, lights, flying objects, wall rapping, and a gauze ghost. Wesley didn't produce anything startling in the way of a solution of the murder. I challenged Wesley to forfeit the fee if, under identical circumstances, I couldn't produce bigger and better ghosts—and maybe trap the murderer to boot."

Banner sniffled to stop his nose from running. "That's inviting danger, Buster."

"Danger?"

Banner pulled a lobster-red bandanna from his coat pocket and gave it a whip that sounded like the pop of a toy cannon. "Just a passing thought." He blew his nose violently.

Drollen started along the hall. "My stage show will be over at eleven. And then I'm off on a broomstick to the séance at Wesley's apartment on Cathedral Parkway. The proceedings start at midnight. I've invited the District Attorney too, for reasons of my own."

Banner listened to the shriek of a youthful banshee outside the window. "You picked a good night for it, warlock," he said.

Ted Wesley, the spiritualist, called the room his parlor. It was eight floors above the fir-lined courtyard. The solitary window was covered with black drapes. The only furniture in the room was a round oak library table, pushed over by the wall, and four chairs arranged facing one another in a tight circle. There were no pictures on the walls. You moved soundlessly on a thick black rug.

Three people were in the cabinet tying Drollen to a carved walnut armchair. The cabinet was a huge box made of fiberboard. A black velvet curtain could be drawn across its front to conceal the opening completely.

Archibald Lang breezed in. "Evening, everybody!" He had a slight

Texas drawl. He was the only District Attorney that New York ever had had who wore tan, polished, high-heeled cowboy short-boots. He took off the moss-green snapbrim that shadowed his plumpish face, uncovering sulphur-yellow hair.

The three people backed out of the cabinet to give Lang a view into it.

Lang grinned at Drollen. "They've got you trusted up like a hog-tied steer."

"Like to add your knots to the collection?" asked Drollen cheerfully.

"No," said Lang. "There're more knots in that rope now than a homeless hound dog has fleas."

Drollen bobbed his head. "You know Mrs. Garrett and Miss Cody, of course."

"Yes," said Lang. "I met them at the start of the murder investigation." Nevertheless he let his eyes drift to the younger of the two.

Ivy Garrett was in her late twenties, but she didn't look it. She had red hair. Her greenish eyes, freckled nose and scarlet lips were registering a sad expression. Lang let his eyes drop from her pie-crust hat, down the straight lines of her box coat, to the leg makeup and the tall-heeled suede porthole pumps.

She smiled faintly back at Lang.

"You have news for us?" asked Letitia Cody anxiously. She had hair as black and thick as a Hopi squaw's. Her skin was muddy colored and her nose a hook. Her whole face was as wrinkled as the palm of an old leather mitten. The long black Chesterfield she was wearing looked as if it had been bequeathed to her by Lord Chesterfield himself. High shoes were laced up over her fat ankles. If you handed her a cup with tea leaves in the bottom, she could read them for you.

"News? No, Miss Cody. I have to depend on Drollen too."

"And," said Drollen, "this is our mystic, Ted Wesley."

Lang looked at the man. "The seventh son of a seventh son?"

"That's exactly what I am," said Wesley in deadly earnest. His hair was so thin against his lumpy skull hat it looked like one coat of brown paint. His skin was sallow, there were deep violet rings under his eyes, and his upper lip was as long as an ape's. There was a light fall of dandruff on the collar of his very conservative dark suit. He was wearing gray spats. And he had the sullen look of a kid about to be parted from his lollipop.

Lang glanced at his wristwatch. "If you want to get started at twelve, Drollen, you'd better get this show on the road. I was able to get the things you wanted."

"The knife, please."

Lang thrust his hand into one of the deep pockets of his coat and took out a long narrow object wrapped in brown paper. He took the paper off a plain, sharp, long-bladed knife with a smooth silver handle. "This's the weapon that killed Garrett," he announced grimly.

A choked sob came from Ivy. "I know," she said. "Must we—?"

"'Fraid so, Mrs. Garrett," said Lang. "Where do you want it, Drollen?"

"First, wipe all your prints off it thoroughly."

Lang polished the knife earnestly with a large cotton handkerchief.

"Now," said Drollen, "put it on the taboret just inside the cabinet."

With his hand wrapped in the handkerchief, Lang placed the knife on a knee-high drum-topped table with three legs.

Drollen raised his eyes. "The straitjackets?"

"Sure. Shannon!" he called out. "Bring in those straitjackets!"

Shannon, a big bluecoat, lumbered in with his arms full.

Drollen gave directions from the cabinet. "Lang, help the others into theirs. When they're all jacketed, your officer can buckle you in too."

"Me?" grinned Lang.

"I want it firmly established that no one is in collusion with me, Lang, so if you want to stay in the room, you'll have to abide by the conditions of the séance."

"I'm staying all right. I stick close to that knife."

With some low-voiced comments and half hearted objections, the straitjackets were put on and buckled at the back. The bluecoat took care of Lang last.

"Fine," smiled Drollen. "Take chairs, please. Any seating arrangement you wish. But once you sit down I want you to reach out your right foot and put your toe on your neighbor's left. Form an unbroken circle."

Lang sat down facing Wesley. On his right was Ivy, and Letitia groped with her heavy shoe on his left.

"Shannon," said Drollen, "draw the cabinet curtain, please." Shannon tugged the black velvet curtain across, shutting the light completely out of the cabinet. Drollen's voice came from inside. "Now turn out the lights and leave the room."

Shannon flicked the wall toggle with his thumb. When he stepped out and closed the door they were left in blinding darkness.

Drollen's voice droned on, "There must be an absolutely unbroken silence before we can have a manifestation."

That was the last thing they heard Drollen say.

The seconds crawled. There was a rustle in the cabinet. There was a very low-pitched exclamation, then the mumbling of voice. This was followed by a scrape, a soft thump, and a cough.

Then there was silence except for the creaking of chairs and the uneven breathing. There were no more verbal sounds or movements from the cabinet. Old Letitia began to mutter to herself.

Lang's voice rang out. "Drollen!" he barked. There were startled movements in the other chairs. "Drollen, if you're not going to produce anything, let's get out of here!"

The bare walls threw his voice back at him in a stinging echo. It was the only answer.

Lang squirmed impatiently. "All right, Drollen. I'm breaking this up. Shannon!" he roared. "Come in here and light the lights!"

Shannon fumbled at the door and light from the outside room poured in. "Yes, sir?"

"Put those lights on! What's the matter with Drollen? Take a look in the cabinet!"

The room was flooded with light. The four people blinked at one another. They unconsciously held their positions. All their toes were still touching.

Shannon stomped across the room. He yanked aside the black velvet drape. "Mr.—" he started to say. He leaned forward, then rocked back on his heels.

His face looked shiny and purple. "Mr. Lang, he's been stabbed—with the knife!"

Lang fought the straitjacket. "Damn it, Shannon. Get me out of this!"

Shannon flipped open the buckles. The others sat helplessly, all looking as if they were holding their breaths. Rubbing his arms, Lang bounded across the room.

The long silver-handled knife that had been so carefully laid on the taboret was now plunged to the hilt in Drollen's starched shirt front. His head was slumped down over the knotted ropes across his breast. He was dead.

Lang's quick eyes noticed things at once. Drollen had never gotten out of the rope ties. There was a tiny flashlight, fitted into the end of a fountain pen, lying in his lap. It was lighted.

"Got your flashlight, Shannon?"

"Yes, sir." Shannon handed it to Lang. With the big flashlight in front of his eyes, Lang bent over the knife handle. Then he straightened up with his lips twisted in a wolfish grin. He stepped out of the cabinet.

"Whichever one of you killed Drollen," he announced savagely, "is going to be safe no longer than it'll take the boys from Homicide to get here. The murderer left his fingerprints on the handle of the knife!"

Later, at police headquarters, Lang looked shocked. The fingerprint expert had taken the prints of Lang himself, Ivy, Letitia, Wesley, Shannon and Drollen. He had compared each set with the set on the knife.

The fingerprints on the knife did not belong to anyone who had been in that room!

It was next afternoon when Banner plodded into the District Attorney's office at Franklin and Lafayette Streets. Banner had appointed himself Drollen's proxy. He was looking after the magician's affairs.

Lang was wearing a cream shirt, an orange tie, and a chocolate suit. He kept his snapbrim on indoors. He was standing in the middle of the rug dry-shooting with an unloaded gun, his favorite .357 Magnum. The target was a pin-up girl calendar pinned to the back wall. He practiced dry shooting for five minutes every day.

"Archie!" boomed Banner. He had endorsed Lang's policies for the last city election.

"The silver-tongued orator himself."

"What do you know, cowboy?"

Lang dropped the Magnum on the desk beside the jettisoned cartridges. "If you mean the Drollen Case, nothing." He slumped in the swivel chair, tilted his hat back on his yellow head, and put his boots on the desk's pull-out leaf. "And for your information," he added dryly, "everybody who comes from Goose Creek isn't a cowboy."

"You always wear cowboy boots," Banner hounded him.

"Did you ever hear about the old feller who put on a pair of these boots and always wore them 'cause he couldn't get them off?"

Banner peeled out of his coat and heaved it onto the leather settee. He sailed his lucky white hat after it. The hat rolled on the floor, but Banner didn't bother to pick it up.

He said disgustedly, "Ask me anything you like about fingerprints. I know all about 'em."

Lang swilled his hands in a mound of papers on the desk. "Me likewise."

Banner lowered himself on a corner of the desk and it creaked under his two hundred seventy pounds. He faced Lang's pin-studded wall map of Manhattan's streets. He said, "Nature never duplicates anything. No two snowflakes are alike, no two leaves, no two blades of grass. The fingerprints of identical sextuplets would be different. And you can't tell race or sex from a fingerprint."

He sighed. "Sounds like I've been at the Bureau of Criminal Investigation all morning. I was. They've got those prints that were on the knife handle blown up till they look like recon photos of a field plowed up by a drunk. There's no thumb print; your thumb overlaps the other four fingers when you grab a knife. The other four show. The index and second fingertips are easily recognizable. They're scarred."

"A fat lot of good it does us to know that," snarled Lang. He viciously zippered open a tobacco pouch and scooped his pipe in it. "The fingerprints have to belong to *somebody* in this country. On an off-chance that it might be a known criminal, I went first to our own Police Department files. The scarred fingerprints don't match anything there. I had the boys phone a description of the fingerprints to the FBI in Washington. The FBI has records of one hundred million sets! No record in Washington either!

"What kind of prints did we find on the knife? Fakes? No, you can't make a convincing fake that will stand up under microscope study. In all genuine fingerprints there's an oily secretion from sweat glands that you can't counterfeit." He put the pipe in his mouth and forgot to light it.

"The fingerprints are real enough," grumbled Banner. "The palm's a little blurred, having slipped down the handle when the knife jarred in the body. Mebbe we can crack it open. Were the fingerprints from spook, human, or animal?"

"Animal!" said Lang in mild surprise.

"Why'd you say animal? Don't you believe in spooks? We'll take them up in the order named. With me, anything that isn't in order goes against the grain." He looked sourly at his hat on the floor. He added, "I'm thinking."

"All right, Banner. Spooks."

Banner ran his tongue around his upper palate, chasing raspberry seeds. "The whole purpose of the séance was to pretend to rake up Garrett's spirit from the vasty deep. Mebbe something backfired and the ghost did it. Were they Garrett's fingerprints?"

"His wife had the corpse cremated. But we took Garrett's prints in the morgue. They're not his on the knife."

"If they had been, what a spot we'd be in. Next, humans." He bobbed his big square head. "Your turn, pard."

Lang sat back, remembered his pipe, and lit it. "I've heard of some beautiful alibis in my time, Banner, but this beats all. Drollen was in that cabinet, all tied up like a turkey gobbler. He couldn't have killed himself. Suicide's out. He had on his lap a fountain pen flashlight that gave out a thin ray as narrow as a pencil. In his clothes were a lot of odd gadgets like—"

"Hush! You'll give away trade secrets. He needed the flashlight to see to manipulate his spooks. He got it out and lit it with his teeth. It served the murderer to see by, too, when he slipped in to join Drollen in the cabinet."

"The four of us in the parlor were squeezed up tight in straitjackets. Have you ever been in one of those things? You're helpless. None of the jackets were phonies. I brought them myself from the asylum." He prodded his chin thoughtfully with the pipestem. "But a magician like Houdini, for instance, could get out of a straitjacket."

"Oh, sure," said Banner. "Houdini did it. But it took a lot of squirming. Even Houdini never tried to get back into one!"

"Even if one of us had squirmed out," said Lang carefully, "none of us left the circle. Our feet were touching. I can swear to Ivy Garrett and Letitia Cody. They were on my right and left. Both of them tell me that Wesley never once moved his own feet."

"How much trust do you put in Shannon, the cop who was on watch outside?"

"I'd trust him with my life. I know he didn't come back in once he turned out the light. That is, until I called him. There was a bright light burning in the outside room where he was stationed. I could see a shaving of it coming through the crack under the door. If he'd turned out the light to sneak back in again, I'd have seen it go out."

"What about an outsider coming in through the window?"

"The only window was locked on the inside and there's no fire escape. It's an eight-story drop to the ground. There's no other way in or out of the parlor."

"I'm coming to the animals. Monkey fingerprints can pass for human's. I knew a spirit medium who hid a monkey in a kettle drum. When he was shut up in his cabinet the monkey would wiggle outta the drum and raise all brands of hell."

"Drollen had no drums, Banner. There was no place in that cabinet to hide a monkey."

"I guess not," mused Banner. "To leave prints that large the monk'd have to be as big as an orangutan."

Lang looked skeptically at Banner. "That covers it. Spook, human, and animal. Where'd we go? Right around the barn. I've been trying to piece together motives for Drollen's killing. My best so far is that Garrett's murderer was afraid that Drollen was onto him, so he killed Drollen to avoid exposure."

Banner reserved comment. "I'll hang around your office for a stretch, pal. I've got some of my people sifting through Drollen's old press clippings in his room at the Sphinx Club. There may be something in his past life that'll latch onto our murderer. They'll call me here if anything turns up."

"Make yourself at home," invited Lang.

The door opened and Tom Neary, one of Lang's special deputies, came in. He said, "Mr. Lang, some of the boys just got him."

Lang raised up. "Got who?"

"The guy who murdered Garrett. It was a snowbird named Mulik. Garrett, being a doctor, was trying to cure Mulik of the cocaine habit. He must have put the brakes on Mulik too hard, because Mulik went berserk in the office and stabbed Garrett. We got a verbal confession. You'll be getting the written statement any minute now."

Lang was recovering from his surprise. "Good work, Neary. Thanks. Send it in when it arrives."

Neary went out.

Banner said, "The snowbird took Garrett for a slay ride. That sinks your motive theory for Drollen's murder. Mulik wasn't at the séance."

Lang was still trying to corral his scattered wits when the phone on his desk rang. Both of them reached for it. Banner got hold of it first.

"Kelly's Pool Hall," said Banner jovially into the phone. "Banner speaking." He listened. "Yup. Yup. I gotcha. Huh? Is that all you could find out? Keep at it, muffin. So long." He hung up.

"What was that?" asked Lang.

"One of my secretaries. She's been going through Drollen's old press notices. Archie, this staggers me. Don't interrupt. Seven years ago Drollen was traveling through the Midwest as part of Colonel Krupp's Amalgamated Shows. That's a high-class name for a carnival. Since then the show's been strewn to the four corners of the country. But the fact that remains is this: seven years ago Drollen married one of the sideshow *freaks!*"

Lang's bellow rattled the window panes. "One of the freaks!"

"Uh-huh. And I never knew he was married. But Drollen was an oyster-mouthed cuss, and some people like to keep marriage strictly private. The press clipping neglects to describe the freak and the name it mentions doesn't mean anything. Anyone can change a name."

"But, Banner, you don't understand. Nobody in that parlor last night was a freak. A couple of them might have been odd, but—"

"I've got detailed descriptions of all of 'em and reports of every move they've made. And I'm not hinting any one of 'em's a freak."

"I see what you mean. One of them, knowing Drollen had at one time married a freak, was up to blackmail. The blackmail scheme was getting out of hand, so the blackmailer killed Drollen. But how are we going to prove anything? You can't loosen that alibi no matter how hard you shake it."

Banner had his eyes on the rug, worrying something with his mind. The phone rang. This time Banner was too slow. Lang got it.

"District Attorney's office. Lang." He listened, then cupped his hand over the mouthpiece to talk to Banner. "It's Wesley, the medium. He wants to know who's representing Drollen."

"Lemme have the phone. Hello, Wesley. This's Senator Banner. You can do business with me. Glad to talk to you. I'll meet you at the—"

He looked up at Lang. "Ivy has gone back to her old job as a table-to-table photo-flasher at the Carnelian Room, hasn't she, Archie!" Lang nodded.

Banner lowered his mouth to the phone. "The Carnelian Room at six, Wesley. Bye-bye." He hung up.

"I'll get three birds with one stone. This'll give me a chance to talk to Wesley and at the same time get a squint at the redhead in the flesh. You said she was a good-looker."

"That's two birds. Where does the third bird come in?"

"I'm gonna *eat* that one."

It was too early for the regular supper crowd, so the tables at the crimson-and-silver Carnelian Room were sparsely occupied. Banner picked out one on the brink of the dance floor. "Sit here, Wesley," he said.

Wesley had his vest buttoned lopsided so that he came out at the bottom with more buttons than buttonholes. He sat down and clasped his hands on the table edge as if he were at an altar rail. "It's big of you to invite me to a place like this, Senator," he said.

"Think nothing of it. What d'you wanna eat?"

"I couldn't eat anything, thanks."

"I'm having a barbecued bird."

A waiter came and Banner gave his order.

After the waiter had gone Wesley cleared the cobwebs out of his throat. "Senator, I don't believe in ghosts."

Banner chuckled. "That sounds strange coming from you."

"What I mean to say is," he said nervously, "I didn't believe in ghosts until last night."

"When Drollen was going to prove there aren't any," said Banner with irony.

"The scarred fingerprints on the knife. Where did they come from? Nobody can explain them. The only explanation is the supernatural. I don't want to have anything to do with *real* ghosts."

"Are you on the level, Wesley, or have you just got a wrinkle in your horn?"

"I mean it. I'm through."

"If you're admitting that you've been shaving without a razor in other words—put it in writing and give it to the D.A."

Banner looked over Wesley's narrow shoulder at the redheaded girl with the flashlight camera who was working her way toward their table.

"Photograph, gentlemen? Oh! Mr. Wesley." Ivy looked pale, almost ill. Wesley didn't say anything.

Banner grinned. "Smile at the birdie, Wesley. Let 'er pop, Ivy."

"I—I'm sorry I don't know you, Mr.—" She let the camera hang.

He had the menu in his hand. "Senator Banner's the name, Ginger. I elected myself a one-man investigating committee to solve Drollen's murder."

Ivy sagged. The camera slipped out of her hand and clattered on the floor. The flash bulb shattered. Ivy became loose joint by joint and toppled after the ruined camera.

"She's fainted," gulped Wesley.

Banner lurched toward her. Some diners and waiters crowded around. One of the women had smelling salts in her handbag. That brought Ivy to in double-quick time.

"She's all right," said Banner. He said to the waiters, "Help her to our table."

When they were all sitting down again Wesley said, "Mrs. Garrett should have a drink. Maybe brandy?"

"Make it milk," said Banner evenly.

Ivy looked up quickly from under her brows. "Why?"

"Well, ma'am. I've heard the story of the flowers and the bees. And I was married once. I'm a widower." He looked at his surroundings with disapproval. "'Tis pity this isn't the Stork Club."

"How did you guess?"

"You fainted. Nowadays gals don't faint unless they're gonna have babies. Nothing scares 'em. What other reason would you have to faint? I didn't say, look, or do anything so frightening." While he was talking his thick fingers were twiddling with a stump of red crayon. He wrote an address with it on the tablecloth. "A detective followed you there this morning. It's the address of Maria Ubertino. She's a midwife."

"Yes, Senator," she said, "I'm going to have a baby. That's why I was so broken up when Gabriel was killed."

"That's understandable," said Banner.

She got up, smiling weakly. "I'll have to see about getting a new camera. I have work to do. Thank you, Senator." She walked away slowly.

Wesley coughed thinly. "I've had my little say to you, Senator. You'll excuse me?"

"Sure. Don't fall off the rug."

Banner was alone, drawing figure-eights on the tablecloth with the red crayon, when his barbecued bird came.

Next afternoon Lang was clicking away at the pin-up girl with his emptied Magnum when Banner trotted into the office. "You always seem to catch the end of my act," said Lang.

"I timed it that way."

While Lang was reloading the gun, Banner took two pieces of stiff cardboard out of his pocket. They were sandwiched together. Out of the sandwich Banner took a piece of flexible, glossy, ivory-colored pasteboard. Its upper edge was ragged where it had been torn. He laid the pasteboard tenderly on the desk in front of Lang.

He said, "See if you can guess what these are."

Lang put down his gun. "Guess! I know what they are! I've been seeing them in my nightmares all night. They're the murderer's scarred fingerprints!"

"Check. I went to the Identification Bureau this morning to see if they matched the originals. Double check."

"Where'd you get them?" exploded Lang.

"From the murderer," grinned Banner. "They were latent when I first got 'em. But black print powder made 'em visible. Beauties."

"But you didn't just reach up into thin air!"

Banner was fiddling around on Lang's desk. "Some people will be here any minute." There was a light tap on the door. "Ha! Come in, Ginger. And bring Grandma with you."

"I'm not a grandmother," said Letitia Cody stiffly, following Ivy Garrett in. In a few minutes Ted Wesley entered.

Telling the three to make themselves comfortable, Banner took Lang by the arm and led him to the outer office. "There're a few things we have to thrash out first, Archie." He closed the connecting door.

Lang looked around. "Where's my secretary? The place is deserted."

Banner hovered over the secretary's desk. "I sent him out for a nickel's worth of uranium. This's private talk anyway. Pard, it's about time you knew who killed Drollen, if you haven't already guessed."

"I haven't guessed," said Lang blankly.

"I'll recap. The hottest clue that came your way was the piece of information that Drollen had married a sideshow freak. Have you ever stopped to figure out what kind of a freak? Which of these was he most likely to marry? Most well-stocked sideshows have an India-rubber man, a tattooed lady, a fat lady, a giant, a Tom Thumb, a strong man, a fire-eater, a dog-faced boy, a bearded lady, Siamese twins, the gal without a head, the living skeleton, the half man-half woman, the ossified man, the three-legged lady. Take your pick.

"Wait a minute! I left one out, didn't I? The armless wonder. Now I've seen Houdini, who had both arms, tie knots in a thread with his bare toes. The average armless wonder on exhibition finds it duck soup to use his feet to cut out cardboard valentines, draw childlike birds and fish, wind a watch, open a penknife, hit a target the size of a quarter with a bow and arrow at ten yards, and beat a mean bull-fiddle. Do you get the drift, Archie? What you found on the knife-handle weren't the murderer's fingerprints, they were the murderer's *toe*-prints!"

"By the great horned spoon!" goggled Lang. "That's it! The straitjacket wouldn't mean anything to an armless wonder!"

"Now you're catching on. You told me that everybody was touching toes in the dark. The next big stunt of the evening was for the killer to slip out of his shoes secretly and leave them there while he moved quietly away over the thick carpet. Think back! It wasn't you. You always wear those fight cowboy boots that take a bootjack to yank off. You couldn't have gotten out of those unknown to the others.

"You told me that Letitia was wearing high-laced shoes. She couldn't have slipped in and outta them. Wesley was wearing spats. It'd be impossible to unbutton and button them with his feet alone.

"Ivy was wearing leg makeup and high-heeled pumps. Leg makeup means no stockings. Ever notice how easily a woman slides in and outta her pumps at a bridge game or a movie? She could have done it without your knowing her foot was outta the pump."

"Ivy Garrett killed Drollen!" said Lang.

"You peg it quick, chum. She's a normal girl who perfected that armless act. Yup. She was in Drollen's cabinet thirty seconds after the light went out. She got to him before he could get out of the ropes. When he saw her he didn't speak aloud for fear of gumming up the act he was about to put on. He probably didn't even see her get her foot on the knife on the low table. The fountain pen flashlight he was using was a direct light, not diffused, and it was directed on him. You heard the sounds in the cabinet when Ivy stabbed him."

"But why?"

"Ivy was the freak Drollen married seven years ago. The marriage was unsuccessful. They drifted apart. Then Ivy committed bigamy by marrying Garrett. Now Garrett's baby is on its way. After Garrett was killed by Mulik, Ivy begged Drollen to take her back as his wife.

"She was the one I heard Drollen talking to over the phone at the Sphinx Club. He wouldn't take her back. She pleaded with him. He called her a no-good and hinted that he could spill things. As it is now, Ivy is the respectable wife of the dead doctor, but Drollen could have ruined all that, so she killed him."

Someone screamed in the other office. Then the echoes of a shot smashed against the walls. "My gosh," yelled Lang. "That's my Magnum! I left it lying on the desk!" He started to plunge toward the closed door of his private office.

Banner's stout arm barred the way. "Wait a minute. When I was at your desk I snapped on the dictograph." He pointed. "That one there's open too. The people in there heard everything I said. I wanted 'em to."

The door jerked open. Wesley's putty-colored face jutted out. "Quick. Mrs. Garrett killed herself. She used your gun. We couldn't get near her to stop her."

Lang looked acidly at Banner. "All over my Persian rug. But I've got to admit you time things well. You never told me how you got her toeprints on that piece of pasteboard."

"You should have looked on the other side of it. It's a Carnelian Room menu. I had it in my hand when she came up to our table to take our pictures last night. In the crowd that gathered round her when she fainted, I slipped off her right shoe and pressed her toes to the back of the menu. She never wore stockings. If you wanna solve these murders, Archie, you gotta grab every opportunity."

THE CALICO DOG
Mignon G. Eberhart

Often described as the Mary Higgins Clark of her day for her ability to combine mystery and romance, Mignon Good Eberhart (1899-
1996) enjoyed a career as one of America's most successful and beloved mystery writers. Her output spanned six decades and produced
sixty books, beginning with *The Patient in Room 18* (1929) and con-
cluding with *Three Days for Emeralds* (1988).

Her first five books featured Sarah Keate, a middle-aged spinster,
nurse, and amateur detective who works closely with Lance O'Leary,
a promising young police detective in an unnamed Midwestern city.
This unlikely duo functions effectively, despite Keate's penchant for
stumbling into dangerous situations from which she must be rescued.
She is inquisitive and supplies O'Leary with valuable information.

The couple were so popular that five films featuring Nurse Keate
and O'Leary were filmed over a three-year period in the 1930s. *While
the Patient Slept* (1935) featured Aline MacMahon as Nurse Keate and
Guy Kibbee as O'Leary. *The Murder of Dr. Harrigan* (1936) starred
Kay Linaker in the lead role, renamed Nurse Sally Keating and now
much younger. *Murder by an Aristocrat* (1936) has Marguerite Chur-
chill as Keating, and *The Great Hospital Mystery* 1937) features a much

older Jane Darwell, before Warner Brothers-First National decided to go younger again with a lovely Ann Sheridan starring in both *The Patient in Room 18* (1938) and *Mystery House* (1938).

Eberhart's other series detective, appearing only in short stories, is Susan Dare who, like her creator, is a mystery writer. Young, attractive, charming, romantic, and gushily emotional, she has a habit of stumbling into real-life murders.

"The Calico Dog" was originally published in the September 1934 issue of *Delineator*; it was first collected in *The Cases of Susan Dare* (New York, Doubleday, Doran, 1934).

The Calico Dog
Mignon G. Eberhart

It was nothing short of an invitation to murder.

"You don't mean to say," Susan Dare said in a small voice, "that both of them—*both* of them are living here?"

Idabelle Lasher—Mrs. Jeremiah Lasher, that is, widow of the patent medicine emperor who died last year (resisting, it is said, his own medicine to the end with the strangest vehemence)—Idabelle Lasher turned large pale blue eyes upon Susan and sighed and said:

"Why, yes. There was nothing else to do. I can't turn my own boy out into the world."

Susan took a long breath. "Always assuming," she said, "that one of them is your own boy."

"Oh, there's no doubt about that, Miss Dare," said Idabelle Lasher simply.

"Let me see," Susan said, "if I have this straight. Your son Derek was lost twenty years ago. Recently he has returned. Rather, two of him has returned."

Mrs. Lasher was leaning forward, tears in her large pale eyes. "Miss Dare," she said, "one of them must be my son. I need him so much."

Her large blandness, her artificiality, the padded ease and softness of her life dropped away before the earnestness and honesty of that brief statement. She was all at once pathetic—no, it was on a larger scale; she was tragic in her need for her child.

"And besides," she said suddenly and with an odd naïveté, "besides, there's all that money. Thirty millions."

"*Thirty*—" began Susan and stopped. It was simply not comprehensible. Half a million, yes; even a million. But thirty millions!

"But if you can't tell yourself which of the two young men is your son, how can I? And with so much money involved—"

"That's just it," said Mrs. Lasher, leaning forward earnestly again. "I'm sure that Papa would have wanted me to be perfectly sure. The last thing he said to me was to warn me. 'Watch out for yourself, Idabelle,' he said. 'People will be after your money. Impostors.' "

"But I don't see how I can help you," Susan repeated firmly.

"You *must* help me," said Mrs. Lasher. "Christabel Frame told me about you. She said you wrote mystery stories and were the only woman who could help me, and that you were right here in Chicago."

Her handkerchief poised, she waited with childlike anxiety to see if the name of Christabel Frame had its expected weight with Susan. But it was not altogether the name of one of her most loved friends that influenced Susan. It was the childlike appeal on the part of this woman.

"How do you feel about the two claimants?" she said. "Do you feel more strongly attracted to one than to the other?"

"That's just the trouble," said Idabelle Lasher. "I like them both."

"Let me have the whole story again, won't you? Try to tell it quite definitely, just as things occurred."

Mrs. Lasher put the handkerchief away and sat up briskly.

"Well," she began. "It was like this: . . ." Two months ago a young man called Dixon March had called on her; he had not gone to her lawyer, he had come to see her. And he had told her a very straight story.

"You must remember something of the story—oh, but, of course, you couldn't. You're far too young. And then, too, we weren't as rich as we are now, when little Derek disappeared. He was four at the time. And his nursemaid disappeared at the same time, and I always thought, Miss Dare, that it was the nursemaid who stole him."

"Ransom?" asked Susan.

"No. That was the queer part of it. There never was any attempt to demand ransom. I always felt the nursemaid simply wanted him for herself—she was a very peculiar woman."

Susan brought her gently back to the present.

"So Dixon March is this claimant's name?"

"Yes. That's another thing. It seemed so likely to me that he could remember his name—Derek—and perhaps in saying Derek in his baby way, the people at the orphanage thought it was Dixon he was trying to say, so they called him Dixon. The only trouble is—"

"Yes," said Susan, as Idabelle Lasher's blue eyes wavered and became troubled.

"Well, you see, the other young man, the other Derek—well, his name is Duane. You see?"

Susan felt a little dizzy. "Just what is Dixon's story?"

"He said that he was taken in at an orphanage at the age of six. That he vaguely remembers a woman, dark, with a mole on her chin, which is an exact description of the nursemaid. Of course, we've had the orphanage records examined, but there's nothing conclusive and no way to identify the woman; she died—under the name of Sarah Gant, which wasn't the nursemaid's name—and she was very poor. A social worker simply arranged for the child's entrance into the orphanage."

"What makes him think he is your son, then?"

"Well, it's this way. He grew up and made as much as he could of the education they gave him and actually was making a nice thing with a construction company when he got to looking into his—his origins, he said—and an account of the description of our Derek, the dates, the fact that he could discover nothing of the woman, Sarah Gant, previous to her life in Ottawa—"

"Ottawa?"

"Yes. That was where he came from. The other one, Duane, from New Orleans. And the fact that, as Dixon remembered her, she looked very much like the newspaper pictures of the nursemaid, suggested the possibility that he was our lost child."

"So, on the evidence of corresponding dates and the likeness of the woman who was caring for him before he was taken to the orphanage, comes to you, claiming to be your son. A year after your husband died."

"Yes, and—well—" Mrs. Lasher flushed pinkly. "There are some things he can remember."

"Things—such as what?"

"The—the green curtains in the nursery. There *were* green curtains in the nursery. And a—a calico dog. And—and a few other things. The lawyers say that isn't conclusive. But I think it's very important that he remembers the calico dog."

"You've had lawyers looking into his claims."

"Oh, dear, yes," said Mrs. Lasher. "Exhaustively."

"But can't they trace Sarah Gant?"

"Nothing conclusive, Miss Dare."

"His physical appearance?" suggested Susan.

"Miss Dare," said Mrs. Lasher. "My Derek was blond with gray eyes. He had no marks of any kind. His teeth were still his baby teeth. Any fair young man with gray eyes might be my son. And both these men—either of these men might be Derek. I've looked long and wearily, searching every feature and every expression for a likeness to my boy. It is equally there—and not there. I feel sure that one of them is my son. I am absolutely sure that he has—has come home."

"But you don't know which one?" said Susan softly.

"I don't know which one," said Idabelle Lasher. "But one of them *is Derek*."

She turned suddenly and walked heavily to a window. Her pale green gown of soft crêpe that trailed behind her, its hem touching a priceless thin rug that ought to have been in a museum. Behind her, against the gray wall, hung a small Mauve, exquisite. Twenty-one stories below, traffic flowed unceasingly along Lake Shore Drive.

"One of them must be an impostor," Idabelle Lasher was saying presently in a choked voice.

"Is Dixon certain he is your son?"

"He says only that he thinks so. But since Duane has come, too, he is more—more positive—"

"Duane, of course." The rivalry of the two young men must be rather terrible. Susan had a fleeting glimpse again of what it might mean: one of them certainly an impostor, both imposters, perhaps, struggling over Idabelle Lasher's affections and her fortune. The thought opened, really, quite appalling and horrid vistas.

"What is Duane's story?" asked Susan.

"That's what makes it so queer, Miss Dare. Duane's story—is— well, it is exactly the same."

Susan stared at her wide green back, cushiony and bulgy in spite of the finest corseting that money could obtain.

"You don't mean *exactly* the same!" she cried.

"Exactly," the woman turned and faced her. "Exactly the same, Miss Dare, except for the names and places. The name of the woman in Duane's case was Mary Miller, the orphanage was in New Orleans, he was going to art school here in Chicago when—when, he says, just as Dixon said—he began to be more and more interested in his parentage and began investigating. And he, too, remembers things, little things from his babyhood and our house that only Derek could remember."

"Wait, Mrs. Lasher," said Susan, grasping at something firm. "Any servant, any of your friends, would know these details also."

Mrs. Lasher's pale, big eyes became more prominent.

"You mean, of course, a conspiracy. The lawyers have talked

nothing else. But, Miss Dare, they authenticated everything possible to authenticate in both statements. I know what has happened to the few servants we had—all, that is, except the nursemaid. And we don't have many close friends, Miss Dare. Not since there was so much money. And none of them—none of them would do this."

"But both young men can't be Derek," said Susan desperately. She clutched at common sense again and said: "How soon after your husband's death did Dixon arrive?"

"Ten months."

"And Duane?"

"Three months after Dixon."

"And they are both living here with you now?"

"Yes." She nodded toward the end of the long room. "They are in the library now."

"Together?" said Susan irresistibly.

"Yes, of course," said Mrs. Lasher. "Playing cribbage."

"I suppose you and your lawyers have tried every possible test?"

"Everything, Miss Dare."

"You have no fingerprints of the baby?"

"No. That was before fingerprints were so important. We tried blood tests, of course. But they are of the same type."

"Resemblances to you or your husband?"

"You'll see for yourself at dinner tonight, Miss Dare. You will help me?"

Susan sighed. "Yes," she said.

The bedroom to which Mrs. Lasher herself took Susan was done in the French manner with much taffeta, inlaid satinwood, and lace cushions. It was very large and overwhelmingly magnificent, and gilt mirrors reflected Susan's small brown figure in unending vistas.

Susan dismissed the maid, thanked fate that the only dinner gown she had brought was a new and handsome one, and felt very awed and faintly dissolute in a great, sunken, black marble pool that she wouldn't have dared call a tub. After all, reflected Susan, finding that she could actually swim a stroke or two, thirty millions was thirty millions.

She got into a white chiffon dress with silver and green at the waist, and was stooping in a froth of white flounces to secure the straps of her flat-heeled silver sandals when Mrs. Lasher knocked.

"It's Derek's baby things," she said in a whisper and with a glance over her fat white shoulder. "Let's move a little farther from the door."

They sat down on a cushioned chaise longue and between them, incongruous against the suave cream satin, Idabelle Lasher spread out certain small objects, touching them lingeringly.

"His little suit—he looked so sweet in yellow. Some pictures. A pink plush teddy bear. His little nursery school reports—he was already in nursery school, Miss Dare—pre-kindergarten, you know. It was in an experimental stage then, and so interesting. And the calico dog, Miss Dare."

She stopped there, and Susan looked at the faded, flabby calico dog held so tenderly in those fat diamonded hands. She felt suddenly a wave of cold anger toward the man who was not Derek and who must know that he was not Derek. She took the pictures eagerly.

But they were only pictures. One at about two, made by a photographer; a round baby face without features that were at all distinctive. Two or three pictures of a little boy playing, squinting against the sun.

"Has anyone else seen these things?"

"You mean either of the two boys—either Dixon or Duane? No, Miss Dare."

"Has anyone at all seen them? Servants? Friends?"

Idabelle's blue eyes became vague and clouded.

"Long ago, perhaps," she said. "Oh, many, many years ago. But they've been in the safe in my bedroom for years. Before that in a locked closet."

"How long have they been in the safe?"

"Since we bought this apartment. Ten—no, twelve years."

"And no one—there's never been anything like an attempted robbery of that safe?"

"Never. No, Miss Dare. There's no possible way for either Dixon or Duane to know of the contents of this box except from memory."

"And Dixon remembers the calico dog?"

"Yes." The prominent blue eyes wavered again, and Mrs. Lasher rose and walked toward the door. She paused then and looked at Susan again.

"And Duane remembers the teddy bear and described it to me," she said definitely and went away.

There was a touch of comedy about it, and, like all comedy, it overlay tragedy.

Left to herself, Susan studied the pictures again thoughtfully. The nursery school reports, written out in beautiful "vertical" handwriting. *Music:* A good ear. *Memory:* Very good. *Adaptability:* Very good. *Sociability:* Inclined to shyness. *Rhythm:* Poor (advise skipping games at home). *Conduct:* (this varied; with at least once a suggestive blank and once a somewhat terse remark to the effect that there had been considerable disturbance during the half hours devoted to naps and a strong suggestion that Derek was at the bottom of it). Susan smiled there and began to like baby Derek. And it was just then that she found the first indication of an identifying trait. And that was after the heading, *Games.* One report said: Quick. Another said: Mentally quick but does not coordinate muscles well. And a third said, definitely pinning the thing down: Tendency to use left hand which we are endeavoring to correct.

Tendency to use left hand. An inborn tendency, cropping out again and again all through life. In those days, of course, it had been rigidly corrected—thereby inducing all manner of ills, according to more recent trends of education. But was it ever altogether conquered?

Presently Susan put the things in the box again and went to Mrs.

Lasher's room. And Susan had the somewhat dubious satisfaction of watching Mrs. Lasher open a delicate ivory panel which disclosed a very utilitarian steel safe set in the wall behind it and place the box securely in the safe.

"Did you find anything that will be of help?" asked Mrs. Lasher, closing the panel.

"I don't know," said Susan. "I'm afraid there's nothing very certain. Do Dixon and Duane know why I am here?"

"No," said Mrs. Lasher, revealing unexpected cunning. "I told them you were a dear friend of Christabel's. And that you were very much interested in their—my—our situation. We talk it over, you know, very frankly, Miss Dare. The boys are as anxious as I am to discover the truth of it."

Again, thought Susan feeling baffled, as the true Derek would be. She followed Mrs. Lasher toward the drawing room again, prepared heartily to dislike both men.

But the man sipping a cocktail in the doorway of the library was much too old to be either Dixon or Duane.

"Major Briggs," said Mrs. Lasher. "Christabel's friend, Susan, Tom." She turned to Susan. "Major Tom Briggs is our closest friend. He was like a brother to my husband, and has been to me."

"Never a brother," said Major Briggs with an air of gallantry. "Say, rather, an admirer. So this is Christabel's little friend." He put down his cocktail glass and bowed and took Susan's hand only a fraction too tenderly.

Then Mrs. Lasher drifted across the room where Susan was aware of two pairs of black shoulders rising to greet her, and Major Briggs said beamingly:

"How happy we are to have you with us, my dear. I suppose Idabelle has told you of our—our problem."

He was about Susan's height; white-haired, rather puffy under the eyes, and a bit too pink, with hands that were inclined to shake. He adjusted his gold-rimmed eyeglasses, then let them drop the length of their black ribbon and said:

"What do you think of it, my dear?"

"I don't know," said Susan. "What do you think?"

"Well, my dear, it's a bit difficult, you know. When Idabelle herself doesn't know. When the most rigid—yes, the most rigid and searching investigation on the part of highly trained and experienced investigators has failed to discover—ah—the identity of the lost heir, how may my own poor powers avail!" He finished his cocktail, gulped, and said blandly: "But it's Duane."

"What—" said Susan.

"I said, it's Duane. He is the heir. Anybody could see it with half an eye. Spittin' image of his dad. Here they come, now."

They were alike and yet not alike at all. Both were rather tall, slender, and well made. Both had medium-brown hair. Both had grayish-blue eyes. Neither was particularly handsome. Neither was exactly unhandsome. Their features were not at all alike in bone structure, yet neither had features that were in any way distinctive. Their description on a passport would not have varied by a single word. Actually they were altogether unlike each other.

With the salad Major Briggs roused to point out a portrait that hung on the opposite wall.

"Jeremiah Lasher," he said, waving a pink hand in that direction. He glanced meaningly at Susan and added: "Do you see any resemblance, Miss Susan? I mean between my old friend and one of these lads here."

One of the lads—it was Dixon—wriggled perceptibly, but Duane smiled.

"We are not at all embarrassed, Miss Susan," he said pleasantly. "We are both quite accustomed to this sort of scrutiny." He laughed lightly, and Idabelle smiled, and Dixon said:

"Does Miss Dare know about this?"

"Oh, yes," said Idabelle, turning as quickly and attentively to him as she had turned to Duane. "There's no secret about it."

"No," said Dixon somewhat crisply. "There's certainly no secret about it."

There was, however, no further mention of the problem of identity during the rest of the evening. Indeed, it was a very calm and slightly dull evening except for the affair of Major Briggs and the draft.

That happened just after dinner. Susan and Mrs. Lasher were sitting over coffee in the drawing room, and the three men were presumably lingering in the dining room.

It had been altogether quiet in the drawing room, yet there had not been audible even the distant murmur of the men's voices. Thus the queer, choked shout that arose in the dining room came as a definite shock to the two women.

It all happened in an instant. They hadn't themselves time to move or inquire before Duane appeared in the doorway. He was laughing but looked pale.

"It's all right," he said. "Nothing's wrong."

"*Duane*," said Idabelle Lasher gaspingly. "*What—*"

"Don't be alarmed," he said swiftly. "It's nothing." He turned to look down the hall at someone approaching and added: "Here he is, safe and sound."

He stood aside, and Major Briggs appeared in the doorway. He looked so shocked and purple that both women moved hurriedly forward, and Idabelle Lasher said: "Here—on the divan. Ring for brandy, Duane. Lie down here, Major."

"Oh, no—no," said Major Briggs stertorously. "No. I'm quite all right."

Duane, however, supported him to the divan, and Dixon appeared in the doorway.

"What happened?" he said.

Major Briggs waved his hands feebly. Duane said:

"The Major nearly went out the window."

"O-h-h-h—"—it was Idabelle in a thin, long scream.

"Oh, it's all right," said Major Briggs shakenly. "I caught hold of the curtain. By God, I'm glad you had heavy curtain rods at that window, Idabelle."

She was fussing around him, her hands shaking, her face ghastly under its make-up.

"But how could you—" she was saying jerkily—"what on earth—how could it have happened—"

"It's the draft," said the Major irascibly. "The confounded draft on my neck. I got up to close the window and—I nearly went out!"

"But how could you—" began Idabelle again.

"I don't know how it happened," said the Major. "Just all at once—" A look of perplexity came slowly over his face. "Queer," said Major Briggs suddenly, "I suppose it was the draft. But it was exactly as if—" He stopped, and Idabelle cried:

"As if what?"

"As if someone had pushed me," said the Major.

Perhaps it was fortunate that the butler arrived just then, and there was the slight diversion of getting the Major to stretch out full length on the divan and sip a restorative.

And somehow in the conversation it emerged that neither Dixon nor Duane had been in the dining room when the thing had happened.

"There'd been a disagreement over—well, it was over inheritance tax," said Dixon flushing. "Duane had gone to the library to look in an encyclopedia, and I had gone to my room to get the evening paper which had some reference to it. So the Major was alone when it happened. I knew nothing of it until I heard the commotion in here."

"I," said Duane, watching Dixon, "heard the Major's shout from the library and hurried across."

That night, late, after Major Briggs had gone home, and Susan was again alone in the paralyzing magnificence of the French bedroom, she still kept thinking of the window and Major Briggs.

And she put up her own window so circumspectly that she didn't get enough air during the night and woke struggling with a silk-covered eiderdown under the impression that she herself was being thrust out the window.

It was only a nightmare, of course, induced as much as anything by her own hatred of heights. But it gave an impulse to the course she proposed to Mrs. Lasher that very morning.

It was true, of course, that the thing may have been exactly what it appeared to be, and that was, an accident. But if it was not accident, there were only two possibilities.

"Do you mean," cried Mrs. Lasher incredulously when Susan had finished her brief suggestion, "that I'm to say openly that Duane is my son! But you don't understand, Miss Dare. I'm not sure. It may be Dixon."

"I know," said Susan. "And I may be wrong. But I think it might help if you will announce to—oh, only to Major Briggs and the two men—that you are convinced that it is Duane and are taking steps for legal recognition of the fact."

"Why? What do you think will happen? How will it help things to do that?"

"I'm not at all sure it will help," said Susan wearily. "But it's the only thing I see to do. And I think that you may as well do it right away."

"Today?" said Mrs. Lasher reluctantly.

"At lunch," said Susan inexorably. "Telephone to invite Major Briggs now."

"Oh, very well," said Idabelle Lasher. "After all, it will please Tom Briggs. He has been urging me to make a decision. He seems certain that it is Duane."

But Susan, present and watching closely, could detect nothing except that Idabelle Lasher, once she was committed to a course, undertook it with thoroughness. Her fondness for Duane, her kindness to Dixon, her air of relief at having settled so momentous a question, left nothing to be desired. Susan was sure that the men were convinced.

There was, to be sure, a shade of triumph in Duane's demeanor, and he was magnanimous with Dixon—as, indeed, he could well afford to be. Dixon was silent and rather pale and looked as if he had not expected the decision and was a bit stunned by it. Major Briggs was incredulous at first, and then openly jubilant, and toasted all of them.

Indeed, what with toasts and speeches on the part of Major Briggs, the lunch rather prolonged itself, and it was late afternoon before the Major had gone and Susan and Mrs. Lasher met alone for a moment in the library.

Idabelle was flushed and worried.

"Was it all right, Miss Dare?" she asked in a stage whisper.

"Perfectly," said Susan.

"Then—then do you know—"

"Not yet," said Susan. "But keep Dixon here."

"Very well," said Idabelle.

The rest of the day passed quietly and not, from Susan's point of view, at all valuably, although Susan tried to prove something about the possible left-handedness of the real Derek. Badminton and several games of billiards resulted only in displaying the more perfectly a consistent right-handedness on the part of both the claimants.

Dressing again for dinner, Susan looked at herself ruefully in the great mirror.

She had never in her life felt so utterly helpless, and the thought of Idabelle Lasher's faith in her hurt. After all, she ought to have realized her own limits: the problem that Mrs. Lasher had set her was one that would have baffled—that, indeed, had baffled—experts. Who was she, Susan Dare, to attempt its solution?

The course of action she had laid out for Idabelle Lasher had certainly, thus far, had no development beyond heightening an already tense situation. It was quite possible that she was mistaken and that nothing at all would come of it. And if not, what then?

Idabelle Lasher's pale eyes and anxious, beseeching hands hovered again before Susan, and she jerked her satin slip savagely over her head—thereby pulling loose a shoulder strap and being obliged to ring for the maid who sewed the strap neatly and rearranged Susan's hair.

"You'll be going to the party tonight, ma'am?" said the maid in a pleasant Irish accent.

"Party?"

"Oh, yes, ma'am. Didn't you know? It's the Charity Ball. At the Dycke Hotel. In the Chandelier Ballroom. A grand, big party, ma'am. Madame is wearing her pearls. Will you bend your head, please, ma'am."

Susan bent her head and felt her white chiffon being slipped deftly over it. When she emerged she said:

"Is the entire family going?"

"Oh, yes, ma'am. And Major Briggs. There you are, ma'am—and I do say you look beautiful. There's orchids, ma'am, from Mr. Duane. And gardenias from Mr. Dixon. I believe," said the maid thoughtfully, "that I could put them all together. That's what I'm doing for Madame."

"Very well," said Susan recklessly. "Put them all together."

It made a somewhat staggering decoration—staggering, thought Susan, but positively abandoned in luxuriousness. So, too, was the long town car which waited for them promptly at ten when they emerged from the towering apartment house. Susan, leaning back in her seat between Major Briggs and Idabelle Lasher, was always afterward to remember that short ride through crowded, lighted streets to the Dycke Hotel.

No one spoke. Perhaps only Susan was aware (and suddenly realized that she was aware) of the surging desires and needs and feelings that were bottled up together in the tonneau of that long, gliding car. She was aware of it quite suddenly and tinglingly.

Nothing had happened. Nothing, all through that long dinner from which they had just come, had been said that was at all provocative.

Yet all at once Susan was aware of a queer kind of excitement.

She looked at the black shoulders of the two men, Duane and Dixon, riding along beside each other. Dixon sat stiff and straight; his shoulders looked rigid and unmoving. He had taken it rather well, she thought; did he guess Idabelle's decision was not the true one? Or was he still stunned by it?

Or was there something back of that silence? Had she underestimated the force and possible violence of Dixon's reaction? Susan frowned: it was dangerous enough without that.

They arrived at the hotel. Their sudden emergence from the silence of the car, with its undercurrent of emotion, into brilliant lights and crowds and the gay lilt of an orchestra somewhere, had its customary tonic effect. Even Dixon shook off his air of brooding and, as they finally strolled into the Chandelier Room, and Duane and Mrs. Lasher danced smoothly into the revolving colors, asked Susan to dance.

They left the Major smiling approval and buying cigarettes from a girl in blue pantaloons.

The momentary gaiety with which Dixon had asked Susan to dance faded at once. He danced conscientiously but without much spirit and said nothing. Susan glanced up at his face once or twice; his direct, dark blue eyes looked straight ahead, and his face was rather pale and set.

Presently Susan said: "Oh, there's Idabelle!"

At once Dixon lost step. Susan recovered herself and her small silver sandals rather deftly, and Idabelle, large and pink and jewel-laden, danced past them in Duane's arms. She smiled at Dixon anxiously and looked, above her pearls, rather worried.

Dixon's eyebrows were a straight dark line, and he was white around the mouth.

"I'm sorry, Dixon," said Susan. She tried to catch step with him, for the moment, and added: "Please don't mind my speaking about it. We are all thinking of it. I do think you behave very well."

He looked straight over her head, danced several somewhat erratic steps, and said suddenly:

"It was so—unexpected. And you see, I was so sure of it."

"Why were you so sure?" asked Susan.

He hesitated, then burst out again:

"Because of the dog," he said savagely, stepping on one of Susan's silver toes. She removed it with Spartan composure, and he said: "The calico dog, you know. And the green curtains. If I had known there was so much money involved, I don't think I'd have come to— Idabelle. But then, when I did know, and this other—fellow turned up, why, of course, I felt like sticking it out!"

He paused, and Susan felt his arm tighten around her waist. She looked up, and his face was suddenly chalk white and his eyes blazing.

"Duane!" he said hoarsely. "I hate him. I could kill him with my own hands."

The next dance was a tango, and Susan danced it with Duane. His eyes were shining, and his face flushed with excitement and gaiety.

He was a born dancer, and Susan relaxed in the perfect ease of his steps. He held her very closely, complimented her gracefully, and talked all the time, and for a few moments Susan merely enjoyed the fast swirl of the lovely Argentine dance. Then Idabelle and Dixon went past, and Susan saw again the expression of Dixon's set white face as he looked at Duane, and Idabelle's swimming eyes above her pink face and bare pink neck.

The rest of what was probably a perfect dance was lost on Susan, busy about certain concerns of her own which involved some adjusting of the flowers on her shoulder. And the moment the dance was over she slipped away.

White chiffon billowed around her, and her gardenias sent up a warm fragrance as she huddled into a telephone booth. She made sure the flowers were secure and unrevealing upon her shoulder, steadied her breath, and smiled a little tremulously as she dialed a number she very well knew. It was getting to be a habit—calling Jim Byrne, her newspaper friend, when she herself had reached an impasse. But she needed him. Needed him at once.

"Jim—Jim," she said. "It's Susan. Listen. Get into a white tie and come as fast as you can to the Dycke Hotel. The Chandelier Room."

"What's wrong?"

"Well," said Susan in a small voice. "I've set something going that—that I'm afraid is going to be more than I meant—"

"You're good at stirring up things, Sue," he said "What's the trouble now?"

"Hurry, Jim," said Susan. "I mean it." She caught her breath. "I—I'm afraid," she said.

His voice changed.

"I'll be right there. Watch for me at the door." The telephone clicked, and Susan leaned rather weakly against the wall of the telephone booth.

She went back to the Chandelier Room. Idabelle Lasher, pink and worried-looking, and Major Briggs and the two younger men made a little group standing together, talking. She breathed a little sigh of relief. So long as they remained together, and remained in that room surrounded by hundreds of witnesses, it was all right. Surely it was all right. People didn't murder in cold blood when other people were looking on.

It was Idabelle who remembered her duties as hostess and suggested the fortune teller.

"She's very good, they say," said Idabelle. "She's a professional, not just doing it for a stunt, you know. She's got a booth in one of the rooms."

"By all means, my dear," said Major Briggs at once. "This way?" She put her hand on his arm and, with Duane at her other side, moved away, and Dixon and Susan followed. Susan cast a worried look toward the entrance. But Jim couldn't possibly get there in less than thirty minutes, and by that time they would have returned.

Dixon said: "Was it the Major that convinced Idabelle that Duane is her son?"

Susan hesitated.

"I don't know," she said cautiously, "how strong the Major's influence has been."

Her caution was not successful. As they left the ballroom and turned down a corridor, he whirled toward her.

"This thing isn't over yet," he said with the sudden savagery that had blazed out in him while they were dancing.

She said nothing, however, for Major Briggs was beckoning jauntily from a doorway.

"Here it is," he said in a stage whisper as they approached him. "Idabelle has already gone in. And would you believe it, the fortune teller charges twenty dollars a throw!"

The room was small: a dining room, probably, for small parties. Across the end of it a kind of tent had been arranged with many gayly striped curtains.

Possibly due to her fees, the fortune teller did not appear to be very popular; at least, there were no others waiting, and no one came to the door except a bellboy with a tray in his hand who looked them over searchingly, murmured something that sounded very much like Mr. Haymow, and wandered away. Duane sat nonchalantly on the small of his back, smoking. The Major seemed a bit nervous and moved restlessly about. Dixon stood just behind Susan. Odd that she could feel his hatred for the man lolling there in the armchair almost as if it were a palpable, living thing flowing outward in waves. Susan's sense of danger was growing sharper. But surely it was safe—so long as they were together.

The draperies of the tent moved confusedly and opened, and Idabelle stood there, smiling and beckoning to Susan.

"Come inside, my dear," she said. "She wants you, too."

Susan hesitated. But, after all, so long as the three men were together, nothing could happen. Dixon gave her a sharp look, and

Susan moved across the room. She felt a slight added qualm when she discovered that in an effort probably to add mystery to the fortune teller's trade, the swathing curtains had been arranged so that one entered a kind of narrow passage among them, which one followed with several turns before arriving at the looped-up curtain which made an entrance to the center of the maze and faced the fortune teller herself.

Susan stifled her uneasiness and sat down on some cushions beside Idabelle. The fortune teller, in Egyptian costume, with French accent and a Sibylline manner began to talk. Beyond the curtains and the drone of her voice Susan could hear little, although once she thought there were voices.

But the thing, when it happened, gave no warning.

There was only, suddenly, a great dull shock of sound that brought Susan taut and upright and left the fortune teller gasping and still and turned Idabelle Lasher's broad pinkness to a queer pale mauve.

"*What was that?*" whispered Idabelle in a choked way.

And the fortune teller cried: "It's a gunshot—out there!"

Susan stumbled and groped through the folds of draperies, trying to find the way through the entangling maze of curtains and out of the tent. Then all at once they were outside the curtains and staring at a figure that lay huddled on the floor, and there were people pouring in the door from the hall, and confusion everywhere.

It was Major Briggs. And he'd been shot and was dead, and there was no revolver anywhere.

Susan felt ill and faint and after one long look backed away to the window. Idabelle was weeping, her faced blotched. Dixon was beside her, and then suddenly someone from the hotel had closed the door into the corridor. And a bellboy's voice, the one who'd wandered into the room looking for Mr. Haymow, rose shrilly above the tumult.

"Nobody at all," he was saying. "Nobody came out of the room. I was at the end of the corridor when I heard the shot and this is the only room on this side that's unlocked and in use tonight. So I ran down here, and I can swear that nobody came out of the room after the shot was fired. Not before I reached it."

"Was anybody here when you came in? What did you see?" It was the manager, fat, worried, but competently keeping the door behind him closed against further intrusion.

"Just this man on the floor. He was dead already."

"And nobody in the room?"

"Nobody. Nobody then. But I'd hardly got to him before there was people running into the room. And these three women came out of this tent."

The manager looked at Idabelle—at Susan.

"He was with you?" he asked Idabelle.

"Oh, yes, yes," sobbed Idabelle. "It's Major Briggs."

The manager started to speak, stopped, began again:

"I've sent for the police," he said. "You folks that were in his party—how many of you are there?"

"Just Miss Dare and me," sobbed Idabelle. "And—" she singled out Dixon and Duane—"these two men."

"All right. You folks stay right here, will you? And you, too, miss—" indicating the fortune teller—"and the bellboy. The rest of you will go to a room across the hall. Sorry, but I'll have to hold you till the police get here."

It was not well received. There were murmurs of outrage and horrified looks over slender bare backs and the indignant rustle of trailing gowns, but the scattered groups that had pressed into the room did file slowly out again under the firm look of the manager.

The manager closed the door and said briskly:

"Now, if you folks will be good enough to stay right here, it won't be long till the police arrive."

"A doctor," faltered Idabelle. "Can't we have a doctor?"

The manager looked at the sodden, lifeless body.

"You don't want a doctor, ma'am," he said. "What you want is an under—" He stopped abruptly and reverted to his professional suavity.

"We'll do everything in our power to save your feelings, Mrs. Lasher," he said. "At the same time we would much appreciate your—er—assistance. You see, the Charity Ball being what it is, we've got to keep this thing quiet." He was obviously distressed but still suave and competent. "Now then," he said, "I've got to make some arrangements—if you'll just stay here." He put his hand on the door knob and then turned toward them again and said quite definitely, looking at the floor: "It would be just as well if none of you were to try to leave."

With that he was gone.

The fortune teller sank down into a chair and said, "Good gracious me," with some emphasis and a Middle-Western accent. The bellboy retired nonchalantly to a corner and stood there, looking very childish in his smart white uniform, but very knowing. And Idabelle Lasher looked at the man at her feet and began to sob again, and Duane tried to comfort her, while Dixon shoved his hands in his pockets and glowered at nothing.

"But I don't see," wailed Idabelle, "how it could have happened!" Odd, thought Susan, that she didn't ask who did it. That would be the natural question. Or why? Why had a man who was—as she had said, like a brother to her—been murdered?

Duane patted Idabelle's heaving bare shoulders and said something soothing, and Idabelle wrung her hands and cried again: "How could it have happened! We were all together—he was not alone a moment—"

Dixon stirred.

"Oh, yes, he was alone," he said. "He wanted a drink, and I'd gone to hunt a waiter."

"And you forget to mention," said Duane icily, "that I had gone with you."

"You left this room at the same time, but that's all I know."

"I went at the same time you did. I stopped to buy cigarettes, and you vanished. I don't know where you went, but I didn't see you again.

Not till I came back with the crowd into this room. Came back to find you already here."

"What do you mean by that?" Dixon's eyes were blazing in his white face, and his hands were working. "If you are accusing me of murder, say so straight out like a man instead of an insolent little puppy."

Duane was white, too, but composed.

"All right," he said. "You know whether you murdered him or not. All I know is when I got back I found him dead and you already here."

"You—"

"*Dixon!*" cried Idabelle sharply, her laces swirling as she moved hurriedly between the two men. "Stop this! I won't have it. There'll be time enough for questions when the police come. When the police—" She dabbed at her mouth, which was still trembling, and at her chin, and her fingers went on to her throat, groped, closed convulsively, and she screamed: "*My pearls!*"

"Pearls?" said Dixon staring, and Duane darted forward.

"Pearls—they're gone!"

The fortune teller had started upward defensively, and the bell-boy's eyes were like two saucers. Susan said:

"They are certainly somewhere in the room, Mrs. Lasher. And the police will find them for you. There's no need to search for them, now."

Susan pushed a chair toward her, and she sank helplessly into it.

"Tom murdered—and now my pearls gone—and I don't know which is Derek, and I—*I don't know what to do*—" Her shoulders heaved, and her face was hidden in her handkerchief, and her corseted fat body collapsed into lines of utter despair.

Susan said deliberately:

"The room will be searched, Mrs. Lasher, every square inch of it— ourselves included. There is nothing," said Susan with soft emphasis. "Nothing that they will miss."

Then Dixon stepped forward. His face was set, and there was an ominous flare of light in his eyes.

He put his hand upon Idabelle's shoulder to force her to look up into his face, and brushed aside Duane, who had moved quickly forward, too, as if his defeated rival had threatened Idabelle.

"Why—why, Dixon," faltered Idabelle Lasher, "you look so strange. What is it? Don't, my dear, you are hurting my shoulder—"

Duane cried: "Let her alone. Let her alone." And then to Idabelle: "Don't pay any attention to him. He's out of his mind. He's—" He clutched at Dixon's arm, but Dixon turned, gave him one black look, and thrust him away so forcefully that Duane staggered backward against the walls of the tent and clutched at the curtains to save himself from falling.

"Look here," said Dixon grimly to Idabelle, "what do you mean when you say as you did just now, that you don't know which is Derek? What do you mean? You must tell me. It isn't fair. *What do you mean?*"

His fingers sank into her bulging flesh. She stared upward as if hypnotized, choking. "I meant just that, Dixon. I don't know yet. I only said I had decided in order to—"

"In order to what?" said Dixon inexorably.

A queer little tingle ran along Susan's nerves, and she edged toward the door. She must get help. Duane's eyes were strange and terribly bright. He still clutched the garishly striped curtains behind him. Susan took another silent step and another toward the door without removing her gaze from the tableau, and Idabelle Lasher looked up into Dixon's face, and her lips moved flabbily, and she said the strangest thing:

"*How like your father you are, Derek.*"

Susan's heart got up into her throat and left a very curious empty place in the pit of her stomach. She probably moved a little farther toward the door, but was never sure, for all at once, while mother and son stared revealingly and certainly at each other, Duane's white face and queer bright eyes vanished.

Susan was going to run. She was going to fling herself out the door and shriek for help. For there was going to be another murder in that room. There was going to be another murder, and she couldn't stop it, she couldn't do anything, she couldn't even scream a warning. Then Duane's black figure was outlined against the tent again. And he held a revolver in his hand. The fortune teller said: "Oh, my God" and the white streak that had been the bellboy dissolved rapidly behind a chair.

"Call him your son if you want to," Duane said in an odd jerky way, addressing Mrs. Lasher and Derek confusedly. "Then your son's a murderer. He killed Briggs. He hid in the folds of this curtain till—the room was full of people—and then he came out again. He left his revolver there. And here it is. *Don't move.* One word or move out of any of you, and I'll shoot." He stopped to take a breath. He was smiling a little and panting. "Don't move," he said again sharply. "I'm going to hand you over to the police, Mr. *Derek*. You won't be so anxious to say he's your son then, perhaps. It's his revolver. He killed Briggs with it because Briggs favored me. He knew it, and he did it for revenge."

He was crossing the room with smooth steps; holding the revolver poised threateningly, and his eyes were rapidly shifting from one to another. Susan hadn't the slightest doubt that the smallest move would bring a revolver shot crashing through someone's brain. *He's going to escape*, she thought, *he's going to escape. I can't do a thing. And he's mad with rage. Mad with the terrible excitement of having already killed once.*

Duane caught the flicker of Susan's eyes. He was near her now, so near that he could have touched her. He cried:

"It's you that's done this! You that advised her! You were on his side! Well—" He'd reached the door now, and there was nothing they could do. He was gloating openly, the way of escape before him. In an excess of dreadful triumphant excitement, he cried: "I'll shoot you first—it's too bad, when you are so pretty. But I'm going to do it."

It's the certainty, thought Susan numbly; *Idabelle is so certain that*

Derek is the other one that Duane knows it, too. He knows there's no use in going on with it. And he knew, when I said what I said about the pearls, that I know.

She felt oddly dizzy. Something was moving. Was she going to faint—was she—something *was* moving, and it was the door behind Duane. It was moving silently, very slowly.

Susan steeled her eyes not to reveal that knowledge. If only Idabelle and Derek would not move—would not see those panels move and betray what they had seen.

Duane laughed.

And Derek moved again, and Idabelle tried to thrust him away from her, and Duane's revolver jerked and jerked again, and the door pushed Duane suddenly to one side and there was a crash of glass, and voices and flashing movement. Susan knew only that someone had pinioned Duane from behind and was holding his arms close to his side. Duane gasped, his hand writhed and dropped the revolver.

Then somebody at the door dragged Duane away; Susan realized confusedly that there were police there. And Jim Byrne stood at her elbow. He looked unwontedly handsome in white tie and tails, but very angry. He said:

"Go home, Sue. Get out of here."

It was literally impossible for Susan to speak or move. Jim stared at her as if nobody else was in the room, got out a handkerchief and wiped his forehead with it.

"I've aged ten years in the last five minutes," he said. He glanced around. Saw Major Briggs' body there on the floor—saw Idabelle Lasher and Derek—saw the fortune teller and the bellboy.

"Is that Mrs. Jeremiah Lasher over there?" he said to Susan.

Mrs. Lasher opened her eyes, looked at him, and closed them again.

Jim looked meditatively at a revolver in his hand, put it in his pocket, and said briskly:

"You can stay for a while, Susan. Until I hear the whole story. Who shot Major Briggs?"

Susan's lips moved and Derek straightened up and cried:

"Oh, it's my revolver all right. But I didn't kill Major Briggs—I don't expect anyone to believe me, but I didn't."

"He didn't," said Susan wearily. "Duane killed Major Briggs. He killed him with Derek's revolver, perhaps, but it was Duane who did the murder."

Jim did not question her statement, but Derek said eagerly:

"How do you know? Can you prove it?"

"I think so," said Susan. "You see, Duane had a revolver when I danced with him. It was in his pocket. That's when I phoned for you, Jim. But I was too late."

"But how—" said Jim.

"Oh, when Duane accused Derek, he actually described the way he himself murdered Major Briggs and concealed himself and the revolver in the folds of the tent until the room was full of people and he could quietly mingle with them as if he had come from the hall. We were all staring at Major Briggs. It was very simple. Duane had got hold of Derek's revolver and knew it would be traced to Derek and the blame put upon him, since Derek had every reason to wish to revenge himself upon Major Briggs."

Idabelle had opened her eyes. They looked a bit glassy but were more sensible.

"Why—" she said—"why did Duane kill Major Briggs?"

"I suppose because Major Briggs had backed him. You see," said Susan gently, "one of the claimants had to be an impostor and a deliberate one. And the attack upon Major Briggs last night suggested either that he knew too much or was a conspirator himself. The exact coinciding of the stories (particularly clever on Major Briggs' part) and the fact that Duane turned up after Major Briggs had had time to search for someone who would fulfill the requirements necessary to make a claim to being your son, seemed to me an indication of conspiracy; besides, the very nature of the case involved imposture. But there had to be a conspiracy; someone had to tell one of the claimants about the things upon which to base his claim, especially about the memories of the baby things—the calico dog," said Susan with a little smile, "and the plush teddy bear. It had to be someone who had known you long ago and could have seen those things before you put them away in the safe. Someone who knew all your circumstances."

"You mean that Major Briggs planned Duane's claim—planned the whole thing? But why—" Idabelle's eyes were full of tears again.

"There's only one possible reason," said Susan. "He must have needed money very badly, and Duane, coming into thirty millions of dollars, would have been obliged to share his spoils."

"Then Derek—I mean Dixon—I mean," said Idabelle confusedly, clutching at Derek, "this one. He really is my son?"

"You know he is," said Susan. "You realized it yourself when you were under emotional stress and obliged to feel instead of reason about it. However, there's reason for it, too. *He is Derek.*"

"He—is—Derek," said Idabelle catching at Susan's words. "You are sure?"

"Yes," said Susan quietly. "He is Derek. You see, I'd forgotten something. Something physical that never changes all through life. That is, a sense of rhythm. Derek has no sense of rhythm and has never had. Duane was a born dancer."

Idabelle said: "Thank God!" She looked at Susan, looked at Derek, and quite suddenly became herself again. She got up briskly, glanced at Major Briggs' body, said calmly: "We'll try to keep some of this quiet. I'll see that things are done decently—after all, poor old fellow, he did love his comforts. Now, then. Oh, yes, if someone will just see the manager of the hotel about my pearls—"

Susan put a startled hand to her gardenias.

"I'd forgotten your pearls, too. Here they are." She fumbled a moment among the flowers, detached a string of flowing beauty, and held it toward Idabelle. "I took them from Duane while we were dancing."

"Duane," said Idabelle. "But—" She took the pearls and said incredulously: "They *are* mine!"

"He had taken them while he danced with you. During the next dance you passed me, and I saw that your neck was bare."

Jim turned to Susan.

"Are you sure about that, Susan?" he said. "I've managed to get the outline of the story, you know. And I don't think the false claimant would have taken such a risk. Not with thirty millions in his pocket, so to speak."

"Oh, they were for the Major," said Susan. "At least, I think that was the reason. I don't know yet, but I think we'll find that he was pretty hard pressed for cash and had to have some right away. Immediately. Duane probably balked at demanding money of Mrs. Lasher so soon, so the Major suggested the pearls. And Duane was in no position to refuse the Major's demands. Then, you see, he had no pearls because I took them; he and the Major must have quarreled, and Duane, who had already foreseen that he would be at Major Briggs' mercy as long as the Major lived, was already prepared for any opportunity to kill him. After he had once got to Idabelle, he no longer needed the Major. He had armed himself with Derek's revolver after what must have seemed to him a heaven-sent chance to stage an accident had failed. Mrs. Lasher's decision removed any remaining small value that the Major was to him and made Major Briggs only a menace. But I think he wasn't sure just what he would do or how—he acceded to the Major's demand for the pearls because it was at the moment the simplest course. But he was ready and anxious to kill him, and when he knew that the pearls had gone from his pocket he must have guessed that I had taken them. And he decided to get rid of Major Briggs at once, before he could possibly tell anything, for any story the Major chose to tell would have been believed by Mrs. Lasher. Later, when I said that the police would search the room, he knew that I knew. And that I knew the revolver was still here."

"Is that why you advised me to announce my decision that Duane was my son?" demanded Idabelle Lasher.

Susan shuddered and tried not to look at that black heap across the room.

"No," she said steadily. "I didn't dream of—murder. I only thought that it might bring the conspiracy that evidently existed somewhere into the open."

Jim said: "Here are the police."

Queer, thought Susan much later, riding along the Drive in Jim's car, with her white chiffon flounces tucked in carefully, and her green velvet wrap pulled tightly about her throat against the chill night breeze, and the scent of gardenias mingling with the scent of Jim's cigarette—queer how often her adventures ended like this: driving silently homeward in Jim's car.

She glanced at the irregular profile behind the wheel and said: "I suppose you know you saved my life tonight."

His mouth tightened in the little glow from the dashlight. Presently he said:

"How did you know he had the pearls in his pocket?"

"Felt 'em," said Susan. "And you can't imagine how terribly easy it was to take them. In all probability a really brilliant career in picking pockets was sacrificed when I was provided with moral scruples."

The light went to yellow and then red, and Jim stopped. He turned and gave Susan a long look through the dusk, and then slowly took her hand in his own warm fingers for a second or two before the light went to green again.

THE EXACT OPPOSITE
Erle Stanley Gardner

It is common to discuss Erle Stanley Gardner (1889-1970) in terms of his prodigious production and his most famous creation, Perry Mason. I am guilty of it, too, in the many times I've written about him. But this focus too often ignores what an excellent storyteller he was, and how meticulously plotted his detective stories were.

Richard Levinson and William Link, the genius creators of *Columbo*, *Murder, She Wrote*, and other television series, ranked Gardner with Ellery Queen and John Dickson Carr among the greatest of the great when it came to fair-play detective stories.

The amazingly prolific author created countless series characters for the pulp magazines before he wrote his first Perry Mason novel, *The Case of the Velvet Claws* (1933). He passed the bar exam in 1911, practicing law for about a decade. He made little money, so started to write fiction, selling his first mystery to a pulp magazine in 1923. For the next decade, he published approximately 1,200,000 words a year, the equivalent of a full-length novel every three weeks.

Mason, the incorruptible lawyer, went on to become the best-selling mystery character in American literature, with 300,000,000 copies sold of more than eighty novels (though Mickey Spillane's Mike Hammer outsold him on a per-book basis). The books inspired the *Perry Mason* television series that starred Raymond Burr for nine hugely successful years (1957-1966).

Most of Gardner's pulp characters were criminals, including Lester Leith, the "hero" of more than seventy novelettes. Leith worked as both a detective and as a Robin Hood figure that was very popular in the Depression era. He stole from the rich, but only those who also were crooks, and gave the money to charities—after taking a twenty per cent "recovery" fee.

He enjoyed the perks of his fortune, checking the newspapers in the comfort of his penthouse apartment for new robberies to solve, from which he could reclaim the stolen treasures. His valet, Beaver, nicknamed "Scuttle" by Leith, is a secret plant of Sergeant Arthur Ackley. Leith, of course, is aware that his manservant is an undercover operative, using that knowledge to plant misinformation to frustrate the policeman again and again.

"The Exact Opposite" was originally published in the March 29, 1941, issue of *Detective Fiction Weekly*.

The Exact Opposite
Erle Stanley Gardner

THERE WAS a glint of amusement in the eyes of Lester Leith as he lazily surveyed the valet, who was in reality no valet at all, but a police undercover operative sent by Sergeant Ackley to spy upon him.

"And so you don't like fanatical East Indian priests, Scuttle?"

"No, sir," he said. "I should hate to have them on *my* trail."

Lester Leith took a cigarette from the humidor and flicked his lighter.

"Scuttle," he said, "why the devil should Indian priests be on anyone's trail?"

"If I were to tell you, sir, you'd think that I was trying to interest you in another crime. As a matter of fact, sir, it *was* a crime which caused me to voice that sentiment about East Indian priests."

"Indeed?" said Lester Leith.

"Yes, sir," he said. "I was thinking about the murder of George Navin."

Lester Leith looked reproachfully at the spy.

"Scuttle," he said, "is it possible that you are trying to interest me in *that* crime?"

"No, sir, not at all," the spy made haste to reassure him. "Although if you *were* interested in the crime, sir, I am satisfied that this is a case made to order for you."

Lester Leith shook his head.

"No, Scuttle," he said. "Much as I like to dabble in crime problems, I don't care to let myself go on them. You see, Scuttle, it's a mental pastime with me. I like to read newspaper accounts of crimes and speculate on what might be a solution."

"Yes, sir," said the spy. "This is just the sort of a crime that you used to like to speculate about, sir."

Lester Leith sighed. "No, Scuttle," he said. "I really don't dare to do it. You see, Scuttle, Sergeant Ackley learned about that fad of mine, and he insists that I am some sort of a super-criminal who goes about hijacking robbers out of their ill-gotten spoils. There's nothing that I can do to convince the man that he is wrong. Therefore, I have found it necessary to give up my fad."

"Well," said the valet, "of course, sir, Sergeant Ackley doesn't need to know everything that happens in the privacy of your own apartment, sir."

Lester Leith shook his head sadly. "One would think so, Scuttle, and yet Sergeant Ackley seems to have some uncanny knowledge of what I am thinking about."

"Yes, sir," he said. "Have you read anything about the murder of George Navin?"

Lester Leith frowned. "Wasn't he mixed up with some kind of a gem robbery, Scuttle?"

"Yes, sir," said the spy eagerly. "He was an explorer, and he had explored extensively in the Indian jungle. Perhaps you've heard something about those jungle temples, sir?"

"What about them, Scuttle?"

"India," the spy said, "is a land of wealth, of gold and rubies. In some of the primitive jungle districts the inhabitants lavish their wealth on idols. Back in a hidden part of the jungle, in a sect known as the Sivaites, there was a huge temple devoted to Vina-ya-ka, the Prince of Evil Spirits, and in that temple was a beautiful ruby, the size of a pigeon egg, set in a gold border which had Sanskrit letters carved in it."

Lester Leith said: "Scuttle, you're arousing my curiosity."

"I'm sorry, sir."

Leith said: "Well, we won't discuss it any more, Scuttle. The way these things go, one thing leads to another, and then—But tell me one thing: is George Navin supposed to have had that gem?"

"Yes, sir. He managed to get it from the temple, although he never admitted it, but in one of his books dealing with some of the peculiar religious sects in India, there's a photographic illustration of this gem—and authorities claim that it would have been absolutely impossible to have photographed it in the temple, that Navin must have managed to get possession of the ruby and brought it to this country."

Lester Leith said: "Wasn't that illustration reproduced in one of the newspapers after Navin's death?"

"Yes, sir. I have it here, sir."

The spy reached inside the pocket of his coat and pulled out a clipping.

Leith hesitated, then reluctantly took it. "I shouldn't look at this. But I'm going to, Scuttle. After that, don't tell me any more about it."

"Very well, sir."

Leith looked at the newspaper illustration. "There'd be a better re-production in Navin's book, Scuttle?"

"Oh, yes, sir—a full-sized photograph."

Leith said: "And, as I gather it, Scuttle, the Hindu priests objected to the spoliation of the temple?"

"Very much, sir. It seems they attached some deep religious significance to the stone. You may remember four or five months ago, shortly after the book was published, there was an attempted robbery of Navin's house. Navin shot a man with a .45 automatic."

"An East Indian?"

"Yes, sir," said the spy. "A Hindu priest of the particular sect which had maintained the jungle temple."

Leith said: "Well, that's enough, Scuttle. I don't want to hear anything more about it. You'd have thought Navin would have taken precautions."

"Oh, but he did, sir. He hired a bodyguard—a chap named Arthur Blaire and a detective, Ed Springer. They were with him all the time."

"Just the three of them in the house?" Lester Leith asked.

"No, sir. There were four. There was a Robert Lamont, a confidential secretary."

"Accompanying Navin on his travels?" Leith asked.

The spy nodded.

"Any servants?" Leith asked.

"Only a housekeeper who came in and worked by the day."

Leith frowned and then said: "Scuttle, don't answer this if it's going to arouse my curiosity any more. But how the devil could a man get murdered if he had two bodyguards and his secretary with him all the time?"

"That, sir, is the thing the police can't understand. Mr. Navin slept in a room which was considered virtually burglar-proof. There were steel shutters on the windows, and a door which locked with a combination, and there was a guard on duty outside of the door all night."

"How did he get ventilation?"

"Through some ventilating system which was installed, and which permitted a circulation of air but wouldn't permit anyone to gain access to the room, sir."

"Don't go on, Scuttle," he said. "I simply mustn't hear about it."

"But, sir," said the spy wheedlingly, "you have heard so much now that it certainly wouldn't hurt to go on and have your natural curiosity satisfied."

Lester Leith sighed. "Very well, Scuttle," he said. "What happened?"

The spy spoke rapidly. "Navin went to bed, sir. Blaire and Springer, the bodyguards, made the rounds of the room, making certain that the steel shutters were locked on the inside, and that the windows were closed and locked. That was about ten o'clock at night. About ten forty Bob Lamont, the secretary, received an important telegram which he wanted to take up to Mr. Navin. He had the bodyguards open the door, and call Navin softly to find out if he was asleep. Navin was sitting up in bed reading.

"They were in there for fifteen or twenty minutes. The guards don't know exactly what happened, because they sat outside on guard, but apparently it was, as Lamont says, just an ordinary business conference. Then Lamont came out, and the guards closed the door. About midnight Arthur Blaire retired, and Ed Springer kept the first watch until four o'clock in the morning. At four, Blaire came on and relieved Springer, and at nine o'clock the secretary came in with the morning mail.

"That was part of the custom, sir. The secretary was the first to go into the room with the morning mail, and he discussed it while Mr. Navin tubbed and shaved.

"The guard opened the door, and Lamont went in.

"The guard heard him say, 'Good morning,' to Mr. Navin, and walk across the room to open the shutters. Then suddenly he heard Lamont give an exclamation.

"George Navin had been murdered by having his throat cut. Everything in the room had been ransacked; even the furniture had been taken to pieces."

Lester Leith made no attempt to disguise his interest now.

"What time was the crime committed, Scuttle?" he asked. "The autopsy surgeon could tell that."

"Yes, sir," said the spy. "At approximately four A.M., sir."

"How did the murderer get into the room?" asked Lester Leith.

"There, sir," said the valet, "is where the police are baffled. The windows were all closed, and the shutters were all locked on the inside."

"And the murder was committed at just about the time the guards were being changed, eh?" said Lester Leith.

"Yes, sir," said the valet.

"So that either one of the guards might be suspected, eh, Scuttle?"

The valet said: "As a matter of fact, sir, both of them are under suspicion. But they have excellent references."

"Well," said Lester Leith, "did the murderer get the ruby, Scuttle?"

"Well, sir, the ruby wasn't in that bedroom at all. The ruby was kept in a specially constructed safe which was in a secret hiding place in the house. No one knew of the existence of that safe, with the exception of George Navin and the two bodyguards. Also, of course, the secretary. Naturally, after discovering the murder, the men went immediately to the safe and opened it. They found that the stone was gone. The police have been unable to find any fingerprints on the safe, but they did discover something else which is rather mystifying.

"The police are satisfied that the murderer entered through one of the windows on the east side of the room. There are tracks in the soft soil of the garden beneath the window, and there are the round marks embedded in the soil where the ends of a bamboo ladder were placed on the ground."

"Bamboo, eh, Scuttle?"

"Yes, sir. That, of course, would indicate that the murderers were Indian, sir."

"But," said Lester Leith, "how could they get through a steel shutter locked on the inside, murder a man, get out through a window, close the window, and leave the shutter still locked on the inside?"

"That is the point, sir."

"Then," said Lester Leith, "the bodyguards weren't mixed up in it. If they were mixed up in it, they would have let the murderer come in through the door.

"But," went on Lester Leith, "there is no evidence as to how the murderer could have secured the gem."

"That's quite true, sir."

"What are the police doing?"

"The police are questioning all the men. That is, sir, the servants and the bodyguards. Lamont left the house right after talking with Navin, and went to a secret conference with Navin's attorney, a man by the name of During. During had his stenographer there, a young lady named Edith Skinner, so that Lamont can account for every minute of his time."

"Do I understand that the conference lasted all night?"

"Yes, sir. The conference was very important. It had to do with certain legal matters in connection with income tax and publishing rights."

"But that's such an unusual time for a conference," said Lester Leith.

"Yes, sir," said the valet, "but it couldn't be helped, Mr. Lamont was very busy with Mr. Navin. It seems that Navin was rather a peculiar individual, and he demanded a great deal of attention. As soon as the lawyer said that the examination of the records and things would take a period of over eight hours, Navin made so much trouble that Lamont finally agreed to work all one night."

"What time did Lamont leave the conference?" asked Leith.

"About eight o'clock in the morning. They went down to breakfast, and then Lamont drove out to the house in time to get the morning mail ready for Mr. Navin."

"The police, of course, are coming down pretty hard on Blaire and Springer, eh, Scuttle?"

"Yes, sir, because it would have been almost impossible for anyone to have entered that room without the connivance of one of the watchmen. And then again, sir, the fact that the murder was timed to take place when the watchmen were changing their shift would seem to indicate that either Blaire was a party to the crime, and fixed the time so that he could put the blame on Springer, or that Springer was the guilty one, and had committed the crime just as soon as he came on duty so that suspicion would attach to Blaire."

"Rather a neat problem, I should say," said Lester Leith. "One that will keep Sergeant Ackley busy."

"Yes, sir," said the valet, "and it just goes to show how ingenious the Hindus are."

"Yes," said Lester Leith dreamily, "it's a very ingenious murder—save for one thing."

The valet's eyes glistened with eagerness.

"What," he asked, "is that one thing, sir?"

"No, no, Scuttle," he said. "If I should tell you, that would be violating the pact which I have made with myself. I have determined that I wouldn't work out any more academic crime solutions."

"I would like very much, sir," said the valet coaxingly, "to know what that one thing is."

Lester Leith took a deep breath.

"No, Scuttle," he said. "Do not tempt me."

Lester Leith reclined in the long chair, his feet crossed on the cushions, his eyes watching the cigarette smoke.

"Do you know, Scuttle," he said, almost dreamily, "I am tempted to conduct an experiment."

"An experiment, sir?"

"Yes," said Lester Leith. "A psychological experiment. It would, however, require certain things. I would want three fifty-dollar bills and fifty one-dollar bills, Scuttle. I would want a diamond tiepin, an imitation of the ruby which was stolen from Navin's house, and a very attractive chorus girl."

Edward H. Beaver, undercover man who was working directly under Sergeant Arthur Ackley, but who was known to Lester Leith as "Scuttle," surveyed the police sergeant across the battered top of the desk at headquarters.

Sergeant Ackley blinked his crafty eyes at the undercover man and said: "Give me that list again, Beaver."

"Three fifty-dollar bills, fifty one-dollar bills, a large diamond stickpin, an imitation of the ruby which was stolen, and a chorus girl."

Sergeant Ackley slammed the pencil down.

"He was taking you for a ride," he said.

The undercover man shook his head stubbornly.

"No, he wasn't," he said. "It's just the way he works. Every time he starts on one of his hijacking escapades, he asks for a bunch of stuff that seems so absolutely crazy there's no sense to it. But every time so far those things have all turned out to be part of a carefully laid plan which results in victory for Leith and defeat for the crooks—and for us."

Sergeant Ackley made a gesture of emphatic dismissal.

"Beaver," he said, "the man is simply stringing you along this time. He couldn't possibly use these things to connect up this crime. As a matter of fact, we have evidence now which indicates very strongly that the crime was actually committed by three Hindus. We've got a straight tip from a stool pigeon who is covering the Hindu section here."

The spy insisted: "It doesn't make any difference, Sergeant, whether or not Hindus committed the crime. I'm telling you that Lester Leith is serious about this, and that he's going to use these things to work out a solution that will leave *him* in possession of that ruby."

"No," went on Sergeant Ackley, "you have overplayed your hand, Beaver. You went too far trying to get him to take an interest in this crime."

"But," protested the harassed spy, "what else could I do? Every time he pulls a job, you come down on him, triumphantly certain that you've cornered him at last, and every time he squirms out of the corner and leaves you holding the sack. As a result, he knows that you have some method of finding out what he is doing all the time. It's a wonder to me that he doesn't suspect me."

"Well," said Sergeant Ackley coldly, "you don't need to wonder any more, Beaver, because he does suspect you. He wouldn't have given you all this line of hooey unless he did."

"If it's hooey," snapped Beaver, "he's spending a lot of money."

"How do you mean?"

Beaver unfolded the morning paper which lay on the sergeant's desk.

"Take a look at the Classified Advertising Section," he said.

"Wanted: A young woman of pleasing personality and attractive looks, who has had at least three years experience on the stage in a chorus, preferably in a musical comedy or burlesque. She must have been out of work for at least eight months."

"And here's another one," said Beaver, and he pointed to another ad.

"Wanted: Ambitious young man to learn detective work at my expense. Must be a man who has had no previous experience and who knows nothing of routine police procedure. I want to train a detective who has a fresh outlook, entirely untrammeled by conventional ideas of police routine. All expenses will be paid, in addition to a generous salary. Preferably someone who has recently arrived from a rural community."

Sergeant Ackley sat back in his chair. "I'll be—"

"Now, then," said the spy, "if he doesn't intend to do something about that Navin murder, what the devil does he want to go to all this trouble for?"

"It doesn't make sense, Beaver," Ackley said. "No matter how you look at it, it's crazy."

The spy shrugged his shoulders.

"Perhaps," he said, "that's why he's always so successful."

"How do you mean, Beaver?"

"Because his stuff doesn't make sense, Sergeant. It's unconventional and so absolutely unique, there's no precedent to help you."

Sergeant Ackley fished a cigar from his waistcoat pocket.

"Beaver," he said, "the real standard of a good detective is his ability to separate the wheat from the chaff. Now, I'm willing to admit that Leith has done some crazy things before, and they've always worked out. But this is once it won't happen."

"Well," said the undercover man, getting to his feet, "you can have it your own way, but I'm willing to bet he's up to something. I'll bet you fifty dollars against that watch that you're so proud of."

Cupidity glittered in Sergeant Ackley's eyes. "Bet me what?"

"Bet you," said Beaver, "that he uses every one of these things to work out a scheme by which he lifts that Indian ruby, and does it all so cleverly that you can't pin anything on him."

Sergeant Ackley's broad hand smacked down on the top of the desk.

"Beaver," he said, "your language verges on insubordination. Just by way of disciplining you, I am going to take that bet. Fifty dollars against my watch.

"However, Beaver, if he is going to use other means to catch that murderer and hijack the ruby, the bet is off. He's got to do it by these particular means."

"That's the bet," said Beaver.

"And you've got to keep me posted as to everything that he's doing, so that if he should use all of the stuff as a smokescreen and try to get the ruby under cover of all this hooey, we can still catch him."

"Certainly," said the undercover man.

Lester Leith smiled urbanely at his valet. "Scuttle," he said, "this is Miss Dixie Dormley, and Mr. Harry Vare. Miss Dormley is a young woman who is doing some special work for me. She has had rather extensive stage experience, but has recently been out of work. In the position that I want her to fill, it will be necessary that she have some rather striking clothes, and I want you to go around with her to the various shops, let her pick out what clothing she desires, and see that it is charged to me."

The valet blinked his eyes.

"Very good, sir," he said. "What is the limit in regard to price, sir?"

"No limit, Scuttle. Also, I have arranged for Miss Dormley to have the apartment next to us, temporarily," said Lester Leith. "She will live there—the one on the left."

"Yes, sir," said the valet.

"And Mr. Harry Vare," said Lester Leith, "is the fortunate young man who has won the free scholarship in my school of deductive reasoning."

The valet stared at Harry Vare.

Vare met that stare with eyes that were hard and appraising. He narrowed the lids and scrutinized the undercover operative as though he were trying to hypnotize the man.

"Harry Vare," said Lester Leith suavely, "is a young man from the country who has recently come to the city in search of some employment which would be worthy of his talents. He felt that he had outgrown the small town in which he lived. He is possessed of that first essential for detective work—an imagination which makes him see an ulterior motive in every action, a crime in every set of circumstances."

The undercover operative was dignified.

"I beg your pardon, sir," he said, "but as I understand it, sir, most of the real detectives are somewhat the other way. They regard it as a business, sir."

Lester Leith shook his head.

"No, Scuttle," he said. "Sergeant Ackley is one of the shrewdest detectives that I know, and you must admit, Scuttle, that he has one of those imaginations which makes him see a crime in everything."

The girl looked from face to face with a twinkle in her eyes. She was a beautiful woman.

"Mr. Vare," said Lester Leith, "will have the apartment on the right—the one adjoining us. He will be domiciled there temporarily, Scuttle."

"Yes, sir," said the valet. "May I ask, what are the duties of these persons?"

"Mr. Vare is going to be a detective," said Lester Leith gravely. "He will detect."

"What will he detect?"

"That is the interesting part of having a professional detective about, Scuttle. One never knows what he is going to detect. There is Sergeant Ackley, for instance. He detects so many things which seem utterly unreasonable at the time, and then, after mature investigation and reflection, they seem to have an entirely different complexion."

The spy cleared his throat.

"And the young lady, sir?"

"Miss Dormley," said Lester Leith, "will engage in dramatic acting upon the stage which was so well described by Shakespeare."

"What stage is that?" asked the undercover man.

"The world," said Lester Leith.

"Very good, sir," the valet said. "And when do I start on this shopping tour?"

"Immediately," said Lester Leith, "And by the way, Scuttle, did you get me the money and the diamond stickpin?"

The valet opened a box which he took from his pocket.

"Yes, sir," he said. "You wanted rather a large diamond with something of a fault in it, something that wasn't too expensive, I believe you said."

"Yes," said Lester Leith. "That's right, Scuttle."

"This is sent on approval," said the valet. "The price tag is on the pin, sir."

Lester Leith looked at the diamond pin, and whistled.

"Rather a low price, Scuttle," he said.

"Yes, sir," said the valet. "There's quite a flaw in the diamond, although it doesn't appear until you examine it closely."

"And the money?"

"Yes, sir," said the valet, and took from his pocket a sheaf of bank notes.

Lester Leith gravely arranged them so that the fifties were on the outside. Then he rolled them and snapped the roll with an elastic.

Lester Leith turned to Vare.

"Vare," he said, "are you ready to start detecting?"

"I thought I was going to be given a course of instruction," he said.

"You are," said Lester Leith, "but you are going to learn by a new method. You know, they used to teach law by reading out of law books, and then they decided that that wasn't the proper way to give the pupils instruction. They switched to what is known as the case method—that is, Vare, they read cases to them and let the students delve into the reported cases until they found the legal principles which had been applied to the facts."

"Yes, sir," said Vare.

"That is the way you are going to learn detective work," said Lester Leith. "By the case method. Are you ready to start?"

Vare nodded.

Lester Leith removed the tiepin from his tie, placed it on the table, and inserted the diamond stickpin.

"Very well, Vare," he said. "Get your hat and come with me. You are about to receive the first lesson."

There was the usual crowd in front of the ticket windows of the big railroad station. Everywhere there was noise, bustle, and confusion.

"Now," said Lester Leith to Harry Vare, "keep about twenty feet behind me and watch sharply. See if you can find anyone who looks like a crook."

Vare cocked a professional eye at the crowd.

"They all look like crooks," he said.

Lester Leith nodded gravely.

"Vare," he said, "you are showing the true detective instincts. But I want you to pick out someone who looks like a crook we can pin something definite on."

"I don't see exactly what you mean," said Vare.

"You will," said Lester Leith. "Just follow me."

Lester Leith pushed his way through the crowd, with Vare tagging along behind him. From time to time Lester Leith pulled out the roll of bills and counted them, apparently anxious to see that they were safe. Then he snapped the elastic back on the roll and pushed it back in his pocket.

Leith kept in the most congested portions of the big depot.

Twice he was bumped into, and each time by a sad-faced individual with mournful eyes and a drooping mouth.

The man was garbed in a dark suit, and his tie was conservative. Everything about him blended into a single drab personality which would attract no attention.

Finally, Lester Leith walked to a closed ticket window, where there was a little elbow room.

"Well, Vare," he said, "did you see anyone?"

Vare said: "Well, I saw several that looked like crooks, but I couldn't see anyone that I could pick out as being a certain particular crook. That is, I couldn't find any proof."

Lester Leith put his hand in his pocket, and then suddenly jumped backwards.

"Robbed!" he said.

Vare stared at him with sagging jaw.

"Robbed?" he asked.

"Robbed," said Lester Leith. "My money—it's gone!"

He pulled his hand from his trousers pocket, and disclosed a slit which had been cut in the cloth so that the contents of the pocket could be reached from the outside.

"Pickpockets," said Harry Vare.

"And you didn't discover them," Leith said.

Vare fidgeted uneasily.

"There was quite a crowd," he said, "and of course I couldn't see everything."

Lester Leith shook his head sadly.

"I can't give you a high mark on the first lesson, Vare," he said. "Now let's take a cab and go home."

"Your tiepin is safe, anyway," said Vare.

Lester Leith gave a sudden start, reached his hand to his tie, and pulled out the diamond scarfpin.

He looked at the diamond and nodded, then suddenly pointed to the pin.

"Look," he said, "the man tried to take it off with nippers. You can see where they left their mark on the pin. I must have pulled away just as he was doing it, so that he didn't get a chance to get the diamond."

Vare's eyes were large; his face showed consternation.

"Really," said Lester Leith, "you have had two lessons in one, and I can't give you a high mark on either. You should have detected the person who was putting nippers on my pin."

Vare looked crestfallen.

Leith said: "Oh, well, you can't expect to become a first-class detective overnight. That's one of the things that training is for. But we'll go back to the apartment and I'll change my clothes, and you can sit back and concentrate for an hour or two on what you saw, and see if you can remember anything significant."

But a little later Lester Leith re-returned to the depot—alone. Once more he mingled with the crowd, moving aimlessly about, but this time his eyes were busy scanning the faces of the stream of people.

He noticed the man in the dark suit with the mournful countenance, moving aimlessly about, a newspaper in his hands, his manner that of one who is waiting patiently for a wife who was to have met him an hour ago.

Lester Leith walked behind this man, keeping him in sight.

After some fifteen minutes, Leith shortened the distance between them and tapped the man sharply on the shoulder.

"I want to talk with you," he said.

The man's face changed expression. The look of mournful listlessness vanished, and the eyes became hard and wary.

"You ain't got nothing on me."

Lester Leith laughed.

"On the contrary," he said, "you have got something of mine on you—a roll of bills with some fifties on the outside and dollar bills in between. Also, you have the scarfpin which you just nipped from that fat gentleman with the scarlet tie."

The man backed away, and turned as though getting ready to run.

Lester Leith said: "I'm not a detective. I just want to talk with you. In fact, I want to employ you."

The pickpocket looked at him with eyes that were wide with surprise.

"Employ me?" he asked.

"Yes," said Lester Leith. "I have been strolling around here all afternoon looking for a good pickpocket."

"I'm not a pickpocket," said the man.

Lester Leith paid no attention to the man's protestation of innocence.

"I am," he said, "running a school for young detectives. I want to employ you as an assistant instructor. I have an idea that the ordinary training of police officers and detectives is exceedingly haphazard. I am looking for someone who can give my students an education in picking pockets."

"What's the pay?"

"Well," said Lester Leith, "you can keep the watch that you got from the tall thin man, the scarfpin which you nipped from the fleshy man, and you can keep the roll of bills which you cut from my trousers pocket. In addition to that, you will draw regular compensation of one hundred dollars a day, and if you feel like risking your liberty, you can, keep anything which you can pick up on the side."

"How do you mean, 'on the side'?"

"By the practice of your profession, of course," said Lester Leith.

The pickpocket stared at him.

"This," he said, "is some kind of a smart game to get me to commit myself."

Lester Leith reached to his inside pocket and took out a well-filled wallet. He opened the wallet, and the startled eyes of the pickpocket caught sight of a number of one-hundred-dollar bills.

Gravely Lester Leith took out one of these hundred-dollar bills and extended it to the pickpocket.

"This," he said, "is the first day's salary."

The man took the one-hundred-dollar bill, and his eyes followed the wallet as Lester Leith returned it to his pocket.

"Okay, boss," he said. "What do you want me to do?"

"Just meet me," said Lester Leith, "at certain regular times and places. Your first job will be to meet me here at nine thirty tonight. I will write a bunch of instructions on a piece of paper, and put that piece of paper in my coat pocket. You can slip the paper out of the coat pocket and follow instructions. Don't let on that you know me at all, unless I should speak to you first."

The pickpocket nodded.

"Okay," he said. "I'll be here at nine thirty. In the meantime, I'll walk as far as your taxicab with you and talk over details. My name is Sid Bentley. What's yours?"

"Leith," Lester Leith told him.

"Pleased to meet you."

After they had finished shaking hands, Lester Leith started toward the taxicab and Bentley walked on his right side, talking rapidly.

"I don't know how you made me, Leith," he said, "but you can believe it or not, it's the first time I've ever been picked up by anybody. I used to be a sleight-of-hand artist on the stage, and then when business got bad, I decided to go out and start work. I haven't a criminal record and the police haven't got a thing on me."

"That's fine," beamed Lester Leith. "You're exactly the man I want. I'll meet you here at nine thirty, eh, Bentley?"

"Nine thirty it is, Captain."

Lester Leith hailed a taxicab. As it swung into the circle in front of the depot, he turned casually to the pickpocket.

"By the way, Bentley," he said, "please don't use that knife. You've already ruined one good suit for me."

As Lester Leith spoke, his left hand shot out and clamped around the wrist of the pickpocket. The light gleamed on the blade of a razor-like knife with which Bentley had been about to cut Lester Leith's coat.

Bentley looked chagrined for a moment, and then sighed.

"You said that it'd be all right for me to pick up anything I could on the side, Captain," he protested.

Lester Leith grinned.

"Well," he said, "I had better amplify that. You can pick up anything you can on the side, provided you leave my pockets alone."

Bentley matched Lester Leith's grin.

"Okay, Captain," he said. "That's a go."

Lester Leith climbed in the taxicab and returned to his apartment. A vision of loveliness greeted him as he opened the door. Dixie Dormley had adorned herself in garments which looked as though they had been tailored to order in the most exclusive shops.

She smiled a welcome to Lester Leith.

"I kept the cost as low as I could," she said, "in order to get the effect that you wanted."

"You certainly got the effect," complimented Lester Leith, staring at her with very evident approval. "Yes, I think you have done very well, indeed, and we will all go to dinner tonight—the four of us. You, Miss Dormley, Mr. Vare, and, Scuttle, I'm going to include you too."

The spy blinked his eyes. "Yes, sir."

"By the way," said Lester Leith, "did you have the imitation ruby made?"

The spy nodded.

"It's rather a swell affair," he said, "so far as the ruby is concerned. The gold setting is rather cleverly done too. The jeweler insisted upon doing it in a very soft gold. He said that the Indian gold was very yellow and very soft, without much alloy in it. He's duplicated the border design very accurately."

"Quite right, Scuttle," said Lester Leith. "The man knows what he is doing. Let's see it."

The spy handed Lester Leith a little casket, which Leith opened.

The girl exclaimed in admiration.

"Good heavens," she said, "it looks genuine!"

Lester Leith nodded. "It certainly does," he said. "They are able to make excellent imitations of rubies these days."

He lifted the imitation jewel from the case and dropped it carelessly in his side pocket.

"All right, Dixie," he said. "If you'll dress for dinner, we'll leave rather early. I have an important appointment at nine thirty. By the way, I don't want either of you to mention to a living soul that this ruby is an imitation."

At dinner that evening Lester Leith was in rare form. He was suave and courteous, acting very much the gentleman, and discharging his duties as host. It was when the dessert had been cleared away that Leith gravely surveyed Harry Vare's countenance.

"Vare," he said, "you have had your first lesson this afternoon. Do you think that you have profited by it?"

Vare flushed.

"I'll say one thing," he said, "no pickpocket will ever get near you again as long as I'm around."

Lester Leith nodded.

"That's fine," he said, "Now then, I have a rather valuable bauble here that I want to have guarded carefully. I am going to ask you to put it in your pocket."

And Lester Leith slipped from his pocket the imitation ruby and passed it across the table to Vare.

Vare gave a gasp, and his eyes bulged.

"Good heavens," he said, "this is worth a fortune!"

Lester Leith shrugged.

"I am making no comments, Vare," he said, "on its value. It is merely something which is entrusted to you for safekeeping, as a part of your training in detective work."

Vare slipped the gem hurriedly into his pocket.

Lester Leith caught the eye of the waiter and secured the check, which he paid.

"I want you folks to take a little walk with me," he said. "Vare is going to have another lesson as a detective, and I would like to have all of you present."

The spy was plainly ill at ease.

"You want me there also, sir?" he asked.

"Certainly," said Lester Leith.

"Very well, sir," said the spy.

Leith helped the young woman on with her wraps, saw that she was seated comfortably in the taxicab, and told the driver to take them to the depot.

The spy stared at him curiously.

"You're leaving town, sir?" he asked.

"Oh, no," said Lester Leith. "We're just going down to the depot, and I'm going to walk around the way I did this afternoon. Vare is going to see that my pocket isn't picked."

There was not as large a crowd in the depot at night, and Lester Leith had some difficulty in finding a crowd of sufficient density to suit his purpose. In his side pocket was a note:

"The young man who is following me around has an imitation ruby in his pocket. He is watching me to make certain that no one picks my pocket. See if you can get the ruby from him, and after you have it, return it to me later."

Bentley, the pickpocket, stood on the outskirts of a crowd of people who were waiting in line at a ticket window, and gave Lester Leith a significant glance. Leith gestured toward his pocket.

Leith pushed his way into the crowd, and, as he did so, felt Bentley's fingers slip the printed instructions from his pocket.

Thereafter, Lester Leith wandered aimlessly about the depot, until suddenly he heard a choked cry from Harry Vare.

Lester Leith turned and retraced his steps to the young man, who was standing with a sickly gray countenance, his eyes filled with despair.

"What is it?" asked Lester Leith.

Vare indicated a gaping cut down the side of his coat and through his vest.

"I put that gem on the inside of my vest," he said, "where I knew that it would be safe from pickpockets, and look what happened!"

Lester Leith summoned the undercover man.

"Scuttle," he said, "will you notice what has happened? This young man whom I was training to be a detective has allowed the property with which I entrusted to him to be stolen."

The valet blinked.

"I didn't see anyone, sir," he said, "and I was keeping my own eye peeled."

"Scuttle," Lester Leith said, "I am going to ask you to take Vare back to his apartment. Let him sit down and meditate carefully for two hours upon everything that happened and every face he saw while he was here at the depot. I want to see if he can possibly identify the man who is guilty of picking his pocket."

Vare said humbly: "I'm afraid, sir, that you picked a poor student."

Lester Leith smiled.

"Tut, tut, Vare," he said, "that's something for me to determine. I told you that I was going to give you an education, and I am. You're getting a free scholarship as well as wages. So don't worry about it. Go on to your apartment, and sit down and concentrate."

Vare said: "It certainly is wonderful of you to take the thing this way."

"That's all right, Vare."

As the undercover man took Vare's arm and piloted him toward a taxicab, Lester Leith turned to Dixie Dormley with a smile.

"I've got to meet a party here in a few minutes," he said, "and then we can go and dance."

They continued to hang around the depot for fifteen or twenty minutes. Lester Leith began to frown and to consult his wrist watch. Suddenly Sid Bentley, the pickpocket, materialized through one of the doorways and hurried toward them.

"It's okay," he said.

Leith frowned at him.

"You took long enough doing it," he said.

"I'm sorry I kept you waiting," Bentley said, "but there was one thing that I had to do. You should have figured it out yourself, Chief."

"What was that?"

"I had to go to a good fence and make sure that the thing I had was an imitation," said Bentley.

"Well," Leith said, "there's nothing like being frank."

"That's the way I figure it, Chief," he said. "You know, I've got a duty to you, but I've got a duty to my profession, too. I certainly would have been a dumb hick to have had my hands on a fortune and let it slip."

Lester Leith felt the weight of the jewel in his pocket. He nodded and turned away.

"That's all right, Bentley," he said. "You meet me here tomorrow night at seven o'clock, and in the meantime there won't be anything more for you unless I should get in touch with you. Can you give me a telephone number where I can get in touch with you if I should need you?"

The pickpocket reached in his pocket and took out a card.

"Here you are, Chief," he said. "Just ring up that number and leave word that you'll be at some particular place at some particular time. Don't try to talk with me over the telephone. Just leave that message. Then you go to that place, and I'll be hanging around. If the thing looks safe to me, I'll be there. And if I don't hear from you I'll be here tomorrow night at seven."

"Okay," said Leith.

"Dixie," he said, "I've got something for you to do which is rather confidential. I am going to take you to a night club where there's a chap by the name of Bob Lamont. He makes this night club his regular hangout. He will probably have a companion with him, but, from what I've heard, he has a roving eye. I want you to see to it that his eye roves your way, and that you dance with him. After that, we'll try and make a foursome if we can. If we can't, you can date him up for tomorrow night. Think you can do it?"

"Brother," she said, "in these clothes, if I can't stop any roving masculine eye, I'm going out of show business."

Sergeant Arthur Ackley banged upon the door of the apartment. Bolts clicked back as Harry Vare opened the door and stared stupidly at Sergeant Ackley.

Sergeant Ackley pushed his way into the apartment without a

word, slammed the door shut behind him, strode across the room to a chair, and sat down.

"Well, young man," he said, "you've got yourself into a pretty pickle."

Harry Vare blinked and started to talk, but words failed him.

Sergeant Ackley flipped back his coat so that Harry Vare's eyes could rest on the gold badge pinned to his vest.

"Well," he said, "what have you got to say for yourself?"

"I—I—I don't know what you're talking about."

"Oh, yes you do," said Sergeant Ackley. "You're teamed up with this super-crook and you're hashing up a scheme to assist in hijacking a big ruby."

Vare shook his head.

"No, sir," he said, "you're mistaken. I had a big ruby which was given to me to keep, but somebody stole it."

Sergeant Ackley let his eyes bore into those of Harry Vare. Then he got to his feet, reached out and thrust a broad hand to the collar of Vare's coat, twisting it tightly.

"Well," he said, "it'll be about ten years for you, and you'd better come along."

Vare stared at Sergeant Ackley with pathetic eyes.

"I haven't done anything," he said. Sergeant Ackley eyed the man shrewdly.

"Listen," he said, "did you ever hear of George Navin?"

"You mean the man who was murdered?" asked Harry Vare.

Ackley nodded.

"I read something about it in the paper," said Vare.

"All right," said Sergeant Ackley. "Navin was murdered for a big Indian ruby. Bob Lamont was his secretary. Does that mean anything to you?"

"No, sir," said Vare. "Not a thing."

"All right," said Sergeant Ackley. "I'll tell you a few things, and you can see how much it means to you. This fellow Lester Leith that you're working for is one of the cleverest crooks this city has ever produced. He makes a living out of robbing crooks of their ill-gotten spoils. He's slick and he's clever, and he usually dopes out the solution of a crime in advance of the police, and then shakes down the crook before we get to him."

"I didn't know that," said Harry Vare.

"Well, maybe you did, and maybe you didn't," said Sergeant Ackley. "That's something for you to tell the jury when you come up for trial. But here's something else that you may like to listen to. Lester Leith picked up this chorus girl, and the two of them went out last night after they left you and picked up Bob Lamont and some other woman.

"Lester Leith is pretty much of a gentleman, and he wears his clothes well, and this chorus girl he had with him looked like a million dollars in a lot of high-priced clothes. The night club was more or less informal, and she gave Bob Lamont the eye. Bob fell for her and started to dance with her, and before the evening was finished they had moved to another table and were having a nice little foursome."

"But," said Harry Vare, gathering courage, "what has that got to do with me?"

Sergeant Ackley studied him in shrewd appraisal.

"So," he said, "they made another date for tonight, and the four of them are going out."

Harry Vare suddenly caught his breath. His eyes grew wide and dark with apprehension.

"Good heavens!" he said.

Sergeant Ackley nodded. "I thought so," he said.

Panic showed in Vare's face.

"You've got just ten seconds to come clean," said Sergeant Ackley. "If you come clean and give me the lowdown on this thing, and agree to work with me, there's a chance that we may give you immunity from prosecution. Otherwise, you're going to jail for at least ten years."

Harry didn't need ten seconds. He was blurting out speech almost before Sergeant Ackley had finished.

"I didn't know the name." he said, "and I didn't know it was Lamont until you told me. But Lester Leith hired me to study detective work. He had his pocket picked once yesterday, and then gave me a jewel to carry, and it was picked from my pocket. I felt all broken up about it, but Mr. Leith said that it was all right, I'd have to learn a step at a time.

"He told me that tonight he was going to teach me how to make an arrest. He said that I was to arrest him, just as though he had been a crook. He said that he was going out to a dinner party tonight with another man and a woman, and that they would probably wind up at the man's apartment; that after they got to the apartment, he had it fixed up that Dixie Dormley—that's the chorus girl—was to take the other girl out for a few moments, and that, as soon as that happened, I was to come busting in as a detective and accuse Lester Leith of some crime, handcuff him, and lead him out."

Sergeant Ackley frowned. "That's everything you know about it?"

"Everything," said Harry Vare, "but I get more instructions later."

"Well," Ackley said, "I'm going to give you a break. If you do exactly as I tell you, and don't tell Lester Leith that I was here, I'll see that you get a break and aren't arrested."

"That's all right, officer," Harry Vare said. "I'll do anything you say—"

Lester Leith handed Sid Bentley, the mournful-faced pickpocket, a one-hundred-dollar bill. "Wages for another day," he said.

Bentley pocketed the hundred and looked with avaricious eyes at the wallet which Leith returned to his breast pocket. "Speaking professionally," he said, "you'd do better to carry your bills in a fold. That breast-pocket stuff is particularly vulnerable."

"I know it," Leith said, "but I like to have my money where I can get at it."

Bentley nodded, his milk-mild eyes without expression. "I," he said, "like people who carry their money where I can get at it."

"Remember our bargain," Leith said.

"What do you suppose makes me feel so bad about getting a hundred bucks?" Bentley asked. "I'm just figuring I made a poor bargain."

"You mean the work's too hard?"

"No, that there are too many restrictions. I'm commencing to think I could make a good living just following *you* around."

Leith lowered his voice. "Where," he asked, "do you suppose I make all this money?"

Bentley said: "Now, buddy, you've got me interested."

Leith said: "We're working on the same side of the street."

"You don't mean you're a dip?"

"No, but I'm a crook. I'm a confidence man."

"What's the game?" Bentley asked.

Leith said: "I have different rackets. Right now, it's sticking a sucker with that imitation ruby. I show the ruby to the man I'm aiming to trim. I tell him I found it on the street, that I don't know whether it's any good or not, that I presume it isn't good, but that even as an imitation, it should have some value. I ask him what he thinks about it.

"If he's a real gem expert, I know it from what he says. He tells me to go home and forget it. I thank him, and that's all there is to it. But if he's a little dubious about whether it's genuine, I gradually let him think I'm a sucker. You see, this ruby is the exact duplicate of a valuable ruby that has been in the newspapers."

Bentley said: "That's what fooled me about it the first time I saw it."

"You recognized it?"

"Sure."

"Well," Leith said, "lots of other people will, too. They'll think it's the genuine priceless ruby. Some of them will want to buy it. Some of them won't. If the guy offers me anything like five hundred dollars for it, I'm perfectly willing to sell."

Bentley said: "I'm still listening."

"The big trouble," Leith said, "is the risk."

"How do you mean?"

"I've got too many of them out," Leith said. "These imitations cost me about fifteen dollars apiece. I've been playing the racket for a week."

"You're afraid some of the suckers have made a squawk?"

"Yes."

Bentley said: "I know just how you feel. When a racket gets hot, you know you should leave it, but there's still coin in it, so you want to hang on."

Leith said: "That's where you come in."

"What do you mean?"

Leith said: "I want you to follow me around from now on whenever I'm going to make a sale."

"What do I do?"

"Just this," Leith said. "A cop can't make a pinch until after I've made a sale. In order to do that, they'll have to plant a ringer on me for a sucker, and have the payments made to me in marked money."

"No, they won't," Bentley said. "You're all wet there, brother. They can *either* have the marked money on you, or they can pinch both you and the sucker and hold the sucker as a material witness."

Leith said: "That last is what I'm afraid of. If that happens, I want you to get the evidence."

"You mean from the sucker?"

"Yes."

"Listen, brother. That evidence will be just as hot as a stove lid. I couldn't—"

Leith took from his pocket a little cloth sack to which was attached a printed tag with a postage stamp on the tag.

"You don't keep it on you for a minute," he said. "You just beat it for the first mailbox, drop it, and let Uncle Sam do the dirty work."

Bentley said: "That's more like it."

"Whenever you do that you get a five-hundred-dollar bonus."

"And that's all I have to do?"

"That's all."

"And my cut is still a hundred bucks a day."

"That's right. You just have to follow me around."

"Lead me to it," Bentley said. "But you'll have to tell me when you're going to make a deal."

Leith said: "In about an hour, Miss Dormley, the young lady who was with me last night, and I are going out to dinner with another couple. I've fixed things up with Miss Dormley so she'll get the other girl out of the way. That will leave me alone with the man. I figure I can put the deal across with him."

"I'll be tagging along."

Leith said: "Carry this mailing sack where you can put your hand on it in an instant. Don't ever be caught without it."

"Listen, buddy," Bentley said, "don't think I was born yesterday. If you think I want to be caught with goods that will hook me up as your confederate, you're cockeyed. And don't pull your stuff in a place where there isn't a mailbox on every corner, because if you do, it's just your hard luck."

Sergeant Arthur Ackley stared reproachfully at Beaver, the undercover operative. "Right under your nose, Beaver," he said, "and you muffed it."

The spy's face colored. "What do you mean, I muffed it? I'm the one that told you he was going after that ruby."

Sergeant Ackley said: "You argued a lot, Beaver, and became personally offensive, but you didn't give me anything constructive."

"What do you mean, constructive?"

"You didn't even smell a rat when he brought that green kid in to act as a detective," Ackley said.

Beaver sighed. "Oh, what's the use. Just don't forget that we have a bet. If all those various things I told you about fit into his plan to get the ruby, I win your watch."

"Not at all, Beaver," said Ackley. "You have overlooked one little fact. It was to have been done so cleverly that I couldn't pin anything on him. You overlooked that little thing, Beaver, and that's going to cost you fifty bucks—because I've already got it pinned on him."

Beaver said: "I suppose you know every step in his campaign."

Sergeant Ackley gloated. "You bet I do."

The spy scraped back his chair and got to his feet.

Sergeant Ackley said: "Don't go to bed until after midnight, Beaver. I'll be calling you some time before then to come down to headquarters. Leith will be booked and in a cell. Then you can have the pleasure of telling him that you helped put him there—and you can pay over the fifty bucks to me."

Beaver lunged toward the door. "You've thought you had him before," he flung back, on the threshold.

Sergeant Ackley laughed. "But this time, Beaver, I *have* got him. I threw a scare into that green kid Vare, and he told me everything."

The four people left the taxicab and walked across the sidewalk to the entrance of die apartment house. Dixie Dormley, attired in soft white was vibrantly beautiful. The other young woman, although expensively gowned, seemed drab and insignificant in comparison.

Lester Leith, well-tailored, faultlessly groomed, wore his evening clothes with an air of distinction. Bob Lamont was quick and nervous. He seemed ill at ease.

The four people chatted as they went up in the elevator, and Bob Lamont opened the door of his apartment with something of a flourish.

It was an apartment which was well and tastefully furnished. As secretary to George Navin, Lamont had drawn a very good salary.

When the two young women were seated, Lamont went to the kitchenette to get the makings of drinks.

Lester Leith gave a significant glance at Dixie Dormley.

She caught the glance, turned at once to the other young woman, and exclaimed "Oh, my heavens, I left my purse in that taxicab! Or else it may have fallen out on the sidewalk; I don't know which. It seems to me that I heard something drop to the running board as I got out."

The young woman said: "Never mind, Dixie, you can telephone the taxicab company, and they'll have it in the Lost and Found Department."

"Yes," wailed Dixie, "but suppose it dropped to the running board. Then it would have spilled off at the corner."

Lester Leith reached for his hat.

"I'll run down and see."

Dixie Dormley got to her feet quickly and started to the door.

"No, please," she said. "You wait here. I can't explain, but I'd much rather go by myself, unless Vivian wants to come with me."

She flashed the other young woman a smile of invitation, and Vivian promptly arose.

"Tell Bob that we'll be right back," she said.

As the door closed behind the two women, Lester Leith strolled out into the kitchenette where Lamont was taking ice cubes from a refrigerator.

"Well, Lamont," said Lester Leith casually, "you pulled that murder pretty cleverly, didn't you?"

Lamont dropped the ice cube tray with a clatter, and stared at Lester Leith with bulging eyes. "What the devil are you talking about?"

"Oh, you know well enough, Lamont," he said. "The police were a little bit slow in catching up with you, that's all, but the scheme wasn't really so clever. The guards shut all of the windows and locked the shutters on the inside when they went into Navin's room, but you were the last one in there. It would have been very easy for you to have moved against one of the windows and unlocked one of the shutters. Then you left the room, went directly to the safe, took out the gem, and went to your conference with the lawyer, which gave you your alibi. In the morning you walked in and locked the shutter again from the inside.

"You'd probably been bribed by the Hindus to leave one of the steel shutters unlocked, and had specified that they must break in and do the job promptly at four o'clock, so that the police would be properly confused.

"Where the police made their mistake was in thinking that whoever had committed the murder had also stolen the gem from the safe. It didn't occur to them that they could have been independent acts. And apparently, so far, it hasn't occurred to the Hindus. They thought simply that they failed to find the gem, and that Navin had placed it in some other hiding place.

"But you can't get away with it long, Lamont. The police will be here inside of half an hour."

"You're crazy!" said Lamont.

Lester Leith shook his head.

"No, Lamont," he said, "you're the one who's crazy. You overlooked the fact that, if the Hindus should start to talk, they had you strapped to the electric chair. And that's exactly what happened. The police got a confession out of one of the Hindus about fifteen minutes ago. My paper telephoned me."

Lamont's face was gray.

"Who—who are you?" he asked.

"I'm a freelance reporter," said Lester Leith, "who works on feature stuff for some of the leading papers. Right now I'm assigned to cover the story of your arrest in the Navin case. The newspaper knew it was going to break sometime within the next twenty-four to forty-eight hours. Now if you would like to pick up a little money that would come in handy when it becomes necessary to retain an attorney to represent you, you can give us an exclusive interview. In fact, the only thing for you to do is to confess and try and get a life sentence. If you want to make your confession through my newspaper, we would bring all the political pressure to bear that we could to see that you got off with life."

There was an imperative knock on the door of the apartment.

Lester Leith strolled to it casually.

"Probably the police now, Lamont."

He opened the door.

Harry Vare burst into the room.

"You're under arrest!" he snapped at Lester Leith.

Lester Leith stepped back and eyed Vare with well-simulated amazement.

"What the devil are you talking about?" he asked.

"Your name's Lamont," said Vare, "and you're under arrest for the murder of George Navin. I'm representing the Indian priests who are trying to recover the gem, and I'm going to take you to police headquarters with me right now."

Lester Leith said: "You're crazy. My name's Leith. I'm not Lamont. That's Lamont over there, the man you want. I'm working for a newspaper."

Harry Vare laughed, scornfully.

"I saw you come in here and had the doorman point out the one who lived here. He pointed to you."

"You fool," Leith said, "he made a mistake, or rather you did. He pointed to this man here, and you thought he was pointing me out."

Vare snapped a gun into view, and fished for handcuffs with his left hand.

"Hold out your wrist," he said, "or I'll blow you apart."

Lester Leith hesitated a moment, then held out his wrist, reluctantly. Vare snapped one of the handcuffs to Leith's wrist, locked the other one around his own wrist, and said "Come on, you slicker, you're going to headquarters."

Leith said: "Listen! You're making the biggest mistake of your life. You're letting the real murderer—"

Bob Lamont laughed.

He turned to Harry Vare and said: "You're quite right, officer, that's Bob Lamont that you've got under arrest, but this comes as quite as a shock to me. I've known him for two or three years, and thought he was above reproach."

"No, he wasn't," said Vare. "He was the man who murdered Navin."

Lester Leith groaned.

"Youngster," he said, "you're making a mistake that is going to make you the laughing stock of the city inside of twenty-four hours."

Vare muttered grimly: "Come along, Lamont."

Lester Leith sighed and accompanied Vare through the doorway to the elevator, down the elevator, across the lobby of the apartment house, and to the street.

"Well," said Leith, "that was pretty well done, Vare. You can let me loose now."

Vare took a key from his pocket and inserted it m the lock of the handcuff only after considerable difficulty. His forehead was beaded with nervous perspiration, and his hand was shaking. He made two attempts to fit the key to the lock. "I can't seem to get it," he said.

Leith glanced at him sharply. "Vare," he said, "what the devil are you trying to do?"

"Nothing."

"Give me that key."

Vare didn't pass over the key but instead looked expectantly back toward the shadows.

The voice of Sergeant Ackley said: "I'll take charge now."

There was motion from the deep shadows of the doorway of an adjoining building. Sergeant Ackley, accompanied by a plainclothes officer, stepped forward.

Leith said to Sergeant Ackley: 'What's the meaning of this?"

Ackley said: "You should know more about it than I do, Leith. You've delivered yourself to me already handcuffed."

For a moment there was consternation on Leith's face, then he masked all expression from his face and eyes.

"Didn't expect to see *me* here, did you?" Sergeant Ackley asked gloatingly.

Leith said nothing.

Sergeant Ackley said to Vare: "Give me the key to those hand-cuffs, young man. I'll slip one off your wrist, and put it on Leith's other wrist."

Vare extended his hand. Sergeant Ackley took the key, clocked the handcuff from Vare's arm, and snapped it around Leith's other wrist.

The rapid *click-clack click-clack* of high heels as two women rounded the corner, walking rapidly, came to Leith's ears. He turned around so that the light fell full on his face.

"Why, Mr. Leith!" Dixie Dormley exclaimed. "What's the matter?"

Lester Leith said nothing.

Sergeant Ackley grinned gloatingly. "Mr. Leith," he said, "is being arrested. You probably didn't know he was a crook."

"A crook!" she exclaimed.

From the doorway of the apartment-house came a hurrying fig-ure, attired in overcoat, hat, and gloves. He carried a light suitcase in one hand, and crossed the strip of sidewalk with three swift strides. It wasn't until he started to signal for a taxicab that he became aware of the little group.

Sergeant Ackley said to the plain-clothesman: "Get that guy."

Lamont heard the order, turned to look over his shoulder, then dropped the suitcase, and started to run.

"Help!" yelled Sergeant Ackley.

Lamont sprinted down the street. He turned to flash an apprehensive glance over his shoulder, and so did not see the figure of Sid Bentley as it slid out from the shadows.

There was a thud, a tangled mass of arms and legs, and then Bentley, sitting up on the sidewalk, said: "I got him for you, officer."

The plainclothesman ran up and grabbed Lamont by the collar. He jerked him to his feet, then said to Bentley: "That was fine work. I'm glad you stopped him."

"No trouble at all," Bentley said.

The officer said: "Come on back with me, and I'll give you a courtesy card which may help you out some time."

Bentley's eyes glistened. "Now, that'll be right nice of you, officer."

The officer pushed the reluctant Lamont back toward the little group which had, by this time, became a small, curious crowd. "Here he is, Sergeant," he said.

Sergeant Ackley said irritably: "All right, Lamont. You'd better come clean."

"I don't know what you're talking about," Lamont said.

Sergeant Ackley laughed. "Come on, Lamont, the jig's up. You killed George Navin and got that ruby. Lester Leith hijacked it from you. Now, if you'll give us the facts, you won't be any worse off for it."

Lamont said: "I don't know what you're talking about. I—I took the custody of the ruby because—"

"Careful, Lamont," Lester Leith said sharply. "Don't put your neck in a noose."

Sergeant Ackley turned and slapped Leith across the mouth. "Keep your trap shut," he said, and to the plainclothes officer: "Go ahead and search him."

"Oh, no," Lamont shouted. "You can't do it. Navin gave it to me to keep for him. I was going to turn it over to the estate."

"Gave you what?" Sergeant Ackley asked.

"The ruby."

Ackley said: "Go ahead, Lamont, tell the truth. You took the ruby, and then Lester Leith took it from you."

Lamont shook his head.

Sergeant Ackley ran his hands over Leith's coat. Abruptly he shot his hand into Leith's inside pocket and pulled out a chamois-skin bag. He reached inside of that bag, and the spectators gasped as the rays from the street light were reflected from a blood-red blob of brilliance.

"There it is," Sergeant Ackley said gloatingly.

Lamont stared, clapped his own hand to his breast pocket, became suddenly silent.

Sergeant Ackley said triumphantly to the crowd: "That's the way we work, folks. Give the crooks rope enough, and they hang themselves. You'll read about it in the paper tomorrow morning. Sergeant Arthur Ackley solves the Navin murder, and at the same time traps a crook who's trying to hijack the East Indian ruby. All right, boys. We're going to the station."

Leith said: "Sergeant, you're making a—"

"Shut up," Ackley said savagely. "I've been laying for you for a long time, and now I've got you."

Dixie Dormley said indignantly: "I think it's an outrage. You've struck this man when he was handcuffed. You won't let him explain."

"Shut up," Ackley growled, "or I'll take you too."

Dixie Dormley fastened glistening, defiant eyes on Sergeant Ackley. "Try to keep me from going," she said. "I'm going to be right there, and complain about your brutality."

Sid Bentley sidled up to the plainclothes officer. "The name's Bentley, Sid Bentley. If you wouldn't mind giving me that card."

The officer nodded, pulled a card from his pocket, and scribbled on it.

"What are you doing?" Sergeant Ackley asked.

"Giving this man a courtesy card. He caught Lamont—stopped him when he was running away."

Sergeant Ackley was in a particularly expansive mood. "Here," he said, "I'll give him one, too."

Sid Bentley took the cards. He stared for a long, dubious moment at Lester Leith, then said: "Gentlemen, I thank you very much. It was a pleasure to help you. Good night."

A police car sirened its way to the curb. Sergeant Ackley loaded his prisoners into the car, and they made a quick run to headquarters with Dixie Dormley, white-faced and determined, following in a taxicab.

Sergeant Ackley said to the desk sergeant: "Well, let's get the boys from the press in here. I've solved the Navin murder, recovered the ruby, and caught a hijacker red-handed."

Dixie Dormley said: "And he's been guilty of unnecessary brutality."

One of the reporters from the press room came sauntering in. "What you got, Sergeant?" he asked.

Sergeant Ackley said: "I've solved the Navin murder."

"Hot dog," the newspaperman said.

The desk sergeant said dubiously: "Sergeant, did you take a good look at this ruby?"

Sergeant Ackley said: "I don't have to. I had the thing all doped out. I knew where it was, and how to get it. That ruby is worth a fortune. There'll be a reward for that, and—"

"There won't be any reward for this," the desk sergeant said, "unless I'm making a big mistake. This is a nice piece of red glass. You see, I know something about gems, Sergeant. I was on the jewelry detail for—"

Sergeant Ackley's jaw sagged. "You mean that isn't a real ruby?"

Lester Leith said to the desk sergeant: "If you'll permit me, I can explain. This was an imitation which I had made. It's rather a good imitation—it cost me fifty dollars. I gave it to a young man who wanted to be a detective to keep for me. His pocket was picked. Naturally, he was very much chagrined. I wanted to get the property returned, so I discreetly offered a reward. The property was returned earlier this evening. What I say can be established by absolute proof."

Sergeant Ackley's eyes were riveted on the red stone. "You didn't get this from Lamont?" he asked.

"Certainly not. Lamont will tell you that I didn't."

Lamont said: "I've never seen that before in my life."

"Then where's the real ruby?" Sergeant Ackley asked.

Lamont took a deep breath. "I haven't the least idea."

"What were you running away for?"

"Probably because of the manner in which you tried to make your arrest," Lester Leith interposed. "You didn't tell him you were an officer. You simply yelled, 'Get him,' and your man started for him with—"

"No such thing!" Sergeant Ackley interrupted.

"That's exactly what happened," Dixie Dormley said indignantly.

The desk sergeant said to Lester Leith: "Why didn't you tell him this was an imitation?"

Dixie Dormley said: "He tried to, and Sergeant Ackley slapped him across the mouth."

Sergeant Ackley blinked his eyes rapidly, then said: "I didn't do any such thing. I didn't touch the man."

Dixie Dormley said: "I thought you'd try to lie out of it. I have the names of a dozen witnesses who feel the same way I do about police brutality, and will join me in making a complaint."

Ackley said savagely: "Give me the list of those witnesses."

Dixie Dormley threw back her head and laughed in his face.

The sergeant said: "You know how the chief feels about that, Sergeant."

Lester Leith said quietly: "I'd like to call up my valet. He can come down here and identify that imitation ruby. It's one which he had made."

The desk sergeant reached for the telephone, but Sergeant Ackley stopped him. "I happen to know there was an imitation ruby made," he said, "if you're sure this is imitation."

The desk sergeant said: "There's no doubt about it."

Sergeant Ackley fitted a key to the handcuffs, unlocked them, said to Lester Leith: "You're getting off lucky this time. I don't know how you did it."

Leith said, with dignity: "You simply went off halfcocked, Sergeant. I wouldn't have held it against you if you'd given me a chance to explain, but you struck me when I tried to tell you that the gem you had was an imitation, that it was my property, that I have a bill of sale for it."

The newspaper reporter scribbled gleefully. "Hot dog," he said, and scurried away toward the press room. A moment later he was back with a camera and a flash bulb. "Let me get a picture of this," he said. "Hold up that imitation gem."

Sergeant Ackley shouted: "You can't publish this!"

The flash of the bulb interrupted his protest.

Edward H. Beaver, the undercover man, was still up when Lester Leith latchkeyed the door of the apartment. "Hello, Scuttle," he said. "Up rather late, aren't you?"

"I was waiting for a phone call."

Leith raised his eyebrows. "Rather late for a phone call, isn't it, Scuttle?"

"Yes, sir. Have you seen Sergeant Ackley tonight, sir?"

"Have I seen him!" Leith said, with a smile. "I'll say I've seen him. You'll read all about it in the papers tomorrow, Scuttle. Do you know what happened? The sergeant arrested me for recovering my own property."

"Your own property, sir?"

"Yes, Scuttle. That imitation ruby. I was rather attached to it, and

Vare felt so chagrined about having lost it that I thought it would be worth a small reward to get it back."

"And you recovered it?"

"Oh, yes." Leith said. "I got it earlier in the evening. Sergeant Ackley found it in my pocket and jumped to the conclusion it was the real ruby."

"What did he do?" the spy asked.

Lester Leith grinned. "He covered himself with glory," he said. "He put on quite a show for a crowd of interested spectators, and then committed the crowning indiscretion of inviting them to read about it in the paper tomorrow morning. They'll read about it, all right. Poor Ackley!"

A slow smile twisted the spy's features. "The sergeant didn't give you anything for me, did he, sir?"

"For you, Scuttle?"

"Yes, sir."

"Why, no. Why the devil would you be getting things from Sergeant Ackley?"

"You see, sir, I happened to run into the sergeant a day or so ago, and he borrowed my watch. He was going to return it. He—"

The phone rang and the spy jumped toward it with alacrity. "I'll answer it, sir," he said.

He picked up the receiver, said: "Hello . . . Yes . . . Oh, he did—" and then listened for almost a minute.

A slow flush spread over the spy's face. He said: "That wasn't the way I understood it. That wasn't the bet—" There was another interval during which the receiver made raucous, metallic sounds, then a bang at the other end of the line announced that the party had hung up.

The undercover man dropped the receiver back into place.

Lester Leith sighed. "Scuttle," he said, "I don't know what we're going to do about Sergeant Ackley. He's a frightful nuisance."

"Yes, sir," the spy said.

"And a very poor loser," Leith remarked.

"I'll say he's a poor loser," the spy blurted. "Any man who will take advantage of his official position as a superior to wriggle out of paying a debt—"

"Scuttle," Lester Leith interrupted, "what the devil are you talking about?"

"Oh, another matter, sir. Something else which happened to be on my mind."

Leith said: "Well, get it off your mind, Scuttle. Bring out that bottle of Scotch and a soda siphon. We'll have a quiet drink. Just the two of us."

Beaver had just finished with the drinks when a knock sounded at the door. "See who it is, Scuttle."

Dixie Dormley and Harry Vare stood on the threshold.

Leith, on his feet, ushered them into the room, seated the actesss, indicated a chair for Vare, and said: "Two more highballs, Scuttle."

Vare said haltingly: "I'm sorry, Mr. Leith. The way the thing was put up to me, I couldn't have done any differently."

Leith dismissed the matter with a gesture.

Dixie Dormley said: "After you left, a Captain Carmichael came in. He seemed terribly upset, and was pretty angry at Sergeant Ackley. It seems that two of the people who had been standing there were friends of Captain Carmichael, and they telephoned in to him about the brutality of the police."

Leith smiled. "Is that so," he commented idly. "What happened?"

Dixie Dormley said: "Well, Sergeant Ackley had just let Lamont go—figured he didn't have any case against him. Captain Carmichael listened to what Ackley had to report, and was furious. He issued an order to have Lamont picked up again, and a radio car got him within a dozen blocks of the police station.

"They brought him back and Carmichael went to work on him,

and in no time had a confession out of him. It seems he'd agreed to open one of the steel shutters for some Hindu priests. They'd paid him for the job. Then he got the idea of doublecrossing them, opened the safe, lifted the ruby, and hid it.

"He had it with him tonight when he was arrested. He swore the plain-clothesman must have taken it from his pocket when they were scuffling. The plainclothesman denied it, and then they thought of this man who had first grabbed Lamont.

"So then they figured *he* was the man they wanted, and it turned out the police had not only let him go, *but given him a couple of courtesy cards*. Well, you should have heard Captain Carmichael! Such language!"

Leith turned to Vare.

"There you are, Vare," he said. "A complete education in the detection of crime by the case method. Just observe Sergeant Ackley, do the exact opposite of what he does, and you're bound to be a success."

And the police spy, resuming his mixing of the drinks, could be seen to nod, unconsciously but perceptibly.

THE LIGHT AT THREE O'CLOCK
MacKinlay Kantor

MacKinlay Kantor (1904-1977) began his writing career as a journalist at seventeen and soon after began selling hardboiled mystery stories to various pulp magazines. He also wrote numerous mystery stories of various types, including the challenging sub-genre of "impossible crimes," producing four that were collected in a single volume, *It's About Crime* (1960).

The highlight of his short story-writing career is the notorious "Gun Crazy," first published *The Saturday Evening Post* in 1940. It served as the basis for the noir cult film of the same title, for which Kantor wrote the screenplay. Released in 1949, it was directed by Joseph H. Lewis. The film, an excellent though more violent expansion of the short story, features a clean-cut gun nut who meets a good-looking sharpshooter and their subsequent spree of bank robberies and shootings.

He also wrote several novels in the mystery genre, such as *Diversey* (1928), about Chicago gangsters, and *Signal Thirty-Two* (1950), an excellent police procedural, given verisimilitude by virtue of receiving permission from the acting police commissioner of New York to accompany the police on their activities to gather background information. His most famous crime novel is *Midnight Lace* (1948), the suspenseful tale of a young woman terrorized by an anonymous telephone caller; it was filmed two years later, starring Doris Day and Rex Harrison.

Kantor is best known for his mainstream novels, such as the sentimental dog story, *The Voice of Bugle Ann* (1936), filmed the same year; the long narrative poem *Glory for Me* (1945), filmed as *The Best Years of Our Lives* (1946), which won the Academy Award for Best Picture; and the outstanding Civil War novel about the notorious Confederate prisoner of war camp, *Andersonville* (1955), for which he won the Pulitzer Prize.

"The Light at Three O'Clock" was first published in the July 1930, issue of *Real Detective Tales and Mystery Stories.*

The Light at Three O'Clock
MacKinlay Kantor

IN THE chill, small hours preceding dawn a switchboard operator gets many unusual calls. But Shultz hardly expected *Red* for *Murder.*

Above the switchboard a little clock ticked fitfully away. There was a certain hesitation in its chatter, as if after each catch of minute cogs it was waiting for something to happen.

It seemed to possess advance information on something relentless and implacable, and much more portentous than the heavy rain outside. Its little white hands registered 2:53. The clock was the only active mechanism, apparently, in all that room. Below it the black surface of the switchboard dozed, unbroken by any gleam of bulbs.

Soon, of course, the bulbs would gleam. A woman would need a doctor for her baby. A man would call up a woman who preferred after-midnight dates. A long-distance call would come in from Milwaukee. People somewhere in the Allan Court would be leaving, even at this hour of the night, and even in this cold rain.

Unlike the clock, Eddie Shultz wasn't functioning. Shultz had fallen asleep, leaning back in his chair, the metal band of the head-phone gleaming tightly across his youthful brow.

Shultz was very young and romantic, and just at this moment he was dreaming of a red-haired waitress with warmth and friendliness in her eyes, and a tantalizing sway to her hips. The job being what it was—night switchboard operator in a large Sheridan Road apartment hotel—Shultz did not receive any enormous salary. But he could sleep—and he could dream.

Suddenly, one red circle exploded amidst the waiting rows of flat bulbs. The buzzer sounded, long and insistently . . . Still the operator slept, stubbornly refusing to turn away from the romance in his dream. The buzzing sound grew louder in its insistency. The office seemed to be alive with it, and its exasperation was almost tangible.

Eddie Shultz came back to the Allan Court with a sudden start. He blinked, jerking forward, and pawed hurriedly at a switch. His groping hand found a plug; rammed it in. The red circle winked into blackness.

"Office."

The board waited blankly. Above, the clock chattered on its ceaseless round.

"Office," said Mr. Shultz.

No answer. Then—it might have been his imagination—there was the sound of a receiver going back on its hook. The red bulb glowed instantly. Very much annoyed, Eddie withdrew the plug, and swore softly to himself.

Then with a quick tightening of his muscles, he bent forward and looked searchingly at the offending light and its accompanying hole. He could hear his own breath, alarmingly close and alarmingly loud. And he could feel an uncomfortable and cool irritation all up and down the back of his neck.

God! he thought. *That was Twenty-two! Hold on—wait. Probably it was Twenty. Yes, it must have been Twenty.* He leaned back and sighed with relief.

Again—the buzzing sound. Again—the little red bulb was gleaming. And this time there was no mistaking the location. The typewritten numerals in the slot beneath were all too plainly visible—twenty-two, they said.

It could hardly be denied that Eddie Shultz would have preferred to remain right where he was—secure and immobile in his chair. But there was that red glow, that waiting connection, and there was the sound of the buzzer.

With one quick lunge he stuffed in the plug and tore open the switch. The bulb winked out, quickly and alarmingly. Shultz found his voice. He said very distinctly: "Office!"

Through the headphone clamped to his ear there came a sound which filled him with sudden horror. It was the sound of some unseen person swallowing. Then the switch clicked, and the red glare of the uncompleted connection danced before his eyes.

He drew out the plug and rose slowly to his feet, his eyes riveted on the calm row of electric bulbs. His dry lips shaped the whispered words. "Twenty-two. I won't let myself believe it. Twenty-two. Oh, God—"

A moaning gust of wind swept around the corner past the basement window. The dark rain sprayed against the pane as if flung from some gigantic ghostly hand, guided by malice. There wasn't any traffic out in the street, not even the welcome sound of one lone car. The neighborhood was dead. The whole world was black and wet and dead. And in Apartment Twenty-two—

The hands of the clock stood at two fifty-eight. He had spent a most frightening five minutes. The job wasn't worth what he had to go through.

Eddie sighed, and sat down very slowly. He had to stay. His self-respect demanded it. Hell, he oughtn't to be so nervous. There wasn't any such thing as a ghost. Any fool would know that. When people were dead, they were done for. Even on a black night in that great U-shaped building, with the rain sweeping down in sheets—

Again the buzzer sounded.

He shrieked in his mind: "I won't look! By God, I don't *have* to look. It just isn't so! That place is—" But his eyes twisted in their sockets, drawn back to the bulb by a hideous fascination. There, in the middle row, the little flat lamp was still registering its rosy gleam.

Eddie's lips were twitching now. He faltered, nerving himself for one final try. It wouldn't be hard. The switch was right there, and he had only to insert the plug— There! The light was gone. It had been easy. Why had he let himself believe—

And then that same ghastly whisper came to him, seemingly nearer than before. For a moment he couldn't speak or move. Then he heard himself screaming, "Office! Answer—Office!"

The switch closed, and the light winked again, and—

Eddie had had enough. He leaped up, ripping off the head-clamp and flinging it down. He plunged across the shadowy little office and threw open the front door. The rain poured down at him in a black, blinding spray. He turned up the collar of his coat, and then—he faltered. He couldn't go out. He just didn't have the nerve to run around the corner and down through the court in that rain. It was too much to expect of him. He didn't have the courage—and he didn't care who knew it.

His eyes were wide and staring as he groped his way back to the switchboard. Hurriedly he thrust a plug into the hole marked "4" and opened a switch. His fingers pushed painfully on the red lever. *Ring.* He must ring. This was too much for anybody in the world to bear alone.

Eddie lifted the headphone. A startled sleepy voice said: "Hello, there. Hello. Hello—"

"Mr. Edwards."

"Well?"

"This is Eddie Shultz—" He hesitated for a moment, his heart pounding tumultuously.

"Well, what is it?"

And then the barriers were swept down in one fearful flood. "My God, Mr. Edwards, I'm quitting! I tell you I'm quitting! I don't want this job. It ain't right for me to go through this. Mr. Edwards, you've got to come down here right away. If you don't come I'll beat it and leave the board. I'll go home. No, I'm not crazy. Listen here: you come down . . . It's Apartment Twenty-two! There's something up there. Three times it's rung in here, and each time it hangs up when I answer. But it sort of chokes and swallows first!

"It's the truth, I tell you! Yes, I know there ain't supposed to be any person up there. I know, I know. Mr. Duncan's dead, too. But it was just about this time last night that he got killed. Mr. Edwards—*that light's on again!*"

Hatless, with his topcoat and trousers drawn loosely over his pajamas, Matt Edwards stood in the office and scowled at the pale and twitching Shultz.

"Now, what's all this damn foolishness about?"

"Nothing, Mr. Edwards. I mean—Well, the light. It keeps coming on. And you know—"

The manager—slim and debonair despite his strange attire—went over to the switchboard and bent to examine the rows of bulbs. "It isn't on now."

"No, it stopped registering just before you came. But wait. It'll come on again."

"Who's this talking right now? Forty-five hooked up with outside? And Thirty-eight hooked up with Seven?" Quickly he opened first one switch, then another. A man's voice said calmly: "Well, heat a little water and give it to her in a teaspoon if she won't take her bottle."

Almost immediately a woman said vengefully: "If you go out to any more poker games this week don't expect to find me here. All right, stay there and lose—"

Edwards made a wry face and clicked the switches. He turned to Shultz. "Nothing there. You're—you're *sure* you weren't mistaken?"

"I ought to know one light from another," protested Shultz.

Edwards frowned, tapping his hand on the back of a-chair. "Look here. The apartment was locked tightly inside—every door and window—when we broke in there with the police last night. I mean, at three o'clock yesterday morning. Duncan's key was on the inside of the front door, and we had to break it open. I had a new lock put on the door afterward. I've got the only key in my pocket. The back door is bolted and has the safety chain on. How could anybody—"

"I tell you it registered, Mr. Edwards," Eddie broke in. "The light was on. Four different times it came on and buzzed. "

The silence was broken only by the splash of water outside—a hollow, lonely drip that somehow reminded Shultz of water seeping out of an old burial vault. In spite of himself, Edwards strove desperately to keep from shuddering.

"We'll sit down here, and watch that board," he said. "I don't want to doubt your word, Shultz. If that light comes on again, and I see it with my own eyes we'll go up to the apartment."

Shultz huddled on a bench by the inner door. Edwards sat down in the chair by the switchboard, and lit a cigarette. His brow creased painfully as he reviewed the events of the preceding twenty-four hours, trying to arrive at some explanation.

Duncan, the tenant in Apartment Twenty-two, had lived at the Allan Court for three years. He had been a man of evident wealth and refinement, though something of a recluse. He belonged to no clubs and attended few theaters. He drove an imported roadster. Few people ever called at his apartment and all of his tastes seemed ordinary, not to say conventional.

He was an ardent collector of old flasks and glassware, and was said to be an authority on early American glass. The management had permitted him, at his own expense, to install many cupboards and cabinets for the housing of his treasures. Tall, gray-haired and slender, he was the perfect picture of a sedate gentleman.

Some time before three o'clock on the previous morning, adjacent tenants had been aroused by a shot. The sound seemed to come from

Mr. Duncan's apartment. The building was old, although it had been remodeled and modernized, and the thick walls prevented voices in one apartment from being heard in another. A few minutes later the woman in the flat above heard an automobile drive down the alley.

The manager was notified. When repeated calls to Apartment Twenty-two failed to elicit any response, Edwards summoned the police. The door of the apartment was locked, with Duncan's key inside, and it was impossible to use a passkey. The police forced the door, and entered the rooms. There was, at first glance, no trace of Duncan. Though every closet and cubbyhole in the place had been ransacked, the tenant could not be found.

Every window was solidly fastened. The lights were burning and the back door was locked, with its inner safety chain in place. The unused kitchen—Duncan took his meals in restaurants—offered no clue. Only the living room bore gruesome testimony that a deadly struggle had taken place. There was a bullet hole in the wall, and Sergeant Sherris dug out a .45 caliber slug. There were fresh bloodstains on two of the rugs—and one splotch of yellowish-white, sickening and unmistakable.

So Duncan was dead—he had been murdered. But where was his body? And what was the motive? The priceless collection of Stiegel glass and curios was untouched and there were diamond studs and platinum cufflinks on the dresser in the bedroom.

A terrified janitor had come hammering at the door. He had been attending to boiler fires in the building next door, and his attention had been drawn to a minor disturbance in the alley outside. Now he saw several men hoisting the inert body of another man into a big sedan.

"What's the matter?" he said.

"Sick man," said one of them ominously. "Get back inside that door, and get back quick!"

The janitor had fled, and they had driven away. No, he hadn't seen the license number—he was too frightened. No, he didn't know how many men there were. Maybe three or four . . .

So Duncan had been murdered, and his body taken away in that unidentified car. But how did the murderers leave the apartment—with every door and every window locked on the inside?

Sergeant Sherris nodded and looked wise. Every so often, for the past few years, some prominent or wealthy man had been kidnapped. Sometimes they got back alive—blindfolded and unable to supply any information. Sometimes they didn't come back at all. The money hadn't been sent as directed. There had been Page, the lumber king. And Rosenblam, the hotel man. And Justessen, that rich Dane visiting at the Drake Hotel. All kidnapped by extortionists . . . It was possible that the same gang had come after Duncan. He had resisted—and had been shot. They had taken his body out of the apartment. But—how? And why?

Edwards twisted uncomfortably in his chair. There could be no denying it. That was where the spooks came in. At least, it was a mystery. And now, this strange call, this alleged lighting up of Apartment Twenty-two's switchboard lamp, when nobody was in the place, and when he had the only key to the new lock.

"Look there!" cried Shultz. "See it? *The light's on again!*"

The rain tore clammily at them as they hurried down the court, as if unseen hands, ghastly and intent, were bent on holding them back from the dark rooms on the floor above. Edwards lifted his eyes as they passed the last concrete flowerbed. The windows of Twenty-two were blank and ominous.

"Come on," he said brusquely, as Shultz halted irresolutely at the vestibule door.

Eddie Shultz turned a greenish face to him. "By God, Mr. Edwards, I don't want to go."

"Neither do I," growled the manager. "We're both going."

Their steps shuddered softly on the carpeted stairway. It was impossible to believe that the opposite door of that first landing opened on an ordinary apartment occupied by ordinary people—a man, his wife, and their two daughters. Apartment Twenty-one. There were human beings there. But across the hall, in Twenty-two—

Edwards fumbled in his pocket for the key. The new lock gleamed ominously on the damaged door; its very brightness an affront.

Shultz whispered, "You got a—a—gun?"

"No, I haven't." Edwards had a spinning, helpless sensation. "But, listen here. There's nothing to hurt us. Nothing—"

The door creaked as it turned on its hinges.

Edwards felt along the wall for the light switch. The pressure of his finger flooded the hall with yellow light. In startled apprehension the eyes of both men turned toward the telephone stand. There was no one beside it, or anywhere else within sight.

The carved walnut telephone stand was of the cabinet type, narrow and high. A small stool had been placed beside it. One door of the cabinet swung partly ajar.

Slowly, Edwards walked toward the telephone. It seemed as if years passed before he reached it, and looked inside, and saw the instrument reposing in the shadows. He lifted the bracket and the connection clicked. Yes, the instrument was in working order. But—

"Nobody here," said Shultz, in a barely audible whisper.

"We'll turn on the lights," the manager said.

They advanced into the living room, the dining room, the bedrooms. Fearfully, they peered under the beds and opened closet doors. Nothing.

In the kitchen they stared at the outer door, which was locked and bolted, its heavy safety chain snugly in place. Still nobody. Nobody in the pantry—a vacant apartment—a ghoulish, threatening place with locked windows, locked doors—and still the thought of something inside.

Once more they toured the rooms, turning on the lights with prodigal haste. The dining room and one bedroom had been refurnished by Duncan to serve as galleries for his rare collections. Electricity gleamed softly on rows of dark flasks and blown glass vases. There were tall cupboards along the walls, each containing an array of glistening treasure.

Nothing had been disturbed. Only that ragged hole in the plaster, and the dark stains on the rugs, remained as grim reminders that stark tragedy had struck. The police had told Edwards to leave everything just as it was. Edwards and Shultz made a last examination. They poked beneath the davenports, and peered into the hamper in the bedroom. The search had been utterly fruitless.

They retreated into the hallway, and the manager once again opened the telephone cabinet and lifted the instrument. No, his ears had not deceived him. He could still hear the click. The telephone was in working order.

"We certainly haven't found anything," he said to Shultz. He tried to laugh, and the sound was eerie and startling in those deserted rooms. "I'm afraid it was just—just something the matter with the switchboard. We might as well go." He reached into his pocket for the key, and brought it out—a shining fragment of metal.

"Mr. Edwards!" The voice of Shultz was deadened with a cold, listless horror. "Look at your hand! You've got blood—all over your hand!"

For a full ten seconds Edwards stared down at those telltale marks on his right hand. It seemed to him that he could hear his own heart, thundering in that oppressive silence. Outside, the rain came down, blackly, dripping on damp ledges.

Then Edwards straightened. There was a tense, quick tightening of his mouth.

"Turn off the rest of those lights," he said. His voice was unnecessarily loud. He waited in the open door, wiping his hand on a handkerchief. Shultz leaped back out of the parlor, his lips trembling. "Let's get out of here," said Edwards, "for good."

At the doorway, with his finger on the light switch, he motioned for the operator to go ahead of him. Then, with a lightning gesture, he had pressed the key into Shultz's hand.

His voice was a hard whisper: "There's something here. I'm going to stay. You turn out that light and slam the door. I'll hide here in the corner. If the light shows on the board again, you call the police and come back up here, and come in! I don't know where it's hidden. I don't even know what it is. But that blood on my hand came off the telephone! Something's here. Now, beat it!"

The electric switch snapped out the one remaining light. Darkness came sweeping down and the door slammed shut.

Quietly, Edwards tiptoed across the hall and slipped into a corner opposite the telephone cabinet. He crouched down in the heavy darkness, scarcely daring to breathe.

The minutes passed like heavy bats, circling low, unwilling to alight.

It seemed an hour before Edwards heard the downstairs door close, and knew that Shultz was in the court, hurrying toward the office. The constant fury of rain had somewhat abated. The water still came down outside, but in an intermittent dribble. Far away, the siren of a fire truck screeched with a horrid earnestness, but in the apartment there was only a dead silence as if unguessed monsters were ominously biding their time, and might at any moment spring out.

He was crouched on the further corner of the hall, opposite the outside door, and between the opening to the bedroom and the wider doorway which gave on the living room. No person—no *thing*—could come from any direction without his seeing it. Lights from the alley and from the court shone in, faintly and bitterly, yet strong enough for Edwards to discern the outlines of the furniture.

His mind returned to the telephone. The first time he held it up, he had not placed his hand on the base of the instrument. The second time, he had done so. And immediately afterward Shultz had pointed to his hand and cried out his awful news.

Far away, in one of the other rooms, a sound broke the stillness. It was unmistakable—the creak of wood, of an opening door. Edwards waited, swallowing fearfully. Something had moved! He was not alone!

Once again he heard the creaking. It was followed by the tinkle of glass and a sound of footsteps, creeping slowly and heavily.

It was coming. It was moving nearer, out of the dining room and into the living room. Its body thudded softly against some obstructing piece of furniture. There was a frightening sound, half human and half animal, a muffled cough and growl. Edwards shrank closer against the wall. His fists were clenched so tightly that the nails cut into his palms.

Nearer it came, and nearer. It moved between him and the court window—a thin shape like a clothed skeleton. Yes, it was coming to the telephone again. It couldn't stay away. It had a call to make, obviously. It was in the doorway now, black and gruesome, an arm's length away.

Edwards heard the choking sound again, and a spasm of strained breathing. The door of the telephone cabinet banged open. There was a faint click and sputter—the sound of a lifting receiver—

Edwards darted forward. His groping hands encountered flesh, cold and moist. He was grappling with the thing, and had it in his arms. But the creature, ghost, or murderer, made no sound, offered no resistance. Quite suddenly and hideously it had collapsed against him there in the close blackness.

Edwards struggled out into the living room, half dragging his terrible burden. And the light from the court shone on the white skin and staring eyes of Duncan, the man who had been murdered.

With a scream, Edwards leaped back. There was the heavy thud of a falling body. The manager felt his own hands fumbling along the wall for a switch. And, then, mercifully, his fingers encountered metal. He pressed down hard—and the room became flooded with light.

Duncan lay before him on the floor, pajama-clad and with stained towels, ghastly and encrusted, tightly wound around his neck.

Trembling, Edwards dropped down and lifted the man in his arms. Duncan's eyes were staring, and his lips moved soundlessly.

"What was it?" Edwards gasped. "What happened?"

The head of the injured man moved slowly. His eyes seemed seeking beyond the hotel manager, searching for something in the room behind him. The other man turned. On the telephone table lay a small bronze-covered notebook and an ornate pencil. He seized them and lifted Duncan to the couch, pressing the book and pencil into his hands. On a side table was a decanter of whiskey. He forced a few drops between Duncan's blue lips.

"Write it," he said. "Write it, if you can. You're going to—"

Falteringly, the pencil slid over the notebook in a weak scrawl:

They came in the back way as always. LeCron started arguing about his split. We had trouble. Baletto cut me with knife but I shot him. They took LeCron away in a car and I was afraid—

Edwards tore off the sheet of paper. The pencil still moved, its words barely legible:

I knew police would come hearing shot, so I hid in my place. Lost a good deal of blood and tonight thought I would give up and send for police and doctor. Tried telephone but could not talk and lost my nerve. When you came I hid again. Thought I might get out alive and get away but it started to bleed again and I came out to phone.

The pencil wavered and dropped from Duncan's stiffening fingers. His head lolled back, jerked once horribly. There was a choking sob. Then his body went limp and his eyes stared glassily upward.

Outside, feet trampled in the hall, and the door shook under the impact of determined blows.

"What I don't see," said Shultz, "is where he was hid."

The sergeant straightened up. "We can find that out in a minute. It's amazing he lived as long as he did. His throat was almost cut in two."

"If you want to look now," Edwards said, "I think we can get to the bottom of this thing. When he came out I heard glass tinkling."

They covered the body with a scarf, and Edwards led the way into the refurnished dining room, Shultz and the officers pressing close behind him.

The manager bent down and inspected the cabinets of glassware with great care. On the bottom shelf of the last cabinet, he found an irregular red circle.

"This must be it," he said, grimly.

It took them some time to ascertain the combination. At length Edwards fumbled with an old flask which seemed cemented on the shelf. Glassware and all, the big bureau began to turn slowly in its place, disclosing a narrow closet behind the shelves. In that narrow compartment were a few cushions, an automatic pistol, a leather brief-case stuffed with papers, and bloodstains which showed all too well how Duncan had weakened and suffered during the hours he had remained in hiding.

The red-faced detective sergeant needed only a few minutes' perusal of the papers in the briefcase to tell him what he wanted to know. "I was partly right and partly wrong," he said. "He must have made that cubbyhole when he installed the cabinets, figuring he would need a hideaway for this stuff—and maybe for himself. We can get the rest of the gang from the names in his dying confession, Mr. Edwards. But I was wrong in one respect. I thought he had been murdered by that kidnapping ring which has been raising so much hell for three years. I thought he was their victim, when all the time he was the brains of the mob. Look at these papers and clippings."

Shultz heaved a vast sigh, and turned to his employer. "Just the same, I think I'll quit my job, Mr. Edwards. I'd go nuts if I was on the board tonight and another call came in from Apartment Twenty-two."

THE EPISODE OF THE NAIL
AND THE REQUIEM
C. Daly King

Although C(harles) Daly King (1895-1963) was an American, his un-doubted masterpiece, the short story collection *The Curious Mr. Tar-rant*, was first published in England in 1935 and, inexplicably, was among the rarest mystery books of the twentieth century until Dover issued the first American edition as a paperback in 1977.

Most of his books were first published in England and two, *Obe-lists en Route* (1934) and *Careless Corpse* (1937), were not published in the United States at all. Because of their uneven nature and the scar-city (most his books never had paperback editions), King's novels are not often read today, despite the ingenuity of their plotting.

In *Obelists at Sea* (1932), four psychologists, each a specialist in a different area of study, investigate a murder from their perspective and knowledge; all are proved wrong. In *Arrogant Alibi* (1938), the nine suspects for two murders all have impeccable, unshakable alibis; Barzun & Taylor's *A Catalogue of Crime* describes it as "excellent from start to finish."

Trevis Tarrant, the amateur detective in the eponymous story col-lection, is a wealthy, cultured gentleman of leisure who believes in cause and effect; they "rule the world," he says. He takes it on himself to explain locked room mysteries and impossible crimes that involve such improbabilities as mysterious footsteps by an invisible entity heard even in broad daylight, horrible images of a hanged man haunting a modern house, headless corpses found on a heavily traveled highway, as well as dealing with apparent ghosts and other supernormal happenings. It entertains him to bring his gift of being able to see things clearly and solve mysteries by the use of inarguable logic. He is accompanied at all times by his valet, Katoh, a Japanese doctor and spy.

"The Episode of the Nail and the Requiem" was first published in *The Curious Mr. Tarrant* (London, Collins, 1935).

The Episode of the Nail and the Requiem
C. Daly King

THE EPISODE of the nail and the requiem was one of the most characteristic of all those in which, over a relatively brief period, I was privileged to watch Trevis Tarrant at work. Characteristic, in that it brought out so well the unusual aptitude of the man to see clearly, to welcome *all* the facts, no matter how apparently contradictory, and to think his way through to the only possible solution by sheer logic, while everyone else boggled at impossibilities and sought to forget them. From the gruesome beginning that November night, when he was confronted by the puzzle of the sealed studio, to the equally gruesome denouement that occurred despite his own grave warning twenty-four hours later, his brain clicked successively and infallibly along the rails of reason to the inevitable, true goal.

We had been to a private address at the Metropolitan Museum by a returning Egyptologist, and had come back to his apartment for a Scotch and soda.

Tarrant was saying, "Cause and effect rule this world; they may be a mirage but they are a consistent mirage; everywhere, except possibly in subatomic physics, there is a cause for each effect, and that cause can be found," when the manager came in. He was introduced to me as Mr. Gleeb. Apparently he had merely dropped in, as was his custom, to assure himself that all was satisfactory with a valued tenant, but the greetings were scarcely over when the phone rang and 'Hido, Tarrant's Filipino butler-valet, indicated that the manager was being called. His monosyllabic answers gave no indication of the conversation from the other end; he finished with "All right; I'll be up in a minute."

He turned back to us. "I'm sorry," he said, "but there is some trouble at the penthouse. Or else my electrician has lost his mind. He says there is a horrible kind of music being played there and that he can get no response to his ringing at the door. I shall have to go up and see what it is all about."

The statement was a peculiar one and Tarrant's eyes, I thought, held an immediate gleam of curiosity. He got out of his seat in a leisurely fashion, however, and declared, "You know, Gleeb, I'd like a breath of fresh night air. Mind if we come up with you? There's a terrace, I believe, where we can take a step or so while you're untangling the matter."

"Not at all, Mr. Tarrant. Come right along. I hardly imagine it's of any importance, but I can guarantee plenty of air."

There was, in fact, a considerable wind blowing across the open terrace that, guarded by a three-foot parapet, surrounded the penthouse on all sides except the north, where its wall was flush with that of the building. The entrance was on the west side of the studio and here stood the electrician who had come to the roof to repair the radio antennae of the apartment house and had been arrested by the strange sounds from within. As we strolled about the terrace, we observed the penthouse itself as well as the lighted view of the city below. Its southern portion possessed the usual windows but the studio part had only blank brick walls; a skylight was just visible above it and there was, indeed, a very large window, covering most of the northern wall, but this, of course, was invisible and inaccessible from the terrace.

Presently the manager beckoned us over to the entrance door, and motioning us to be silent, asked, "What do you make of that, Mr. Tarrant?"

In the silence the sound of doleful music was more than audible. It appeared to emanate from within the studio; slow, sad and mournful, it was obviously a dirge and its full-throated quality suggested that it was being played by a large orchestra. After a few moment's listening Tarrant said, "That is the rendition of a requiem mass and very competently done, too. Unless I'm mistaken, it is the requiem of Palestrina. . . . There; there's the end of it. . . . Now it's beginning again."

"Sure, it goes on like that all the time," contributed Wicks, the electrician. "There must be some one in there, but I can't get no answer." He banged on the door with his fist but obviously without hope of response.

"Have you looked in at the windows?"

"Sure."

We, too, stepped to the available windows and peered in what was obviously a dark and empty bedroom, but nothing was visible. The door from the bedroom to the studio was closed. The windows were all locked.

"I suggest," said Tarrant, "that we break in."

The manager hesitated. "I don't know. After all, he has a right to play any music he likes, and if he doesn't want to answer the door—"

"Who has the penthouse, anyhow?"

"A man named Michael Salti. An eccentric fellow, like many of these artists. I don't know much about him, to tell the truth; we can't insist on as many references as we used to, nowadays. He paid a year's rent in advance and he hasn't bothered anyone in the building, that's about all I can tell you."

"Well," Tarrant considered, "this performance *is* a little peculiar.

How does he know we may not be trying to deliver an important message? How about his phone?"

"Tried it," Wicks answered. "The operator says there isn't any answer."

"I'm in favor of taking a peek. Look here, Gleeb, if you don't want to take the responsibility of breaking in, let us procure a ladder and have a look through the skylight. Ten to one that will pass unobserved; and if everything seems all right, we can simply sneak away."

To this proposal the manager consented, although it seemed to me that he did so most reluctantly. Possibly the eerie sounds that continued to issue through the closed door finally swayed him, for their quality, though difficult to convey, was certainly upsetting. In any event the ladder was brought and Tarrant himself mounted it, once it had been set in place. I saw him looking through the skylight, then leaning closer, peering intently through hands cupped about his eyes. Presently he straightened, and came down the ladder in some haste.

His face, when he stood beside us, was strained. "I think you should call the police," he grated. "At once. And wait till they get here before you go in."

"The police? But—what is it?"

"It's not pleasant," Tarrant said slowly. "I think it's murder."

Nor would he say anything further until the police, in the person of a traffic patrolman from Park Avenue, arrived. Then we all went in together, Gleeb's passkey having failed and the door being broken open.

The studio was a large, square room, and high, and the lamps which strangely enough were alight, illuminated it almost garishly. It was comfortably furnished in the modern note; an easel and a cabinet for paints and supplies stood on a hardwood floor which a soft rug did not completely cover. The question of the music was soon settled; in one corner was an electric victrola with an automatic arrangement for turning the record and starting it off again when it had reached its end. The record was of Palestrina's Requiem Mass, played by a well-known orchestra. Someone, I think it was Tarrant, crossed the room and turned it off, while we stood huddled near the door, gazing stupidly at the twisted, bloody figure on the couch.

It was that of a girl, altogether naked; although she was young—not older than twenty-two, certainly—her body was precociously voluptuous. One of her legs was contorted into a bent position, her mouth was awry, her left hand held a portion of the couch covering in an agonized clutch. Just beneath her left breast the hilt of a knife protruded shockingly. The bleeding had been copious.

It was Tarrant again who extinguished the four tall candles, set on the floor and burning at the corners of the couch. As he did so he murmured, "You will remember that the candles were burning at ten forty-seven, officer."

Then I was out on the terrace again, leaning heavily against the western parapet, while I gasped deep intakes of clear, cold air. I wasn't used to violence of this sort.

When I came back into the studio, a merciful blanket covered the girl's body. And for the first time I noticed the easel. It stood in the southeast corner of the room, diagonally opposite the couch and across the studio from the entrance doorway. It should have faced northwest, to receive the light from the big north window, and in fact the stool to its right indicated that position. But the easel had been partly turned, so that it faced southwest, toward the bedroom door, and one must walk almost to that door to observe its canvas.

This, stretched tightly on it's frame, bore a painting in oil of the murdered girl. She was portrayed in a nude, half crouching pose, her arms extended, and her features held a revoltingly lascivious leer. The portrait was entitled "La Seduction." In the identical place where the knife had pierced her actual body, a large nail had been driven through the web of the canvas. It was halfway through, the head protruding two inches on the opposite side of the picture; and a red gush of blood had been painted down the torso from the point where the nail entered.

Tarrant stood with his hands in his pockets, surveying this work of art. His gaze seemed focussed upon the nail, incongruous in its strange position and destined to play so large a part in the tragedy. He was murmuring to himself and his voice was so low that I scarcely caught his words.

"Madman's work. . . . But why is the easel turned away from the room. . . . Why is that? . . ."

It was midnight in Tarrant's apartment and much activity had gone forward. The Homicide Squad in charge of Lieutenant Mullins had arrived and unceremoniously ejected everyone else from the penthouse, Tarrant included. Thereupon he had called a friend at headquarters and been assured of a visit from Deputy Inspector Peake, who would be in command of the case, a visit which had not yet eventuated.

'Hido, who was certainly an excellent butler, had immediately provided me with a fine bottle of Irish whiskey (Bushmill's, bottled in 1919). I was sipping my second highball and Tarrant was quietly reading across the room, when Inspector Peake rang the bell.

He advanced into the room with hand outstretched. "Mr. Tarrant, I believe? . . . Ah, glad to know you, Mr. Phelan." He was a tall, thin man in mufti, with a voice unexpectedly soft. I don't know why, but I was also surprised that a policeman should wear so well-cut a suit of tweeds. As he sank into a chair, he continued, "I understand you were among the first to enter the penthouse, Mr. Tarrant. But I'm afraid there isn't much to add now. The case is cut and dried."

"You have the murderer?"

"Not yet. But the dragnet is out. We shall have him, if not today, then tomorrow or the next day."

"The artist, I suppose?"

"Michael Salti, yes. An eccentric man, quite mad. . . . By the way, I must thank you for that point about the candles. In conjunction with the medical examiner's evidence it checked the murder definitely at between three and four P.M."

"There is no doubt, then, I take it, about the identity of the criminal."

"No," Peake asserted, "none at all. He was seen alone with his model at 12:50 P.M. by one of the apartment house staff and the elevator operators are certain no one was taken to the penthouse during the afternoon or evening. His fingerprints were all over the knife, the candlesticks, the victrola record. There was a lot more corroboration, too."

"And was he seen to leave the building after the crime?"

"No, he wasn't. That's the one missing link. But since he isn't here, he must have left. Perhaps by the fire stairs; we've checked it and it's possible. . . . The girl is Barbara Brebant—a wealthy family." The inspector shook his head. "A wild one, though. She has played around with dubious artists from the Village and elsewhere for some years; gave most of 'em more than they could take, by all accounts. Young, too; made her debut only about a year ago. Apparently she had made something of a name for herself in the matter of viciousness; three of our men brought in the very same description—a vicious beauty."

"The old Roman type," Tarrant surmised. "Not so anachronistic in this town, at that. . . . Living with Salti?"

"No. She lived at home. When she bothered to go home. No one doubts, though, that she was Salti's mistress. And from what I've learned, when she was any man's mistress, he was pretty certain to be dragged through the mire. Salti, being mad, finally killed her."

"Yes, that clicks," Tarrant agreed. "The lascivious picture and the nail driven through it. Madmen, of course, act perfectly logically. He was probably a loose liver himself, but she showed him depths he had not suspected. Then remorse. His insanity taking the form of an absence of the usual values, he made her into a symbol of his own vice, through the painting, and then killed her, just as he mutilated the painting with the nail. . . . Yes, Salti is your man, all right."

Peake ground out a cigarette. "A nasty affair. But not especially mysterious. I wish all our cases were as simple." He was preparing to take his leave.

Tarrant also got up. He said, "Just a moment. There were one or two things—"

"Yes?"

"I wonder if I could impose upon you a little more, Inspector. Just to check some things I noticed tonight. Can I be admitted to the penthouse now?"

Peake shrugged, as if the request were a useless one, but took it with a certain good grace. "Yes, I'll take you up. All our men have left now, except a patrolman who will guard the premises until we make the arrest. I still have an hour to spare."

It was two hours, however, before they returned. The inspector didn't come in, but I caught Tarrant's parting words at the entrance. "You will surely assign another man to the duty tonight, won't you?" The policeman's reply sounded like a grunt of acquiescence.

I looked at my friend in amazement when he came into the lounge. His clothes, even his face, were covered with dirt; his nose was a long, black smudge. By the time he had bathed and changed into his pajamas, it was nearly dawn.

During the next few minutes Tarrant was unaccustomedly silent. Even after 'Hido had brought us a nightcap, he sat deep in thought, and in the light of the standing lamp behind him I thought his face wore a slight frown.

Presently he gave that peculiar whistle that summoned his man and the butler-valet appeared almost immediately from the passage to the kitchen. "Sit down, doctor," he spoke without looking up.

Doubtless a small shift in my posture expressed my surprise, for he continued, for my benefit, "I've told you that 'Hido is a doctor in his own country, a well educated man. When I wish his advice as a friend, I call him doctor—a title to which he is fully entitled. Usually I do it when I'm worried. . . . I'm worried now."

'Hido, meantime, had hoisted himself onto the divan, where he sat smiling and helping himself to one of Tarrant's Dimitrines. "Social custom, matter of convenience," he acknowledged. "Conference about what?"

"About this penthouse murder," said Tarrant without further ado. "You know the facts related by Inspector Peake. You heard them?"

"I listen. Part my job."

"Yes, well that portion is all right. Salti's the man. There's no mystery about that, not even interesting, in fact. But there's something else, something that isn't right. It stares you in the face but the police don't care. Their business is to arrest the murderer; they know who he is and they're out looking for him. That's enough for them. But there is a mystery up above, a real one. I'm not concerned with chasing crooks, but their own case won't hold unless this curious fact fits in. It is as strange as anything I've ever met."

'Hido's grin had faded; his face was entirely serious. "What this mystery?"

"It's the most perfect sealed room, or rather sealed house, problem ever reported. There was no way out and yet the man isn't there. No possibility of suicide; the fingerprints on the knife are only one element that rules that out. No, he was present all right. But where did he go, and how? . . . Listen carefully. I've checked this from my own observations, from the police investigations and from my later search with Peake.

"When we entered the penthouse tonight, Gleeb's passkey didn't suffice; we had to break the entrance door in because it was bolted on the inside by a strong bar. The walls of the studio are of brick and they have no windows except on the northern side where there is a sheer drop to the ground. The window there was fastened on the inside and the skylight was similarly fastened. The only other exit from the studio is the door to the bedroom. This was closed and the key turned in the lock; the key was on the studio side of the door.

"Yes, I know." Tarrant went on, apparently forestalling an interruption, "it is sometimes possible to turn a key in a lock from the wrong side, by means of a pair of pincers or some similar contrivance. That makes the bedroom, the lavatory, and the kitchenette adjoining it, possibilities. There is no exit from any of them except by the windows. They were all secured from the inside and I am satisfied that they cannot be so secured by anybody already out of the penthouse."

He paused and looked over at 'Hido whose head nodded up and down as he made the successive points. "Two persons in penthouse when murder committed. One is victim, other is Salti man. After murder only victim is visible. One door, windows and skylight are only exits and they are all secured on inside. Cannot be secured from outside. Therefore, Salti man still in penthouse when you enter."

"But he wasn't there when we entered. The place was thoroughly searched. I was there then myself."

"Maybe trap door. Maybe space under floor or entrance to floor below."

"Yes," said Tarrant. "Well, now, get this. There are no trap doors in the flooring of the penthouse, there are none in the walls and there are not even any in the roof. I have satisfied myself of that with Peake. Gleeb, the manager who was on the spot when the penthouse was built, further assures me of it."

"Only place is floor," 'Hido insisted. "Salti man could make this himself."

"He couldn't make a trap door without leaving at least a minute crack," was Tarrant's counter. "At least I don't see how he could. The flooring of the studio is hard wood, the planks closely fitted together and I have been over every inch of it. Naturally there are cracks between the planks, lengthwise; but there are no transverse cracks anywhere. Gleeb has shown me the specifications of that floor. The planks are grooved together and it is impossible to raise any plank without splintering that grooving. From my own examination I am sure none of the planks has been, or can be, lifted.

"All this was necessary because there is a space of something like two and a half feet between the floor of the penthouse and the roof of the apartment building proper. One has to mount a couple of steps at the entrance of the penthouse. Furthermore I have been in part of this space. Let me make it perfectly clear how I got there.

"The bedroom adjoins the studio on the south, and the lavatory occupies the northwest corner of the bedroom. It is walled off, of course. Along the northern wall of the lavatory (which is part of the southern wall of the studio) is the bathtub; and the part of the flooring under the bathtub has been cut away, leaving an aperture to the space beneath."

I made my first contribution. "But how can that be? Wouldn't the bathtub fall through?"

"No. The bathtub is an old-fashioned one, installed by Salti himself only a few weeks ago. It is not flush with the floor, as they make them now, but stands on four legs. The flooring has only been cut away in the middle of the tub, say two or three planks, and the opening extended only to the outer edge of the tub. Not quite that far, in fact."

"There is Salti man's trap door," grinned 'Hido. "Not even door; just trap."

"So I thought," Tarrant agreed grimly. "But it isn't. Or if it is, he didn't use it. As no one could get through the opening without moving the tub—which hadn't been done, by the way—Peake and I pulled up some more of the cut planks and I squeezed myself into the space beneath the lavatory and bedroom. There was nothing there but dirt; I got plenty of that."

"How about space below studio?"

"Nothing doing. The penthouse is built on a foundation, as I said about two and a half feet high, of concrete building blocks. A line of these blocks runs underneath the penthouse, directly below the wall between the studio and bedroom. As the aperture in the floor is on the southern side of the wall, it is likewise to the south of the transverse line of building blocks in the foundation. The space beneath the studio is to the north of these blocks, and they form a solid wall that is impassable. I spent a good twenty minutes scrummaging along the entire length of it."

"Most likely place," 'Hido confided, "just where hole in lavatory floor."

"Yes, I should think so, too. I examined it carefully. I could see the ends of the planks that form the studio floor part way over the beam above the building blocks. But there isn't a trace of a loose block at that point, any more than there is anywhere else. . . . To make everything certain, we also examined the other three sides of the foundation of the bedroom portion of the penthouse. They are solid and haven't been touched since it was constructed. So the whole thing is just a cul-de-sac; there is no possibility of exit from the penthouse even through the aperture beneath the bathtub."

"You examine also foundations under studio part?"

"Yes, we did that, too. No result."

He looked at 'Hido long and searchingly and the other, after a pause, replied slowly, "Can only see this. Salti man construct this trap, probably for present use. Then he do not use. Must go some other way."

"But there *is* no other way."

"Then Salti man still there."

"He isn't there."

"Harumph," said 'Hido reflectively. It was evident that he felt the same respect for a syllogism that animated Tarrant; and was stopped, for the time being, at any rate. He went off on a new tack. "What else especially strange about setting?"

"There are two other things that strike me as peculiar," Tarrant answered, and his eyes narrowed. "On the floor, about one foot from the northern window, there is a fairly deep indentation in the floor of the studio. It is a small impression and is almost certainly made by a nail partly driven through the planking and then pulled up again."

I thought of the nail through the picture. "Could he have put the picture down on that part of the floor in order to drive the nail through it? But what if he did?"

"I can see no necessity for it, in any case. The nail would go through the canvas easily enough, just as it stood on the easel."

'Hido said, "With nail in plank, perhaps plank could be pulled up! You say no?"

"I tried it. Even driving the nail in sideways, instead of vertically, as the original indentation was made, the plank can't be lifted at all."

"O. K. You say some other thing strange, also."

"Yes. The position of the easel that holds the painting of the dead girl. When we broke in this morning, it was turned away from the room, toward the bedroom door, so that the picture was scarcely visible even from the studio entrance, let alone the rest of the room. I don't believe that was the murderer's intention. He had set the rest of the stage too carefully. The requiem; the candles. It doesn't fit; I'm sure he meant the first person who entered to be confronted by the whole scene, and especially by that symbolic portrait. It doesn't accord even with the position of the stool, which agrees with the intended position of the easel. It doesn't fit at all with the mentality of the murderer. It seems a small thing but I'm sure it's important. I'm certain the position of the easel is an important clue."

"To mystery of disappearance?"

"Yes. To the mystery of the murderer's escape from that sealed room."

"Not see how," 'Hido declared, after some thought. As for me, I couldn't even appreciate the suggestion of any connection.

"Neither do I," grated Tarrant. He had risen and begun to pace the floor. "Well, there you have it all. A little hole in the floor near the north window, an easel turned out of position and a sealed room without an occupant who certainly ought to be there. . . . There's an answer to this; damn it, there must be an answer."

Suddenly he glanced at an electric clock on the table he was passing and stopped abruptly. "My word," he exclaimed, "it's nearly five o'clock. Didn't mean to keep you up like this, Jerry. You either, doctor. Well, the conference is over. We've got nowhere."

'Hido was on his feet, in an instant once more the butler. "Sorry could not help. You wish nightcap, Misster Tarrant?"

"No. Bring the scotch. And a siphon. And ice. I'm not turning in."

I had been puzzling my wits without intermission over the problem above, and the break found me more tired than I had realized. I yawned prodigiously. I made a half hearted attempt to persuade Tarrant to come to bed but it was plain that he would have none of it.

I said, "Good-night, 'Hido. I'm no good for anything until I get a little sleep . . . Night, Tarrant."

I left him once more pacing the floor; his face, in the last glimpse I had of it, was set in the stern lines of thought.

It seemed no more than ten seconds after I got into bed that I felt my shoulder being shaken and, through the fog of sleep, heard 'Hido's hissing accents. "—Misster Tarrant just come from penthouse. He excited. Maybe you wish wake up." As I rolled out and shook myself free from slumber, I noticed that my wrist watch pointed to six thirty.

When I had thrown on some clothes and come into the living room, I found Tarrant standing with the telephone instrument to his head, his whole posture one of grimness. Although I did not realize it at once, he had been endeavoring for some time to reach Deputy Inspector Peake. He accomplished this finally a moment or so after I reached the room.

"Hello, Peake? Inspector Peake? This is Tarrant. How many men did you leave to guard that penthouse last night? . . . What, only one? But I said two, man. Damn it all, I don't make suggestions like that for amusement! . . . All right, there's nothing to be accomplished arguing about it. You'd better get here, and get here pronto. . . . That's all I'll say." He slammed down the receiver viciously.

I had never before seen Tarrant upset; my surprise was a measure of his own disturbance, which resembled consternation. He paced the floor, muttering below his breath, his long legs carrying him swiftly up and down the apartment. ". . . Damned fools . . . everything must fit. . . . Or else. . . ." For once I had sense enough to keep my questions to myself for the time being.

Fortunately I had not long to wait. Hardly had 'Hido had opportunity to brew some coffee, with which he appeared somewhat in the manner of a dog wagging its tail deprecatingly, than Peake's ring sounded at the entrance. He came in hurriedly, but his smile, as well as his words, indicated his opinion that he had been roused by a false alarm.

"Well, well, Mr. Tarrant, what *is* this trouble over?"

Tarrant snapped, "Your man's gone. Disappeared. How do you like that?"

"The patrolman on guard?" The policeman's expression was incredulous.

"The *single* patrolman you left on guard."

Peake stepped over to the telephone, called headquarters. After a few brief words he turned back to us, his incredulity at Tarrant's statement apparently confirmed.

"You must be mistaken, sir," he asserted. "There have been no reports from Officer Weber. He would never leave the premises without reporting such an occasion."

Tarrant's answer was purely practical. "Come and see."

And when we reached the terrace on the building's roof, there was, in fact, no sign of the patrolman who should have been at his station. We entered the penthouse and, the lights having been turned on, Peake himself made a complete search of the premises. While Tarrant watched the proceedings in a grim silence, I walked over to the north window of the studio, gray in the early morning light, and sought for the nail hole he had mentioned as being in the floor. There it was, a small indentation, about an inch deep, in one of the hardwood planks. This, and everything else about the place appeared just as Tarrant had described it to us some hours before, previous to my turning in. I was just in time to see Peake emerge from the enlarged opening in the lavatory floor, dusty and sorely puzzled.

"Our man is certainly not here," the inspector acknowledged. "I cannot understand it. This is a serious breach of discipline."

"Hell," said Tarrant sharply, speaking for the first time since we had come to the roof. "This is a serious breach of intelligence, not discipline."

"I shall broadcast an immediate order for the detention of Patrolman Weber." Peake stepped into the bedroom and approached the phone to carry out his intention.

"You needn't broadcast it. I have already spoken to the night operator in the lobby on the ground floor. He told me a policeman left the building in great haste about 3:30 this morning. If you will have the local precinct check up on the all-night lunch rooms along Lexington Avenue in this vicinity, you will soon pick up the first step of the trail that man left. . . . You will probably take my advice, now that it is too late."

Peake did so, putting the call through at once; but his bewilderment was no whit lessened. Nor was mine. As he put down the instrument, he said, "All right. But it doesn't make sense. Why should he leave his post without notifying us? And why should he go to a lunch room?"

"Because he was hungry."

"But—. There has been a crazy murderer here already. And now Weber, an ordinary cop, if I ever saw one. Does this place make everybody mad?"

"Not as mad as you're going to be in a minute. But perhaps you weren't using the word in that sense?"

Peake let it pass. "Everything," he commented slowly, "is just as we left it last night. Except for Weber's disappearance."

"Is that so?" Tarrant led us to the entrance from the roof to the studio and pointed downwards. The light was now bright enough to disclose an unmistakable spattering of blood on one of the steps before the door. "That blood wasn't there when we left last night. I came up here about five thirty, the moment I got onto this thing," he continued bitterly. "Of course I was too late. . . . Damnation, let us make an end to this farce. I'll show you some more things that have altered during the night."

We followed him into the studio again as he strode over to the easel with its lewd picture, opposite the entrance. He pointed to the nail still protruding through the canvas. "I don't know how closely you observed the hole made in this painting by the nail yesterday. But it's a little larger now and the edges are more frayed. In other words the nail has been removed and once more inserted."

I turned about to find that Gleeb, somehow appraised of the excitement, had entered the penthouse and now stood a little behind us. Tarrant acknowledged his presence with a curt nod; and in the air of tension that his tenant was building up the manager ventured no questions.

"Now," Tarrant continued, pointing out the locations as he spoke, "possibly they have dried, but when I first got here this morning, there was a trail of moist spots still leading from the entrance doorway to the vicinity of the north window. You will find that they were places where a trail of blood had been wiped away with a wet cloth."

He turned to the picture beside him and withdrew the nail, pulling himself up as if for a repugnant job. He walked over to the north window and motioned us to take our places on either side of him. Then he bent down and inserted the nail, point first, into the indentation in the plank, as firmly as he could. He braced himself and apparently strove to pull the nail toward the south, away from the window.

I was struggling with an obvious doubt. I said, "But you told us the planks could not be lifted."

"Can't," Tarrant grunted. "But they can be *slid*."

Under his efforts the plank was, in fact, sliding. Its end appeared from under the footboard at the base of the north wall below the window and continued to move over a space of several feet. When this had been accomplished, he grasped the edges of the planks on both sides of the one already moved and slid them back also. An opening quite large enough to squeeze through was revealed.

But that was not all. The crumpled body of a man lay just beneath; the man was clad only in underwear and was obviously dead from the beating in of his head.

As we bent over, gasping at the unexpectedly gory sight, Gleeb suddenly cried, "But that is not Michael Salti! What is this, a murder farm? I don't know this man."

Inspector Peake's voice was ominous with anger. "I do. That is the body of Officer Weber. But how could he—"

Tarrant had straightened up and was regarding us with a look that said plainly he was anxious to get an unpleasant piece of work finished. "It was simple enough," he ground out. "Salti cut out the planks beneath the bathtub in the lavatory so that *these* planks in the studio could be slid back over the beam along the foundation under the south wall; their farther ends in this position will now be covering the hole in the lavatory floor. The floor here is well fitted and the planks are grooved, thus making the sliding possible. They can be moved back into their original position by someone in the space below here; doubtless we shall find a small block nailed to the under portion of all three planks for that purpose.

"He murdered his model, set the scene and started his phonograph, which will run interminably on the electric current. Then he crawled into his hiding place. The discovery of the crime could not be put off any later than the electrician's visit to fix the aerial.

"When the place was searched and the murderer not discovered, his pursuit passed elsewhere, while he himself lay concealed here all night. It was even better than doubling back upon his tracks, for he had never left the starting post. Eventually, of course, he had to get out, but by that time the vicinity of this building would be the last place in which he was being searched for.

"This morning he pushed back the planks from underneath and came forth. I don't know whether he had expected anyone to be left on guard, but that helped rather than hindered him. Creeping up upon the unsuspecting guard he knocked him out—doubtless with that mallet I can just see beside the body—and beat him to death. Then he put his second victim in the hiding place, returning the instrument that closes it from above, the nail, to its position in the painting. He had already stripped off his own clothes, which you will find down in that hole, and in the officer's uniform and coat he found no difficulty in leaving the building. His first action was to hurry to a lunch room, naturally, since after a day and a night without food under the floor here, he must have been famished. I have no doubt that your man will get a report of him along Lexington Avenue, Peake; but even so, he now has some hours' start on you."

"We'll get him," Peake assured us. "But if you knew all this, why in heaven's name didn't you have this place opened up last night, before he had any chance to commit a second murder? We should have taken him red-handed."

"Yes, but I didn't know it last night," Tarrant reminded him. "It was not until early this morning that I had any proper opportunity to examine the penthouse. What I found was a sealed room and a sealed house. There was no exit that had not been blocked nor, after our search, could I understand how the man could still be in the penthouse. On the other hand I could not understand how it was possible that he had left. As a precaution, in case he were still here in some manner I had not fathomed, I urged you to leave at least two men on guard, and it was my understanding that you agreed. I think it is obvious, although I was unable then to justify myself, that the precaution was called for."

Peake said, "It was."

"I have been up all night working this out. What puzzled me completely was the absence of any trap doors. Certainly we looked for them thoroughly. But it was there right in front of us all the time; we even investigated a portion of it, the aperture in the lavatory floor, which we supposed to be a trap door itself, although actually it was only a part of the real arrangement. As usual the trick was based upon taking advantage of habits of thought, of our habitized notion of a trap door as something that is lifted or swung back. I have never heard before of a trap door that slides back. Nevertheless, that was the simple answer, and it took me until five thirty to reach it."

'Hido whom for the moment I had forgotten completely, stirred uneasily and spoke up. "I not see, Misster Tarrant, how you reach answer then."

"Four things," was the reply. "First of all, the logical assumption that, since there was no way out, the man was still here. As to the mechanism by which he managed to remain undiscovered, three things. We mentioned them last night. First, the nail hole in the plank; second, the position of the easel; third, the hole in the lavatory floor. I tried many ways to make them fit together, for I felt sure they must *all* fit.

"It was the position of the easel that finally gave me the truth. You remember we agreed that it was wrong, that the murderer had never intended to leave it facing away from the room. But if no one had entered until we did and still its position was wrong, what could have moved it in the meantime? Except for the phonograph, which could scarcely be responsible, the room held nothing but motionless objects. *But if the floor under one of its legs had moved, the easel would have been slid around.* That fitted with the other two items, the nail hole in the plank, the opening under the bathtub.

"The moment it clicked, I got an automatic and ran up here. I was too late. As I said, I've been up all night. I'm tired; I'm going to bed."

He walked off without another word, scarcely with a parting nod. Tarrant, as I know now, did not often fail. He was a man who offered few excuses for himself, and he was humiliated.

It was a week or so later when I had an opportunity to ask him if Salti had been captured. I had seen nothing of it in the newspapers, and the case had now passed to the back pages with the usual celerity of sensations.

Tarrant said, "I don't know."

"But haven't you followed it up with that man, Peake?"

"I'm not interested. It's nothing but a straight police case now."

He stopped and added after an appreciable pause, "Damn it, Jerry, I don't like to think of it even now. I've blamed the stupidity of the police all I can; their throwing me out when I might have made a real investigation that evening; that delay; then the negligence in overlooking my suggestion for a pair of guards, which I made as emphatic as I could. But it's no use. I should have solved it in time, even so. There could only be that one answer and I took too long to find it.

"The human brain works too slowly, Jerry, even when it works straight. . . . It works too slowly."

THE RIDDLE OF THE
YELLOW CANARY
Stuart Palmer

The inverted detective story was invented by R. Austin Freeman and, while it remains an occasional form of mystery fiction, it is uncommon, though it enjoyed huge popularity when brought to near-perfection in the *Columbo* television series.

It is challenging to write a murder story when the reader knows immediately—not only who the guilty person is, but how the crime was committed. This is especially risky in a locked room story, which projects the appearance of an impossible crime and the puzzle element of learning how it was accomplished is generally what fascinates the reader.

The tour-de-force in this collection was written by Charles Stuart Palmer (1905-1968), the creator of the popular spinster-sleuth Hildegarde Withers who was introduced in *The Penguin Pool Murder* (1931). Formerly a schoolteacher, the thin, angular, horse-faced snoop devoted her energy to aiding Inspector Oliver Piper of the New York City Police Department, driving him slightly crazy in the process. She is noted for her odd, even eccentric, choice of hats. Palmer stated that she was based on his high school English teacher, Miss Fern Hackett, and on his father.

There were thirteen more novels in the Miss Withers series, the last, *Hildegarde Withers Makes the Scene* (1969), being completed by Fletcher Flora after Palmer died. There also were three short story collections, with the first, *The Riddles of Hildegarde Withers* (1947), being selected as a *Queen's Quorum* title. It was followed by *The Monkey Murders and Other Hildegarde Withers Stories* (1950), and *People vs. Withers and Malone* (1963), in conjunction with Craig Rice, which also featured her series character, John J. Malone.

The film version of *The Penguin Pool Murder* was released in 1932 and spurred five additional comic mystery films, the first three featuring Edna May Oliver in a perfect casting decision, followed by Helen Broderick, and the last, *Forty Naughty Girls* (1937), with Zasu Pitts; Piper was played by James Gleason in all films.

"The Riddle of the Yellow Canary" was originally published in the April 1934 issue of *Mystery*; it was first collected in *The Riddles of Hildegarde Withers* (New York, Jonathan Press, 1947).

The Riddle of the Yellow Canary
Stuart Palmer

THE SOFT April rain was beating against the windows of Arthur Reese's private office, high above Times Square. Reese himself sat tensely before his desk, studying a sheet of paper still damp from the presses. He had just made the most important decision of his life. He was going to murder the Thorens girl.

For months he had been toying with the idea, as a sort of mental chess problem. Now, when Margie Thorens was making it so necessary that she be quietly removed, he was almost surprised to find that the idle scheme had reached sheer perfection. It was as if he had completed a jigsaw puzzle while thinking of something else.

Beyond his desk was a door. On the glass Reese could read his own name and the word "Private" spelled backwards. As he watched, a shadow blotted out the light, and he heard a soft knock.

"Yes?" he called out.

It was plump, red-haired Miss Kelly—excellent secretary, Kelly, in spite of her platinum fingernails. "Miss Thorens is still waiting to see you," said Kelley.

She had not held her job long enough to realize just how often, and how long, Margie Thorens had been kept waiting.

"Oh, Lord!" Reese made his voice properly weary. He looked at his watch, and saw that it was five past five. "Tell her I'm too busy," he began. Then—"No, I'll stop in the reception room and see her for just a moment before I go. Bad news for her again, I'm afraid."

Miss Kelly knew all about would-be songwriters. She smiled. "Don't forget your appointment with Mr. Larry Foley at five thirty. G'night, Mr. Reese." She closed the door.

Reese resumed his study of the sheet of music. "'May Day'—a song ballad with words and music by Art Reese, published by Arthur Reese and Company." He opened the page, found the chorus, and hummed a bar of the catchy music. "I met you on a May day, a wonderful okay day. . . ."

He put the song away safely, and reached into his desk for a large flask of hammered silver. He drank deeply, but not too deeply, and shoved it into his hip pocket.

The outer office was growing suddenly quiet as the song pluggers left their pianos. Vaudeville sister teams, torch singers, and comics were temporarily giving up the search for something new to interest a fretful and jaded public. Stenographers and clerks were covering their typewriters. The day's work was over for them—and beginning for Reese.

From his pocket he took an almost microscopic capsule. It was colorless, and no larger than a pea. Yet it was potentially more dangerous than a dozen cobras . . . a dark gift of fortune which had started the whole plot working in his mind.

Three years ago an over-emotional young lady, saddened at the prospect of being tossed aside "like a worn glove," had made a determined effort to end her own life under circumstances which would have been very unpleasant indeed for Arthur Reese. He had luckily been able to take the cyanide of potassium from her in time. She was married and in Europe now. There would be no way of tracing the stuff. It was pure luck.

The capsule was his own idea, a stroke of genius. He rolled it in his fingers, then looked at his watch. It was fifteen minutes past five. The lights of Times Square were beginning to come on, clashing with the lingering dullness of the April daylight. Reese picked up a brown envelope which lay on his desk, crossed to his topcoat and pocketed a pair of light gloves. Then he stepped out into the brilliantly lighted but deserted outer office.

The first door on his right bore only the figure "I" on the glass. It was unlocked, and he stepped quickly through. It did not matter if anyone saw him, he knew, yet it would be safer if not.

Margie Thorens leaped up from the piano stool—the room was furnished so that it could be used by Reese's staff if necessary—and came toward him. Reese smiled with his mouth, but his eyes stared at her as if he had never seen her before.

There had been a time not so long ago when Arthur Reese had thought this helpless, babyish girl very attractive, with her dark eyes, darker hair, and the hot sullen mouth. But that time was over and done. He steeled himself to bear her kiss, but he was saved from completing that Judas gesture. She stopped, searching his face.

"Sit down, Margie," he said.

She dropped to the stool. "Sit down yourself," she told him. Her voice was husky. "Or do you have to rush away? Making another trip to Atlantic City this weekend?" Her words dripped with meaning. She played three notes on the black keys.

"Forget your grouch," said Reese. "I've got news."

"You'd better have!" She swung on him. "You've got to do something about me. I'm not going to sit out in the cold. Not with what I've got on you, Lothario."

She had raised her voice, and he didn't want that. "Good news," he said hastily. Her eyes widened a little. "Oh, it's not the Tennessee song. That stuff is passé. But I finally got Larry Foley to listen to 'May Day,' and he thinks it's great. 'Another Echo in the Valley,' he says. So I'm going to publish it. He's willing to plug it with his band over the air, and he'll make a play to get it in the picture he's going to do in Hollywood. You're a success! You're a songwriter at last!"

Margie Thorens looked as though she might fall. "It's all true," he assured her. As a matter of fact it was. Reese had known that it would be easier to tell the truth than to invent a lie. And it wouldn't matter afterward. "I'm rushing publication, and there'll be a contract for you in the morning."

She was still dizzy. "You—you're not going to horn in as co-author or anything? Truly, Art?"

"You look dizzy," he said. He pulled out his flask. "How about a drink to celebrate?"

Margie shook her head. "Not on an empty stomach," she pleaded. "I'd like a glass of water, though."

The carefully designed plan of Arthur Reese rearranged itself, like a shaken kaleidoscope. He hurried to the water-cooler in the corner, and after a second's pause returned with a conical paper cup nearly full. "This will fix you up," he told her.

Margie drained it at one gulp, and he breathed again. He looked at his watch, and saw that it was five twenty. The capsule would hold for four to six minutes. . . .

"Better still," he rushed on. "I got an idea for a lyric the other day, and Foley likes it. If you can concoct a good sobby tune to go with it . . ."

He fumbled at his pockets. "I've lost the notes," he said. "But I can remember the lyric if you'll write it down." He handed her a yellow pencil and the brown envelope which held her rejected manuscript of "Tennessee Sweetheart." "It begins— Goodbye, goodbye—"

He dictated, very slowly, for what seemed to him an hour. He stole a glance at his watch, and saw that four minutes had elapsed. He found himself improvising, repeating a line. . . ."

"You gave me that once," protested Margie. "And the rhymes are bad." She raised her head as if she had suddenly remembered some unspeakable and ancient secret. "Turn on the lights!" she cried. "It's getting—Art! I can't see you!" She groped to her feet. "Art—oh, God, what have you done to me. . . ."

Her voice trailed away, and little bubbles were at her lips. She plunged forward, before he could catch her.

Reese found himself without any particular emotion except gratitude that her little body had not been heavy enough to shake the floor. He left her there, and went swiftly to the door. There was no sign that anyone had been near to hear that last desperate appeal. He congratulated himself on his luck. This sort of thing was far simpler than the books had made him suppose.

He closed the door, and shot the bolt which was designed to insure privacy for the musicians. Then he began swiftly to complete his picture—a picture that was to show to the whole world the inevitable suicide of Margie Thorens.

He first donned his light gloves. It was no effort at all to lift the girl to the wicker settee, although he had to resist a temptation to close the staring dark eyes.

He reached for the tiny gold-washed strap-watch that Margie Thorens wore around her left wrist. Here he struck a momentary snag. Reese had meant to set the hands at five of six, and then smash the thing in order to set the time of the "suicide," but the crystal had broken when she fell.

The watch was not ticking. He removed one glove, and carefully forced the hands of the little timepiece ahead. The shards of broken glass impeded their movement, but they moved. He put his glove back on.

Reese did not neglect to gather up the fragment or two of glass which had fallen on the oak floor, and place them where they would naturally have been if the watch had been broken against the arm of the settee in her death agony. Luckily the daylight lingered.

The paper cup was on the floor. He was not sure that fingerprints could be wiped from paper, so he crumpled it into his pocket. Taking another from the rack, he sloshed a bit of water into it, and then dropped in a few particles of the poison which he had saved for some such purpose. The mixture he spilled about the dead mouth and face, and let the cup fall where it would have fallen from the nerveless fingers. On second thought, he picked it up, placed it in the limp hand of Margie Thorens, and crumpled it there with his gloved hand.

It was finished—and water-tight, he knew that. Who could doubt that a young and lonely girl, stranded in New York without friends or family, disappointed in her ambitions and low in funds, might be moved to take her own life?

Reese looked at his watch. The hands had barely passed the hour of five thirty-five. He had twenty minutes to establish a perfect alibi, if he should ever need one.

There still remained a ticklish bit of fine work. He unlocked the door and looked out into the main office. It was still deserted. He stepped out, leaving the door ajar, and put his arm inside to turn the brass knob which shot the bolt.

Pressing the large blade of his jackknife against the spring lock, he withdrew his arm and swung the door shut. Then he'pulled away the knife, and the latch clicked. Margie Thorens was dead in a room which had a window without a fire escape, and a door locked on the inside.

In two minutes Reese was laughing with the elevator boy on his way down. In five more he stepped out of the men's room at the Roxy

Grill, washed and groomed, and with the paper cup and the folded paper which had held poison and capsule all gone forever via the plumbing. When the big clock above the bar pointed to ten of six, Reese had already stood Larry Foley his second round of drinks. He was softly humming "May Day."

Inspector Oscar Piper called Spring 7-3100 before he put on his slippers. "Anything doing, Sergeant?"

"Nothing but a lousy suicide of a dame up in Tin Pan Alley," the phone sergeant said. "Scrub woman found her, and the precinct boys are there now."

"I'll stop in and have a look in the morning," decided the Inspector. "These things are all alike."

The morrow was a Saturday, and Miss Hildegarde Withers was thus relieved of the necessity of teaching the young how to sprout down in Jefferson School's third grade. But if she had any ideas of lying abed in luxurious idleness, they were rudely shattered by the buzzing of the telephone.

"Yes, Oscar," she said wearily.

"You've often asked me how the police can spot a suicide from a murder," Piper was saying. "Well, I'm on the scene of a typical suicide, perfect in every detail but one and that doesn't matter. Want to have a look? If you hurry you'll have a chance to see the stiff before she goes to the morgue."

"I'll come," decided the schoolteacher. "But I shall purposely dawdle in hopes of missing your exhibit."

Dawdle as she did, she still rode up the ten stories in the elevator and entered the offices of Arthur Reese, Music Publisher, before the white-clad men from the morgue arrived. Her long face, somewhat resembling that of a well-bred horse, made a grimace as the Inspector showed her the broken lock of the little reception and music room, and what lay beyond.

"Scrub women came in at midnight, and found the door locked. They got the night watchman to break it, since it couldn't have been locked from the outside, and thought somebody was ill inside or something. Somebody was. The medical examiner was out on Long Island over that latest gang killing, and couldn't get here till a couple of hours ago, but he found traces of cyanide on her mouth. The autopsy will confirm if, he says." Miss Withers nodded. "She looks awfully—young," she said.

"She was," Piper told her. "We've checked up on the kid. Ran away from an Albany high school to make her fortune as a songwriter, so she's even younger than you thought. Been in New York five months and got nothing but rejections. Yesterday afternoon she got another one and she waited until everyone else had gone, and bumped herself off. Left a suicide note on the piano, too." The Inspector handed over the brown envelope. "Wrote it on the envelope which held the bad—news—her rejected manuscript. And notice how firm and steady the writing is, right to the last word almost."

Miss Withers noticed. She bent to squint over the rhymed note. She saw:

"Goodbye, goodbye I cry
A long and last goodbye
Goodbye to Broadway and the lights
Goodbye sad days and lonely nights
I've waited alone
To sing this last song
Goodbye . . .

. . .

. . .

. . .

. . ."

She read it through again. "She didn't sign it," Piper went on. "But it's her handwriting all right. Checks with the manuscript of the rejected song in the envelope, and also with a letter in her handbag that she was going to mail."

"A letter?" Miss Withers handed back the envelope. But the letter was a disappointment. It was a brief note to the Metropolitan Gas Company, promising that a check would be mailed very shortly to take care of the overdue bill, and signed "Margery Thorens."

Miss Withers gave it back. She took the tiny handbag that had been the dead girl's, and studied it for a moment. "She had a miniature fountain pen, I-see," said the school teacher. "It writes, too. Wonder why she used a pencil?"

"Well, use it she did, because here it is." Piper handed her the long yellow pencil which had laid on the floor. The school teacher looked at it for a long time.

"The picture is complete," said Piper jovially. "There's only one tiny discrepancy, and that doesn't matter."

Miss Withers wanted to know what it was. "Only this," said the Inspector. "We know the time she died, because she smashed her wrist watch in her death throes. That was five minutes to six. But at that hour it's pretty dark—and this is the first time I ever heard of a suicide going off in the dark. They usually want the comfort of a light."

"Perhaps," said Miss Withers, "perhaps she died earlier, and the watch was wrong? Or it might have run a little after she died?"

The Inspector shook his head. "The watch was too badly smashed to run a tick after she fell," he said. "Main stem broken. And she must have died after dark because there was somebody here in the offices until around five thirty. I tell you . . ."

He was interrupted by a sergeant in a baggy blue uniform. "Reese has just come in, Inspector. I told him you said he should wait in his office."

"Right!" Oscar Piper turned to Miss Withers. "Reese is the boss of this joint, and ought to give us a line on the girl. Come along if you like."

Miss Withers liked. She followed him into the outer office and through a door marked "Arthur Reese, Private." The Inspector, introduced her as his stenographer.

Reese burst out, a little breathlessly, with, "What a thing to happen—here! I came down as soon as I heard. What a—"

"What a thing to happen anywhere," Miss Withers said under her breath.

"Poor little Margie!" finished the man at the desk.

Piper grew suddenly Inspectorish. "Margie, eh? You knew her quite well, then?"

"Of course!" Reese was as open as a book. "She's been hounding the life out of me for months because I have the reputation of sometimes publishing songs by beginners. But what could I do? She had more ambition than ability. . . ."

"You didn't know her personally, then?"

Reese shook his head. "Naturally, I took a friendly interest in her, but anyone in my office will tell you that I never run around with would-be songwriters. It would make things too difficult. Somebody is always trying to take advantage of friendship, you know."

"When did you last see the Thorens girl?" Piper cut in.

Reese turned and looked out of the window. "I am very much afraid," he said, "that I was the last person to see her alive. If I had only known . . ."

"Get this, Hildegarde!" commanded Piper.

"I am and shall," she came back:

"Several weeks ago," began Reese, "Margie Thorens submitted to me a song called 'Tennessee Sweetheart,' in manuscript form. It was her fifth or sixth attempt, but it was a lousy—I beg your pardon, a terrible song. Couldn't publish it. Last night she came in, and I gave her the bad news. Made it as easy as I could, but she looked pretty disappointed. I had to rush off and leave her, as I had an appointment for five thirty with Larry Foley, the radio crooner. So I saw her last in the reception room where she died—it must have been five thirty or a little earlier."

Miss Withers whispered to the Inspector. "Oh," said he, "how did you know that the Thorens girl died in the reception room?"

"I didn't," admitted Reese calmly. "I guessed it. You haven't got that cop standing guard at the broken door for exercise. Anyway, I was a few minutes late for my date because of the rain, but I met Foley at about twenty to six. He'll testify to that, and fifty others."

Piper nodded. He took a glittering gadget from his pocket. "Can you identify this, Mr. Reese?"

Reese studied the watch. "On first glance, I should say that it was Margie's. But I wouldn't know . . ."

"You wouldn't know, then, if it was usually on time?"

Reese was thoughtful. "Of course I wouldn't. But Margie was usually on time, if that is anything. I said when she phoned me yesterday morning that I'd see her if she came in at quarter to five, and on the dot she arrived. I was busy, and she had to wait."

The Inspector started to put the watch back into its envelope, but Miss Withers held out her hand. She wrinkled her brows above it, as the Inspector put his last question.

"You don't know, then, anything about any private love affairs Miss Thorens might have had?"

"Absolutely not. I don't even know where she lived, or anything except that she came from somewhere upstate—Albany I think it was. One of her attempts at songwriting was titled 'Amble to Albany.' "

Piper and the music publisher walked slowly out of the office, toward where a wicker basket was being swiftly carried through a broken door by two brawny men in white. Miss Withers lingered behind to study the wrist watch which had been Margie Thorens'. It was a trumpery affair with a square modernistic face. Miss Withers found it hard to tell time by such a watch. She noted that the minute hand pointed to five before the hour, and that the hour hand was in the exactly opposite direction. She put it safely away, and hurried after the Inspector.

With the departure of the mortal remains of Margie Thorens, the offices of Arthur Reese and Company seemed to perk up a bit. The red-haired Miss Kelly returned to her desk outside Reese's office, wearing a dress which Miss Withers thought cut a bit too low in front for business purposes. The clerks and stenographers were permitted to fill the large room again, somewhere a man began to bang very loudly upon a piano, and an office boy rushed past Miss Withers with a stack of sheet music fresh from the printer's.

"Well, we'll be off," said the Inspector suddenly, in her ear.

Miss Hildegarde Withers jumped. "Eh? Well what?"

"We'll leave. This case is plain as the nose—I mean, plain as day. Nothing here for the Homicide Squad."

"Naturally," said Miss Withers. But her thoughts were somewhere else.

The Inspector had learned to heed her suggestions. "Anything wrong? You haven't found anything that I've missed, have you?"

Hildegarde Withers shook her head. "That's just the trouble," she said. "I'm beginning to suspect myself of senility."

"Tell me," said Miss Withers that evening, "just what are the clues which spell suicide so surely?"

"First, the locked door to insure privacy," said the Inspector. "Second, the suicide note, for it's human nature to leave word behind. Third, the motive—in this case, melancholy. Fourth, the suicide must be an emotional, neurotic person. Get me?"

"Clear as crystal," said Hildegarde Withers. "But granted that a girl chooses to die in darkness, why does she write a suicide note in darkness? And why does she bend a pencil?"

"But the pencil wasn't bent!"

"Exactly!" said Hildegarde Withers, thoughtfully.

To all intents and purposes, that ended the Thorens case. Inspector Oscar Piper turned his attention to weightier matters. Medical Examiner Bloom reported, on completion of the autopsy, that the deceased had met death at her own hands through taking a lethal dose of cyanide of potassium, probably obtained in a college or high school laboratory, or perhaps from a commercial orchard spray.

Miss Hildegarde Withers attended to her usual duties down at

Jefferson School, and somewhere in the back of her mind a constant buzzing continued to bother her. The good lady was honestly bewildered by her own stubbornness. It was perfectly possible that the obvious explanation was the true one. For the life of her she could think of no other that fit even some of the known facts. And yet—

On Tuesday, the fourth day after the death of Margie Thorens, Miss Withers telephoned to Inspector Piper, demanding further information. "Ask Max Van Donnen how long the girl could have lived after taking the poison, will you?"

But the old German laboratory expert had not analyzed the remains, said Piper. Dr. Bloom had summarized the findings of the autopsy—and Margie Thorens had died an instant death. In her vital organs was a full grain of cyanide of potassium, one of the quickest known poisons.

"She couldn't have taken the poison and then written the note?" asked Miss Withers.

"Impossible," said the Inspector. "But what in the name of—"

Miss Withers had hung up. Again she had struck a stone wall. But too many stone walls were in themselves proof that something was a little wrong in this whole business.

That afternoon Miss Withers called upon a Mrs. Blenkinsop, the landlady who operated the rooming house in which Margie Thorens had lived. She found that lady fat, dingy, and sympathetic.

"I read in the papers that the poor darling is to be sent home to her aunt in Albany, and that her class is to be let out of high school to be honorary pallbearers," said Mrs. Blenkinsop. "Such a quiet one she was, the poor child. But it's them that runs deep."

Miss Withers agreed to this.

"Do you suppose I could see her rooms?"

"Of course," agreed the landlady. "Everything is just as she left it, because her rent was paid till the end of April, and that's a week yet." She led the way up a flight of stairs. "You know, the strangest thing, about the whole business was her going off and making no provision for her pets. You'd a thought—"

"Pets?"

The landlady threw open a door. "Yes'm. A fine tortoise shell cat, and a bird. A happy family if ever I saw one. I guess Miss Thorens was lonesome here in the city, and she gave all her love to them. Feed and water 'em I've done ever since I heard the news . . ." She snapped her fat fingers as they came into a dark, bare room furnished with little more than the bare necessities of life. It was both bedroom and sitting room, with the kitchenette in a closet and a bath across the hall. One large window looked out upon bare rooftops. One glance told Miss Withers that the room existed only for the rented grand piano which stood near the window.

Mrs. Blenkinsop snapped her fingers again, and a rangy, half grown cat arose from the bed and stretched itself. "Nice Pussy," said Mrs. Blenkinsop.

Pussy refused to be patted, and as soon as she had made sure that neither visitor carried food she returned to her post on the pillow. Both great amber eyes were staring up at the gilt cage which hung above the piano, in the full light of the window. Inside the cage was a small yellow canary, who eyed the intruders balefully and muttered, "Cheep, cheep."

"I've got no instructions about her things, poor darling," said the landlady. "I suppose they'll want me to pack what few clothes she had. If nobody wants Pussy, I'll keep her, for there's mice in the basement. I don't know what to do with the bird, for I hate the dratted things. I got a radio, anyhow. . . ."

The woman ran on interminably. Miss Withers listened carefully, but she soon saw that Mrs. Blenkinsop knew less about Margie Thorens than she did herself. The woman was sure, she insisted, that Margie had never had men callers in her room.

More than anything, Miss Withers wanted to look around, though she knew the police had done a routine job already. She wondered if she must descend to the old dodge of the fainting spell and the request for a glass of water, but she was saved from it by a ring at the bell downstairs.

"I won't be a minute," promised Mrs. Blenkinsop. She hastened out of the door. Miss Withers made a hurried search of bureau drawers, of the little desk, the music on the piano . . . and found nothing that gave her an inkling. There were reams of music paper, five or six rejected songs in manuscript form . . . that was the total. The room had no character.

Miss Withers sat down at the piano and struck a chord. If only this instrument, Margie's one outlet in the big city, could speak! There was a secret here somewhere . . . for the understanding eye and heart to discover. Miss Withers let her fingers ramble over the keys, in the few simple chords she knew. And then the canary burst into song!

"Dickie!" said the school teacher. "You surprise me." All canaries are named Dickie, and none of them know it. The bird sang on, improvising, trilling, swinging gaily by its tiny talons from the bottom of its trapeze. Miss Withers realized that there was a rare singer indeed. Her appreciation was shared by Pussy, who dug shining claws into the cover of the bed and narrowed his amber eyes. The song went on and on. . . .

Miss Withers thought of something. She had once read that the key to a person's character lies in the litter which accumulates beneath the paper in his bureau drawers. She hurried back to the bureau, and explored again. She found two dance programs, a stub of pencil, pins, a button, and a smashed cigarette, beneath the lining.

She was about to replace the paper when she heard someone ascending the stairs. That would be Mrs. Blenkinsop. Hastily she jammed the wearing apparel back in the drawer, and thrust the folded newspaper which had lined it into her handbag. When the door opened she was talking to the still twittering canary.

She took her departure as soon as she could, leaving Mrs. Blenkinsop completely in the dark as to the reasons for her call. "I hope you're not from a tabloid," said the landlady. "I don't want my house to get a bad name. . . ."

Down the street Miss Withers paused to take the bulky folded newspaper from her bag. But she didn't throw it away. It was a feature story clipped from the "scandal sheet" of a Sunday paper—a story which dealt with the secrets behind some of America's song hits, how they were adapted from classics, revamped every ten years and put out under new names, together with photographs of famous songwriters.

But the subject of the story was not what attracted Miss Withers' eagle eye. Across the top margin of the paper a rubber stamp had placed the legend—"With the compliments of the Hotel Rex—America's Riviera—Boardwalk."

"Dr. Bloom? This is Hildegarde Withers. Yes, Withers. I have a very delicate question to ask you, doctor. In making your autopsy of the Thorens girl's body, did you happen to notice whether or not she was—er, enceinte? It is very important, doctor, or I wouldn't bother you. If you say yes, it will turn suicide into murder."

"I say no," said crusty Dr. Bloom. *"I did and she wasn't."* And that was the highest stone wall of all for Hildegarde Withers.

"Where in heaven's name have you been hiding yourself?" inquired the Inspector when Miss Withers entered his office on Friday of that week after the death of Margie Thorens.

"I've been cutting classes," she said calmly. "A substitute is enduring my troop of hellions, and I'm doing scientific research."

"Yeah? And in what direction?" The Inspector was in a jovial mood, due to the fact that both his Commissioner and the leading gangster of the city were out of town—not together, but still far enough out of town to insure relative peace and quiet to New York City.

"I'm an expert locksmith," Miss Withers told him. "I've spent three hours learning something about poisons from Max Van Donnen, who has forgotten more than the Medical Examiner ever knew!

He says you can't swallow a lethal dose of cyanide without dying before it gets to the stomach—*unless it's in a capsule.*"

"You're not still hopped up about the Thorens suicide?" The Inspector was very amused. "Why, that's the clearest, open and shut case . . ."

"Oscar, did you ever hear of a murder without the ghost of a motive?"

He shook his head. "Doesn't exist," he told her. She nodded slowly. "See you later," she said.

Miss Withers rode uptown on the subway, crossed over to Times Square, and came into the offices of Arthur Reese, Music Publisher.

The red-headed Miss Kelly looked up with a bright smile. "Mr. Reese is very busy just now," she said. Miss Withers took a chair, and stared around the long office. It was a scene of redoubled activity since her last visit, with vaudevillians, song pluggers, office boys and radio artists rushing hither and yon. On the wall opposite her was an enlargement in colors of the cover of the new song, "May Day"—by Art Reese. On every desk and table were stacks of copies of the new song, "May Day."

"So Mr. Reese is a composer as well as a publisher?" Miss Withers asked conversationally.

Miss Kelly was in a friendly mood. "Oh, yes! You know, he wrote that big hit, 'Sunny Jim,' which is how he got started in the music business. Of course, that was before I came here. . . ."

"When was it?" asked Miss Withers.

"Two years ago, at least. But 'May Day' is going to be a bigger hit than any of them. It's going to be the sensation of the season. All the crooners want it, and the contracts for records are being signed this week."

Miss Withers nodded. "There's a lot of money in writing a song, isn't there?"

"A hit—oh, yes. Berlin made a quarter of a million out of 'Russian Lullaby.'" Miss Kelly had to raise her voice, as a dozen pianos in a dozen booths were clashing out lilting, catchy music. A door opened somewhere, and Miss Withers heard a sister team warbling soft, close-harmony . . . "I met you on a May day, a wonderful okay day, and that was my hey-hey day . . . a day I can't forget. . . ."

"It's published the first of May," Miss Kelly went on chattily. "And that's why Mr. Reese is so busy. He's got to go out of town this afternoon, and I'm afraid he won't be able to see you today without an appointment."

"Eh?" Miss Withers started. "Yes, of course. No, he won't. I mean . . . I mean . . ." She rose suddenly to her feet, humming the lilting music of "May Day." It was familiar, hauntingly familiar. Of course, she had read of how popular tunes were stolen. And yet—suddenly the mists cleared and she knew. Knew where she had heard those first few bars of music—knew what the meaning of it all must be—knew the answer to the riddle. She turned and walked swiftly from the room.

She rode down in the elevator somehow, and stumbled out of it into the main hall. There she stopped short. She could waste no energy in walking. Every ounce of her strength was needed to think with. The whole puzzle was assembling itself in her mind—all the hundred odd and varied bits flying into place. Everything—

She stood there for a long time, wondering what to do. Should she do anything? Wasn't it better to let well enough alone? Nobody would believe her, not even Oscar Piper. Certainly not Oscar Piper.

She stood there until one o'clock struck, and the hall was filled with luncheon-bound clerks and stenographers. Her head was aching and her hands were icy-cold. There was a glitter in her eyes, and her nostrils were extraordinarily wide.

Miss Withers was about to move on when she stopped, frozen into immobility. She saw the elevator descend, saw the doors open . . . and out stepped the plump, red-haired Miss Kelly.

She was laughing up into the face of Arthur Reese. Reese was talking, softly yet clearly, oblivious of everything except the warm and desirable girl who smiled at him. . . .

Miss Withers pressed closer, and caught one sentence—one only. "You'll be crazy about the American Riviera. . . ." he was promising.

Then they were gone.

Miss Withers had three nickels. She made three phone calls. The first was to Penn Station, the second to Mrs. Blenkinsop, and the third to Spring 7-3100. She asked for Inspector Piper.

"Quick!" she cried. "Oscar, I've got it! The Thorens suicide wasn't—I mean! It was murder!"

"Who?" asked Piper sensibly.

"Reese, of course," she snapped. "I want you to arrest him quick . . ."

"But the locked door?"

Miss Withers said she could duplicate that trick, given a knife and the peculiar type of lock that Reese had installed on his music reception room.

"But the suicide note?"

Miss Withers gave as her opinion that it was dictated, judging by the spaces between words and the corrections made by the writer.

"But—but, Hildegarde, you can't force a person to take poison!"

Miss Withers said you could give them poison under the guise of something more innocent.

"You're still crazy," insisted the Inspector. "Why—"

Miss Withers knew what he was thinking. "The alibi? Well, Oscar, the murder was committed at a time when Reese was still in his office, which explains the daylight. He smashed the girl's watch, and then set the hands ahead. But you didn't have sense enough to know that with the minute hand at five of six, the hour hand cannot naturally be exactly opposite! Particles of glass interfered, and the hands of her watch were at an impossible angle!"

Piper had one last shot in his locker. "But the motive?"

"I can't explain, and the train leaves in twenty minutes!" Miss Withers was a bit hysterical. "She's a nice girl, Oscar, even if she has platinum fingernails. She mustn't go with him, I tell you. If they get out of the state, it means extradition and God knows what—it'll be too late . . ."

"Take an aspirin and go to bed," said the Inspector kindly. "You're too wrought up over this. My dear woman . . ." He got the receiver crashed in his ear.

Mr. Arthur Reese was out to enjoy a pleasant weekend. The first balmy spring weather of the year had come, aptly enough, on the heels of his first happy week in many a month. To have 'May Day' showing such excellent signs of becoming a hit upon publication day was almost too much.

He made no mistakes. He did not try to kiss Kelly in the taxi, not even after they had picked up her suitcase and were approaching Penn Station.

There would be time enough for that later.

"This trip, is partly pleasure as well as business," he said to Miss Kelly. "We both need a rest after everything that's happened this week—and I want you to play with me a little. Call me Art. . . ."

"Sure," said Kelly. "You can call me Gladys, too. But I like Kelly better." She snuggled a little closer to her employer. "Gee, this is thrilling," she said. "I've never been to Atlantic City even—let alone with a man and adjoining rooms and everything . . . what my mother would say!"

"Very few people would understand about things like this," said Reese comfortably. "About how a man and a girl can have a little adventure together like this—really modern. . . ."

"If you say so," said Kelly, "it's true. You know I've had a crush on you ever since I came to work for you, Mr. Reese—Art. . . ."

"Sure," he said. "And I'm crazy about you, too." He paused, and his eyes very imperceptibly narrowed. "How old are you, Kelly?"

"Twenty," she said wonderingly. "Why?"

"Nice age, twenty," said Reese, taking a deep breath. "Well, Kelly—here we are."

Reese had a stateroom on the Atlantic City Special, and Kelly was naturally pleased and excited by that. She was greener than he had thought. Well, he owed this to himself, Reese thought. A sort of reward after a hard week. It was a week ago today that—

"What are you thinking of?" asked Kelly. "You look so mad."

"Business." Reese told her. He took a hammered silver flask from his pocket. "How about a stiff one?" She shook her head, and then gave in.

He took a longer one, because he needed it even worse than Kelly. Then he took her hungrily in his arms. "I mustn't let him know how green I am," thought Kelly.

The door opened, and they sprang apart.

A middle-aged, fussy school teacher was coming into the stateroom. Both Kelly and Reese thought her vaguely familiar, but the world is full of thinnish elderly spinsters.

"This is a private stateroom," blurted Reese.

"Excuse me," said Hildegarde Withers. When she spoke, they knew who she was.

She neither advanced nor retreated. She had a feeling that she had taken hold of a tiger's tail and couldn't let go.

"Don't go with him," she said to Kelly. "You don't know what you're doing."

Kelly, very naturally, said, "Why don't you mind your own business?"

"I am," said Miss Withers. She shut the door behind her. "This man is a murderer, with blood on his hands."

Kelly looked at Reese's hands. They had no red upon them, but they were moving convulsively.

"He poisoned Margie Thorens," said Miss Withers conversationally. "He probably will poison you, too, in one way or another."

"She's stark mad," said Arthur Reese nervously. "Stark, staring mad!" He rose to his feet and advanced. "Get out of here," he said. "You don't know what you're saying. . . ."

"Be quiet," Miss Withers told him. "Young lady, are you going to follow my advice? I tell you that Margie Thorens once took a weekend trip with this man to Atlantic City—America's Riviera—and she's having her high school class as honorary pallbearers as a result of it."

"Will you go?" cried Reese.

"I will not." There was a lurch of the car as the train got under way. Shouts of "all aboard" rang down the platform. "This man is going to be arrested at the other end of the line—arrested for murdering Margie Thorens by giving her poison and then dictating a suicide note to her as—"

Reese moved rather too quickly for Miss Withers to scream. She had counted on screaming, but his hands caught her throat. They closed, terribly. . . .

The murderer had only one thought, and that was to silence forever that sharp, accusing voice. He was rather well on to succeeding when he heard a clear soprano in his ear. "Stop! Stop hurting her, I tell you!"

He pressed the tighter as the train got really under way. And then Kelly hit him in the face with his own flask. She hit him again.

Reese choked, caught the flask and flung it wildly through the window, and dropped his victim. He was swearing horribly, in a low and expressionless voice. He shoved Kelly aside, stepped over Miss Withers, and tore out into the corridor. The porter was standing there, worried and a little scared about the sounds he had heard. Reese threw him aside and trampled on him. He fought his way to the vestibule, and found that a blue-clad conductor was just closing up the doors.

Reese knocked him down, and leaped for the end of the platform.

One foot plunged into the recess between train and platform, and his hands clawed at the air. He fell sidewise, struck a wooden partition which bounded the platform, and scrambled forward.

He leaped to his feet. He was free! It would take a minute for the train to stop. He whirled and ran back along the platform. . . .

He knocked over a child, kicked a dog savagely because its leash almost tripped him, and flung men and women out of his way. The train was stopping with a hissing of air brakes. He ran faster. . . .

He saw his way cleared, except for a smallish middle-aged man in a gray suit who was hurrying down the stairs—a man who blinked stupidly at him. Arthur Reese knocked him aside—and was then very deftly flung forward in a double somersault. Deft hands caught his arm, and raised it to the back of his neck, excruciatingly.

"What's all this?" said Inspector Oscar Piper. "What's your blasted hurry?"

Miss Withers came to life to find a porter splashing water in her face, and red-haired Miss Kelly praying unashamed. The train had stopped. "I'm all right," she said. "But where did he go—he got away!"

They came out on the platform to find the Inspector sitting on his captive. "This was the only train that left any station in twenty minutes," said Piper. "I changed my mind and thought I'd better rally around."

An hour or so later Miss Withers sat in an armchair, surrounded by the grim exhibits which line the walls of the Inspector's office in Center Street. She still felt seedy, but not too seedy to outline her deductions as to the manner in which Reese had committed the "suicide" of Margie Thorens. One by one she checked off the points. "I knew that a girl who had a fountain pen in her handbag wouldn't use a pencil to write something unless it was given to her," she said. "It wasn't her own, because it was too long to fit into the bag, unless it miraculously bent. From then on the truth came slowly but surely . . ."

"But the motive!" insisted Piper. "We've got to have a motive. I've got Reese detained downstairs, but we can't book him without a motive."

Miss Withers nodded. Then—"Did a woman come down to see you, a Mrs. Blenkinsop?"

The Inspector shook his head. "No—wait a minute. She came

and went again. But she left a package for you with the desk lieutenant. . . ."

"Good enough," said Miss Withers. "If you'll call Reese in here I'll produce the motive."

Arthur Reese, strangely enough, came quietly and pleasantly, with a smile on his face.

There was an officer on either side, but Piper had them go outside the door.

"I'm sorry, madam," said Reese when he saw Miss Withers. "But I lost my head when you said those terrible things. I didn't know what I was doing. If I'd realized that you were a policewoman. . . ."

"You're under arrest for the murder of Margie Thorens," cut in Piper. "Under the law, you may make a confession but you may not make a plea of guilty to a charge of murder. . . ."

"Guilty? But I'm not guilty! This woman here may have made a lot of wild guesses as to how I might have killed Margie Thorens, but man alive—where's my motive? Just because I made love to her months ago . . ."

"And took her to Atlantic City—before she was eighteen," cut in Miss Withers. "That gave her a hold over you, for she was under the age of consent. Being an ambitious and precocious little thing, she tried desperately to blackmail you into publishing one of her songs. And then you found that she had accidently struck a masterpiece of popular jingles—this famous 'May Day.' So you took the song, and made it your own property by removing Margie. She wrote 'May Day'—not you! That's your motive!"

Reese shook his head. "You haven't got any proof," he said confidently. "Where's one witness? That's all I ask! Just one—"

"Here's the one," said Hildegarde Withers calmly. From behind the desk she took up a paper-wrapped bundle. Stripping the newspapers away, she brought out a gilt cage, in which a small yellow bird blinked and muttered indignantly.

Miss Withers put it on the desk. "That was Margie Thorens' family," she said. "One of her only two companions in the long days and nights she spent, a bewildered little girl, trying to make a name for herself in an adult's world." She clucked to the little bird, and then, as the ruffled feathers subsided, Miss Withers began to whistle. Over and over again she whistled the first bar of the unpublished song hit, "May Day."

"I met you on a May day. . . ."

"Who-whew whew-whee whee whee," continued Dickie happily, swelling his throat. On through the second, through the third bar. . . . The Inspector gripped the table top.

"Reese, you said yourself that you never called on Miss Thorens and never knew where she lived," said Hildegarde Withers triumphantly. "Then I wish you'd tell me how her canary learned the chorus of your unpublished song hit!"

Arthur Reese started to say something, but there was nothing to say. "I talked to a pet store man this morning," said Miss Withers, "and he said that it's perfectly possible to teach a clever canary any tune, provided he hears it over and over and over. Well, Dickie here is first witness for the prosecution!" Arthur Reese's shrill hysterical laughter drowned out anything else she might have said. He was dragged away, while the canary still whistled.

"I'm going to keep him," said Miss Withers impulsively. She did keep Dickie, for several months, only giving him away to Mrs. Macfarland, wife of the Principal, when she learned that he would never learn any other tune but "May Day." . . .

It was December when Inspector Oscar Piper received an official communication. "You are invited to attend, as a witness for the State of New York, the execution of Arthur Reese at midnight, January 7th. . . . Sing Sing, Ossining, New York per L. E. I."

"With pleasure," said the Inspector.

THE HOUSE OF HAUNTS
Ellery Queen

While it may be unfair to some other very good writers, it would be hard to argue with Anthony Boucher when he declared that "Ellery Queen *is* the American detective story."

In what remains one of the most brilliant marketing decisions of all time, the two Brooklyn cousins who collaborated under the pseudonym Ellery Queen, Frederic Dannay (born Daniel Nathan) (1905-1982) and Manfred B(ennington) Lee (born Manford Lepofsky) (1905-1971), also named their detective Ellery Queen. They reasoned that if readers forgot the name of the author, *or* the name of the character, they might remember the other. It worked, as Ellery Queen is counted among the handful of best known names in the history of mystery fiction.

Lee was a full collaborator on the fiction created as Ellery Queen, but Dannay on his own was also one of the most important figures in the mystery world. He founded *Ellery Queen's Mystery Magazine* in 1941 and it remains, more than seventy years later, the most significant periodical in the genre. He also formed one of the first great collections of detective fiction first editions, the rare contents leading to reprinted stories in the magazines and anthologies he edited, which are among the best ever produced, most notably *101 Years' Entertainment* (1941), which gets my vote as the greatest mystery anthology ever published. He also produced such landmark reference books as *Queen's Quorum* (1951), a listing and appreciation of the 106 (later expanded to 125) most important short story collections in the genre, and *The Detective Short Story* (1942), a bibliography of all the collections Dannay had identified up to the publication date. More than a dozen movies were based on Queen books, there were several radio and television shows as well as comics; it was not far-fetched to describe the ubiquitous Ellery Queen in the 1930s, 1940s and 1950s as the personification of the American detective story.

"The House of Haunts" was first published in the February 1935 issue of *American Magazine*; it was retitled "The Lamp of God" when it was collected in *The New Adventures of Ellery Queen* (New York, Stokes, 1940). It was also published in 1951 as a single story by Dell in its short-lived ten cent series.

The House of Haunts
Ellery Queen

I

IF A story began: "Once upon a time in a house cowering in wilderness there lived an old and eremitical creature named Mayhew, a crazy man who had buried two wives and lived a life of death; and this house was known as 'The Black House'"—if a story began in this fashion, it would strike no one as especially remarkable. There are people like that who live in houses like that, and very often mysteries materialize like ectoplasm about their wild-eyed heads.

Now however disorderly Mr. Ellery Queen may be by habit, mentally he is an orderly person. His neckties and shoes may be strewn about his bedroom helter-skelter, but inside his skull hums a perfectly oiled machine, functioning as neatly and inexorably as the planetary system. So if there was a mystery about one Sylvester Mayhew, deceased, and his buried wives and gloomy dwelling, you may be sure the Queen brain would seize upon it and worry it and pick it apart and get it all laid out in neat and shiny rows.

Rationality, that was it. No esoteric mumbo jumbo could fool *that* fellow.

Lord, no! His two feet were planted solidly on God's good earth, and one and one made two—always—and that's all there was to that.

Of course, Macbeth had said that stones have been known to move and trees to speak; but, pshaw! for these literary fancies. In this day and age, with its Cominforms, its wars of peace and its rocketry experiments?

Nonsense! The truth is, Mr. Queen would have said, there is something about the harsh, cruel world we live in that's very rough on miracles.

Miracles just don't happen any more, unless they are miracles of stupidity or miracles of national avarice. Everyone with a grain of intelligence knows that.

"Oh, yes," Mr. Queen would have said; "there are yogis, voodoos, fakirs, shamans, and other tricksters from the effete East and primitive Africa, but nobody pays any attention to such pitiful monkeyshines—I mean, nobody with sense. This is a reasonable world and everything that happens in it must have a reasonable explanation."

You couldn't expect a sane person to believe, for example, that a three-dimensional, flesh-and-blood, veritable human being could suddenly stoop, grab his shoelaces, and fly away. Or that a water buffalo could change into a golden-haired little boy before your eyes. Or that a man dead one hundred and thirty-seven years could push aside his tombstone, step out of his grave, yawn, and then sing three verses of "Mademoiselle from Armentières." Or even, for that matter, that a stone could move or a tree speak—yea, though it were in the language of Atlantis or Mu.

Or . . . could you?

The tale of Sylvester Mayhew's house is a strange tale. When what happened happened, proper minds tottered on their foundations and porcelain beliefs threatened to shiver into shards. Before the whole fantastic and incomprehensible business was done, God Himself came into it. Yes, God came into the story of Sylvester Mayhew's house, and that is what makes it quite the most remarkable adventure in which Mr. Ellery Queen, that lean and indefatigable agnostic, has ever become involved.

The early mysteries in the Mayhew case were trivial—mysteries merely because certain pertinent facts were lacking; pleasantly provocative mysteries, but scarcely savorous of the supernatural.

Ellery was sprawled on the hearthrug before the hissing fire that raw January morning, debating with himself whether it was more desirable to brave the slippery streets and biting wind on a trip to Centre Street in quest of amusement, or to remain where he was in idleness but comfort, when the telephone rang.

It was Thorne on the wire. Ellery, who never thought of Thorne without perforce visualizing a human monolith—a long-limbed, gray-thatched male figure with marbled cheeks and agate eyes, the whole man coated with a veneer of ebony, was rather startled. Thorne was excited; every crack and blur in his voice spoke eloquently of emotion. It was the first time, to Ellery's recollection, that Thorne had betrayed the least evidence of human feeling.

"What's the matter?" Ellery demanded. "Nothing's wrong with Ann, I hope?" Ann was Thorne's wife.

"No, no." Thorne spoke hoarsely and rapidly, as if he had been running.

"Where the deuce have you been? I saw Ann only yesterday and she said she hadn't heard from you for almost a week. Of course, your wife's used to your preoccupation with those interminable legal affairs, but an absence of six days—"

"Listen to me, Queen, and don't hold me up. I must have your help. Can you meet me at Pier 54 in half an hour? That's North River."

"Of course."

Thorne mumbled something that sounded absurdly like: "Thank God!" and hurried on: "Pack a bag. For a couple of days. And a revolver. Especially a revolver, Queen."

"I see," said Ellery, not seeing at all.

"I'm meeting the Cunarder *Caronia*. Docking this morning. I'm with a man by the name of Reinach, Dr. Reinach. You're my colleague; get that? Act stern and omnipotent. Don't be friendly. Don't ask him—or me—questions. And don't allow yourself to be pumped. Understood?"

"Understood," said Ellery, "but not exactly clear. Anything else?"

"Call Ann for me. Give her my love and tell her I shan't be home for days yet, but that you're with me and that I'm all right. And ask her to telephone my office and explain matters to Crawford."

"Do you mean to say that not even your partner knows what you've been doing?"

But Thorne had hung up.

Ellery replaced the receiver, frowning. It was stranger than strange.

Thorne had always been a solid citizen, a successful attorney who led an impeccable private life and whose legal practice was dry and unexciting. To find old Thorne entangled in a web of mystery . . .

Ellery drew a happy breath, telephoned Mrs. Thorne, tried to sound reassuring, yelled for Djuna, hurled some clothes into a bag, loaded his .38 police revolver with a grimace, scribbled a note for Inspector Queen, dashed downstairs and jumped into the cab Djuna had summoned, and landed on Pier 54 with thirty seconds to spare.

There was something terribly wrong with Thorne, Ellery saw at once, even before he turned his attention to the vast fat man by the lawyer's side.

Thorne was shrunken within his Scotch-plaid greatcoat like a pupa which had died prematurely in its cocoon. He had aged years in the few weeks since Ellery had last seen him. His ordinarily sleek cobalt cheeks were covered with a straggly stubble. Even his clothing looked tired and uncared for. And there was a glitter of furtive relief in his bloodshot eyes as he pressed Ellery's hand that was, to one who knew Thorne's self-sufficiency and aplomb, almost pathetic.

But he merely remarked: "Oh, hello, there, Queen. We've a longer wait than we anticipated, I'm afraid. Want you to shake hands with Dr. Herbert Reinach. Doctor, this is Ellery Queen."

"'D'you do," said Ellery curtly, touching the man's immense gloved hand. If he was to be omnipotent, he thought, he might as well be rude, too.

"Surprise, Mr. Thorne?" said Dr. Reinach in the deepest voice Ellery had ever heard; it rumbled up from the caverns of his chest like the echo of thunder. His little purplish eyes were very, very cold.

"A pleasant one, I hope," said Thorne.

Ellery snatched a glance at his friend's face as he cupped his hands about a cigarette, and he read approval there. If he had struck the right tone, he knew how to act thenceforth. He flipped the match away and turned abruptly to Thorne. Dr. Reinach was studying him in a half puzzled, half amused way.

"Where's the *Caronia*?"

"Held up in quarantine," said Thorne. "Somebody's seriously ill aboard with some disease or other and there's been difficulty in clearing her passengers. It will take hours, I understand. Suppose we settle down in the waiting room for a bit."

They found places in the crowded room, and Ellery set his bag between his feet and disposed himself so that he was in a position to catch every expression on his companions' faces. There was something in Thorne's repressed excitement, an even more piquing aura enveloping the fat doctor, that violently whipped his curiosity.

"Alice," said Thorne in a casual tone, as if Ellery knew who Alice was, "is probably becoming impatient. But that's a family trait with the Mayhews, from the little I saw of old Sylvester. Eh, Doctor? It's trying, though, to come all the way from England only to be held up on the threshold."

So they were to meet an Alice Mayhew, thought Ellery, arriving from England on the *Caronia*. Good old Thorne! He almost chuckled aloud.

"Sylvester" was obviously a senior Mayhew, some relative of Alice's.

Dr. Reinach fixed his little eyes on Ellery's bag and rumbled politely: "Are you going away somewhere, Mr. Queen?"

Then Reinach did not know Ellery was to accompany them— wherever they were bound for.

Thorne stirred in the depths of his greatcoat, rustling like a sack of desiccated bones. "Queen's coming back with me, Dr. Reinach." There was something brittle and hostile in his voice.

The fat man blinked, his eyes buried beneath half moons of damp flesh.

"Really?" he said, and by contrast his bass voice was tender.

"Perhaps I should have explained," said Thorne abruptly. "Queen is a colleague of mine, Doctor. This case has interested him."

"Case?" said the fat man.

"Legally speaking. I really hadn't the heart to deny him the pleasure of helping me—ah—protect Alice Mayhew's interests. I trust you won't mind?"

This was a deadly game, Ellery became certain. Something important was at stake, and Thorne in his stubborn way was determined to defend it by force or guile.

Reinach's puffy lids dropped over his eyes as he folded his paws on his stomach. "Naturally, naturally not," he said in a hearty tone. "Only too happy to have you, Mr. Queen. A little unexpected, perhaps, but delightful surprises are as essential to life as to poetry. Eh?" And he chuckled.

Samuel Johnson, thought Ellery, recognizing the source of the doctor's remark. The physical analogy struck him. There was iron beneath those layers of fat and a good brain under that dolichocephalic skull. The man sat there on the waiting room bench like an octopus, lazy and inert and peculiarly indifferent to his surroundings. Indifference—that was it, thought Ellery! The man was a colossal remoteness, as vague and darkling as a storm cloud on an empty horizon.

Thorne said in a weary voice: "Suppose we have lunch. I'm famished."

By three in the afternoon Ellery felt old and worn. Several hours of nervous, cautious silence, threading his way smiling among treacherous shoals, had told him just enough to put him on guard. He often felt knotted-up and tight inside when a crisis loomed or danger threatened from an unknown quarter. Something extraordinary was going on.

As they stood on the pier watching the *Caronia*'s bulk being nudged alongside, he chewed on the scraps he had managed to glean during the long, heavy, pregnant hours. He knew definitely now that the man called Sylvester Mayhew was dead, that he had been pronounced paranoic, that his house was buried in an almost inaccessible wilderness on Long Island.

Alice Mayhew, somewhere on the decks of the *Caronia* doubtless straining her eyes pierward, was the dead man's daughter, parted from her father since childhood.

And he had placed the remarkable figure of Dr. Reinach in the puzzle.

The fat man was Sylvester Mayhew's half brother. He had also acted as Mayhew's physician during the old man's last illness. This illness and death seemed to have been very recent, for there had been some talk of "the funeral" in terms of fresh if detached sorrow. There was also a Mrs. Reinach glimmering unsubstantially in the background, and a queer old lady who was the dead man's sister. But what the mystery was, or why Thorne was so perturbed, Ellery could not figure out.

The liner tied up to the pier at last. Officials scampered about, whistles blew, gangplanks appeared, passengers disembarked in droves to the accompaniment of the usual howls and embraces.

Interest crept into Dr. Reinach's little eyes, and Thorne was shaking.

"There she is!" croaked the lawyer. "I'd know her anywhere from her photographs. That slender girl in the brown turban!"

As Thorne hurried away Ellery studied the girl eagerly. She was anxiously scanning the crowd, a tall charming creature with an elasticity of movement more aesthetic than athletic and a harmony of delicate feature that approached beauty. She was dressed so simply and inexpensively that he narrowed his eyes.

Thorne came back with her, patting her gloved hand and speaking quietly to her. Her face was alight and alive, and there was a natural gaiety in it which convinced Ellery that whatever mystery or tragedy lay before her, it was still unknown to her. At the same time there were certain signs about her eyes and mouth—fatigue, strain, worry, he could not put his finger on the exact cause—which puzzled him.

"I'm so glad," she murmured in a cultured voice, strongly British in accent. Then her face grew grave and she looked from Ellery to Dr. Reinach.

"This is your uncle, Miss Mayhew," said Thorne. "Dr. Reinach. This other gentleman is not, I regret to say, a relative. Mr. Ellery Queen, a colleague of mine."

"Oh," said the girl; and she turned to the fat man and said tremulously:

"Uncle Herbert. How terribly odd. I mean—I've felt so all alone. You've been just a legend to me, Uncle Herbert, you and Aunt Sarah and the rest, and now . . ." She choked a little as she put her arms about the fat man and kissed his pendulous cheek.

"My dear," said Dr. Reinach solemnly; and Ellery could have struck him for the Judas quality of his solemnity.

"But you must tell me everything! Father—how is Father? It seems so strange to be . . . to be saying that."

"Don't you think, Miss Mayhew," said the lawyer quickly, "that we had better see you through the Customs? It's growing late and we have a long trip before us. Long Island, you know."

"Island?" Her candid eyes widened. "That sounds so exciting!"

"Well, it's not what you might think—"

"Forgive me. I'm acting the perfect gawk." She smiled. "I'm entirely in your hands, Mr. Thorne. Your letter was more than kind."

As they made their way toward the Customs, Ellery dropped a little behind and devoted himself to watching Dr. Reinach. But that vast lunar countenance was as inscrutable as a gargoyle.

Dr. Reinach drove. It was not Thorne's car; Thorne had a regal new Lincoln limousine and this was a battered if serviceable old Buick sedan.

The girl's luggage was strapped to the back and sides; Ellery was puzzled by the scantness of it—three small suitcases and a tiny steamer trunk. Did these four pitiful containers hold all of her worldly possessions?

Sitting beside the fat man, Ellery strained his ears. He paid little attention to the road Reinach was taking.

The two behind were silent for a long time. Then Thorne cleared his throat with an oddly ominous finality. Ellery saw what was coming; he had often heard that throat-clearing sound emanate from the mouths of judges pronouncing sentence of doom.

"We have something sad to tell you, Miss Mayhew. You may as well learn it now."

"Sad?" murmured the girl after a moment. "Sad? Oh, it's not—"

"Your father," said Thorne inaudibly. "He's dead."

She cried: "Oh!" in a small helpless voice; and then she grew quiet.

"I'm dreadfully sorry to have to greet you with such news," said Thorne in the silence. "We'd anticipated. . . . And I realize how awkward it must be for you. After all, it's quite as if you had never known him at all. Love for a parent, I'm afraid, lies in direct ratio to the degree of childhood association. Without any association at all . . ."

"It's a shock, of course," Alice said in a muffled voice. "And yet, as you say, he was a stranger to me, a mere name. As I wrote you, I was only a toddler when Mother got her divorce and took me off to England. I don't remember Father at all. And I've not seen him since, or heard from him."

"Yes," muttered the attorney.

"I might have learned more about Father if Mother hadn't died when I was six; but she did, and my people—her people—in England . . . Uncle John died last fall. He was the last one. And then I was left all alone. When your letter came I was—I was so glad, Mr. Thorne. I didn't feel lonely any more. I was really happy for the first time in years. And now—" She broke off to stare out the window.

Dr. Reinach swiveled his massive head and smiled benignly. "But you're not alone, my dear. There's my unworthy self, and your Aunt Sarah, and Milly—Milly's my wife, Alice; naturally you wouldn't know anything about her—and there's even a husky young fellow named Keith who works about the place—bright lad who's come down in the world." He chuckled.

"So you see there won't be a dearth of companionship for you."

"Thank you, Uncle Herbert," she murmured. "I'm sure you're all terribly kind. Mr. Thorne, how did Father . . . When you replied to my letter you wrote me he was ill, but—"

"He fell into a coma unexpectedly nine days ago. You hadn't left England yet and I cabled you at your antique shop address. But somehow it missed you."

"I'd sold the shop by that time and was flying about, patching up things. When did he . . . die?"

"A week ago Thursday. The funeral . . . Well, we couldn't wait, you see. I might have caught you by cable or telephone on the *Caronia*, but I didn't have the heart to spoil your voyage."

"I don't know how to thank you for all the trouble you've taken."

Without looking at her Ellery knew there were tears in her eyes. "It's good to know that someone—"

"It's been hard for all of us," rumbled Dr. Reinach.

"Of course, Uncle Herbert. I'm sorry." She fell silent. When she spoke again, it was as if there were a compulsion expelling the words. "When Uncle John died, I didn't know where to reach Father. The only American address I had was yours, Mr. Thorne, which some patron or other had given me. It was the only thing I could think of. I was sure a solicitor could find Father for me. That's why I wrote to you in such detail, with photographs and all."

"Naturally we did what we could." Thorne seemed to be having difficulty with his voice. "When I found your father and went out to see him the first time and showed him your letter and photographs, he . . . I'm sure this will please you, Miss Mayhew. He wanted you badly. He'd apparently been having a hard time of late years—ah, mentally, emotionally. And so I wrote you at his request. On my second visit, the last time I saw him alive, when the question of the estate came up—"

Ellery thought that Dr. Reinach's paws tightened on the wheel. But the fat man's face bore the same bland, remote smile.

"Please," said Alice wearily. "Do you greatly mind, Mr. Thorne? I—I don't feel up to discussing such matters now."

The car was fleeing along the deserted road as if it were trying to run away from the weather. The sky was gray lead; a frowning, gloomy sky under which the countryside lay cowering. It was growing colder, too, in the dark and drafty tonneau; the cold seeped in through the cracks and their overclothes.

Ellery stamped his feet a little and twisted about to glance at Alice Mayhew. Her oval face was a glimmer in the murk; she was sitting stiffly, her hands clenched into tight little fists in her lap. Thorne was slumped miserably by her side, staring out the window.

"By George, it's going to snow," announced Dr. Reinach with a cheerful puff of his cheeks.

No one answered.

The drive was interminable. There was a dreary sameness about the landscape that matched the weather's mood. They had long since left the main highway to turn into a frightful byroad; along which they jolted in an unsteady eastward curve between ranks of leafless woods. The road was pitted and frozen hard; the woods were tangles of dead trees and underbrush densely packed but looking as if they had been repeatedly seared by fire.

The whole effect was one of widespread and oppressive desolation.

"Looks like No Man's Land," said Ellery at last from his bouncing seat beside Dr. Reinach. "And feels like it, too."

Dr. Reinach's cetaceous back heaved in a silent mirth. "Matter of fact, that's exactly what it's called by the natives. Land-God-forgot, eh? But then Sylvester always swore by the Greek unities."

The man seemed to live in a dark and silent cavern, out of which he maliciously emerged at intervals to poison the atmosphere.

"It isn't very inviting-looking, is it?" remarked Alice in a low voice. It was clear she was brooding over the strange old man who had lived in this wasteland, and of her mother who had fled from it so many years before.

"It wasn't always this way," said Dr. Reinach, swelling his cheeks like a bullfrog. "Once it was pleasant enough; I remember it as a boy. Then it seemed as if it might become the nucleus of a populous community. But progress has passed it by, and a couple of uncontrollable forest fires did the rest."

"It's horrible," murmured Alice, "simply horrible."

"My dear Alice, it's your innocence that speaks there. All life is a frantic struggle to paint a rosy veneer over the ugly realities. Why not be honest with yourself? Everything in this world is stinking rotten; worse than that, a bore. Hardly worth living, in any impartial analysis. But if you have to live, you may as well live in surroundings consistent with the rottenness of everything."

The old attorney stirred beside Alice, where he was buried in his greatcoat. "You're quite a philosopher, Doctor," he snarled.

"I'm an honest man."

"Do you know, Doctor," murmured Ellery, despite himself, "you're beginning to annoy me."

The fat man glanced at him. Then he said: "And do you agree with this mysterious friend of yours, Thorne?"

"I believe," snapped Thorne, "that there is a platitude extant which says that actions speak with considerably more volume than words. I haven't shaved for six days, and today has been the first time I left Sylvester Mayhew's house since his funeral."

"Mr. Thorne!" cried Alice, turning to him. "Why?"

The lawyer muttered: "I'm sorry, Miss Mayhew. All in good time, in good time."

"You wrong us all," smiled Dr. Reinach, deftly skirting a deep rut in the road. "And I'm afraid you're giving my niece quite the most erroneous impression of her family. We're odd, no doubt, and our blood is presumably turning sour after so many generations of cold storage; but then don't the finest vintages come from the deepest cellars? You've only to glance at Alice to see my point. Such vital loveliness could only have been produced by an old family."

"My mother," said Alice, with a faint loathing in her glance, "had something to do with that, Uncle Herbert."

"Your mother, my dear," replied the fat man, "was merely a contributory factor. You have the typical Mayhew features."

Alice did not reply. Her uncle, whom until today she had not seen, was an obscene enigma; the others, waiting for them at their destination, she had never seen at all, and she had no great hope that they would prove better. A livid streak ran through her father's family; he had been a paranoiac with delusions of persecution. The Aunt Sarah in the dark distance, her father's surviving sister, was apparently something of a character. As for Aunt Milly, Dr. Reinach's wife, whatever she might have been in the past, one had only to glance at Dr. Reinach to see what she undoubtedly was in the present.

Ellery felt prickles at the nape of his neck. The farther they penetrated this wilderness the less he liked the whole adventure. It smacked vaguely of a foreordained theatricalism, as if some hand of monstrous power were setting the stage for the first act of a colossal tragedy. . . . He shrugged this sophomoric foolishness off, settling deeper into his coat. It was queer enough, though. Even the lifelines of the most indigent community were missing; there were no telephone poles and, so far as he could detect, no electric cables. That meant candles. He detested candles.

The sun was behind them, leaving them. It was a feeble sun, shivering in the pallid cold. Feeble as it was, Ellery wished it would stay.

They crashed on and on, endlessly, shaken like dolls. The road kept lurching toward the east in a stubborn curve. The sky grew more and more leaden. The cold seeped deeper and deeper into their bones.

When Dr. Reinach finally rumbled: "Here we are," and steered the jolting car leftward off the road into a narrow, wretchedly graveled driveway, Ellery came to with a start of surprise and relief. So their journey was really over, he thought. Behind him he heard Thorne and Alice stirring; they must be thinking the same thing.

He roused himself, stamping his icy feet, looking about. The same desolate tangle of woods to either side of the byroad. He recalled now that they had not once left the main road nor crossed another road since turning off the highway. No chance, he thought grimly, to stray off this path to perdition.

Dr. Reinach twisted his fat neck and said: "Welcome home, Alice."

Alice murmured something incomprehensible; her face was buried to the eyes in the moth-eaten laprobe Reinach had flung over her. Ellery glanced sharply at the fat man; there had been a note of mockery, of derision, in that heavy rasping voice. But the face was smooth and damp and bland, as before.

Dr. Reinach ran the car up the driveway and brought it to a rest a little before, and between, two houses. These structures flanked the drive, standing side by side, separated by only the width of the drive, which led straight ahead to a ramshackle garage. Ellery caught a glimpse of Thorne's glittering Lincoln within its crumbling walls.

The three buildings huddled in a ragged clearing, surrounded by the tangle of woods, like three desert islands in an empty sea.

"That," said Dr. Reinach heartily, "is the ancestral mansion, Alice. To the left."

The house to the left was of stone; once gray, but now so tarnished by the elements and perhaps the ravages of fire that it was almost black. Its face was blotched and streaky, as if it had succumbed to an insensate leprosy.

Rising three stories, elaborately ornamented with stone flora and gargoyles, it was unmistakably Victorian in its architecture. The façade had a neglected, granular look that only the art of great age could have etched.

The whole structure appeared to have thrust its roots immovably into the forsaken landscape.

Ellery saw Alice Mayhew staring at it with a sort of speechless horror; it had nothing of the pleasant hoariness of old English mansions. It was simply old, old with the dreadful age of this seared and blasted countryside.

He cursed Thorne beneath his breath for subjecting the girl to such a shocking experience.

"Sylvester called it 'the Black House,'" said Dr. Reinach cheerfully as he turned off the ignition. "Not pretty, I admit, but as solid as the day it was built, seventy-five years ago."

"Black House," grunted Thorne. "Rubbish."

"Do you mean to say," whispered Alice, "that Father . . . Mother lived *here*?"

"Yes, my dear. Quaint name, eh, Thorne? Another illustration of Sylvester's preoccupation with the morbidly colorful. Built by your grandfather, Alice. The old gentleman built this one, too, later; I believe you'll find it considerably more habitable. Where the devil is everyone?"

He descended heavily and held the rear door open for his niece. Ellery Queen slipped down to the driveway on the other side and glanced about with the sharp, uneasy sniff of a wild animal. The old mansion's companion house was a much smaller and less pretentious dwelling, two stories high and built of an originally white stone which had turned gray.

The front door was shut and the curtains at the lower windows were drawn.

But there was a fire burning somewhere inside; he caught the tremulous glimmers. In the next moment they were blotted out by the head of an old woman, who pressed her face to one of the panes for a single instant and then vanished. But the door remained shut.

"You'll stop with us, of course," he heard the doctor say genially; and Ellery circled the car. His three companions were standing in the driveway, Alice pressed close to old Thorne as if for protection. "You won't want to sleep in the Black House, Alice. No one's there, it's in rather a mess; and a house of death, y'know . . ."

"Stop it," growled Thorne. "Can't you see the poor child is half dead from fright as it is? Are you trying to scare her away?"

"Scare me away?" repeated Alice, dazedly.

"Tut, tut," smiled the fat man. "Melodrama doesn't become you at all, Thorne. I'm a blunt old codger, Alice, but I mean well. It will really be more comfortable in the White House." He chuckled suddenly again.

"White House. That's what *I* named it to preserve a sort of atmospheric balance."

"There's something frightfully wrong here," said Alice in a tight voice.

"Mr. Thorne, what is it? There's been nothing but innuendo and concealed hostility since we met at the pier. And just why *did* you spend six days in Father's house after the funeral? I think I've a right to know."

Thorne licked his lips. "I shouldn't—"

"Come, come, my dear," said the fat man. "Are we to freeze here all day?"

Alice drew her thin coat more closely about her. "You're all being beastly. Would you mind, Uncle Herbert? I should like to see the inside—where Father and Mother . . ."

"I don't think so, Miss Mayhew," said Thorne hastily.

"Why not?" said Dr. Reinach tenderly, and he glanced once over his shoulder at the building he had called the White House. "She may as well do it now and get it over with. There's still light enough to see by. Then we'll go over, wash up, have a hot dinner, and you'll feel worlds better." He seized the girl's arm and marched her toward the dark building, across the dead, twig-strewn ground. "I believe," continued the doctor blandly, as they mounted the steps of the stone porch, "that Mr. Thorne has the keys."

The girl stood quietly waiting, her dark eyes studying the faces of the three men. The attorney was pale, but his lips were set in a stubborn line.

He did not reply. Taking a bunch of large rusty keys out of a pocket, he fitted one into the lock of the front door. It turned over with a creak. Then Thorne pushed open the door and they stepped into the house.

It was a tomb. It smelled of must and damp. The furniture, ponderous pieces which once no doubt had been regal, was uniformly dilapidated and dusty. The walls were peeling, showing broken, discolored laths beneath.

There was dirt and debris everywhere. It was inconceivable that a human being could once have inhabited this grubby den.

The girl stumbled about, her eyes a blank horror, Dr. Reinach steering her calmly. How long the tour of inspection lasted Ellery did not know; even to him, a stranger, the effect was so oppressive as to be almost unendurable.

They wandered about, silent, stepping over trash from room to room, impelled by something stronger than themselves.

Once Alice said in a strangled voice: "Uncle Herbert, didn't anyone . . . take care of Father? Didn't anyone ever clean up this horrible place?"

The fat man shrugged. "Your father had notions in his old age, my dear. There wasn't much anyone could do with him. Perhaps we had better not go into that."

The sour stench filled their nostrils. They blundered on, Thorne in the rear, watchful as an old cobra. His eyes never left Dr. Reinach's face.

On the middle floor they came upon a bedroom in which, according to the fat man, Sylvester Mayhew had died. The bed was unmade; indeed, the impress of the dead man's body on the mattress and tumbled sheets could still be discerned.

It was a bare and mean room, not as filthy as the others, but infinitely more depressing. Alice began to cough.

She coughed and coughed, hopelessly, standing still in the center of the room and staring at the dirty bed in which she had been born.

Then suddenly she stopped coughing and ran over to a lopsided bureau with one foot missing. A large, faded chromo was propped on its top against the yellowed wall. She looked at it for a long time without touching it. Then she took it down.

"It's Mother," she said slowly. "It's really Mother. I'm glad now I came. He did love her, after all. He's kept it all these years."

"Yes, Miss Mayhew," muttered Thorne. "I thought you'd like to have it."

"I've only one portrait of Mother, and that's a poor one. This— why, she was beautiful, wasn't she?"

She held the chromo up proudly, almost laughing in her hysteria. The time-dulled colors revealed a stately young woman with her hair worn high.

The features were piquant and regular. There was little resemblance between Alice and the woman in the picture.

"Your father," said Dr. Reinach with a sigh, "often spoke of your mother toward the last, and of her beauty."

"If he had left me nothing but this, it would have been worth the trip from England." Alice trembled a little. Then she hurried back to them, the chromo pressed to her breast. "Let's get out of here," she said in a shriller voice. "I—I don't like it here. It's ghastly. I'm . . . afraid."

They left the house with half running steps, as if someone were after them. The old lawyer turned the key in the lock of the front door with great care, glaring at Dr. Reinach's back as he did so. But the fat man had seized his niece's arm and was leading her across the driveway to the White House, whose windows were now flickeringly bright with light and whose front door stood wide open.

As they crunched along behind, Ellery said sharply to Thorne: "Thorne. Give me a clue. A hint. Anything. I'm completely in the dark."

Thorne's unshaven face was haggard in the setting sun. "Can't talk now," he muttered. "Suspect everything, everybody. I'll see you to-night, in your room. Or wherever they put you, if you're alone. . . . Queen, for God's sake, be careful!"

"Careful?" frowned Ellery.

"As if your life depended on it." Thorne's lips made a thin, grim line. "For all I know, it does."

Then they were crossing the threshold of the White House.

Ellery's impressions were curiously vague. Perhaps it was the effect of the sudden smothering heat after the hours of cramping cold outdoors; perhaps he thawed out too suddenly, and the heat went to his brain.

He stood about for a while in a state of almost semi-consciousness, basking in the waves of warmth that eddied from a roaring fire in a fireplace black with age. He was only dimly aware of the two people who greeted them, and of the interior of the house. The room was old, like everything else he had seen, and its furniture might have come from an antique shop.

They were standing in a large living room, comfortable enough; strange to his senses only because it was so old-fashioned in its appointments. There were actually antimacassars on the overstuffed chairs! A wide staircase with worn brass treads wound from one corner to the sleeping quarters above.

One of the two persons awaiting them was Mrs. Reinach, the doctor's wife. The moment Ellery saw her, even as she embraced Alice, he knew that this was inevitably the sort of woman the fat man would choose for a mate. She was a pale and wizened midge, almost fragile in her delicacy of bone and skin; and she was plainly in a silent convulsion of fear. She wore a hunted look on her dry and bluish face; and over Alice's shoulder she glanced timidly, with the fascinated obedience of a whipped bitch, at her husband.

"So, you're Aunt Milly," sighed Alice, pushing away. "You'll forgive me if I . . . It's all so very new to me."

"You must be exhausted, poor darling," said Mrs. Reinach in the chirping twitter of a bird; and Alice smiled wanly and looked grateful. "And I quite understand. After all, we're no more than strangers to you. Oh!" she said, and stopped. Her faded eyes were fixed on the chromo in the girl's hands.

"Oh," she said again. "I see you've been over to the other house *already.*"

"Of course she has," said the fat man; and his wife grew even paler at the sound of his bass voice. "Now, Alice, why don't you let Milly take you upstairs and get you comfortable?"

"I am rather done in," confessed Alice; and then she looked at her mother's picture and smiled again. "I suppose you think I'm very silly, dashing in this way with just—" She did not finish; instead, she went to the fireplace. There was a broad flame-darkened mantel above it, crowded with gewgaws of a vanished era. She set the chromo of the handsome Victorian-garbed woman among them. "There! Now I feel ever so much better."

"Gentlemen, gentlemen," said Dr. Reinach. "Please don't stand on ceremony. Nick! Make yourself useful. Miss Mayhew's bags are strapped to the car."

A gigantic young man, who had been leaning against the wall, nodded in a surly way. He was studying Alice Mayhew's face with a dark absorption. He went out.

"Who," murmured Alice, flushing, "is that?"

"Nick Keith." The fat man slipped off his coat and went to the fire to warm his flabby hands. "My morose protégé. You'll find him pleasant company, my dear, if you can pierce that thick defensive armor he wears. Does odd jobs about the place, as I believe I mentioned, but don't let that hold you back. This is a democratic country."

"I'm sure he's very nice. Would you excuse me? Aunt Milly, if you'd be kind enough to . . ."

The young man reappeared under a load of baggage, clumped across the living room, and plodded up the stairs. And suddenly, as if at a signal, Mrs. Reinach broke out into a noisy twittering and took Alice's arm and led her to the staircase. They disappeared after Keith.

"As a medical man," chuckled the fat man, taking their wraps and depositing them in a hall closet, "I prescribe a large dose of . . . this, gentlemen." He went to a sideboard and brought out a decanter of brandy.

"Very good for chilled bellies." He tossed off his own glass with an amazing facility, and in the light of the fire the finely etched capillaries in his bulbous nose stood out clearly. "Ah-h! One of life's major compensations. Warming, eh? And now I suppose you feel the need of a little sprucing up yourselves. Come along, and I'll show you to your rooms."

Ellery shook his head in a dogged way, trying to clear it. "There's something about your house, Doctor, that's unusually soporific. Thank you, I think both Thorne and I would appreciate a brisk wash."

"You'll find it brisk enough," said the fat man, shaking with silent laughter. "This is the forest primeval, you know. Not only haven't we any electric light or gas or telephone, but we've no running water, either. Well behind the house keeps us supplied. The simple life, eh? Better for you than the pampering influences of modern civilization. Our ancestors may have died more easily of bacterial infections, but I'll wager they had a greater body immunity to coryza! . . . Well, well, enough of this prattle. Up you go."

The chilly corridor upstairs made them shiver, but the very shiver revived them; Ellery felt better at once. Dr. Reinach, carrying candles and matches, showed Thorne into a room overlooking the front of the house, and Ellery into one on the side. A fire burned crisply in the large fireplace in one corner, and the basin on the old-fashioned washstand was filled with icy-looking water.

"Hope you find it comfortable," drawled the fat man, lounging in the doorway. "We were expecting only Thorne and my niece, but one more can always be accommodated. Ah—colleague of Thorne's, I believe he said?"

"Twice," replied Ellery. "If you don't mind—"

"Not at all." Reinach lingered, eyeing Ellery with a smile. Ellery shrugged, stripped off his coat, and made his ablutions. The water *was* cold; it nipped his fingers like the mouths of little fishes. He scrubbed his face vigorously.

"That's better," he said, drying himself. "Much. I wonder why I felt so peaked downstairs."

"Sudden contrast of heat after cold, no doubt." Dr. Reinach made no move to go.

Ellery shrugged again. He opened his bag with pointed nonchalance.

There, plainly revealed on his haberdashery, lay the .38 police revolver. He tossed it aside.

"Do you always carry a gun, Mr. Queen?" murmured Dr. Reinach.

"Always." Ellery picked up the revolver and slipped it into his hip pocket.

"Charming!" The fat man stroked his triple chin. "Charming. Well, Mr. Queen, if you'll excuse me I'll see how Thorne is getting on. Stubborn fellow, Thorne. He could have taken pot luck with us this past week, but he insisted on isolating himself in that filthy den next door."

"I wonder," murmured Ellery, "why."

Dr. Reinach eyed him. Then he said: "Come downstairs when you're ready. Mrs. Reinach has an excellent dinner prepared and if you're as hungry as I am, you'll appreciate it." Still smiling, the fat man vanished.

Ellery stood still for a moment, listening. He heard the fat man pause at the end of the corridor; a moment later the heavy tread was audible again, this time descending the stairs.

Ellery went swiftly to the door on tiptoe. He had noticed that the instant he had come into the room.

There was no lock. Where a lock had been there was a splintery hole, and the splinters had a newish look about them. Frowning, he placed a rickety chair against the doorknob and began to prowl.

He raised the mattress from the heavy wooden bedstead and poked beneath it, searching for he knew not what. He opened closets and drawers; he felt the worn carpet for wires.

But after ten minutes, angry with himself, he gave up and went to the window. The prospect was so dismal that he scowled in sheer misery. Just brown stripped woods and the leaden sky; the old mansion picturesquely known as the Black House was on the other side, invisible from this window.

A veiled sun was setting; a bank of storm clouds slipped aside for an instant and the brilliant rim of the sun shone directly into his eyes, making him see colored, dancing balls. Then other clouds, fat with snow, moved up and the sun slipped below the horizon. The room darkened rapidly.

Lock taken out, eh? Someone had worked fast. They could not have known he was coming, of course. Then someone must have seen him through the window as the car stopped in the drive. The old woman who had peered out for a moment? Ellery wondered where she was. At any rate, a few minutes' work by a skilled hand at the door . . . He wondered, too, if Thorne's door had been similarly mutilated. And Alice Mayhew's.

Thorne and Dr. Reinach were already seated before the fire when Ellery came down, and the fat man was rumbling: "Just as well. Give the poor girl a chance to return to normal. With the shock she's had today, it might be the finisher. I've told Mrs. Reinach to break it to Sarah gently. . . . Ah, Queen. Come over here and join us. We'll have dinner as soon as Alice comes down."

"Dr. Reinach was just apologizing," said Thorne casually, "for this Aunt Sarah of Miss Mayhew's—Mrs. Fell, Sylvester Mayhew's sister. The excitement of anticipating her niece's arrival seems to have been a bit too much for her."

"Indeed," said Ellery, sitting down and planting his feet on the nearest firedog.

"Fact is," said the fat man, "my poor half sister is cracked. The family paranoia. She's off-balance; not violent, you know, but it's wise to humor her. She isn't normal, and for Alice to see her—"

"Paranoia," said Ellery. "An unfortunate family, it seems. Your half brother Sylvester's weakness seems to have expressed itself in rubbish and solitude. What's Mrs. Fell's delusion?"

"Common enough—she thinks her daughter is still alive. As a matter of fact, poor Olivia was killed in an automobile accident three years ago. It shocked Sarah's maternal instinct out of plumb. Sarah's been looking forward to seeing Alice, her brother's daughter, and it may prove awkward. Never can tell how a diseased mind will react to an unusual situation."

"For that matter," drawled Ellery, "I should have said the same remark might be made about any mind, diseased or not."

Dr. Reinach laughed silently. Thorne, hunched by the fire, said: "This Keith boy."

The fat man set his glass down slowly. "Drink, Queen?"

"No, thank you."

"This Keith boy," said Thorne again.

"Eh? Oh, Nick. Yes, Thorne? What about him?"

The lawyer shrugged. Dr. Reinach picked up his glass again. "Am I imagining things, or is there the vaguest hint of hostility in the circumambient ether?"

"Reinach—" began Thorne harshly.

"Don't worry about Keith, Thorne. We let him pretty much alone. He's sour on the world, which demonstrates his good sense; but I'm afraid he's unlike me in that he hasn't the emotional buoyancy to rise above his wisdom. You'll probably find him anti-social. . . . Ah, there you are, my dear! Lovely, lovely."

Alice was wearing a different gown, a simple unfrilled frock, and she had freshened up. There was color in her cheeks and her eyes were sparkling with a light and tinge they had not had before. Seeing her for the first time without her hat and coat, Ellery thought she looked different, as all women contrive to look different divested of their outer clothing and refurbished by the mysterious activities which go on behind the closed doors of feminine dressing rooms. Apparently the ministrations of another woman, too, had cheered her; there were still rings under her eyes, but her smile was more cheerful.

"Thank you, Uncle Herbert." Her voice was slightly husky. "But I do think I've caught a nasty cold."

"Whiskey and hot lemonade," said the fat man promptly. "Eat lightly and go to bed early."

"To tell the truth, I'm famished."

"Then eat as much as you like. I'm one hell of a physician, as no doubt you've already detected. Shall we go in to dinner?"

"Yes," said Mrs. Reinach in a frightened voice. "We shan't wait for Sarah or Nicholas."

Alice's eyes dulled a little. Then she sighed and took the fat man's arm and they all trooped into the dining room.

Dinner was a failure. Dr. Reinach divided his energies between gargantuan inroads on the viands and copious drinking. Mrs. Reinach donned an apron and served, scarcely touching her own food in her haste to prepare the next course and clear the plates; apparently the household employed no domestic. Alice gradually lost her color, the old strained look reappearing on her face; occasionally she cleared her throat. The oil lamp on the table flickered badly, and every mouthful Ellery swallowed was flavored with the taste of oil. Besides, the *pièce de résistance* was curried lamb; if there was one dish he detested, it was lamb, and if there was one culinary style that sickened him, it was curry. Thorne ate stolidly, not raising his eyes from his plate.

As they returned to the living room the old lawyer managed to drop behind. He whispered to Alice: "Is everything all right? Are you?"

"I'm a little scarish, I think," she said quietly. "Mr. Thorne, please don't think me a child, but there's something so strange about—everything. . . . I wish now I hadn't come."

"I know," muttered Thorne. "And yet it was necessary, quite necessary. If there was any way to spare you this, I should have taken it. But you obviously couldn't stay in that horrible hole next door—"

"Oh, no," she shuddered.

"And there isn't a hotel for miles and miles. Miss Mayhew, has any of these people—"

"No, no. It's just that they're so strange to me. I suppose it's my imagination and this cold. Would you greatly mind if I went to bed? Tomorrow will be time enough to talk."

Thorne patted her hand. She smiled gratefully, murmured an apology, kissed Dr. Reinach's cheek, and went upstairs with Mrs. Reinach again.

They had just settled themselves before the fire again and were lighting cigarettes when feet stamped somewhere at the rear of the house.

"Must be Nick," wheezed the doctor. "Now where's *he* been?"

The gigantic young man appeared in the living room archway, glowering. His boots were soggy with wet. He growled, "Hello," in his surly manner and went to the fire to toast his big reddened hands. He paid no attention whatever to Thorne, although he glanced once, swiftly, at Ellery in passing.

"Where've you been, Nick? Go in and have your dinner."

"I ate before you came."

"What's been keeping you?"

"I've been hauling in firewood. Something you didn't think of doing."

Keith's tone was truculent, but, Ellery noticed that his hands were shaking. Damnably odd! His manner was noticeably not that of a servant, and yet he was apparently employed in a menial capacity. "It's snowing."

"Snowing?"

They crowded to the front windows. The night was moonless and palpable, and big fat snowflakes were sliding down the panes.

"Ah, snow," sighed Dr. Reinach; and for all the sigh there was something in his tone that made the nape of Ellery's neck prickle. " 'The whited air hides hills and woods, the river, and the heaven, and veils the farmhouse at the garden's end.' "

"You're quite the countryman, Doctor," said Ellery.

"I like Nature in her more turbulent moods. Spring is for milksops. Winter brings out the fundamental iron." The doctor slipped his arm about Keith's broad shoulders. "Smile, Nick. Isn't God in His heaven?"

Keith flung the arm off without replying.

"Oh, you haven't met Mr. Queen. Queen, this is Nick Keith. You know Mr. Thorne already." Keith nodded shortly. "Come, come, my boy, buck up. You're too emotional, that's the trouble with you. Let's all have a drink. The disease of nervousness is infectious."

Nerves! thought Ellery grimly. His nostrils were pinched, sniffing the little mysteries in the air. They tantalized him. Thorne was tied up in knots, as if he had cramps; the veins at his temples were pale blue swollen cords and there was sweat on his forehead. Above their heads the house was soundless. Dr. Reinach went to the sideboard and began hauling out bottles—gin, bitters, rye, vermouth. He busied himself mixing drinks, talking incessantly. There was a purr in his hoarse undertones, a vibration of pure excitement. What in Satan's name, thought Ellery in a sort of agony, was going on here?

Keith passed the cocktails around, and Ellery's eyes warned Thorne.

Thorne nodded slightly; they had two drinks apiece and refused more. Keith drank doggedly, as if he were anxious to forget something.

"Now that's better," said Dr. Reinach, settling his bulk into an easy chair.

"With the women out of the way and a fire and liquor, life becomes almost endurable."

"I'm afraid," said Thorne, "that I shall prove an unpleasant influence, Doctor. I'm going to make it unendurable."

Dr. Reinach blinked. "Well, now," he said. "Well, now." He pushed the brandy decanter carefully out of the way of his elbow and folded his pudgy paws on his stomach. His purple little eyes shone.

Thorne went to the fire and stood looking down at the flames, his back to them. "I'm here in Miss Mayhew's interests, Dr. Reinach," he said, without turning. "In her interests alone. Sylvester Mayhew died last week very suddenly. Died while waiting to see the daughter whom he hadn't seen since his divorce from her mother almost twenty years ago."

"Factually exact," rumbled the doctor, without stirring.

Thorne spun about. "Dr. Reinach, you acted as Mayhew's physician for over a year before his death. What was the matter with him?"

"A variety of things. Nothing extraordinary. He died of cerebral hemorrhage."

"So your certificate claimed." The lawyer leaned forward. "I'm not entirely convinced," he said slowly, "that your certificate told the truth."

The doctor stared at him for an instant, then he slapped his bulging thigh.

"Splendid!" he roared. "Splendid! a man after my own heart. Thorne, for all your desiccated exterior you have juicy potentialities." He turned on Ellery, beaming. "You heard that, Mr. Queen? Your friend openly accuses me of murder. This is becoming quite exhilarating. So! Old Reinach's a fratricide. What do you think of that, Nick? Your patron accused of cold-blooded murder. Dear, dear."

"That's ridiculous, Mr. Thorne," growled Nick Keith. "You don't believe it yourself."

The lawyer's gaunt cheeks sucked in. "Whether I believe it or not is immaterial. The possibility exists. But I'm more concerned with Alice Mayhew's interests at the moment than with a possible homicide. Sylvester Mayhew is dead, no matter by what agency—divine or human; but Alice Mayhew is very much alive."

"And so?" asked Reinach softly.

"And so I say," muttered Thorne, "it's damnably queer her father should have died when he did. Damnably."

For a long moment there was silence. Keith put his elbows on his knees and stared into the flames, his shaggy boyish hair over his eyes. Dr. Reinach sipped a glass of brandy with enjoyment.

Then he set his glass down and said with a sigh: "Life is too short, gentlemen, to waste in cautious skirmishings. Let us proceed without feinting movements to the major engagement. Nick Keith is in my confidence and we may speak freely before him." The young man did not move. "Mr. Queen, you're very much in the dark, aren't you?" went on the fat man with a bland smile.

Ellery did not move, either. "And how," he murmured, "did you know that?"

Reinach kept smiling. "Pshaw. Thorne hadn't left the Black House since Sylvester's funeral. Nor did he receive or send any mail during his self-imposed vigil last week. This morning he left me on the pier to telephone someone. You showed up shortly after. Since he was gone only a minute or two, it was obvious that he hadn't had time to tell you much, if anything. Allow me to felicitate you, Mr. Queen, upon your conduct today. It's been exemplary. An air of omniscience covering a profound and desperate ignorance."

Ellery removed his pince-nez and began to polish their lenses. "You're a psychologist as well as a physician, I see."

Thorne said abruptly: "This is all beside the point."

"No, no, it's all very much *to* the point," replied the fat man in a sad bass. "Now the canker annoying your friend, Mr. Queen—since it seems a shame to keep you on tenterhooks any longer—is roughly this: My half brother Sylvester, God rest his troubled soul, was a miser. If he'd been able to take his gold with him to the grave—with any assurance that it would remain there—I'm sure he would have done it."

"Gold?" asked Ellery, raising his brows.

"You may well titter, Mr. Queen. There was something medieval about Sylvester; you almost expected him to go about in a long black velvet gown muttering incantations in Latin. At any rate, unable to take his gold with him to the grave, he did the next best thing. He hid it."

"Oh, lord," said Ellery. "You'll be pulling clanking ghosts out of your hat next."

"Hid," beamed Dr. Reinach, "the filthy lucre in the Black House."

"And Miss Alice Mayhew?"

"Poor child, a victim of circumstances. Sylvester never thought of her until recently, when she wrote from London that her last maternal relative had died. Wrote to friend Thorne, he of the lean and hungry eye, who had been recommended by some friend as a trustworthy lawyer. As he is, as he is! You see, Alice didn't even know if her father was alive, let alone where he was. Thorne, good Samaritan, located us, gave Alice's exhaustive letters and photographs to Sylvester, and has acted as liaison officer ever since. And a downright circumspect one, too, by thunder!"

"This explanation is wholly unnecessary," said the lawyer stiffly. "Mr. Queen knows—"

"Nothing," smiled the fat man, "to judge by the attentiveness with which he's been following my little tale. Let's be intelligent about this, Thorne."

He turned to Ellery again, nodding very amiably. "Now, Mr. Queen, Sylvester clutched at the thought of his newfound daughter with the pertinacity of a drowning man clutching a life preserver. I betray no secret when I say that my half brother, in his paranoiac dotage, suspected his own family—imagine!—of having evil designs on his fortune."

"A monstrous slander, of course."

"Neatly put, neatly put! Well, Sylvester told Thorne in my presence that he had long since converted his fortune into specie, that he'd hidden this gold somewhere in the house next door, and that he wouldn't reveal the hiding place to anyone but Alice, his daughter, who was to be his sole heir. You see?"

"I see," said Ellery.

"He died before Alice's arrival, unfortunately. Is it any wonder, Mr. Queen, that Thorne thinks dire things of us?"

"This is fantastic," snapped Thorne, coloring. "Naturally, in the interests of my client, I couldn't leave the premises unguarded with that mass of gold lying about loose somewhere—"

"Naturally not," nodded the doctor.

"If I may intrude my still, small voice," murmured Ellery, "isn't this a battle of giants over a mouse? The possession of gold is a clear violation of the law in this country, and has been for several years. Even if you found it, wouldn't the government confiscate it?"

"There's a complicated legal situation, Queen," said Thorne; "but one which cannot come into existence before the gold is found. Therefore my efforts to—"

"And successful efforts, too," grinned Dr. Reinach. "Do you know, Mr. Queen, your friend has slept behind locked, barred doors, with an old cutlass in his hand—one of Sylvester's prized mementoes of a grandfather who was in the Navy? It's terribly amusing."

"I don't find it so," said Thorne shortly. "If you insist on playing the buffoon—"

"And yet—to go back to this matter of your little suspicions, Thorne—have you analyzed the facts? Whom do you suspect, my dear fellow? Your humble servant? I assure you that I am spiritually an ascetic—"

"An almighty fat one!" snarled Thorne.

"—and that money, *per se*, means nothing to me," went on the doctor imperturbably. "My half sister Sarah? An anile wreck living in a world of illusion, quite as antediluvian as Sylvester—they were twins, you know—who isn't very long for this world. Then that leaves my estimable Milly and our saturnine young friend Nick. Milly? Absurd; she hasn't had an idea, good or bad, for two decades. Nick? Ah, an outsider—we may have struck something there. Is it Nick you suspect, Thorne?" chuckled Dr. Reinach.

Keith got to his feet and glared down into the bland, damp, lunar countenance of the fat man. He seemed quite drunk. "You damned porker," he said thickly.

Dr. Reinach kept smiling, but his little porcine eyes were wary. "Now, now, Nick," he said in a soothing rumble.

It all happened very quickly. Keith lurched forward, snatched the heavy cut-glass brandy decanter, and swung it at the doctor's head. Thorne cried out and took an instinctive forward step; but he might have spared himself the exertion. Dr. Reinach jerked his head back like a fat snake and the blow missed. The violent effort pivoted Keith's body completely about; the decanter slipped from his fingers and flew into the fireplace, crashing to pieces. The fragments splattered all over the fireplace, strewing the hearth, too; the little brandy that remained in the bottle hissed into the fire, blazing with a blue flame.

"That decanter," said Dr. Reinach angrily, "was almost a hundred and fifty years old!"

Keith stood still, his broad back to them. They could see his shoulders heaving. Ellery sighed with the queerest feeling. The room was shimmering as in a dream, and the whole incident seemed unreal, like a scene in a play on a stage. Were they acting? Had the scene been carefully planned? But, if so, why? What earthly purpose could they have hoped to achieve by pretending to quarrel and come to blows? The sole result had been the wanton destruction of a lovely old decanter. It didn't make sense.

"I think," said Ellery, struggling to his feet, "that I shall go to bed before the Evil One comes down the chimney. Thank you for an altogether extraordinary evening, gentlemen. Coming, Thorne?"

He stumbled up the stairs, followed by the lawyer, who seemed as weary as he. They separated in the cold corridor, without a word, to stumble to their respective bedrooms. From below came a heavy silence.

It was only as he was throwing his trousers over the footrail of his bed that Ellery recalled hazily Thorne's whispered intention hours before to visit him that night and explain the whole fantastic business. He struggled into his dressing gown and slippers and shuffled down the hall to Thorne's room. But the lawyer was already in bed, snoring stertorously.

Ellery dragged himself back to his room and finished undressing. He knew he would have a head the next morning; he was a notoriously poor drinker. His brain spinning, he crawled between the blankets and fell asleep almost instantly.

He opened his eyes after a tossing, tiring sleep with the uneasy conviction that something was wrong. For a moment he was aware only of the ache in his head and the fuzzy feel of his tongue; he did not remember where he was. Then, as his glance took in the faded wallpaper, the pallid patches of sunlight on the worn blue carpet, his trousers tumbled over the footrail where he had left them the night before, memory returned; and, shivering, he consulted his wristwatch, which he had forgotten to take off on going to bed. It was five minutes to seven. He raised his head from the pillow in the frosty air of the bedroom; his nose was half frozen. But he could detect nothing wrong; the sun looked brave if weak in his eyes; the room was quiet and exactly as he had seen it on retiring; the door was closed. He snuggled between the blankets again.

Then he heard it. It was Thorne's voice. It was Thorne's voice raised in a thin faint cry, almost a wail, coming from somewhere outside the house.

He was out of bed and at the window in his bare feet in one leap. But Thorne was not visible at this side of the house, upon which the dead woods encroached directly; so he scrambled back to slip shoes on his feet and his gown over his pajamas, darted toward the footrail and snatched his revolver out of the hip pocket of his trousers, and ran out into the corridor, heading for the stairs, the revolver in his hand.

"What's the matter?" grumbled someone, and he turned to see Dr. Reinach's vast skull protruding nakedly from the room next to his.

"Don't know. I heard Thorne cry out," and Ellery pounded down the stairs and flung open the front door.

He stopped within the doorway, gaping.

Thorne, fully dressed, was standing ten yards in front of the house, facing Ellery obliquely, staring at something outside the range of Ellery's vision with the most acute expression of terror on his gaunt face Ellery had ever seen on a human countenance. Beside him crouched Nicholas Keith, only half dressed; the young man's jaws gaped foolishly and his eyes were enormous glaring discs.

Dr. Reinach shoved Ellery roughly aside and growled: "What's the matter? What's wrong?" The fat man's feet were encased in carpet slippers and he had pulled a raccoon coat over his nightshirt, so that he looked like a particularly obese bear.

Thorne's Adam's apple bobbed nervously. The ground, the trees, the world were blanketed with snow of a peculiarly unreal texture; and the air was saturated with warm woolen flakes, falling softly. Deep drifts curved upwards to clamp the boles of trees.

"Don't move," croaked Thorne as Ellery and the fat man stirred. "Don't move, for the love of God. Stay where you are." Ellery's grip tightened on the revolver and he tried perversely to get past the doctor; but he might have been trying to budge a stone wall. Thorne stumbled through the snow to the porch, paler than his background, leaving two deep ruts behind him. "Look at me," he shouted. "*Look at me.* Do I seem all right? Have I gone mad?"

"Pull yourself together, Thorne," said Ellery sharply. "What's the matter with you? I don't see anything wrong."

"Nick!" bellowed Dr. Reinach. "Have you gone crazy, too?"

The young man covered his sunburned face suddenly with his hands; then he dropped his hands and looked again.

He said in a strangled voice: "Maybe we all have. This is the most—Take a look yourself."

Reinach moved then, and Ellery squirmed by him to land in the soft snow beside Thorne, who was trembling violently. Dr. Reinach came lurching after. They plowed through the snow toward Keith, squinting, straining to see.

They need not have strained. What was to be seen was plain for any seeing eye to see. Ellery felt his scalp crawl as he looked; and at the same instant he was aware of the sharp conviction that this was inevitable, this was the only possible climax to the insane events of the previous day. The world had turned topsy-turvy. Nothing in it meant anything reasonable or sane.

Dr. Reinach gasped once; and then he stood blinking like a huge owl. A window rattled on the second floor of the White House. None of them looked up. It was Alice Mayhew in a wrapper, staring from the window of her bedroom, which was on the side of the house facing the driveway. She screamed once; and then she, too fell silent.

There was the house from which they had just emerged, the house Dr. Reinach had dubbed the White House, with its front door quietly swinging open and Alice Mayhew at an upper side window. Substantial, solid, an edifice of stone and wood and plaster and glass and the patina of age. It was everything a house should be. That much was real, a thing to be grasped.

But beyond it, beyond the driveway and the garage, where the Black House had stood, the house in which Ellery himself had set foot only the afternoon before, the house of the filth and the stench, the house of the equally stone walls, wooden facings, glass windows, chimneys, gargoyles, porch; the house of the blackened look; the old Victorian house built during the Civil War where Sylvester Mayhew had died, where Thorne had barricaded himself with a cutlass for a week; the house which they had all seen, touched, smelled . . . there, *there stood nothing.* No walls. No chimney. No roof. No ruins. No debris. No house. Nothing.

Nothing but empty space covered smoothly and warmly with snow.

The house had vanished during the night.

II

"There's even," thought Mr. Ellery Queen dully, "a character named Alice."

He looked again. The only reason he did not rub his eyes was that it would have made him feel ridiculous; besides, his sight, all his senses, had never been keener. He simply stood there in the snow and looked and looked and looked at the empty space where a three-story stone house seventy-five years old had stood the night before.

"Why, it isn't there," said Alice feebly from the upper window. "It . . . isn't . . . there."

"Then I'm not insane." Thorne stumbled toward them. Ellery watched the old man's feet sloughing through the snow, leaving long tracks. A man's weight still counted for something in the universe, then. Yes, and there was his own shadow; so material objects still cast shadows. Absurdly, the discovery brought a certain faint relief.

"It *is* gone!" said Thorne in a cracked voice.

"Apparently." Ellery found his own voice thick and slow; he watched the words curl out on the air and become nothing. "Apparently, Thorne." It was all he could find to say.

Dr. Reinach arched his fat neck, his wattles quivering like a gobbler's. "Incredible. Incredible!"

"Incredible," said Thorne in a whisper.

"Unscientific. It can't be. I'm a man of sense. Of senses. My mind is clear. Things like this—damn it, they just don't happen!"

"As the man said who saw a giraffe for the first time," sighed Ellery. "And yet . . . there it was."

Thorne began wandering helplessly about in a circle. Alice stared, bewitched into stone, from the upper window. And Keith cursed and began to run across the snow-covered driveway toward the invisible house, his hands outstretched before him like a blind man's.

"Hold on," said Ellery. "Stop where you are."

The giant halted, scowling. "What d'ye want?"

Ellery slipped his revolver back into his pocket and sloshed through the snow to pause beside the young man in the driveway. "I don't know precisely. Something's wrong. Something's out of kilter either with us or with the world. It isn't the world as we know it. It's almost . . . almost a matter of transposed dimensions. Do you suppose the solar system has slipped out of its niche in the universe and gone stark crazy in the uncharted depths of space-time? I suppose I'm talking nonsense."

"You know best," shouted Keith. "I'm not going to let this screwy business stampede *me*. There was a solid house on that plot last night, by God, and nobody can convince me it still isn't there. Not even my own eyes. We've—we've been hypnotized! The hippo could do it here—he could do anything. Hypnotized. You hypnotized us, Reinach!"

The doctor mumbled: "What?" and kept glaring at the empty lot.

"I tell you it's there!" cried Keith angrily.

Ellery sighed and dropped to his knees in the snow; he began to brush aside the white, soft blanket with chilled palms. When he had laid the ground bare, he saw wet gravel and a rut.

"This *is* the driveway, isn't it?" he asked without looking up.

"The driveway," snarled Keith, "or the road to hell. You're as mixed up as we are. Sure it's the driveway! Can't you see the garage? Why shouldn't it be the driveway?"

"I don't know." Ellery got to his feet, frowning. "I don't know anything. I'm beginning to learn all over again. Maybe—maybe it's a matter of gravitation. Maybe we'll all fly into space any minute now."

Thorne groaned: "My God."

"All I can be sure of is that something very strange happened last night."

"I tell you," growled Keith, "it's an optical illusion!"

"Something strange." The fat man stirred. "Yes, decidedly. What an inadequate word! A house has disappeared. Something strange." He began to chuckle in a choking, mirthless way.

"Oh that," said Ellery impatiently. "Certainly. Certainly, Doctor. That's a *fact*. As for you, Keith, you don't really believe this mass hypnosis bilge. The house is gone, right enough. . . . It's not the fact of its being gone that bothers me. It's the agency, the *means*. It smacks of—of—" He shook his head. "I've never believed in . . . this sort of thing, damn it all!"

Dr. Reinach threw back his vast shoulders and glared, red-eyed, at the empty snow-covered space. "It's a trick," he bellowed. "A rotten trick, that's what it is. That house is right there in front of our noses. Or—or— They can't fool *me*!"

Ellery looked at him. "Perhaps," he said, "Keith has it in his pocket?"

Alice clattered out on the porch in high-heeled shoes over bare feet, her hair streaming, a cloth coat flung over her night clothes. Behind her crept little Mrs. Reinach. The women's eyes were wild.

"Talk to them," muttered Ellery to Thorne. "Anything; but keep their minds occupied. We'll all go balmy if we don't preserve at least an air of sanity. Keith, get me a broom."

He shuffled up the driveway, skirting the invisible house very carefully and not once taking his eyes off the empty space. The fat man hesitated; then he lumbered along in Ellery's tracks. Thorne stumbled back to the porch and Keith strode off, disappearing behind the White House.

There was no sun now. A pale and eerie light filtered down through the cold clouds. The snow continued its soft, thick fall. They looked like dots, small and helpless, on a sheet of blank paper.

Ellery pulled open the folding doors of the garage and peered. A healthy odor of raw gasoline and rubber assailed his nostrils. Thorne's car stood within, exactly as Ellery had seen it the afternoon before, black monster with glittering chrome work. Beside it, apparently parked by Keith after their arrival, stood the battered Buick in which Dr. Reinach had driven them from the city. Both cars were perfectly dry.

He shut the doors and turned back to the driveway. Aside from the catenated links of their footprints in the snow, made a moment before, the white covering on the driveway was virgin.

"Here's your broom," said the giant. "What are you going to do— ride it?"

"Hold your tongue, Nick," growled Dr. Reinach.

Ellery laughed. "Let him alone, Doctor. His angry sanity is infectious. Come along, you two. This may be the Judgment Day, but we may as well go through the motions."

"What do you want with a broom, Queen?"

"It's hard to decide whether the snow was an accident or part of the plan," murmured Ellery. "Anything may be true today. Literally anything."

"Rubbish," snorted the fat man. "Abracadabra. *Om mani padme hum*. How could a man have planned a snowfall? You're talking gibberish."

"I didn't say a human plan, Doctor."

"Rubbish, rubbish, rubbish!"

"You may as well save your breath. You're a badly scared little boy whistling in the dark—for all your bulk, Doctor."

Ellery gripped the broom tightly and stamped out across the driveway. He felt his own foot shrinking as he tried to make it step upon the white rectangle. His muscles were gathered in, as if in truth he expected to encounter the adamantine bulk of a house which was still there but unaccountably impalpable. When he felt nothing but cold air, he laughed a little self-consciously and began to wield the broom on the snow in a peculiar manner. He used the most delicate of sweeping motions, barely brushing the surface crystals away, so that layer by layer he reduced the depth of the snow. He scanned each layer with anxiety as it was uncovered. And he continued to do this until the ground itself lay revealed; and at no depth did he come across the minutest trace of a human imprint.

"Elves," he complained. "Nothing less than elves. I confess it's beyond me."

"Even the foundation—" began Dr. Reinach heavily.

Ellery poked the tip of the broom at the earth. It was hard as corundum.

The front door slammed as Thorne and the two women crept into the White House. The three men outside stood still, doing nothing.

"Well," said Ellery at last, "this is either a bad dream or the end of the world." He made off diagonally across the plot, dragging the broom behind him like a tired charwoman, until he reached the snow-covered drive; and then he trudged down the drive towards the invisible road, disappearing around a bend under the stripped white-dripping trees.

It was a short walk to the road. Ellery remembered it well. It had curved steadily in a long arc all the way from the turn-off at the main highway. There had been no crossroad in all the jolting journey.

He went out into the middle of the road, snow-covered now but plainly distinguishable between the powdered tangles of woods as a gleaming, empty strip. There was the long curve exactly as he remembered it.

Mechanically he used the broom again, sweeping a small area clear. And there were the pits and ruts of the old Buick's journeys.

"What are you looking for," said Nick Keith quietly, "gold?"

Ellery straightened up by degrees, turning about slowly until he was face to face with the giant. "So you thought it was necessary to follow me? Or—no, I beg your pardon. Undoubtedly it was Dr. Reinach's idea."

The sun-charred features did not change expression.

"You're crazy as a bat. Follow you? I've got all I can do to follow myself."

"Of course," said Ellery. "But did I understand you to ask me if I was looking for gold, my dear young Prometheus?"

"You're a queer one," said Keith as they made their way back toward the house.

"Gold," repeated Ellery. "Hmm. There was gold in that house, and now the house is gone. In the shock of the discovery that houses fly away like birds, I'd quite forgotten that little item. Thank you, Mr. Keith," said Ellery grimly, "for reminding me."

"Mr. Queen," said Alice. She was crouched in a chair by the fire, white to the lips. "What's happened to us? What are we to do? Have we . . . Was yesterday a dream? Didn't we walk into that house, go through it, touch things? . . . I'm frightened."

"If yesterday *was* a dream," smiled Ellery, "then we may expect that tomorrow will bring a vision; for that's what holy Sanskrit says, and we may as well believe in parables as in miracles." He sat down, rubbing his hands briskly. "How about a fire, Keith? It's arctic in here."

"Sorry," said Keith with surprising amiability, and he went away.

"We could see a vision," shivered Thorne. "My brain is—sick. It just isn't possible. It's horrible." His hands slapped his side and something jangled in his pocket.

"Keys," said Ellery, "and no house. It *is* staggering."

Keith came back under a mountain of firewood. He grimaced at the litter in the fireplace, dropped the wood, and began sweeping together the fragments of glass, the remains of the brandy decanter he had smashed against the brick wall the night before. Alice glanced from his broad back to the chromo of her mother on the mantel. As for Mrs. Reinach, she was as silent as a sacred bird; she stood in a corner like a wizened little gnome, her wrapper drawn about her, her stringy sparrow-colored hair hanging down her back, and her glassy eyes fixed on the face of her husband.

"Milly," said the fat man.

"Yes, Herbert, I'm going," said Mrs. Reinach instantly, and she crept up the stairs and out of sight.

"Well, Mr. Queen, what's the answer? Or is this riddle too esoteric for your taste?"

"No riddle is esoteric," muttered Ellery, "unless it's the riddle of God; and that's no riddle—it's a vast blackness. Doctor, is there any way of reaching assistance?"

"Not unless you can fly."

"No phone," said Keith without turning, "and you saw the condition of the road for yourself. You'd never get a car through those drifts."

"If you had a car," chuckled Dr. Reinach. Then he seemed to remember the disappearing house, and his chuckle died.

"What do you mean?" demanded Ellery. "In the garage are—"

"Two useless products of the machine age. Both cars are out of fuel."

"And mine," said old Thorne suddenly, with a resurrection of grim personal interest, "mine has something wrong with it besides. I left my chauffeur in the city, you know, Queen, when I drove down last time. Now I can't get the engine running on the little gasoline that's left in the tank."

Ellery's fingers drummed on the arm of his chair. "Bother! Now we can't even call on the other eyes to test whether we've been bewitched or not. By the way, Doctor, how far is the nearest community? I'm afraid I didn't pay attention on the drive down."

"Over fifteen miles by road. If you're thinking of footing it, Mr. Queen, you're welcome to the thought."

"You'd never get through the drifts," muttered Keith. The drifts appeared to trouble him.

"And so we find ourselves snowbound," said Ellery, "in the middle of the fourth dimension—or perhaps it's the fifth. A pretty kettle! Ah there, Keith, that feels considerably better."

"You don't seem bowled over by what's happened," said Dr. Reinach, eyeing him curiously. "I'll confess it's given even me a shock."

Ellery was silent for a moment. Then he said lightly: "There wouldn't be any point to losing our heads, would there?"

"I fully expect dragons to come flying over the house," groaned Thorne.

He eyed Ellery a bit bashfully. "Queen . . . perhaps we had better . . . try to get out of here."

"You heard Keith, Thorne."

Thorne bit his lips. "I'm frozen," said Alice, drawing nearer the fire.

"That was well done, Mr. Keith. It—it—a fire like this makes me think of home, somehow." The young man got to his feet and turned around. Their eyes met for an instant.

"It's nothing," he said shortly. "Nothing at all."

"You seem to be the only one who— *Oh*!"

An enormous old woman with a black shawl over her shoulders was coming downstairs. She might have been years dead, she was so yellow and emaciated and mummified. And yet she gave the impression of being very much alive, with a sort of ancient, ageless life; her black eyes were young and bright and cunning, and her face was extraordinarily mobile. She was sidling down stiffly, feeling her way with one foot and clutching the banister with two dried claws, while her lively eyes remained fixed on Alice's face. There was a curious hunger in her expression, the flaring of a long-dead hope suddenly, against all reason.

"Who—who—" began Alice, shrinking back.

"Don't be alarmed," said Dr. Reinach quickly. "It's unfortunate that she got away from Milly. . . . Sarah!" In a twinkling he was at the foot of the staircase, barring the old woman's way. "What are you doing up at this hour? You should take better care of yourself, Sarah."

She ignored him, continuing her snail's pace down the stairs until she reached his pachyderm bulk. "Olivia," she mumbled, with a vital eagerness.

"It's Olivia come back to me. Oh, my sweet, sweet darling . . ."

"Now, Sarah," said the fat man, taking her hand gently. "Don't excite yourself. This isn't Olivia, Sarah. It's Alice—Alice Mayhew, Sylvester's girl, come from England. You remember Alice, little Alice? Not Olivia, Sarah."

"Not Olivia?" The old woman peered across the banister, her wrinkled lips moving. "Not Olivia?"

The girl jumped up. "I'm Alice, Aunt Sarah. Alice—"

Sarah Fell darted suddenly past the fat man and scurried across the room to seize the girl's hand and glare into her face. As she studied those shrinking features her expression changed to one of despair. "Not Olivia. Olivia's beautiful black hair . . . Not Olivia's voice. Alice? Alice?" She dropped into Alice's vacated chair, her skinny broad shoulders sagging, and began to weep. They could see the yellow skin of her scalp through the sparse gray hair.

Dr. Reinach roared: "Milly!" in an enraged voice. Mrs. Reinach popped into sight like a jack-in-the-box. "Why did you let her leave her room?"

"B-but I thought she was—" began Mrs. Reinach, stammering.

"Take her upstairs at once!"

"Yes, Herbert," whispered the sparrow, and Mrs. Reinach hurried downstairs in her wrapper and took the old woman's hand and, unopposed, led her away. Mrs. Fell kept repeating, between sobs: "Why doesn't Olivia come back? Why did they take her away from her mother?" until she was out of sight.

"Sorry," panted the fat man, mopping himself. "One of her spells. I knew it was coming on from the curiosity she exhibited the moment she heard you were coming, Alice. There *is* a resemblance; you can scarcely blame her."

"She's—she's horrible," said Alice faintly. "Mr. Queen—Mr. Thorne, must we stay here? I'd feel so much easier in the city. And then my cold, these frigid rooms—"

"By heaven," burst out Thorne, "I feel like chancing it on foot!"

"And leave Sylvester's gold to our tender mercies?" smiled Dr. Reinach. Then he scowled.

"I don't want Father's legacy," said Alice desperately. "At this moment I don't want anything but to get away. I—I can manage to get along all right. I'll find work to do—I can do so many things. I want to go away. Mr. Keith, couldn't you possibly—"

"*I'm* not a magician," said Keith rudely; and he buttoned his mackinaw and strode out of the house. They could see his tall figure stalking off behind a veil of snowflakes.

Alice flushed, turning back to the fire.

"Nor are any of us," said Ellery. "Miss Mayhew, you'll simply have to be a brave girl and stick it out until we can find a means of getting out of here."

"Yes," murmured Alice, shivering; and stared into the flames.

"Meanwhile, Thorne, tell me everything you know about this case, especially as it concerns Sylvester Mayhew's house. There may be a clue in your father's history, Miss Mayhew. If the house has vanished, so has the gold *in* the house; and whether you want it or not, it belongs to you. Consequently we must make an effort to find it."

"I suggest," muttered Dr. Reinach, "that you find the house first. House!" he exploded, waving his furred arms. And he made for the sideboard.

Alice nodded listlessly. Thorne mumbled: "Perhaps, Queen, you and I had better talk privately."

"We made a frank beginning last night; I see no reason why we shouldn't continue in the same candid vein. You needn't be reluctant to speak before Dr. Reinach. Our host is obviously a man of parts—unorthodox parts."

Dr. Reinach did not reply. His globular face was dark as he tossed off a water goblet full of gin.

Through air metallic with defiance, Thorne talked in a hardening voice; not once did he take his eyes from Dr. Reinach.

His first suspicion that something was wrong had been germinated by Sylvester Mayhew himself.

Hearing by post from Alice, Thorne had investigated and located Mayhew. He had explained to the old invalid his daughter's desire to find her father, if he still lived. Old Mayhew, with a strange excitement, had acquiesced; he was eager to be reunited with his daughter; and he seemed to be living, explained Thorne defiantly, in mortal fear of his relatives in the neighboring house.

"Fear, Thorne?" The fat man sat down, raising his brows. "You know he was afraid, not of us, but of poverty. He was a miser."

Thorne ignored him. Mayhew had instructed Thorne to write Alice and bid her come to America at once; he meant to leave her his entire estate and wanted her to have it before he died. The repository of the gold he had cunningly refused to divulge, even to Thorne; it was "in the house," he had said, but he would not reveal its hiding place to anyone but Alice herself.

The "others," he had snarled, had been looking for it ever since their "arrival."

"By the way," drawled Ellery, "how long have you good people been living in this house, Dr. Reinach?"

"A year or so. You certainly don't put any credence in the paranoiac ravings of a dying man? There's no mystery about our living here. I looked Sylvester up over a year ago after a long separation and found him still in the old homestead, and this house boarded up and empty. The White House, this house, incidentally, was built by my stepfather—Sylvester's father—on Sylvester's marriage to Alice's mother; Sylvester lived in it until my stepfather died, and then moved back to the Black House. I found Sylvester, a degenerated hulk of what he'd once been, living on crusts, absolutely alone and badly in need of medical attention."

"Alone—here, in this wilderness?" said Ellery incredulously.

"Yes. As a matter of fact, the only way I could get his permission to move back to this house, which belonged to him, was by dangling the bait of free medical treatment before his eyes. I'm sorry, Alice; he was quite unbalanced. . . . And so Milly and Sarah and I—Sarah had been living with us ever since Olivia's death—moved in here."

"Decent of you," remarked Ellery. "I suppose you had to give up your medical practice to do it, Doctor?"

Dr. Reinach grimaced. "I didn't have much of a practice to give up, Mr. Queen."

"But it was an almost pure brotherly impulse, eh?"

"Oh, I don't deny that the possibility of falling heir to some of Sylvester's fortune had crossed our minds. It was rightfully ours, we believed, not knowing anything about Alice. As it's turned out—" he shrugged his fat shoulders. "I'm a philosopher."

"And don't deny, either," shouted Thorne, "that when I came back here at the time Mayhew sank into that fatal coma you people watched me like a—like a band of spies! I was in your way!"

"Mr. Thorne," whispered Alice, paling.

"I'm sorry, Miss Mayhew, but you may as well know the truth. Oh, you didn't fool me, Reinach! You wanted that gold, Alice or no Alice. I shut myself up in that house just to keep you from getting your hands on it!"

Dr. Reinach shrugged again; his rubbery lips compressed.

"You want candor; here it is!" rasped Thorne. "I was in that house, Queen, for six days after Mayhew's funeral and before Miss Mayhew's arrival, *looking for the gold*. I turned that house upside down. And I didn't find the slightest trace of it. I tell you it isn't there." He glared at the fat man. "I tell you it was stolen before Mayhew died!"

"Now, now," sighed Ellery. "That makes less sense than the other. Why then has somebody intoned an incantation over the house and caused it to disappear?"

"I don't know," said the old lawyer fiercely. "I know only that the most dastardly thing's happened here, that everything is unnatural, veiled in that—that false creature's smile! Miss Mayhew, I'm sorry I must speak this way about your own family. But I feel it my duty to warn you that you've fallen among human wolves. Wolves!"

"I'm afraid," said Reinach sourly, "that I shouldn't come to you, my dear Thorne, for a reference."

"I wish," said Alice in a very low tone, "I truly wish I were dead."

But the lawyer was past control. "That man Keith," he cried. "Who is he? What's he doing here? He looks like a gangster. I suspect him, Queen—"

"Apparently," smiled Ellery, "you suspect everybody."

"Mr. Keith?" murmured Alice. "Oh, I'm sure not. I—I don't think he's that sort at all, Mr. Thorne. He looks as if he's had a hard life. As if he's suffered terribly from something."

Thorne threw up his hands, turning to the fire.

"Let us," said Ellery amiably, "confine ourselves to the problem at hand. We were, I believe, considering the problem of a disappearing house. Do any architect's plans of the so-called Black House exist?"

"Lord, no," said Dr. Reinach.

"Who has lived in it since your stepfather's death besides Sylvester Mayhew and his wife?"

"Wives," corrected the doctor, pouring himself another glassful of gin. "Sylvester married twice; I suppose you didn't know that, my dear." Alice shivered by the fire. "I dislike raking over old ashes, but since we're at confessional . . . Sylvester treated Alice's mother abominably."

"I—guessed that," whispered Alice.

"She was a woman of spirit and she rebelled; but when she'd got her final decree and returned to England, the reaction set in and she died very shortly afterward, I understand. Her death was recorded in the New York papers."

"When I was a baby," whispered Alice.

"Sylvester, already unbalanced, although not so anchoretic in those days as he became later, then wooed and won a wealthy widow and brought her out here to live. She had a son, a child by her first husband, with her. Father'd died by this time, and Sylvester and his second wife lived in the Black House. It was soon evident that Sylvester had married the widow for her money; he persuaded her to sign it over to him—a considerable fortune for those days—and promptly proceeded to devil the life out of her. Result: the woman vanished one day, taking her child with her."

"Perhaps," said Ellery, seeing Alice's face, "we'd better abandon the subject, Doctor."

"We never did find out what actually happened—whether Sylvester drove her out or whether, unable to stand his brutal treatment any longer, she left voluntarily. At any rate, I discovered by accident, a few years later, through an obituary notice, that she died in the worst sort of poverty."

Alice was staring at him with a wrinkle-nosed nausea. "Father . . . did that?"

"Oh, stop it," growled Thorne. "You'll have the poor child gibbering in another moment. What has all this to do with the house?"

"Mr. Queen asked," said the fat man mildly. Ellery was studying the flames as if they fascinated him.

"The real point," snapped the lawyer, "is that you've watched me from the instant I set foot here, Reinach. Afraid to leave me alone for a moment. Why, you even had Keith meet me in your car on both my visits—to 'escort' me here! And I didn't have five minutes alone with the old gentleman—you saw to that. And then he lapsed into the coma and was unable to speak again before he died. Why? Why all this surveillance? God knows I'm a forbearing man; but you've given me every ground for suspecting your motives."

"Apparently," chuckled Dr. Reinach, "you don't agree with Caesar."

"I beg your pardon?"

"'Would,'" quoted the fat man, "'he were fatter.' Well, good people, the end of the world may come, but that's no reason why we shouldn't have breakfast. Milly!" he bellowed.

Thorne awoke sluggishly, like a drowsing old hound dimly aware of danger. His bedroom was cold; a pale morning light was struggling in through the window. He groped under his pillow.

"Stop where you are!" he said harshly.

"So you have a revolver, too?" murmured Ellery. He was dressed and looked as if he had slept badly. "It's only I, Thorne, stealing in for a conference. It's not so hard to steal in here, by the way."

"What do you mean?" grumbled Thorne, sitting up and putting his old-fashioned revolver away.

"I see your lock has gone the way of mine, Alice's, the Black House, and Sylvester Mayhew's elusive gold."

Thorne drew the patchwork comforter about him, his old lips blue. "Well, Queen?"

Ellery lit a cigarette and for a moment stared out Thorne's window at the streamers of crêpy snow still dropping from the sky. The snow had fallen without a moment's let-up the entire previous day. "This is a curious business all round, Thorne. The queerest medley of spirit and matter. I've just reconnoitered. You'll be interested to learn that our young friend the Colossus is gone."

"Keith gone?"

"His bed hasn't been slept in at all. I looked."

"And he was away most of yesterday, too!"

"Precisely. Our surly Crichton, who seems afflicted by a particularly acute case of *Weltschmerz*, periodically vanishes. Where does he go? I'd give a good deal to know the answer to that question."

"He won't get far in those nasty drifts," mumbled the lawyer.

"It gives one, as the French say, to think. Comrade Reinach is gone, too."

Thorne stiffened. "Oh, yes; his bed's been slept in, but briefly, I judge. Have they eloped together? Separately? Thorne," said Ellery thoughtfully, "this becomes an increasingly subtle devilment."

"It's beyond me," said Thorne with another shiver. "I'm just about ready to give up. I don't see that we're accomplishing a thing here. And then there's always that annoying, incredible fact . . . the house—vanished."

Ellery sighed and looked at his wristwatch. It was a minute past seven.

Thorne threw back the comforter and groped under the bed for his slippers. "Let's go downstairs," he snapped.

"Excellent bacon, Mrs. Reinach," said Ellery. "I suppose it must be a trial carting supplies up here."

"We've the blood of pioneers," said Dr. Reinach cheerfully, before his wife could reply. He was engulfing mounds of scrambled eggs and bacon.

"Luckily, we've enough in the larder to last out a considerable siege. The winters are severe out here—we learned that last year."

Keith was not at the breakfast table. Old Mrs. Fell was. She ate voraciously, with the unconcealed greed of the very old, to whom nothing is left of the sensual satisfactions of life but the filling of the belly.

Nevertheless, although she did not speak, she contrived as she ate to keep her eyes on Alice, who wore a haunted look.

"I didn't sleep very well," said Alice, toying with her coffee cup. Her voice was huskier. "This abominable snow! Can't we manage somehow to get away today?"

"Not so long as the snow keeps up, I'm afraid," said Ellery gently. "And you, Doctor? Did you sleep badly, too? Or hasn't the whisking away of a whole house from under your nose affected your nerves at all?"

The fat man's eyes were red-rimmed and his lids sagged. Nevertheless, he chuckled and said: "I? I always sleep well. Nothing on my conscience. Why?"

"Oh, no special reason. Where's friend Keith this morning? He's a seclusive sort of chap, isn't he?"

Mrs. Reinach swallowed a muffin whole. Her husband glanced at her and she rose and fled to the kitchen. "Lord knows," said the fat man. "He's as unpredictable as the ghost of Banquo. Don't bother yourself about the boy; he's harmless."

Ellery sighed and pushed back from the table. "The passage of twenty-four hours hasn't softened the wonder of the event. May I be excused? I'm going to have another peep at the house that isn't there any more." Thorne started to rise. "No, no, Thorne; I'd rather go alone."

He put on his warmest clothes and went outdoors. The drifts reached the lower windows now; and the trees had almost disappeared under the snow.

A crude path had been hacked by someone from the front door for a few feet; already it was half refilled with snow.

Ellery stood still in the path, breathing deeply of the raw air and staring off to the right at the empty rectangle where the Black House had once stood. Leading across that expanse to the edge of the woods beyond were barely discernible tracks. He turned up his coat collar against the cutting wind and plunged into the snow waist-deep.

It was difficult going, but not unpleasant. After a while he began to feel quite warm. The world was white and silent—a new, strange world.

When he had left the open area and struggled into the woods, it was with a sensation that he was leaving even that new world behind. Everything was so still and white and beautiful, with a pure beauty not of the earth; the snow draping the trees gave them a fresh look, making queer patterns out of old forms.

Occasionally a clump of snow fell from a low branch, pelting him.

Here, where there was a roof between ground and sky, the snow had not filtered into the mysterious tracks so quickly. They were purposeful tracks, unwandering, striking straight as a dotted line for some distant goal. Ellery pushed on more rapidly, excited by a presentiment of discovery.

Then the world went black.

It was a curious thing. The snow grew gray, and grayer, and finally very dark gray, becoming jet black at the last instant, as if flooded from underneath by ink. And with some surprise he felt the cold wet kiss of the drift on his cheek.

He opened his eyes to find himself flat on his back in the snow and Thorne in the greatcoat stooped over him, nose jutting from blued face like a winter thorn.

"Queen!" cried the old man, shaking him. "Are you all right?"

Ellery sat up, licking his lips. "As well as might be expected," he groaned. "What hit me? It felt like one of God's angrier thunder-bolts." He caressed the back of his head, and staggered to his feet. "Well, Thorne, we seem to have reached the border of the enchanted land."

"You're not delirious?" asked the lawyer anxiously.

Ellery looked about for the tracks which should have been there. But except for the double line at the head of which Thorne stood, there were none. Apparently he had lain unconscious in the snow for a long time.

"Farther than this," he said with a grimace, "we may not go. Hands off. Nose out. Mind your own business. Beyond this invisible boundary line lie Sheol and Domdaniel and Abaddon. *Lasciate ogni speranza voi ch'entrate*. . . . Forgive me, Thorne. Did you save my life?"

Thorne jerked about, searching the silent woods. "I don't know. I think not. At least I found you lying here, alone. Gave me quite a start—thought you were dead."

"As well," said Ellery with a shiver, "I might have been."

"When you left the house Alice went upstairs, Reinach said something about a catnap, and I wandered out of the house. I waded through the drifts on the road for a spell, and then I thought of you and made my way back. Your tracks were almost obliterated; but they were visible enough to take me across the clearing to the edge of the woods, and I finally blundered upon you. By now the tracks are gone."

"I don't like this at all," said Ellery, "and yet in another sense I like it very much."

"What do you mean?"

"I can't imagine," said Ellery, "a divine agency stooping to such a mean assault."

"Yes, it's open war now," muttered Thorne. "Whoever it is—he'll stop at nothing."

"A benevolent war, at any rate. I was quite at his mercy, and he might have killed me as easily as—"

He stopped. A sharp report, like a pine knot snapping in a fire or an ice-stiffened twig breaking in two, but greatly magnified, had come to his ears.

Then the echo came to them, softer but unmistakable.

It was the report of a gun.

"From the house!" yelled Ellery. "Come on!"

Thorne was pale as they scrambled through the drifts. "Gun . . . I forgot. I left my revolver under the pillow in my bedroom. Do you think—?"

Ellery scrabbled at his own pocket. "Mine's still here. . . . No, by George, I've been scotched!" His cold fingers fumbled with the cylinder. "Bullets taken out. And I've no spare ammunition." He fell silent, his mouth hardening.

They found the women and Reinach running about like startled animals, searching for they knew not what.

"Did you hear it, too?" cried the fat man as they burst into the house. He seemed extraordinarily excited. "Someone fired a shot!"

"Where?" asked Ellery, his eyes on the rove. "Keith?"

"Don't know where he is. Milly says it might have come from behind the house. I was napping and couldn't tell. Revolvers! At least he's come out in the open."

"Who has?" asked Ellery.

The fat man shrugged. Ellery went through to the kitchen and opened the back door. The snow outside was smooth, untrodden. When he returned to the living room Alice was adjusting a scarf about her neck with fingers that shook.

"I don't know how long you people intend to stay in this ghastly place," she said in a passionate voice. "But I've had *quite* enough, thank you. Mr. Thorne, I insist you take me away at once. At once! I shan't stay another instant."

"Now, now, Miss Mayhew," said Thorne in a distressed way, taking her hands. "I should like nothing better. But can't you see—"

Ellery, on his way upstairs three steps at a time, heard no more. He made for Thorne's room and kicked the door open, sniffing. Then, with rather a grim smile, he went to the tumbled bed and pulled the pillow away. A long-barreled, old-fashioned revolver lay there. He examined the cylinder; it was empty. Then he put the muzzle to his nose.

"Well?" said Thorne from the doorway. The English girl was clinging to him.

"Well," said Ellery, tossing the gun aside, "we're facing fact now, not fancy. It's war, Thorne, as you said. The shot was fired from your revolver. Barrel's still warm, muzzle still reeks, and you can smell the burned gunpowder if you sniff this cold air hard enough. *And* the bullets are gone."

"But what does it mean?" moaned Alice.

"It means that somebody's being terribly cute. It was a harmless trick to get Thorne and me back to the house. Probably the shot was a warning as well as a decoy."

Alice sank into Thorne's bed. "You mean we—"

"Yes," said Ellery, "from now on we're prisoners, Miss Mayhew. Prisoners who may not stray beyond the confines of the jail. I wonder," he added with a frown, "precisely why."

The day passed in a timeless haze. The world of outdoors became more and more choked in the folds of the snow. The air was a solid white sheet. It seemed as if the very heavens had opened to admit all the snow that ever was, or ever would be.

Young Keith appeared suddenly at noon, taciturn and leaden-eyed, gulped down some hot food, and without explanation retired to his bedroom. Dr. Reinach shambled about quietly for some time; then he disappeared, only to show up, wet, grimy, and silent, before dinner. As the day wore on, less and less was said. Thorne in desperation took up a bottle of whiskey. Keith came down at eight o'clock, made himself some coffee, drank three cups, and went upstairs again. Dr. Reinach appeared to have lost his good nature; he was morose, almost sullen, opening his mouth only to snarl at his wife.

And the snow continued to fall.

They all retired early, without conversation.

At midnight the strain was more than even Ellery's iron nerves could bear. He had prowled about his bedroom for hours, poking at the brisk fire in the grate, his mind leaping from improbability to fantasy until his head throbbed with one great ache. Sleep was impossible.

Moved by an impulse which he did not attempt to analyze, he slipped into his coat and went out into the frosty corridor.

Thorne's door was closed; Ellery heard the old man's bed creaking and groaning. It was pitch dark in the hall as he groped his way about. Suddenly Ellery's toe caught in a rent in the carpet and he staggered to regain his balance, coming up against the wall with a thud, his heels clattering on the bare planking at the bottom of the baseboard.

He had no sooner straightened up than he heard the stifled exclamation of a woman. It came from across the corridor; if he guessed right, from Alice Mayhew's bedroom. It was such a weak, terrified exclamation that he sprang across the hall, fumbling in his pockets for a match as he did so. He found match and door in the same instant; he struck one and opened the door and stood still, the tiny light flaring up before him.

Alice was sitting up in bed, quilt drawn about her shoulders, her eyes gleaming in the quarter-light. Before an open drawer of a tallboy across the room, one hand arrested in the act of scattering its contents about, loomed Dr. Reinach, fully dressed. His shoes were wet; his expression was blank; his eyes were slits.

"Please stand still, Doctor," said Ellery softly as the match sputtered out.

"My revolver is useless as a percussion weapon, but it still can inflict damage as a blunt instrument." He moved to a nearby table, where he had seen an oil lamp before the match went out, struck another match, lighted the lamp, and stepped back again to stand against the door.

"Thank you," whispered Alice.

"What happened, Miss Mayhew?"

"I . . . don't know. I slept badly. I came awake a moment ago when I heard the floor creak. And then you dashed in." She cried suddenly: "Bless you!"

"You cried out."

"Did I?" She sighed like a tired child. "I . . . Uncle Herbert!" she said suddenly, fiercely. "What's the meaning of this? What are you doing in my room?"

The fat man's eyes came open, innocent and beaming; his hand withdrew from the drawer and closed it; and he shifted his elephantine bulk until he was standing erect. "Doing, my dear?" he rumbled. "Why, I came in to see if you were all right." His eyes were fixed on a patch of her white shoulders visible above the quilt. "You were so overwrought today. Purely an avuncular impulse, my child. Forgive me if I startled you."

"I think," sighed Ellery, "that I've misjudged you, Doctor. That's not clever of you at all. Downright clumsy, in fact; I can only attribute it to a certain understandable confusion of the moment. Miss Mayhew isn't normally to be found in the top drawer of a tallboy, no matter how capacious it may be." He said sharply to Alice: "Did this fellow touch you?"

"Touch me?" Her shoulders twitched with repugnance. "No. If he had, in the dark, I—I think I should have died."

"What a charming compliment," said Dr. Reinach ruefully.

"Then what," demanded Ellery, "*were* you looking for, Dr. Reinach?"

The fat man turned until his right side was toward the door. "I'm notoriously hard of hearing," he chuckled, "in my right ear. Good night, Alice; pleasant dreams. May I pass, Sir Launcelot?"

Ellery kept his gaze on the fat man's bland face until the door closed. For some time after the last echo of Dr. Reinach's chuckle died away they were silent.

Then Alice slid down in the bed and clutched the edge of the quilt. "Mr. Queen, please! Take me away tomorrow. I mean it. I truly do. I—can't tell you how frightened I am of . . . all this. Every time I think of that—that. . . . How can such things be? We're not in a place of sanity, Mr. Queen. We'll all go mad if we remain here much longer. Won't you take me away?"

Ellery sat down on the edge of her bed. "Are you really so upset, Miss Mayhew?" he asked gently.

"I'm simply terrified," she whispered.

"Then Thorne and I will do what we can tomorrow." He patted her arm through the quilt. "I'll have a look at his car and see if something can't be done with it. He said there's some gas left in the tank. We'll go as far as it will take us and walk the rest of the way."

"But with so little petrol . . . Oh, I don't care!" She stared up at him wide-eyed. "Do you think . . . he'll let us?"

"He?"

"Whoever it is that . . ."

Ellery rose with a smile. "We'll cross that bridge when it gets to us. Meanwhile, get some sleep; you'll have a strenuous day tomorrow."

"Do you think I'm—he'll—"

"Leave the lamp burning and set a chair under the doorknob when I leave." He took a quick look about. "By the way, Miss Mayhew, is there anything in your possession which Dr. Reinach might want to appropriate?"

"That's puzzled me, too. I can't imagine what I've got he could possibly want. I'm so poor, Mr. Queen—quite the Cinderella. There's nothing; just my clothes, the things I came with."

"No old letters, records, mementoes?"

"Just one very old photograph of Mother."

"Hmm, Dr. Reinach doesn't strike me as that sentimental. Well, good night. Don't forget the chair. You'll be quite safe, I assure you."

He waited in the frigid darkness of the corridor until he heard her creep out of bed and set a chair against the door. Then he went into his own room.

And there was Thorne in a shabby dressing gown, looking like an ancient and disheveled specter of gloom.

"What ho! The ghost walks. Can't you sleep, either?"

"Sleep!" The old man shuddered. "How can an honest man sleep in this God-forsaken place? I notice you seem rather cheerful."

"Not cheerful. Alive." Ellery sat down and lit a cigarette. "I heard you tossing about your bed a few minutes ago. Anything happen to pull you out into this cold?"

"No. Just nerves." Thorne jumped up and began to pace the floor. "Where have you been?"

Ellery told him. "Remarkable chap, Reinach," he concluded. "But we mustn't allow our admiration to overpower us. We'll really have to give this thing up, Thorne, at least temporarily. I had been hoping. . . . But there! I've promised the poor girl. We're leaving tomorrow as best we can."

"And be found frozen stiff next March by a rescue party," said Thorne miserably. "Pleasant prospect! And yet even death by freezing is preferable to this abominable place." He looked curiously at Ellery. "I must say I'm a trifle disappointed in you, Queen. From what I'd heard about your professional cunning . . ."

"I never claimed," shrugged Ellery, "to be a magician. Or even a theologian. What's happened here is either the blackest magic or palpable proof that miracles can happen."

"It would seem so," muttered Thorne. "And yet, when you put your mind to it . . . It goes against reason, by thunder!"

"I see," said Ellery dryly, "the man of law is recovering from the initial shock. Well, it's a shame to have to leave here now, in a way. I detest the thought of giving up—especially at the present time."

"At the present time? What do you mean?"

"I dare say, Thorne, you haven't emerged far enough from your condition of shock to have properly analyzed this little problem. I gave it a lot of thought today. The goal eludes me—but I'm near it," he said softly, "very near it."

"You mean," gasped the lawyer, "you mean you actually—"

"Remarkable case," said Ellery. "Oh, extraordinary—there isn't a word in the English language or any other, for that matter, that properly describes it. If I were religiously inclined . . ." He puffed away thoughtfully. "It gets down to the very simple elements, as all truly great problems do. A fortune in gold exists. It is hidden in a house. The house disappears. To find the gold, then, you must first find the house. I believe. . . ."

"Aside from that mumbo-jumbo with Keith's broom the other day," cried Thorne, "I can't recall that you've made a single effort in that direction. Find the house!—why, you've done nothing but sit around and wait."

"Exactly," murmured Ellery.

"What?"

"Wait. That's the prescription, my lean and angry friend. That's the sigil that will exorcise the spirit of the Black House."

"Sigil?" Thorne stared. "Spirit?"

"Wait. Precisely. Lord, how I'm waiting!"

Thorne looked puzzled and suspicious, as if he suspected Ellery of a contrary midnight humor. But Ellery sat soberly smoking. "Wait! For what, man? You're more exasperating than that fat monstrosity! What are you waiting for?"

Ellery looked at him. Then he rose and flung his butt into the dying fire and placed his hand on the old man's arm. "Go to bed, Thorne. You wouldn't believe me if I told you."

"Queen, you *must*. I'll go mad if I don't see daylight on this thing soon!"

Ellery looked shocked, for no reason that Thorne could see. And then, just as inexplicably, he slapped Thorne's shoulder and began to chuckle.

"Go to bed," he said, still chuckling.

"But you must tell me!"

Ellery sighed, losing his smile. "I can't. You'd laugh."

"I'm not in a laughing mood!"

"Nor is it a laughing matter. Thorne, I began to say a moment ago that if I, poor sinner that I am, possessed religious susceptibilities, I should have become permanently devout in the past three days. I suppose I'm a hopeless case. But even I see a power not of earth in this."

"Play-actor," growled the old lawyer. "Professing to see the hand of God in . . . Don't be sacrilegious, man. We're not all heathen."

Ellery looked out his window at the moonless night and the glimmering grayness of the snow-swathed world.

"Hand of God?" he murmured. "No, not hand, Thorne. If this case is ever solved, it will be by . . . a lamp."

"Lamp?" said Thorne faintly. "Lamp?"

"In a manner of speaking. *The lamp of God.*"

III

The next day dawned sullenly, as ashen and hopeless a morning as ever was. Incredibly, it still snowed in the same thick fashion, as if the whole sky were crumbling bit by bit.

Ellery spent the better part of the day in the garage, tinkering at the big black car's vitals. He left the doors wide open, so that anyone who wished might see what he was about. He knew little enough of automotive mechanics, and he was engaged in a futile business.

But in the late afternoon, after hours of vain experimentation, he suddenly came upon a tiny wire which seemed to him to be out of joint with its environment. It simply hung, a useless thing. Logic demanded a connection. He experimented. He found one.

As he stepped on the starter and heard the cold motor sputter into life, a shape darkened the entrance of the garage. He turned off the ignition quickly and looked up.

It was Keith, a black mass against the background of snow, standing with widespread legs, a large can hanging from each big hand.

"Hello, there," murmured Ellery. "You've assumed human shape again I see. Back on one of your infrequent jaunts to the world of men, Keith?"

Keith said quietly: "Going somewhere, Mr. Queen?"

"Certainly. Why—do you intend to stop me?"

"Depends on where you're going."

"Ah, a treat. Well, suppose I tell *you* where to go?"

"Tell all you want. You don't get off these grounds until I know where you're bound for."

Ellery grinned. "There's a naive directness about you, Keith, that draws me in spite of myself. Well, I'll relieve your mind. Thorne and I are taking Miss Mayhew back to the city."

"In that case it's all right." Ellery studied his face; it was worn deep with ruts of fatigue and worry. Keith dropped the cans to the cement floor of the garage. "You can use these, then. Gas."

"Gas! Where on earth did you get it?"

"Let's say," said Keith grimly, "I dug it up out of an old Indian tomb."

"Very well."

"You've fixed Thorne's car, I see. Needn't have. I could have done it."

"Then why didn't you?"

"Because nobody asked me to." The giant swung on his heel and vanished.

Ellery sat still, frowning. Then he got out of the car, picked up the cans, and poured their contents into the tank. He reached into the car again, got the engine running, and leaving it to purr away like a great cat he went back to the house.

He found Alice in her room, a coat over her shoulders, staring out her window. She sprang up at his knocks.

"Mr. Queen, you've got Mr. Thorne's car going!"

"Success at last," smiled Ellery. "Are you ready?"

"Oh, yes! I feel so much better, now that we're actually to leave. Do you think we'll have a hard time? I saw Mr. Keith bring those cans in. Petrol, weren't they? Nice of him. I never did believe such a nice young man—"

She flushed. There were hectic spots in her cheeks and her eyes were brighter than they had been for days. Her voice seemed less husky, too.

"It may be hard going through the drifts, but the car is equipped with chains. With luck we should make it. It's a powerful—"

Ellery stopped very suddenly indeed, his eyes fixed on the worn carpet at his feet, stony yet startled.

"Whatever is the matter, Mr. Queen?"

"Matter?" Ellery raised his eyes and drew a deep, deep breath. "Nothing at all. God's in His heaven and all's right with the world."

She looked down at the carpet. "Oh . . . the sun!" With a little squeal of delight she turned to the window. "Why, Mr. Queen, it's stopped snowing. There's the sun setting—at last!"

"And high time, too," said Ellery briskly. "Will you please get your things on? We leave at once." He picked up her bags and left her, walking with a springy vigor that shook the old boards. He crossed the corridor to his room opposite hers and began, whistling, to pack his bag.

The living room was noisy with a babble of adieux. One would have said that this was a normal household, with normal people in a normal human situation. Alice was positively gay, quite as if she were not leaving a fortune in gold for what might turn out to be all time.

She set her purse down on the mantel next to her mother's chromo, fixed her hat, flung her arms about Mrs. Reinach, pecked gingerly at Mrs. Fell's withered cheek, and even smiled forgivingly at Dr. Reinach. Then she dashed back to the mantel, snatched up her purse, threw one long enigmatic glance at Keith's drawn face, and hurried outdoors as if the devil himself were after her.

Thorne was already in the car, his old face alight with incredible happiness, as if he had been reprieved at the very moment he was to set foot beyond the little green door. He beamed at the dying sun.

Ellery followed Alice more slowly. The bags were in Thorne's car; there was nothing more to do. He climbed in, raced the motor, and then released the brake.

The fat man filled the doorway, shouting: "You know the road, now, don't you? Turn to the right at the end of this drive. Then keep going in a straight line. You can't miss. You'll hit the main highway in about. . . ."

His last words were drowned in the roar of the engine. Ellery waved his hand. Alice, in the tonneau beside Thorne, twisted about and laughed a little hysterically. Thorne sat beaming at the back of Ellery's head.

The car, under Ellery's guidance, trundled unsteadily out of the drive and made a right turn into the road.

It grew dark rapidly. They made slow progress. The big machine inched its way through the drifts, slipping and lurching despite its chains. As night fell, Ellery turned the powerful headlights on.

He drove with unswerving concentration.

None of them spoke.

It seemed hours before they reached the main highway. But when they did the car leaped to life on the road, which had been partly cleared by snowplows, and it was not long before they were entering the nearby town.

At the sight of the friendly electric lights, the paved streets, the solid blocks of houses, Alice gave a cry of sheer delight. Ellery stopped at a gasoline station and had the tank filled.

"It's not far from here, Miss Mayhew," said Thorne reassuringly. "We'll be in the city in no time. The Triborough Bridge . . ."

"Oh, it's wonderful to be alive!"

"Of course you'll stay at my house. My wife will be delighted to have you. After that . . ."

"You're so kind, Mr. Thorne. I don't know how I shall ever be able to thank you enough." She paused, startled. "Why, what's the matter, Mr. Queen?"

For Ellery had done a strange thing. He had stopped the car at a traffic intersection and asked the officer on duty something in a low tone. The officer stared at him and replied with gestures. Ellery swung the car off into another street. He drove slowly.

"What's the matter?" asked Alice again, leaning forward.

Thorne said, frowning: "You can't have lost your way. There's a sign which distinctly says. . . ."

"No, it's not that," said Ellery in a preoccupied way. "I've just thought of something."

The girl and the old man looked at each other, puzzled. Ellery stopped the car at a large stone building with green lights outside and went in, remaining there for fifteen minutes. He came out whistling.

"Queen!" said Thorne abruptly, eyes on the green lights. "What's up?"

"Something that must be brought down." Ellery swung the car about and headed it for the traffic intersection. When he reached it he turned left.

"Why, you've taken the wrong turn," said Alice nervously. "This is the direction from which we've just come. I'm sure of that."

"And you're quite right, Miss Mayhew. It is." She sank back, pale, as if the very thought of returning terrified her. "We're going back, you see," said Ellery.

"Back!" exploded Thorne, sitting up straight.

"Oh, can't we just forget all those horrible people?" moaned Alice.

"I've a viciously stubborn memory. Besides, we have reinforcements. If you'll look back you'll see a car following us. It's a police car, and in it are the local Chief of Police and a squad of picked men."

"But why, Mr. Queen?" cried Alice. Thorne said nothing; his happiness had quite vanished, and he sat gloomily staring at the back of Ellery's neck.

"Because," said Ellery grimly, "I have my own professional pride. Because I've been on the receiving end of a damnably cute magician's trick."

"Trick?" she repeated dazedly.

"Now I shall turn magician myself. You saw a house disappear." He laughed softly. "I shall make it appear again!"

They could only stare at him, too bewildered to speak.

"And then," said Ellery, his voice hardening, "even if we chose to overlook such trivia as dematerialized houses, in all conscience we can't overlook . . . *murder*."

IV

And there was the Black House again. Not a wraith. A solid house, a strong dirty time-encrusted house, looking as if it would never dream of taking wings and flying off into space. It stood on the other side of the driveway, where it had always stood.

They saw it even as they turned into the drive from the drift-covered road, its bulk looming black against the brilliant moon, as substantial a house as could be found in the world of sane things.

Thorne and the girl were incapable of speech; they could only gape, dumb witnesses of a miracle even greater than the disappearance of the house in the first place.

As for Ellery, he stopped the car, sprang to the ground, signaled to the car snuffling up behind, and darted across the snowy clearing to the White House, whose windows were bright with lamp- and firelight. Out of the police car swarmed men, and they ran after Ellery like hounds. Thorne and Alice followed in a daze.

Ellery kicked open the White House door. There was a revolver in his hand and there was no doubt, from the way he gripped it, that its cylinder had been replenished.

"Hello again," he said, stalking into the living room. "Not a ghost; Inspector Queen's little boy in the too, too solid flesh. Nemesis, perhaps. I bid you good evening. What—no welcoming smile, Dr. Reinach?"

The fat man had paused in the act of lifting a glass of Scotch to his lips. It was wonderful how the color seeped out of his pouchy cheeks, leaving them gray. Mrs. Reinach whimpered in a corner, and Mrs. Fell stared stupidly. Only Nick Keith showed no great astonishment. He was standing by a window, muffled to the ears; and on his face there was bitterness and admiration and, strangely, a sort of relief.

"Shut the door." The detectives behind Ellery spread out silently. Alice stumbled to a chair, her eyes wild, studying Dr. Reinach with a fierce intensity. . . . There was a sighing little sound and one of the detectives lunged toward the window at which Keith had been standing. But Keith was no longer there. He was bounding through the snow toward the woods like a huge deer.

"Don't let him get away!" cried Ellery. Three men dived through the window after the giant, their guns out. Shots began to sputter. The night outside was streaked with orange lightning.

Ellery went to the fire and warmed his hands. Dr. Reinach slowly, very slowly, sat down in the armchair. Thorne sank into a chair, too, putting his hands to his head.

Ellery turned around and said: "I've told you, Captain, enough of what's happened since our arrival to allow you an intelligent understanding of what I'm about to say." A stocky man in uniform nodded curtly.

"Thorne, last night for the first time in my career," continued Ellery whimsically, "I acknowledged the assistance of . . . Well, I tell you, who are implicated in this extraordinary crime, that had it not been for the good God above you would have succeeded in your plot against Alice Mayhew's inheritance."

"I'm disappointed in you," said the fat man from the depths of the chair.

"A loss I keenly feel." Ellery looked at him, smiling. "Let me show you, skeptic. When Mr. Thorne, Miss Mayhew and I arrived the other day, it was late afternoon. Upstairs, in the room you so thoughtfully provided, I looked out the window and saw the sun setting. This was nothing and meant nothing, surely: sunset. Mere sunset. A trivial thing, interesting only to poets, meteorologists, and astronomers. But this was the one time when the sun was vital to a man seeking truth . . . a veritable lamp of God shining in the darkness.

"For, see. Miss Mayhew's bedroom that first day was on the opposite side of the house from mine. If the sun set in my window, then I faced west and she faced east. So far, so good. We talked, we retired. The next morning I awoke at seven—shortly after sunrise in this winter month—and what did I see? *I saw the sun streaming into my window.*"

A knot hissed in the fire behind him. The stocky man in the blue uniform stirred uneasily.

"Don't you understand?" cried Ellery. "The sun had *set* in my window, and now it was *rising* in my window!"

Dr. Reinach was regarding him with a mild ruefulness. The color had come back to his fat cheeks. He raised the glass he was holding in a gesture curiously like a salute. Then he drank, deeply.

And Ellery said: "The significance of this unearthly reminder did not strike me at once. But much later it came back to me; and I dimly saw that chance, cosmos, God, whatever you may choose to call it, had given me the instrument for understanding the colossal, the mind-staggering phenomenon of a house which vanished overnight from the face of the earth."

"Good lord," muttered Thorne.

"But I was not sure; I did not trust my memory. I needed another demonstration from heaven, a bulwark to bolster my own suspicions. And so, as it snowed and snowed and snowed, the snow drawing a blanket across the face of the sun through which it could not shine, I waited. I waited for the snow to stop, and for the sun to shine again."

He sighed. "When it shone again, there could no longer be any doubt. It appeared first to me in Miss Mayhew's room, which had faced the east the afternoon of our arrival. But what was it I saw in Miss Mayhew's room late this afternoon? I saw the sun *set*."

"Good lord," said Thorne again; he seemed incapable of saying anything else.

"Then her room faced west today. How could her room face west today when it had faced east the day of our arrival? How could my room face west the day of our arrival and face east today? Had the sun stood still? Had the world gone mad? Or was there another explanation—one so extraordinarily simple that it staggered the imagination?"

Thorne muttered: "Queen, this is the most—"

"Please," said Ellery, "let me finish. The only logical conclusion, the only conclusion that did not fly in the face of natural law, of science itself, was that while the house we were in today, the rooms we occupied, *seemed* to be identical with the house and the rooms we had occupied on the day of our arrival, *they were not*. Unless this solid structure had been turned about on its foundation like a toy on a stick, which was palpably absurd, then *it was not the same house*. It looked the same inside and out, it had identical furniture, identical carpeting, identical decorations . . . but it was not the same house. It was another house. It was another house exactly like the first in every detail except one: and that was its terrestrial position in relation to the sun."

A detective outside shouted a message of failure, a shout carried away by the wind under the bright cold moon.

"See," said Ellery softly, "how everything fell into place. If this White House we were in was not the same White House in which we had slept that first night, but was a twin house in a different position in relation to the sun, then the Black House, which apparently had vanished, had not vanished at all. It was where it had always been. It was not the Black House which had vanished, but we who had vanished. It was not the Black House which had moved away, but we who had moved away. We had been transferred during that first night to a new location, where the surrounding woods looked similar, where there was a similar driveway with a similar garage at its terminus, where the road outside was similarly old and pitted, where everything was similar except that there was no Black House, only an empty clearing.

"So we must have been moved, body and baggage, to this twin White House during the time we retired the first night and the time we awoke the next morning. We, Miss Mayhew's chromo on the mantel, the holes in our doors where locks had been, even the fragments of a brandy decanter which had been shattered the night before in a cleverly staged scene against the brick wall of the fireplace at the original house . . . all, all transferred to the twin house to further the illusion that we were still in the original house the next morning."

"Drivel," said Dr. Reinach, smiling. "Such pure drivel that it smacks of phantasmagoria."

"It was beautiful," said Ellery. "A beautiful plan. It had symmetry, the polish of great art. And it made a beautiful chain of reasoning, too, once I was set properly at the right link. For what followed? Since we had been transferred without our knowledge during the night, it must have been while we were unconscious. I recalled the two drinks Thorne and I had had, and the fuzzy tongue and head that resulted the next morning. Mildly drugged, then; and the drinks had been mixed the night before by Dr. Reinach's own hand. Doctor—drugs; very simple." The fat man shrugged with amusement, glancing sidewise at the stocky man in blue. But the stocky man in blue wore a hard, unchanging mask.

"But Dr. Reinach alone?" murmured Ellery. "Oh, no, impossible.

One man could never have accomplished all that was necessary in the scant few hours available . . . fix Thorne's car, carry us and our clothes and bags from the one White House to its duplicate—by machine—put Thorne's car out of commission again, put us to bed again, arrange our clothing identically, transfer the chromo, the fragments of the cut-glass decanter in the fireplace, perhaps even a few knickknacks and ornaments not duplicated in the second White House, and so on. A prodigious job, even if most of the preparatory work had been done before our arrival. Obviously the work of a whole group. Of accomplices. Who but everyone in the house? With the possible exception of Mrs. Fell, who in her condition could be swayed easily enough, with no clear perception of what was occurring."

Ellery's eyes gleamed. "And so I accuse you all—including young Mr. Keith who has wisely taken himself off—of having aided in the plot whereby you would prevent the rightful heiress of Sylvester Mayhew's fortune from taking possession of the house in which it was hidden."

Dr. Reinach coughed politely, flapping his paws together like a great seal.

"Terribly interesting, Queen, terribly. I don't know when I've been more captivated by sheer fiction. On the other hand, there are certain personal allusions in your story which, much as I admire their ingenuity, cannot fail to provoke me." He turned to the stocky man in blue. "Certainly, Captain," he chuckled, "you don't credit this incredible story? I believe Mr. Queen has gone a little mad from sheer shock."

"Unworthy of you, Doctor," sighed Ellery. "The proof of what I say lies in the very fact that we are here, at this moment."

"You'll have to explain that," said the police chief, who seemed out of his depth.

"I mean that we are now in the original White House. I led you back here, didn't I? And I can lead you back to the twin White House, for now I know the basis of the illusion. After our departure this evening, incidentally, all these people returned to this house. The other White House had served its purpose and they no longer needed it.

"As for the geographical trick involved, it struck me that this side road we're on makes a steady curve for miles. Both driveways lead off this same road, one some six miles farther up the road; although, because of the curve, which is like a number 9, the road makes a wide sweep and virtually doubles back on itself, so that as the crow flies the two settlements are only a mile or so apart, although by the curving road they are six miles apart.

"When Dr. Reinach drove Thorne and Miss Mayhew and me out here the day the *Caronia* docked, he deliberately passed the almost imperceptible drive leading to the substitute house and went on until he reached this one, the original. We didn't notice the first driveway.

"Thorne's car was put out of commission deliberately to prevent his driving. The driver of a car will observe landmarks when his passengers notice little or nothing. Keith even met Thorne on both Thorne's previous visits to Mayhew—ostensibly to lead the way, actually to prevent Thorne from familiarizing himself with the road. And it was Dr. Reinach who drove the three of us here that first day. They permitted me to drive away tonight for what they hoped was a one-way trip because we started from the substitute house—of the two, the one on the road nearer to town. We couldn't possibly, then, pass the telltale second drive and become suspicious. And they knew the relatively shorter drive would not impress our consciousness."

"But even granting all that, Mr. Queen," said the policeman, "I don't see what these people expected to accomplish. They couldn't hope to keep you folks fooled forever."

"True," cried Ellery, "but don't forget that by the time we caught on to the various tricks involved they hoped to have laid hands on Mayhew's fortune and disappeared with it. Don't you see that the whole illusion was planned *to give them time*? Time to dismantle the Black House without interference, raze it to the ground if necessary, to find that hidden hoard of gold? I don't doubt that if you examine the house next door you'll find it a shambles and a hollow shell. That's why Reinach and Keith kept disappearing. They were taking turns at the Black House, picking it apart, stone by stone, in a frantic search for the cache, while we were occupied in the duplicate White House with an apparently supernatural phenomenon. That's why someone—probably the worthy doctor here—slipped out of the house behind your back, Thorne, and struck me over the head when I rashly attempted to follow Keith's tracks in the snow. I could not be permitted to reach the original settlement, for if I did the whole preposterous illusion would be revealed."

"How about that gold?" growled Thorne.

"For all I know," said Ellery with a shrug, "they've found it and salted it away again."

"Oh, but we didn't," whimpered Mrs. Reinach, squirming in her chair. "Herbert, I *told* you not to—"

"Idiot," said the fat man. "Stupid swine." She jerked as if he had struck her.

"If you hadn't found the loot," said the police chief to Dr. Reinach brusquely, "why did you let these people go tonight?"

Dr. Reinach compressed his blubbery lips; he raised his glass and drank quickly.

"I think I can answer that," said Ellery in a gloomy tone. "In many ways it's the most remarkable element of the whole puzzle. Certainly it's the grimmest and least excusable. The other illusion was child's play compared to it. For it involves two apparently irreconcilable elements—Alice Mayhew and a murder."

"A murder!" exclaimed the policeman, stiffening.

"Me?" said Alice in bewilderment.

Ellery lit a cigarette and flourished it at the policeman. "When Alice Mayhew came here that first afternoon, she went into the Black House with us. In her father's bedroom she ran across an old chromo—I see it's not here, so it's still in the other White House—portraying her long-dead mother as a girl. Alice Mayhew fell on the chromo like a Chinese refugee on a bowl of rice. She had only one picture of her mother, she explained, and that a poor one. She treasured this unexpected discovery so much that she took it with her, then and there, to the White House—this house. And she placed it on the mantel over the fireplace here in a prominent position."

The stocky man frowned; Alice sat very still; Thorne looked puzzled.

And Ellery put the cigarette back to his lips and said: "Yet when Alice Mayhew fled from the White House in our company tonight for what seemed to be the last time, *she completely ignored her mother's chromo*, that treasured memento over which she had gone into such raptures the first day! She could not have failed to overlook it in, let us say, the excitement of the moment. She had placed her purse on the mantel, a moment before, next to the chromo. She returned to the mantel for her purse. And yet she passed the chromo up without a glance. Since its sentimental value to her was overwhelming, by her own admission, it's the one thing in all this property *she would not have left*. If she had taken it in the beginning, she would have taken it on leaving."

Thorne cried: "What in the name of heaven are you saying, Queen?" His eyes glared at the girl, who sat glued to her chair, scarcely breathing.

"I am saying," said Ellery curtly, "that we were blind. I am saying that not only was a house impersonated, but a woman as well. *I am saying that this woman is not Alice Mayhew.*"

The girl raised her eyes after an infinite interval in which no one, not even the policemen present, so much as stirred a foot.

"I thought of everything," she said with the queerest sigh, and quite without the husky tone, "but that. And it was going off so beautifully."

"Oh, you fooled me very neatly," drawled Ellery. "That pretty little bedroom scene last night. . . . I know now what happened. This precious Dr. Reinach of yours had stolen into your room at midnight to report to you on the progress of the search at the Black House, perhaps to urge you to persuade Thorne and me to leave today—at any cost. I happened to pass along the hall outside your room, stumbled, and fell against the wall with a clatter; not knowing who it might be or what the intruder's purpose, you both fell instantly into that cunning deception. . . . Actors! Both of you missed a career on the stage."

The fat man closed his eyes; he seemed asleep. And the girl murmured, with a sort of tired defiance: "Not missed, Mr. Queen. I spent several years in the theater."

"You were devils, you two. Psychologically this plot has been the conception of evil genius. You knew that Alice Mayhew was unknown to anyone in this country except by her photographs. Moreover, there was a startling resemblance between the two of you, as Miss Mayhew's photographs showed. And you knew Miss Mayhew would be in the company of Thorne and me for only a few hours, and then chiefly in the murky light of a sedan."

"Good lord," groaned Thorne, staring at the girl in horror.

"Alice Mayhew," said Ellery grimly, "walked into this house and was whisked upstairs by Mrs. Reinach. *And Alice Mayhew, the English girl, never appeared before us again.* It was you who came downstairs; you, who had been secreted from Thorne's eyes during the past six days deliberately, so that he would not even suspect your existence; you who probably conceived the entire plot when Thorne brought the photographs of Alice Mayhew here, and her gossipy, informative letters; you, who looked enough like the real Alice Mayhew to get by with an impersonation in the eyes of two men to whom Alice Mayhew was a total stranger. I did think you looked different, somehow, when you appeared for dinner that first night; but I put it down to the fact that I was seeing you for the first time refreshed, brushed up, and without your hat and coat. Naturally, after that, the more I saw of you the less I remembered the details of the real Alice Mayhew's appearance and so became more and more convinced, unconsciously,

that you were Alice Mayhew. As for the husky voice and the excuse of
having caught cold on the long automobile ride from the pier, that was
a clever ruse to disguise the inevitable difference between your voices.
The only danger that existed lay in Mrs. Fell, who gave us the answer
to the whole riddle the first time we met her. She thought you were
her own daughter Olivia. Of course. *Because that's who you are!*"

Dr. Reinach was sipping brandy now with a steady indifference to
his surroundings. His little eyes were fixed on a point miles away. Old
Mrs. Fell sat gaping stupidly at the girl.

"You even covered that danger by getting Dr. Reinach to tell us
beforehand that trumped-up story of Mrs. Fell's 'delusion' and Olivia
Fell's 'death' in an automobile accident several years ago. Oh, admirable! Yet even this poor creature, in the frailty of her anile faculties,
was fooled by a difference in voice and hair—two of the most easily
distinguishable features. I suppose you fixed up your hair at the time
Mrs. Reinach brought the real Alice Mayhew upstairs and you had a
living model to go by. . . . I could find myself moved to admiration if
it were not for one thing."

"You're so clever," said Olivia Fell coolly. "Really a fascinating
monster. What do you mean?"

Ellery went to her and put his hand on her shoulder. "Alice Mayhew vanished and you took her place. Why did you take her place?
For two possible reasons. One—to get Thorne and me away from the
danger zone as quickly as possible, and to keep us away by 'aban-
doning' the fortune or dismissing us, which as Alice Mayhew would
be your privilege: in proof, your vociferous insistence that we take
you away. Two—of infinitely greater importance to the scheme: if
your confederates did not find the gold at once, you were still Alice
Mayhew in our eyes. You could then dispose of the house when and
as you saw fit. Whenever the gold was found, it would be yours and
your accomplices'.

"But the real Alice Mayhew vanished. For you, her impersonator,
to be in a position to go through the long process of taking over Al-

ice Mayhew's inheritance, it was necessary that Alice Mayhew remain *permanently invisible.* For you to get possession of her rightful inheritance and live to enjoy its fruits, it was necessary that Alice Mayhew die. And that, Thorne," snapped Ellery, gripping the girl's shoulder hard, "is why I said that there was something besides a disappearing house to cope with tonight. Alice Mayhew was murdered."

There were three shouts from outside which rang with tones of great excitement. And then they ceased, abruptly.

"Murdered," went on Ellery, "by the only occupant of the house who was not *in* the house when this imposter came downstairs that first evening—Nicholas Keith. A hired killer. Although these people are all accessories to that murder."

A voice said from the window: "Not a hired *killer.*"

They wheeled sharply, and fell silent. The three detectives who had sprung out of the window were there in the background, quietly watchful. Before them were two people.

"Not a killer," said one of them, a woman. "That's what he was supposed to be. Instead, and without their knowledge, he saved my life . . . dear Nick."

And now the pall of grayness settled over the faces of Mrs. Fell, and of Olivia Fell, and of Mrs. Reinach, and of the burly doctor. For by Keith's side stood Alice Mayhew. She was the same woman who sat near the fire only in general similitude of feature. Now that both women could be compared in proximity, there were obvious points of difference. She looked worn and grim, but happy withal; and she was holding to the arm of bitter-mouthed Nick Keith with a grip that was quite possessive.

ADDENDUM

Afterwards, when it was possible to look back on the whole amazing fabric of plot and event, Mr. Ellery Queen said: "The scheme would have been utterly impossible except for two things: the character of

Olivia Fell and the—in itself—fantastic existence of that duplicate house in the woods."

He might have added that both of these would in turn have been impossible except for the aberrant strain in the Mayhew blood. The father of Sylvester Mayhew—Dr. Reinach's stepfather—had always been erratic, and he had communicated his unbalance to his children. Sylvester and Sarah, who became Mrs. Fell, were twins, and they had always been insanely jealous of each other's prerogatives. When they married in the same month, their father avoided trouble by presenting each of them with a specially built house, the houses being identical in every detail. One he had erected next to his own house and presented to Mrs. Fell as a wedding gift; the other he built on a piece of property he owned some miles away and gave to Sylvester.

Mrs. Fell's husband died early in her married life; and she moved away to live with her half brother Herbert. When old Mayhew died, Sylvester boarded up his own house and moved into the ancestral mansion. And there the twin houses stood for many years, separated by only a few miles by road, completely and identically furnished inside—fantastic monuments to the Mayhew eccentricity.

The duplicate White House lay boarded up, waiting, idle, requiring only the evil genius of an Olivia Fell to be put to use. Olivia was beautiful, intelligent, accomplished, and as unscrupulous as Lady Macbeth. It was she who had influenced the others to move back to the abandoned house next to the Black House for the sole purpose of coercing or robbing Sylvester Mayhew. When Thorne appeared with the news of Sylvester's long-lost daughter, she recognized the peril to their scheme and, grasping her own resemblance to her English cousin from the photographs Thorne brought, conceived the whole extraordinary plot.

Then obviously the first step was to put Sylvester out of the way. With perfect logic, she bent Dr. Reinach to her will and caused him to murder his patient before the arrival of Sylvester's daughter. (A later exhumation and autopsy revealed traces of poison in the corpse.)

Meanwhile, Olivia perfected the plans of the impersonation and illusion.

The house illusion was planned for the benefit of Thorne, to keep him sequestered and bewildered while the Black House was being torn down in the search for gold. The illusion would perhaps not have been necessary had Olivia felt certain that her impersonation would succeed perfectly.

The illusion was simpler, of course, than appeared on the surface. The house was there, completely furnished, ready for use. All that was necessary was to take the boards down, air the place out, clean up, put fresh linen in.

There was plenty of time before Alice's arrival for this preparatory work.

The one weakness of Olivia Fell's plot was objective, not personal. That woman would have succeeded in anything. But she made the mistake of selecting Nick Keith for the job of murdering Alice Mayhew. Keith had originally insinuated himself into the circle of plotters, posing as a desperado prepared to do anything for sufficient pay. Actually, he was the son of Sylvester Mayhew's second wife, who had been so brutally treated by Mayhew and driven off to die in poverty.

Before his mother expired she instilled in Keith's mind a hatred for Mayhew that waxed, rather than waned, with the ensuing years. Keith's sole motive in joining the conspirators was to find his stepfather's fortune and take that part of it which Mayhew had stolen from his mother. He had never intended to murder Alice—his ostensible role. When he carried her from the house that first evening under the noses of Ellery and Thorne, it was not to strangle and bury her, as Olivia had directed, but to secrete her in an ancient shack in the nearby woods known only to himself.

He had managed to smuggle provisions to her while he was ransacking the Black House. At first he had held her frankly prisoner, intending to keep her so until he found the money, took his share, and escaped. But as he came to know her, he came to love her, and he soon confessed the whole story to her in the privacy of the shack. Her sympathy gave him new courage; concerned now with her safety above everything else, he prevailed upon her to remain in hiding until he could find the money and outwit his fellow conspirators. Then they both intended to unmask Olivia.

The ironical part of the whole affair, as Mr. Ellery Queen was to point out, was that the goal of all this plotting and counterplotting— Sylvester Mayhew's gold—remained as invisible as the Black House apparently had been. Despite the most thorough search of the building and grounds no trace of it had been found.

"I've asked you to visit my poor diggings," smiled Ellery a few weeks later, "because something occurred to me that simply cried out for investigation."

Keith and Alice glanced at each other blankly; and Thorne, looking clean, rested, and complacent for the first time in weeks, sat up straighter in Ellery's most comfortable chair.

"I'm glad something occurred to somebody," said Nick Keith with a grin. "I'm a pauper; and Alice is only one jump ahead of me."

"You haven't the philosophic attitude towards wealth," said Ellery dryly, "that's so charming a part of Dr. Reinach's personality. Poor Colossus! I wonder how he likes our jails. . . ." He poked a log into the fire. "By this time, Miss Mayhew, our common friend Thorne has had your father's house virtually annihilated. No gold. Eh, Thorne?"

"Nothing but dirt," said the lawyer sadly. "Why, we've taken that house apart stone by stone."

"Exactly. Now there are two possibilities, since I am incorrigibly categorical: either your father's fortune exists, Miss Mayhew, or it does not. If it does not and he was lying, there's an end to the business, of course, and you and your precious Keith will have to put your heads together and agree to live either in noble, rugged individualistic poverty or by the grace of the Relief Administration. But suppose there was a fortune, as your father claimed, and suppose he did secrete it somewhere in that house. What then?"

"Then," sighed Alice, "it's flown away."

Ellery laughed. "Not quite; I've had enough of vanishments for the present, anyway. Let's tackle the problem differently. Is there anything which was in Sylvester Mayhew's house before he died which is not there now?"

Thorne stared. "If you mean the—er—the body . . ."

"Don't be gruesome, Literal Lyman. Besides, there's been an exhumation. No, guess again."

Alice looked slowly down at the package in her lap. "So that's why you asked me to fetch this with me today!"

"You mean," cried Keith, "the fellow was deliberately putting everyone off the track when he said his fortune was gold?"

Ellery chuckled and took the package from the girl. He unwrapped it and for a moment gazed appreciatively at the large old chromo of Alice's mother.

And then, with the self-assurance of the complete logician, he stripped away the back of the frame.

Gold-and-green documents cascaded into his lap.

"Converted into bonds," grinned Ellery. "Who said your father was cracked, Miss Mayhew? A very clever gentleman! Come, come, Thorne, stop rubbernecking and let's leave these children of fortune alone!"

OFF THE FACE OF THE EARTH
Clayton Rawson

Combining his skills as one of America's most famous illusionists and his talents as a mystery writer, all the fiction that Clayton Rawson (1906-1971) wrote using his own name featured the Great Merlini, a professional magician and amateur detective. Merlini opened a magic shop in New York City's Times Square, where he often is visited by his friendly rival, Inspector Homer Gavigan of the NYPD whenever he is utterly baffled by a seemingly impossible crime.

Merlini's adventures are recounted by freelance writer Ross Harte. There are only four Merlini novels, two of which have been adapted for motion pictures. *Miracles for Sale* (1939) was based on Rawson's first novel, *Death from a Top Hat* (1938). In this film, the protagonist is named Mike Morgan, played by Robert Young; it was directed by Tod Browning. The popular Mike Shayne series used Rawson's second book, *The Footprints on the Ceiling* (1939), as the basis for *The Man Who Wouldn't Die* (1942), with Lloyd Nolan starring as Shayne, who consults a professional magician for help.

The other Merlini books are *The Headless Lady* (1940), *No Coffin for the Corpse* (1942), and *The Great Merlini* (1979), a complete collection of Merlini stories. Under the pseudonym Stuart Towne, Rawson wrote four pulp novellas featuring Don Diavolo.

Rawson was a member of the American Society of Magicians and wrote on the subject frequently. Born in Elyria, Ohio, he graduated from Ohio State University and worked as an illustrator for advertising agencies and magazines before turning to writing. He used his extensive knowledge of stage magic to create elaborate locked room and impossible crime novels and short stories. The author was one of the four founding members of the Mystery Writers of America and created its motto: "Crime Does Not Pay—Enough."

"Off the Face of the Earth" was first published in the September 1949 issue of *Ellery Queen's Mystery Magazine*; it was first collected in *The Great Merlini* (Boston, Gregg Press, 1979).

Off the Face of the Earth
Clayton Rawson

THE LETTERING in neat gilt script on the door read: *Miracles For Sale*, and beneath it was the familiar rabbit-from-a-hat trademark. Inside, behind the glass showcase counter, in which was displayed as unlikely an assortment of objects as could be got together in one spot, stood The Great Merlini.

He was wrapping up half a dozen billiard balls, several bouquets of feather flowers, a dove pan, a Talking Skull, and a dozen decks of cards for a customer who snapped his fingers and nonchalantly produced the needed number of five-dollar bills from thin air. Merlini rang up the sale, took half a carrot from the cash drawer, and gave it to the large white rabbit who watched proceedings with a pink skeptical eye from the top of a nearby escape trunk. Then he turned to me.

"Clairvoyance, mind reading, extrasensory perception," he said. "We stock only the best grade. And it tells me that you came to pick up the two Annie Oakleys I promised to get you for that new hit musical. I have them right here."

But his occult powers slipped a bit. He looked in all his coat pockets one after another, found an egg, a three-foot length of rope, several brightly colored silk handkerchiefs, and a crumpled telegram reading: NEED INVISIBLE MAN AT ONCE. SHIP UNIONTOWN BY MONDAY—NEMO THE ENIGMA. Then he gave a surprised blink and scowled darkly at a sealed envelope that he had fished out of his inside breast pocket.

"That," I commented a bit sarcastically, "doesn't look like a pair of theater tickets."

He shook his head sadly. "No. It's a letter my wife asked me to mail a week ago."

I took it from him. "There's a mail chute by the elevators about fifteen feet outside your door. I'm no magician, but I can remember to put this in it on my way out." I indicated the telegram that lay on the counter. "Since when have you stocked a supply of invisible men? That I would like to see."

Merlini frowned at the framed slogan: *Nothing Is Impossible* which hung above the cash register. "You want real miracles, don't you? We guarantee that our invisible man can't be seen. But if you'd like to see how impossible it is to see him, step right this way."

In the back, beyond his office, there is a larger room that serves as workshop, shipping department and, on occasion, as a theater. I stood there a moment later and watched Merlini step into an upright coffin-shaped box in the center of the small stage. He faced me, smiled, and snapped his fingers. Two copper electrodes in the side walls of the cabinet spat flame, and a fat, green, electric spark jumped the gap just above his head, hissing and writhing. He lifted his arms; the angry stream of energy bent, split in two, fastened on his fingertips, and then disappeared as he grasped the gleaming spherical electrodes, one with each hand.

For a moment nothing happened; then, slowly, his body began to fade into transparency as the cabinet's back wall became increasingly visible through it. Clothes and flesh melted until only the bony skeletal structure remained. Suddenly, the jawbone moved and its grinning white teeth clicked as Merlini's voice said:

"You must try this, Ross. On a hot day like today, it's most comfortable."

As it spoke, the skeleton also wavered and grew dim. A moment later it was gone and the cabinet was, or seemed to be, empty. If Merlini still stood there, he was certainly invisible.

"Okay, Gypsy Rose Lee," I said. "I have now seen the last word in striptease performances." Behind me I heard the office door open and I looked over my shoulder to see Inspector Gavigan giving me a fishy stare. "You'd better get dressed again," I added. "We have company."

The Inspector looked around the room and at the empty stage, then at me again, cautiously this time. "If you said what I think you did—"

He stopped abruptly as Merlini's voice, issuing from nowhere, chuckled and said, "Don't jump to conclusions, Inspector. Appearances are deceptive. It's not an indecent performance, nor has Ross gone off his rocker and started talking to himself. I'm right here. On the stage."

Gavigan looked and saw the skeleton shape taking form within the cabinet. He closed his eyes, shook his head, then looked again. That didn't help. The grisly spectre was still there and twice as substantial. Then, wraithlike, Merlini's body began to form around it and, finally, grew opaque and solid. The magician grinned broadly, took his hands from the electrodes, and bowed as the spitting, green discharge of energy crackled once more above him. Then the stage curtains closed.

"You should be glad that's only an illusion," I told Gavigan. "If it were the McCoy and the underworld ever found out how it was done, you'd face an unparalleled crime wave and you'd never solve a single case."

"It's the Pepper's Ghost illusion brought up to date," Merlini said as he stepped out between the curtains and came toward us. "I've got more orders than I can fill. It's a sure-fire carnival draw." He frowned at Gavigan. "But *you* don't look very entertained."

"I'm not," the Inspector answered gloomily. "Vanishing into thin air may amuse some people. Not me. Especially when it really happens. Off stage in broad daylight. In Central Park."

"Oh," Merlini said. "I see. So that's what's eating you. Helen Hope, the chorus girl who went for a walk last week and never came back. She's still missing then, and there are still no clues?"

Gavigan nodded. "It's the Dorothy Arnold case all over again. Except for one thing we haven't let the newspapers know about—Bela Zyyzk."

"Bela what?" I asked.

Gavigan spelled it.

"Impossible," I said. "He must be a typographical error. A close relative of Etoain Shrdlu."

The Inspector wasn't amused. "Relatives," he growled. "I wish I could find some. He not only claims he doesn't have any—he swears he never has had any! And so far we haven't been able to prove different."

"Where does he come from?" Merlini asked. "Or won't he say?"

"Oh, he talks all right," Gavigan said disgustedly. "Too much. And none of it makes any sense. He says he's a momentary visitor to this planet—from the dark cloud of Antares. I've seen some high, wide, and fancy screwballs in my time, but this one takes the cake—candles and all."

"Helen Hope," Merlini said, "vanishes off the face of the earth. And Zyyzk does just the opposite. This gets interesting. What else does he have to do with her disappearance?"

"Plenty," Gavigan replied. "A week ago Tuesday night she went to a Park Avenue party at Mrs. James Dewitt-Smith's. She's another candidate for Bellevue. Collects Tibetan statuary, medieval relics, and crackpots like Zyyzk. He was there that night—reading minds."

"A visitor from outer space," Merlini said, "and a mindreader to boot. I won't be happy until I've had a talk with that gentleman."

"I have talked with him," the Inspector growled. "And I've had indigestion ever since. He does something worse than read minds. He makes predictions." Gavigan scowled at Merlini. "I thought fortune tellers always kept their customers happy by predicting good luck?"

Merlini nodded. "That's usually standard operating procedure. Zyyzk does something else?"

"He certainly does. He's full of doom and disaster. A dozen witnesses testify that he told Helen Hope she'd vanish off the face of the earth. And three days later that's exactly what she does do."

"I can see," Merlini said, "why you view him with suspicion. So you pulled him in for questioning and got a lot of answers that weren't very helpful?"

"Helpful!" Gavigan jerked several typewritten pages from his pocket and shook them angrily. "Listen to this. He's asked: 'What's your age?' and we get: 'According to which time—solar, sidereal, galactic, or universal?' Murphy of Missing Persons, who was questioning him, says: 'Any kind. Just tell us how old you are.' And Zyyzk replies: 'I can't answer that. The question, in that form, has no meaning.' " The Inspector threw the papers down disgustedly.

Merlini picked them up, riffled through them, then read some of the transcript aloud. "Question: How did you know that Miss Hope would disappear? Answer: Do you understand the basic theory of the fifth law of interdimensional reaction? Murphy: Huh? Zyyzk: Explanations are useless. You obviously have no conception of what I am talking about."

"He was right about that," Gavigan muttered. "Nobody does."

Merlini continued. "Question: Where is Miss Hope now? Answer: Beyond recall. She was summoned by the Lords of the Outer Darkness." Merlini looked up from the papers. "After that, I suppose, you sent him over to Bellevue?"

The Inspector nodded. "They had him under observation a week. And they turned in a report full of eight-syllable jawbreakers all meaning he's crazy as a bedbug—but harmless. I don't believe it. Anybody who predicts in a loud voice that somebody will disappear into thin air at twenty minutes after four on a Tuesday afternoon, just before it actually happens, knows plenty about it!"

Merlini is a hard man to surprise, but even he blinked at that. "Do you mean to say that he foretold the exact time, too?"

"Right on the nose," Gavigan answered. "The doorman of her apartment house saw her walk across the street and into Central Park at four eighteen. We haven't been able to find anyone who has seen her since. And don't tell me his prediction was a long shot that paid off."

"I won't," Merlini agreed. "Whatever it is, it's not coincidence. Where's Zyyzk now? Could you hold him after that psychiatric report?"

"The D.A.," Gavigan replied, "took him into General Sessions before Judge Keeler and asked that he be held as a material witness." The Inspector looked unhappier than ever. "It would have to be Keeler."

"What did he do?" I asked. "Deny the request?"

"No. He granted it. That's when Zyyzk made his second prediction. Just as they start to take him out and throw him back in the can, he makes some funny motions with his hands and announces, in that confident manner he's got, that the Outer Darkness is going to swallow Judge Keeler up, too!"

"And what," Merlini wanted to know, "is wrong with that? Knowing how you've always felt about Francis X. Keeler, I should think that prospect would please you."

Gavigan exploded. "Look, blast it! I have wished dozens of times that Judge Keeler would vanish into thin air, but that's exactly what I don't want to happen right now. We've known at headquarters that he's been taking fix money from the Castelli mob ever since the day he was appointed to the bench. But we couldn't do a thing. Political-ly he was dynamite. One move in his direction and there'd be a new Commissioner the next morning, with demotions all down the line. But three weeks ago the Big Guy and Keeler had a scrap, and we get a tip straight from the feed box that Keeler is fair game. So we start working overtime collecting the evidence that will send him up the river for what I hope is a ninety-nine-year stretch. We've been afraid he might tumble and try to pull another 'Judge Crater.' And now, just when we're almost, but not quite, ready to nail him and make it stick, this has to happen."

"Your friend, Zyyzk," Merlini said, "becomes more interesting by the minute. Keeler is being tailed, of course?"

"Twenty-four hours a day, ever since we got the word that there'd be no kickback." The phone on Merlini's desk rang as Gavigan was speaking. "I get hourly reports on his movements. Chances are that's for me now."

It was. In the office, we both watched him as he took the call. He listened a moment, then said, "Okay. Double the number of men on him immediately. And report back every fifteen minutes. If he shows any sign of going anywhere near a railroad station or airport, notify me at once."

Gavigan hung up and turned to us. "Keeler made a stop at the First National and spent fifteen minutes in the safety deposit vaults. He's carrying a suitcase, and you can have one guess as to what's in it now. This looks like the payoff."

"I take it," Merlini said, "that, this time, the Zyyzk forecast did not include the exact hour and minute when the Outer Darkness would swallow up the Judge?"

"Yeah. He sidestepped that. All he'll say is that it'll happen before the week is out."

"And today," Merlini said, "is Friday. Tell me this. The Judge seems to have good reasons for wanting to disappear which Zyyzk may or may not know about. Did Miss Hope also have reasons?"

"She had one," Gavigan replied. "But I don't see how Zyyzk could have known it. We can't find a thing that shows he ever set eyes on her before the night of that party. And her reason is one that few people knew about." The phone rang again and Gavigan reached for it. "Helen Hope is the girlfriend Judge Keeler visits the nights he doesn't go home to his wife!"

Merlini and I both tried to assimilate that and take in what Gavigan was telling the telephone at the same time. "Okay, I'm coming. And grab him the minute he tries to go through a gate." He slammed the receiver down and started for the door.

"Keeler," he said over his shoulder, "is in Grand Central. There's room in my car if you want to come."

He didn't need to issue that invitation twice. On the way down in the elevator Merlini made one not very helpful comment.

"You know," he said thoughtfully, "if the Judge does have a reservation on the extraterrestrial express—destination: the Outer Darkness—we don't know what gate that train leaves from."

We found out soon enough. The Judge stepped through it just two minutes before we hurried into the station and found Lieutenant Malloy exhibiting all the symptoms of having been hit over the head with a sledgehammer. He was bewildered and dazed, and had difficulty talking coherently.

Sergeant Hicks, a beefy, unimaginative, elderly detective who had also seen the thing happen looked equally groggy.

Usually, Malloy's reports were as dispassionate, precise, and factual as a logarithmic table. But not today. His first paragraph bore a much closer resemblance to a first-person account of a dope addict's dream.

"Malloy," Gavigan broke in icily. "Are you tight?"

The Lieutenant shook his head sadly. "No, but the minute I go off duty, I'm going to get so plas—"

Gavigan cut in again. "Are all the exits to this place covered?"

Hicks replied, "If they aren't, somebody is sure going to catch it."

Gavigan turned to the detective who had accompanied us in the inspector's car. "Make the rounds and double check that, Brady. And tell headquarters to get more men over here fast."

"They're on the way now," Hicks said. "I phoned right after it happened. First thing I did."

Gavigan turned to Malloy. "All right. Take it easy. One thing at a time—and in order."

"It don't make sense that way either," Malloy said hopelessly. "Keeler took a cab from the bank and came straight here. Hicks and I were right on his tail. He comes down to the lower level and goes into the Oyster Bar and orders a double brandy. While he's working on that, Hicks phones in for reinforcements with orders to cover every exit. They had time to get here, too; Keeler had a second brandy. Then, when he starts to come out, I move out to the center of the station floor by the information booth so I'm ahead of him and all set to make the pinch no matter which gate he heads for. Hicks stands pat, ready to tail him if he heads upstairs again.

"At first, that's where I think he's going because he starts up the ramp. But he stops here by this line of phone booths, looks in a directory and then goes into a booth halfway down the line. And as soon as he closes the door, Hicks moves up and goes into the next booth to the left of Keeler's." Malloy pointed. "The one with the Out-of-Order sign on it."

Gavigan turned to the Sergeant. "All right. You take it."

Hicks scowled at the phone booth as he spoke. "The door was closed and somebody had written 'Out of Order' on a card and stuck it in the edge of the glass. I lifted the card so nobody'd wonder why I was trying to use a dead phone, went in, closed the door and tried to get a load of what the Judge was saying. But it's no good. He was talking, but so low I couldn't get it. I came out again, stuck the card back in the door and walked back toward the Oyster Bar so I'd be set to follow him either way when he came out. And I took a gander into the Judge's booth as I went past. He was talking with his mouth up close to the phone."

"And then," Malloy continued, "we wait. And we wait. He went into that booth at five ten. At five twenty I get itchy feet. I begin to think maybe he's passed out or died of suffocation or something. Nobody in his right mind stays in a phone booth for ten minutes when the temperature is ninety like today. So I start to move in just as Hicks gets the same idea. He's closer than I am, so I stay put.

"Hicks stops just in front of the booth and lights a cigarette, which gives him a chance to take another look inside. Then I figure I must be right about the Judge having passed out. I see the match Hicks is holding drop, still lighted, and he turns quick and plasters his face against the glass. I don't wait. I'm already on my way when he turns and motions for me."

Malloy hesitated briefly. Then, slowly and very precisely, he let us have it. "I don't care if the Commissioner himself has me up on the carpet, one thing I'm sure of—*I hadn't taken my eyes off that phone booth for one single split second since the Judge walked into it.*"

"And neither," Hicks said with equal emphasis, "did I. Not for one single second."

"I did some fancy open-field running through the commuters," Malloy went on, "skidded to a stop behind Hicks and looked over his shoulder."

Gavigan stepped forward to the closed door of the booth and looked in.

"And what you see," Malloy finished, "is just what I saw. You can ship me down to Bellevue for observation, too. It's impossible. It doesn't make sense. I don't believe it. But that's exactly what happened."

For a moment Gavigan didn't move. Then, slowly, he pulled the door open.

The booth was empty.

The phone receiver dangled off the hook, and on the floor there was a pair of horn-rimmed spectacles, one lens smashed.

"Keeler's glasses," Hicks said. "He went into that booth and I had my eyes on it every second. He never came out. And he's not in it."

"And that," Malloy added in a tone of utter dejection, "isn't the half of it. I stepped inside, picked up the phone receiver Keeler had been using, and said, 'Hello' into the mouthpiece. There was a chance the party he'd been talking to might still be on the other end." Malloy came to a full stop.

"Well?" Gavigan prodded him. "Let's have it. Somebody answered?"

"Yes. Somebody said: '*This is the end of the trail, Lieutenant.*' Then—hung up."

"You didn't recognize the voice?"

"Yeah, I recognized it. That's the trouble. It was—*Judge Keeler!*"
Silence.

Then, quietly, Merlini asked, "You are quite certain that it was his voice, Malloy?"

The Lieutenant exploded. "I'm not sure of anything any more. But if you've ever heard Keeler—he sounds like a bullfrog with a cold—you'd know it couldn't be anyone else."

Gavigan's voice, or rather, a hollow imitation of it, cut in. "Merlini. Either Malloy and Hicks have both gone completely off their chumps or this is the one phone booth in the world that has two exits. The back wall is sheet metal backed by solid marble, but if there's a loose panel in one of the side walls, Keeler could have moved over into the empty booth that is supposed to be out of order. . ."

"Is supposed to be. . ." Malloy repeated. "So that's it! The sign's a phony. That phone isn't on the blink, and his voice—" Malloy took two swift steps into the booth. He lifted the receiver, dropped a nickel, and waited for the dial tone. He scowled. He jiggled the receiver. He repeated the whole operation.

This specimen of Mr. Bell's invention was definitely not working.

A moment or two later Merlini reported another flaw in the Inspector's theory. "There are," he stated after a quick but thorough inspection of both booths, "no sliding panels, hinged panels, removable sections, trapdoors, or any other form of secret exit. The sidewalls are single sheets of metal, thin but intact. The back wall is even more solid. There is one exit and one only—the door through which our vanishing man entered."

"He didn't come out," Sergeant Hicks insisted again, sounding like a cracked phonograph record endlessly repeating itself. "I was watching that door every single second. Even if he turned himself into an invisible man like in a movie I saw once, he'd still have had to open the door. And the door didn't budge. I was watching it every single—"

"And that," Merlini said thoughtfully, "leaves us with an invisible man who can also walk through closed doors. In short—a ghost. Which brings up another point. Have any of you noticed that there are a few spots of something on those smashed glasses that look very much like—blood?"

Malloy growled. "Yeah, but don't make any cracks about there being another guy in that booth who sapped Keeler—that'd mean *two* invisible men. . ."

"If there can be one invisible man," Merlini pointed out, "then there can be two."

Gavigan said, "Merlini, that vanishing gadget you were demonstrating when I arrived. . . It's just about the size and shape of this phone booth. I want to know—"

The magician shook his head. "Sorry, Inspector. That method wouldn't work here under these conditions. It's not the same trick. Keeler's miracle, in some respects, is even better. He should have been a magician; he's been wasting his time on the bench. Or has he? I wonder how much cash he carried into limbo with him in that suitcase?" He paused, then added, "More than enough, probably, to serve as a motive for murder."

And there, on that ominous note, the investigation stuck. It was as dead an end as I ever saw. And it got deader by the minute. Brady, returning a few minutes later, reported that all station exits had been covered by the time Keeler left the Oyster Bar and that none of the detectives had seen hide nor hair of him since.

"Those men stay there until further notice," Gavigan ordered. "Get more men—as many as you need—and start searching this place. I want every last inch of it covered. And every phone booth, too. If it was Keeler's voice Malloy heard, then he was in one of them, and—"

"You know, Inspector," Merlini interrupted, "this case not only takes the cake but the marbles, all the blue ribbons, and a truck load of loving cups too. That is another impossibility."

"What is?"

"The voice on the telephone. Look at it. If Keeler left the receiver in this booth off as Malloy and Hicks found it, vanished, then reappeared in another booth and tried to call this number, he'd get a busy signal. He couldn't have made a connection. And if he left the receiver on the hook, he could have called this number, but someone would have had to be here to lift the receiver and leave it off as it was found. It keeps adding up to two invisible men no matter how you look at it."

"I wish," Malloy said acidly, "that you'd disappear, too."

Merlini protested. "Don't. You sound like Zyyzk."

"That guy," Gavigan predicted darkly, "is going to wish he never heard of Judge Keeler. "

Gavigan's batting average as a prophet was zero. When Zyyzk, whom the Inspector ordered brought to the scene and who was delivered by squad car twenty minutes later, discovered that Judge Keeler had vanished, he was as pleased as punch.

An interstellar visitor from outer space should have three eyes, or at least green hair. Zyyzk, in that respect, was a disappointment. He was a pudgy little man in a wrinkled gray suit. His eyes, two only, were a pale, washed-out blue behind gold-rimmed bi-focals, and his hair, the color of weak tea, failed miserably in its attempt to cover the top of his head.

His manner, however, was charged with an abundant and vital confidence, and there was a haughty, imperious quality in his high, thin voice which hinted that there was much more to Mr. Zyyzk than met the eye.

"I issued distinct orders," he told Gavigan in an icy tone, "that I was never, under any circumstances, to be disturbed between the sidereal hours of five and seven postmeridian. You know that quite well, Inspector. Explain why these idiots have disobeyed. At once!"

If there is any quicker way of bringing an inspector of police to a boil, I don't know what it is. The look Gavigan gave the little man would have wrecked a Geiger counter. He opened his mouth. But the searing blast of flame which I expected didn't issue forth. He closed his mouth and swallowed. The Inspector was speechless.

Zyyzk calmly threw more fuel on the fire. "Well," he said impatiently tapping his foot. "I'm waiting."

A subterranean rumble began deep in Gavigan's interior and then, a split second before he blew his top, Merlini said quietly, "I understand, Mr. Zyyzk, that you read minds?"

Zyyzk, still the Imperial Roman Emperor, gave Merlini a scathing look. "I do," he said. "And what of it?"

"For a mind reader," Merlini told him, "you ask a lot of questions. I should think you'd know why you've been brought here."

That didn't bother the visitor from Outer Space. He stared intently at Merlini for a second, glanced once at Gavigan, then closed his eyes. The fingertips of one white hand pressed against his brow. Then he smiled.

"I see. Judge Keeler."

"Keeler?" Gavigan pretended surprise. "What about him?" Zyyzk wasn't fooled. He shook his head. "Don't try to deceive me, Inspector. It's childish. The Judge has vanished. Into the Outer Darkness—as I foretold." He grinned broadly. "You will, of course, release me now."

"I'll—I'll *what*?"

Zyyzk spread his hands. "You have no choice. Not unless you want to admit that I could sit in a police cell surrounded on all sides by steel bars and cause Judge Keeler to vanish off the face of the earth by willpower alone. Since that, to your limited, earthly intelligence, is impossible, I have an impregnable alibi. Good day, Inspector."

The little man actually started to walk off. The detectives who stood on either side were so dazed by his treatment of the Inspector that Zyyzk had gone six feet before they came to life again and grabbed him.

Whether the strange powers he claimed were real or not, his ability to render Gavigan speechless was certainly uncanny. The Inspector's mouth opened, but again nothing came out.

Merlini said, "You admit then that you are responsible for the Judge's disappearance?"

Zyyzk, still grinning, shook his head. "I predicted it. Beyond that I admit nothing."

"But you know how he vanished?"

The little man shrugged. "In the usual way, naturally. Only an adept of the seventh order would understand."

Merlini suddenly snapped his fingers and plucked a shiny silver dollar from thin air. He dropped it into his left hand, closed his fingers over it and held his fist out toward Zyyzk. "Perhaps Judge Keeler vanished—like this." Slowly he opened his fingers. The coin was gone.

For the first time a faint crack appeared in the polished surface of Zyyzk's composure. He blinked. "Who," he asked slowly, "are you?"

"An adept," Merlini said solemnly, "of the eighth order. One who is not yet satisfied that you are what you claim to be." He snapped his fingers again, almost under Zyyzk's nose, and the silver dollar reappeared. He offered it to Zyyzk. "A test," he said. "Let me see you send that back into the Outer Darkness from which I summoned it."

Zyyzk no longer grinned. He scowled and his eyes were hard. "It will go," he said, lifting his hand and rapidly tracing a cabalistic figure in the air. "And you with it!"

"Soon?" Merlini asked.

"Very soon. Before the hour of nine strikes again you will appear before the Lords of the Outer Darkness in far Antares. And there—"

Gavigan had had enough. He passed a miracle of his own. He pointed a cabalistic but slightly shaking finger at the little man and roared an incantation that had instant effect.

"*Get him out of here!*"

In the small space of time that it took them to hurry down the corridor and around a corner, Zyyzk and the two detectives who held him both vanished.

Gavigan turned on Merlini. "Isn't one lunatic enough without you acting like one, too?"

The magician grinned. "Keep your eyes on me, Inspector. If I vanish, as predicted, you may see how Keeler did it. If I don't, Zyyzk is on the spot and he may begin to make more sense."

"That," Gavigan growled, "is impossible."

Zyyzk, as far as I was concerned, wasn't the only thing that made no sense. The Inspector's men turned Grand Central station inside out and the only trace of Judge Keeler to be found were the smashed spectacles on the floor of that phone booth. Gavigan was so completely at a loss that he could think of nothing else to do but order the search made again.

Merlini, as far as I could tell, didn't seem to have any better ideas. He leaned against the wall opposite the phone booth and scowled darkly at its empty interior. Malloy and Hicks looked so tired and dispirited that Gavigan told them both to go home and sleep it off. An hour later, when the second search had proved as fruitless as the first, Gavigan suddenly told Lieutenant Doran to take over, turned, and started to march off.

Then Merlini woke up. "Inspector," he asked, "where are you going?"

Gavigan turned, scowling. "Anywhere," he said, "where I don't have to look at telephone booths. Do you have any suggestions?"

Merlini moved forward. "One, yes. Let's eat."

Gavigan didn't look as if he could keep anything in his stomach stronger than weak chicken broth, but he nodded absently. We got into Gavigan's car and Brady drove us crosstown, stopping, at Merlini's direction, in front of the Williston building.

The Inspector objected, "There aren't any decent restaurants in this neighborhood. Why—"

"Don't argue," Merlini said as he got out. "If Zyyzk's latest prediction comes off, this will be my last meal on earth. I want to eat here. Come on." He crossed the pavement toward a flashing green and purple neon sign that blinked: *Johnson's Cafeteria. Open All Night.*

Merlini was suddenly acting almost as strangely as Zyyzk. I knew very well that this wasn't the sort of place he'd pick for his last meal and, although he claimed to be hungry, I noticed that all he put on his tray was crackers and a bowl of soup. Pea soup at that—something he heartily disliked.

Then, instead of going to a table off in a corner where we could talk, he chose one right in the center of the room. He even selected our places for us. "You sit there, Inspector. You there, Ross. And excuse me a moment. I'll be right back." With that he turned, crossed to the street door through which we had come, and vanished through it.

"I think," I told Gavigan, "that he's got a bee in his bonnet."

The Inspector grunted. "You mean bats. In his belfry." He gave the veal cutlet on his plate a glum look.

Merlini was gone perhaps five minutes. When he returned, he made no move to sit down. He leaned over the table and asked, "Either of you got a nickel?"

I found one and handed it to him. Suspiciously, Gavigan said, "I thought you wanted to eat?"

"I must make a phone call first," the magician answered. "And with Zyyzk's prediction hanging over me, I'd just as soon you both watched me do it. Look out the window behind me, watch that empty booth—the second from the right. And keep your eyes on it every second." He glanced at his wrist watch. "If I'm not back here in exactly three minutes, you'd better investigate."

I didn't like the sound of that. Neither did Gavigan. He started to object. "Now, wait a minute. You're not going—"

But Merlini had already gone. He moved with long strides toward the street door, and the Inspector half rose from his chair as if to go after him. Then, when Gavigan saw what lay beyond the window, he stopped. The window we both faced was in a side wall at right angles to the street, and it opened, not to the outside, but into the arcade that runs through the Williston building.

Through the glass we could see a twenty-foot stretch of the arcade's opposite wall and against it, running from side to side, was a row of half a dozen phone booths.

I took a quick look at the clock on the wall above the window just as Merlini vanished through the street door. He reappeared at once in the arcade beyond the window, went directly to the second booth from the right, and went inside. The door closed.

"I don't like this," I said. "In three minutes the time will be exactly—"

"Quiet!" Gavigan commanded.

"—exactly nine o'clock," I finished. "Zyyzk's deadline!"

"He's not going to pull this off," Gavigan said. "You keep your eyes on that booth. I'm going outside and watch it from the street entrance. When the time's up, join me."

I heard his chair scrape across the floor as he got up, but I kept my eyes glued to the scene beyond the window—more precisely to one section of it—the booth into which Merlini had gone. I could see the whole face of the door from top to bottom and the dim luminescence of the light inside.

Nothing happened.

The second hand on the wall clock moved steadily, but much too slowly. At five seconds to the hour I found myself on my feet. And when the hand hit twelve I moved fast. I went through the door, turned left, and found Gavigan just inside the arcade entrance, his eyes fixed on the booth.

"Okay," he said without turning his head. "Come on."

We hurried forward together. The Inspector jerked the door of the second booth open. The light inside blinked out.

Inside, the telephone receiver dangled, still swaying, by its cord.

The booth was empty.

Except for one thing. I bent down and picked it up off the floor—Merlini's shiny silver dollar.

Gavigan swore. Then he pushed me aside, stepped into the booth and lifted the receiver. His voice was none too steady. He said one word into the phone.

"Hello?"

Leaning in behind him, I heard the voice that replied—Merlini's voice making a statement that was twice as impossible as anything that had happened yet.

"Listen carefully," it said. "And don't ask questions now. I'm at 1462-12 Astoria Avenue, the Bronx. Got that? 1462-12 Astoria. Keeler's here—and a murderer! *Hurry!*"

The tense urgency of that last command sent a cold shiver down my spine. Then I heard the click as the connection was broken.

Gavigan stood motionless for a second, holding the dead phone. Then the surging flood of his emotions spilled over. He jiggled the receiver frantically and swore again.

"Blast it! This phone is dead!"

I pulled myself out of a mental tailspin, found a nickel, and dropped it in the slot. Gavigan's verbal fireworks died to a mutter as he heard the dial tone and he jabbed savagely at the dial.

A moment later the Telegraph Bureau was broadcasting a bowdlerized version of Gavigan's orders to the prowl cars in the Astoria Avenue neighborhood. And Gavigan and I were running for the street and his own car. Brady saw us coming, gunned his motor, and the instant we were aboard, took off as though jet-powered. He made a banked turn into Fifth Avenue against a red light, and we raced uptown, siren screaming.

If Zyyzk had been there beside us, handing out dire predictions that we were headed straight for the Pearly Gates, I wouldn't have doubted him for a moment. We came within inches of that destination half a dozen times as we roared swerving through the crosstown traffic.

The Astoria address wasn't hard to find. There were three prowl cars parked in front of it and two uniformed cops on the front porch. One sat on the floor, his back to the wall, holding a limp arm whose sleeve was stained with blood. There were two round bullet holes in the glass of the door above him. As we ran up the walk, the sound of gun fire came from the rear of the house and the second cop lifted his foot, kicked in a front window, and crawled in through the opening, gun in hand.

The wounded man made a brief report as we passed him. "Nobody answered the door," he said. "But when we tried to crash the joint, somebody started shooting."

Somebody was still shooting. Gavigan, Brady, and I went through the window and toward the sound. The officer who had preceded us was in the kitchen, firing around the jamb of the back door. An answering gun blazed in the dark outside and the cop fired at the flash.

"Got him, I think," the cop said. Then he slipped out through the door, moved quickly across the porch and down the steps. Brady followed him.

Gavigan's pocket flash suddenly sent out a thin beam of light. It started a circuit of the kitchen, stopped for a moment as it picked up movement just outside the door, and we saw a third uniformed man pull himself to a sitting position on the porch floor, look at the bloodstain on his trouser leg, and swear.

Then the Inspector's flash found the open cellar door.

And down there, beside the beginning of a grave, we found Judge Keeler.

His head had been battered in.

But he couldn't find Merlini anywhere in the house. It wasn't until five minutes later, when we were opening Keeler's suitcase, that Merlini walked in.

He looked at the cash and negotiable securities that tumbled out. "You got here," he said, "before that vanished, too, I see."

Gavigan looked up at him. "But you just arrived this minute. I heard a cab out front."

Merlini nodded. "My driver refused to ignore the stop lights the way yours did. Did you find the Judge?"

"Yes, we found him. And I want to know how of all the addresses in Greater New York, you managed to pick this one out of your hat?"

Merlini's dark eyes twinkled. "That was the easy part. Keeler's disappearance, as I said once before, added up to two invisible men. As soon as I knew who the second one must be, I simply looked the name up in the phone book."

"And when you vanished," I asked, "was that done with two invisible men?"

Merlini grinned. "No. I improved on the Judge's miracle a bit. I made it a one-man operation."

Gavigan had had all the riddles he could digest. "We found Keeler's body," he growled ominously, "beside an open grave. And if *you* don't stop—"

"Sorry," Merlini said, as a lighted cigarette appeared mysteriously between his fingers. "As a magician I hate to have to blow the gaff on such a neatly contrived bit of hocus pocus as The Great Phone Booth Trick. But if I must—well, it began when Keeler realized he was going to have to take a runout powder. He knew he was being watched. It was obvious that if he and Helen Hope tried to leave town by any of the usual methods, they'd both be picked up at once. Their only chance was to vanish as abruptly and completely as Judge Crater and Dorothy Arnold once did. I suspect it was Zyyzk's first prediction that Miss Hope would disappear that gave Keeler the idea. At any rate, that was what set the wheels in motion."

"I thought so," Gavigan said. "Zyyzk was in on it."

Merlini shook his head. "I'm afraid you can't charge him with a thing. He was in on it—but he didn't know it. One of the subtlest deceptive devices a magician uses is known as 'the principle of the impromptu stooge.' He so manages things that an unrehearsed spectator acts as a confederate, often without ever realizing it. That's how Keeler used Zyyzk. He built his vanishing trick on Zyyzk's predictions and used them as misdirection. But Zyyzk never knew that he was playing the part of a red herring."

"He's a fraud though," Gavigan insisted. "And he does know it."

Merlini contradicted that, too. "No. Oddly enough he's the one thing in this whole case that is on the level. As you, yourself, pointed out, no fake prophet would give such precisely detailed predictions. He actually does believe that Helen Hope and Judge Keeler vanished into the Outer Darkness."

"A loony," Gavigan muttered.

"And," Merlini added, "a real problem, at this point, for any psychiatrist. He's seen two of his prophecies come true with such complete and startling accuracy that he'll never believe what really happened. I egged him into predicting my disappearance in order to show him that he wasn't infallible. If he never discovers that I did vanish right on time, it may shake his belief in his occult powers. But if he does, the therapy will backfire; he'll be convinced when he sees me, that I'm a doppelganger or an astral double the police have conjured up to discredit him."

"If you don't stop trying to psychoanalyze Zyyzk," Gavigan growled impatiently, "the police are going to conjure up a charge of withholding information in a murder case. Get on with it. Helen Hope wasn't being tailed, so her disappearance was a cinch. She simply walked out, without even taking her toothbrush—to make Zyyzk's prediction look good—and grabbed a plane for Montana or Mexico or some such place where Keeler was to meet her later. But how did Keeler evaporate? And don't you give me any nonsense about two invisible men."

Merlini grinned. "Then we'd better take my disappearance first. That used only one invisible man—and, of course, too many phone booths."

Then, quickly, as Gavigan started to explode, Merlini stopped being cryptic. "In that restaurant you and Ross sat at a table and in the seats that I selected. You saw me, through the window, enter what I had been careful to refer to as the second booth from the right. Seen through the window, that is what it was.

But the line of phone booths extended on either side beyond the window and your field of vision. Viewed from outside, there were nine—not six—booths, and the one I entered was actually the third in line."

"Do you mean," Gavigan said menacingly, "that when I was outside watching the second booth, Ross, inside, was watching the third—and we both thought we were watching the same one?"

"Yes. It isn't necessary to deceive the senses if the mind can be misdirected. You saw what you saw, but it wasn't what you thought you saw. And that—"

Then Gavigan did explode, in a muffled sort of way. "Are you saying that we searched the *wrong* phone booth? And that you were right there all the time, sitting in the next one?"

Merlini didn't need to answer. That was obviously just what he did mean.

"Then your silver dollar," I began, "and the phone receiver—"

"Were," Merlini grinned, "what confidence men call 'the convincer'—concocted evidence which seemed to prove that you had the right booth, prevented any skeptical second thoughts, and kept you from examining the other booths just to make sure you had the right one."

I got it then. "That first time you left the restaurant, before you came back with that phony request for the loan of a nickel—that's when you left the dollar in the second booth."

Merlini nodded. "I made a call, too. I dialed the number of the second booth. And when the phone rang, I stepped into the second booth, took the receiver off the hook, dropped the silver dollar on the floor, then hurried back to your table. Both receivers were off and the line was open."

"And when we looked into the second booth, you were sitting right next door, three feet away, telling Gavigan via the phone that you were in the Bronx?"

Merlini nodded. "And I came out after you had gone. It's a standard conjuring principle. The audience doesn't see the coin, the rabbit, or the girl vanish because they actually disappear either before or after the magician pretends to conjure them into thin air. The audience is watching most carefully at the wrong time."

"Now wait a minute," the Inspector objected. "That's just exactly the way you said Keeler couldn't have handled the phone business. What's more he couldn't. Ross and I weren't watching you the first time you left the restaurant. But we'd been watching Keeler for a week."

"And," I added, "Malloy and Hicks couldn't have miscounted the booths at the station and searched the wrong one. They could see both ends of that line of booths the whole time."

"They didn't miscount," Merlini said. "They just didn't count. The booth we examined was the fifth from the right end of the line, but neither Malloy nor Hicks ever referred to it in that way."

Gavigan scowled. "They said Keeler went into the booth '*to the right of the one that was out of order.*' And the phone in the next booth *was* out of order."

"I know, but Keeler didn't enter the booth next to the one we found out of order. He went into a booth next to one that was marked Out of Order. That's not quite the same."

Gavigan and I both said the same thing at the same time: "The sign had been moved!"

"Twice," Merlini said, nodding. "First, when Keeler was in the Oyster Bar. The second invisible man—invisible because no one was watching him—moved it one booth to the right. And when Keeler, a few minutes later, entered the booth to the right of the one bearing the sign, he was actually in the second booth from the one whose phone didn't work.

"And then our second invisible man went into action again. He walked into the booth marked out of order, smashed a duplicate pair of blood-smeared glasses on the floor, and dialed the Judge's phone. When Keeler answered, he walked out again, leaving the receiver off the hook. It was as neat a piece of misdirection as I've seen in a long time. Who would suspect him of putting through a call from a phone booth that was plainly labeled out of order?"

Cautiously, as if afraid the answer would blow up in his face, I the Inspector asked, "He did all this with Malloy and Hicks both watching? And he wasn't seen—because he was invisible?"

"No, that's not quite right. He was invisible—because he wasn't suspected."

I still didn't see it. "But," I objected, "the only person who went anywhere near the booth next to the one Keeler was in—"

Heavy footsteps sounded on the back porch and then Brady's voice from the doorway said, "We found him, Inspector. Behind some bushes the other side of the wall. Dead. And do you know who—"

"I do now," Gavigan cut in. "Sergeant Hicks."

Brady nodded.

Gavigan turned to Merlini. "Okay, so Hicks was a crooked cop and a liar. But not Malloy. He says he was watching that phone booth every second. How did Hicks switch that Out of Order sign back to the original booth again without being seen?"

"He did it when Malloy wasn't watching quite so closely—*after*

Malloy thought Keeler had vanished. Malloy saw Hicks look into the booth, act surprised, then beckon hurriedly. Those actions, together with Hicks' later statement that the booth was already empty, made Malloy think the Judge had vanished sooner than he really did. Actually Keeler was still right there, sitting in the booth into which Hicks stared. It's the same deception as to time that I used."

"Will you," Gavigan growled, "stop lecturing on the theory of deception and just explain when Hicks moved that sign."

"All right. Remember what Malloy did next? He was near the information booth in the center of the floor and he ran across toward the phones. Malloy said, 'I did some fancy open-field running through the commuters.' Of course he did. At five twenty the station is full of them and he was in a hell of a hurry. He couldn't run fast and keep his eyes glued to Hicks and that phone booth every step of the way; he'd have had half a dozen head-on collisions. But he didn't think the fact that he had had to use his eyes to steer a course rather than continue to watch the booth was important. He thought the dirty work—Keeler's disappearance—had taken place.

"As Malloy ran toward him through the crowd, Hicks simply took two steps sideways to the left and stared into the phone booth that was tagged with the Out-of-Order card. And, behind his body, his left hand shifted the sign one booth to the left—back to the booth that was genuinely out of order. Both actions took no more than a second or two. When Malloy arrived, 'the booth next to the one that was out of order' was empty. Keeler had vanished into Zyyzk's Outer Darkness *by simply sitting still and not moving at all!*"

"And he really vanished," Gavigan said, finally convinced, "by walking out of the next booth as soon as he had spoken his piece to Malloy on the phone."

"While Malloy," Merlini added, "was still staring goggle-eyed at the phone. Even if he had turned to look out of the door, all he'd have seen was the beefy Hicks standing smack in front of him carefully blocking the view. And then Keeler walked right out of the station. Every exit was guarded—except one. An exit big enough to drive half a dozen trains through!"

"Okay," the Inspector growled. "You don't have to put it in words of one syllable. He went out through one of the train gates which Malloy himself had been covering, boarded a train a moment before it pulled out, and ten minutes later he was getting off again up at 125th Street."

"Which," Merlini added, "isn't far from Hicks' home where we are now and where Keeler intended to hide out until the cops, baffled by the dead end he'd left, relaxed their vigilance a bit. The judge was full of cute angles. Who'd ever think of looking for him in the home of one of the cops who was supposed to be hunting him?"

"After which," I added, "he'd change the cut of his whiskers or trim them off altogether, go to join Miss Hope, and they'd live happily ever after on his ill-gotten gains. Fadeout."

"That was the way the script read," Merlini said. "But Judge Keeler forgot one or two little things. He forgot that a man who has just vanished off the face of the earth, leaving a deadend trail, is a perfect prospective murder victim. And he forgot that a suitcase full of folding money is a temptation one should never set before a crooked cop."

"Forgetfulness seems to be dangerous," I said. "I'm glad I've got a good memory."

"I have a hunch that somebody is going to have both our scalps," Merlini said ominously. "I've just remembered that when we left the shop—"

He was right. I hadn't mailed Mrs. Merlini's letter.

HIS HEART COULD BREAK
Craig Rice

Craig Rice (1908-1957) was one of the most beloved and successful mystery writers in America from the 1930s to the 1960s, famed for the zany humor she brought to her mystery novels.

Born Georgiana Ann Randolph Craig, Rice's real-life mysteries were a match for her fiction. Because of her enormous popularity in the 1940s and 1950s (she was the first mystery writer to appear on the cover of *Time* magazine), she was often interviewed but was as forthcoming as a deep-cover agent for the Central Intelligence Agency. How her pseudonym was created is a question that remains unanswered more than sixty years after her premature death. Equally murky is the questions about her marriages, the number of which remain a subject of conjecture. She was married a minimum of four times, and it is possible the number reached seven; that she had numerous affairs is not in dispute. She had three children.

Born in Chicago where she spent much of her life, her parents took off for Europe when she was only three years old so she was raised by various family members. She worked in radio and public relations but sought a career in music and writing poetry and general novels, with which she had no success, so she turned to writing detective novels with spectacular results.

Rice is perhaps best known for the series featuring John J. Malone, whose fictional career began as a friend of a madcap couple, the handsome but dim press agent Jake Justus and his socially prominent bride-to-be, Helene Brand. Malone's "Personal File" usually contains a bottle of rye. Despite his seeming irresponsibility, Malone inspired great loyalty among his friends, including the Justuses, Maggie Cassidy, his long-suffering and seldom-paid secretary, and Captain Daniel von Flanagan of the Chicago homicide squad. The series began with *Eight Faces at Three* in 1939 and ran for a dozen novels.

"His Heart Could Break" was originally published in the March 1943 issue of *Ellery Queen's Mystery Magazine*; it was first collected in *The Name Is Malone* (New York, Pyramid, 1958).

His Heart Could Break
Craig Rice

John J. Malone shuddered. He wished he could get the insidious melody out of his mind—or, remember the rest of the words.

As I passed by the ol' state's prison,
Ridin' on a stream-line' train—

It had been annoying him since three o'clock that morning, when he'd heard it sung by the janitor of Joe the Angel's City Hall Bar.

It seemed like a bad omen, and it made him uncomfortable. Or maybe it was the cheap gin he'd switched to between two and four A.M. that was making him uncomfortable. Whichever it was, he felt terrible.

"I bet your client's happy today," the guard said cordially, leading the way towards the death house.

"He ought to be," Malone growled. He reminded himself that he too ought to be happy. He wasn't. Maybe it was being in a prison that depressed him. John J. Malone didn't like prisons. He devoted his life to keeping his clients out of them.

Then the warden told me gently—

That song again! How did the next line go?

"Well," the guard said, "they say you've never lost a client yet." It wouldn't do any harm, he thought, to get on the good side of a smart guy like John J. Malone.

"Not yet," Malone said. He'd had a close call with this one, though.

"You sure did a wonderful job, turning up the evidence to get a new trial," the guard rattled on. Maybe Malone could get him a better appointment, with his political drag. "Your client sure felt swell when he heard about it last night, he sure did."

"That's good," Malone said noncommittally. It hadn't been evidence that had turned the trick, though. Just a little matter of knowing some interesting facts about the judge's private life. The evidence would have to be manufactured before the trial, but that was the least of his worries. By that time, he might even find out the truth of what had happened. He hummed softly under his breath. Ah, there were the next lines!

Then the warden told me gently,
He seemed too young, too young to die,
We cut the rope and let him down—

John J. Malone tried to remember the rhyme for "die." By, cry, lie, my, and sigh. Then he let loose a few loud and indignant remarks about whoever had written that song, realized that he was entering the death house and stopped, embarrassed. That particular cell block always inspired him with the same behavior he would have shown at a high class funeral. He took off his hat and walked softly.

And at that moment hell broke loose. Two prisoners in the block began yelling like banshees. The alarms began to sound loudly, causing the outside siren to chime in with its hideous wail.

Guards were running through the corridor, and John J. Malone instinctively ran with them toward the center of disturbance, the fourth cell on the left.

Before the little lawyer got there, one of the guards had the door open. Another guard cut quickly through the bright new rope from which the prisoner was dangling, and eased the limp body down to the floor.

The racket outside was almost deafening now, but John J. Malone scarcely heard it. The guard turned the body over, and Malone recognized the very young and rather stupid face of Paul Palmer.

"He's hung himself," one of the guards said.

"With me for a lawyer?" Malone said angrily. "Hung himself—" He started to say "hell," then remembered he was in the presence of death.

"Hey," the other guard said excitedly. "He's alive. His neck's broke, but he's breathing a little."

Malone shoved the guard aside and knelt down beside the dying man. Paul Palmer's blue eyes opened slowly, with an expression of terrible bewilderment. His lips parted.

"It wouldn't break," Paul Palmer whispered. He seemed to recognize Malone, and stared at him, with a look of frightful urgency. "*It wouldn't break*," he whispered to Malone. Then he died. . . .

"You're damned right I'm going to sit in on the investigation," Malone said angrily. He gave Warden Garrity's wastebasket a vicious kick. "The inefficient way you run your prison has done me out of a client." Out of a fat fee, too, he reminded himself miserably. He hadn't been paid yet, and now there would be a long tussle with the lawyer handling Paul Palmer's estate, who hadn't wanted him engaged for the defense in the first place. Malone felt in his pocket, found three crumpled bills and a small handful of change. He wished now that he hadn't got into that poker game last week.

The warden's dreary office was crowded. Malone looked around, recognized an assistant warden, the prison doctor—a handsome gray-haired man named Dickson—the guards from the death house, and the guard who had been ushering him in—Bowers was his name, Malone remembered, a tall, flat-faced, gangling man.

"Imagine him hanging himself," Bowers was saying incredulously. "Just after he found out he was gonna get a new trial."

Malone had been wondering the same thing. "Maybe he didn't get my wire," he suggested coldly.

"I gave it to him myself," Bowers stated positively. "Just last night. Never saw a man so happy in my life."

Dr. Dickson cleared his throat. Everyone turned to look at him.

"Poor Palmer was mentally unstable," the doctor said sadly. "You may recall I recommended, several days ago, that he be moved to the prison hospital. When I visited him last night he appeared hilariously—hysterically—happy. This morning, however, he was distinctly depressed."

"You mean the guy was nuts?" Warden Garrity asked hopefully.

"He was nothing of the sort," Malone said indignantly. Just let a hint get around that Paul Palmer had been of unsound mind, and he'd never collect that five thousand dollar fee from the estate. "He was saner than anyone in this room, with the possible exception of myself."

Dr. Dickson shrugged his shoulders. "I didn't suggest that he was insane. I only meant he was subject to moods."

Malone wheeled to face the doctor. "Say. Were you in the habit of visiting Palmer in his cell a couple of times a day?"

"I was," the doctor said, nodding. "He was suffering from a serious nervous condition. It was necessary to administer sedatives from time to time."

Malone snorted. "You mean he was suffering from the effect of being sober for the first time since he was sixteen."

"Put it any way you like," Dr. Dickson said pleasantly. "You remember, too, that I had a certain personal interest."

"That's right," Malone said slowly. "He was going to marry your niece."

"No one was happier than I to hear about the new trial," the doctor said. He caught Malone's eye and added, "No, I wasn't fond enough of him to smuggle in a rope. Especially when he'd just been granted a chance to clear himself."

"Look here," Warden Garrity said irritably. "I can't sit around listening to all this stuff. I've got to report the result of an investigation. Where the hell did he get that rope?"

There was a little silence, and then one of the guards said, "Maybe from the guy who was let in to see him last night."

"What guy?" the warden snapped.

"Why—" The guard paused, confused. "He had an order from you admitting him. His name was La Cerra."

Malone felt a sudden tingling along his spine. Georgie La Cerra was one of Max Hook's boys. What possible connection could there be between Paul Palmer, socialite, and the big gambling boss?

Warden Garrity had recognized the name too. "Oh yes," he said quickly. "That must have been it. But I doubt if we could prove it." He paused just an instant, and looked fixedly at Malone, as though daring him to speak. "The report will read that Paul Palmer obtained a rope, by means which have not yet been ascertained, and committed suicide while of unsound mind."

Malone opened his mouth and shut it again. He knew when he was licked. Temporarily licked, anyway. "For the love of mike," he said, "leave out the unsound mind."

"I'm afraid that's impossible," the warden said coldly.

Malone had kept his temper as long as he could. "All right," he said, "but I'll start an investigation that'll be a pip." He snorted. "Letting a gangster smuggle a rope in to a guy in the death house!" He glared at Dr. Dickson. "And you, foxy, with two escapes from the prison hospital in six months." He kicked the wastebasket again, this time sending it halfway across the room. "I'll show you from investigations! And I'm just the guy who can do it, too."

Dr. Dickson said quickly, "We'll substitute 'temporarily depressed' for the 'unsound mind.'"

But Malone was mad, now. He made one last, long comment regarding the warden's personal life and probably immoral origin, and slammed the door so hard when he went out that the steel engraving of Chester A. Arthur over the warden's desk shattered to the floor.

"Mr. Malone," Bowers said in a low voice as they went down the hall, "I searched that cell, after they took the body out. Whoever smuggled in that rope smuggled in a letter, too. I found it hid in his mattress, and it wasn't there yesterday, because the mattress was changed." He paused, and added, "And the rope couldn't of been there last night either, because there was no place he could of hid it."

Malone glanced at the envelope the guard held out to him—pale grey expensive stationery, with "Paul Palmer" written across the front of it in delicate, curving handwriting.

"I haven't any money with me," the lawyer said.

Bowers shook his head. "I don't want no dough. But there's gonna be an assistant warden's job open in about three weeks."

"You'll get it," Malone said. He took the envelope and stuffed it in an inside pocket. Then he paused, frowned, and finally added, "And keep your eyes open and your mouth shut. Because there's going to be an awful stink when I prove Paul Palmer was murdered. . . ."

The pretty, black-haired girl in Malone's anteroom looked up as he opened the door. "Oh, Mr. Malone," she said quickly. "I read about it in the paper. I'm so sorry."

"Never mind, Maggie," the lawyer said. "No use crying over spilled clients." He went into his private office and shut the door.

Fate was treating him very shabbily, evidently from some obscure motive of personal spite. He'd been counting heavily on that five thousand buck fee.

He took a bottle of rye out of the filing cabinet marked "Personal," poured himself a drink, noted that there was only one more left in the bottle, and stretched out on the worn red leather davenport to think things over.

Paul Palmer had been an amiable, stupid young drunk of good family, whose inherited wealth had been held in trust for him by an uncle considered to be the stingiest man in Chicago. The money was to be turned over to him on his thirtieth birthday—some five years off—or on the death of the uncle, Carter Brown. Silly arrangement, Malone reflected, but rich men's lawyers were always doing silly things.

Uncle Carter had cramped the young man's style considerably, but he'd managed pretty well. Then he'd met Madelaine Starr.

Malone lit a cigar and stared dreamily through the smoke. The Starrs were definitely social, but without money. A good keen eye for graft, too. Madelaine's uncle was probably making a very good thing out of that political appointment as prison doctor.

Malone sighed, wished he weren't a lawyer, and thought about Madelaine Starr. An orphan, with a tiny income which she augmented by modeling in an exclusive dress shop—a fashionable and acceptable way of making a living. She had expensive tastes. (The little lawyer could spot expensive tastes in girls a mile away.)

She'd had to be damned poor to want to marry Palmer, Malone reflected, and damned beautiful to get him. Well, she was both.

But there had been another girl, one who had to be paid off. Lillian Claire by name, and a very lovely hunk of girl, too. Lovely, and smart enough to demand a sizable piece of money for letting the Starr-Palmer nuptials go through without a scandalous fuss.

Malone shook his head sadly. It had looked bad at the trial. Paul Palmer had taken his bride-to-be night clubbing, delivering her back to her kitchenette apartment just before twelve. He'd been a shade high, then, and by the time he'd stopped off at three or four bars, he was several shades higher. Then he'd paid a visit to Lillian Claire, who claimed later at the trial that he'd attempted—unsuccessfully—to talk her out of the large piece of cash money, and had drunk up all the whiskey in the house. She'd put him in a cab and sent him home.

No one knew just when Paul Palmer had arrived at the big, gloomy apartment he shared with Carter Brown. The manservant had the night off. It was the manservant who discovered, next morning, that Uncle Carter had been shot neatly through the forehead with Paul Palmer's gun, and that Paul Palmer had climbed into his own bed, fully dressed, and was snoring drunk.

Everything had been against him, Malone reflected sadly. Not only had the jury been composed of hard-working, poverty-stricken men who liked nothing better than to convict a rich young wastrel of murder, but worse still, they'd all been too honest to be bribed. The trial had been his most notable failure. And now, this.

But Paul Palmer would never have hanged himself. Malone was sure of it. He'd never lost hope. And now, especially, when a new trial had been granted, he'd have wanted to live.

It had been murder. But how had it been done?

Malone sat up, stretched, reached in his pocket for the pale gray envelope Bowers had given him, and read the note through again.

> My dearest Paul:
>
> I'm getting this note to you this way because I'm in terrible trouble and danger. I need you—no one else can help me. I know there's to be a new trial, but even another week may be too late. Isn't there *any* way?
>
> > Your own
> >
> > *M.*

"M.", Malone decided, would be Madelaine Starr. She'd use that kind of pale gray paper, too.

He looked at the note and frowned. If Madelaine Starr had smuggled that note to her lover, would she have smuggled in a rope by the same messenger? Or had someone else brought in the rope?

There were three people he wanted to see. Madelaine Starr was one. Lillian Claire was the second. And Max Hook was the third.

He went out into the anteroom, stopped halfway across it and said aloud, "But it's a physical impossibility. If someone smuggled that rope into Paul Palmer's cell and then Palmer hanged himself, it isn't murder. But it must have been murder." He stared at Maggie without seeing her. "Damn it, though, no one could have got into Paul Palmer's cell and hanged him."

Maggie looked at him sympathetically, familiar from long experience with her employer's processes of thought. "Keep on thinking and it'll come to you."

"Maggie, have you got any money?"

"I have ten dollars, but you can't borrow it. Besides, you haven't paid my last week's salary yet."

The little lawyer muttered something about ungrateful and heartless wenches, and flung himself out of the office.

Something had to be done about ready cash. He ran his mind over a list of prospective lenders. The only possibility was Max Hook. No, the last time he'd borrowed money from the Hook, he'd got into no end of trouble. Besides, he was going to ask another kind of favor from the gambling boss.

Malone went down Washington street, turned the corner, went into Joe the Angel's City Hall Bar, and cornered its proprietor at the far end of the room.

"Cash a hundred dollar check for me, and hold it until a week from,"—Malone made a rapid mental calculation—"Thursday?"

"Sure," Joe the Angel said. "Happy to do you a favor." He got out ten ten-dollar bills while Malone wrote the check. "Want I should take your bar bill out of this?"

Malone shook his head. "I'll pay next week. And add a double rye to it."

As he set down the empty glass, he heard the colored janitor's voice coming faintly from the back room.

"They hanged him for the thing you done,
You knew it was a sin,
You didn't know his heart could break—"

The voice stopped suddenly. For a moment Malone considered calling for the singer and asking to hear the whole thing, all the way through. No, there wasn't time for it now. Later, perhaps. He went out on the street, humming the tune.

What was it Paul Palmer had whispered in that last moment? *"It wouldn't break!"* Malone scowled. He had a curious feeling that there was some connection between those words and the words of that damned song. Or was it his Irish imagination, tripping him up again? *"You didn't know his heart could break."* But it was Paul Palmer's neck that had been broken.

Malone hailed a taxi and told the driver to take him to the swank Lake Shore Drive apartment-hotel where Max Hook lived.

The gambling boss was big in two ways. He took in a cut from every crooked gambling device in Cook County, and most of the honest ones. And he was a mountain of flesh, over six feet tall and three times too fat for his height. His pink head was completely bald and he had the expression of a pleased cherub.

His living room was a masterpiece of the gilt-and-brocade school of interior decoration, marred only by a huge, battle-scarred rolltop desk in one corner. Max Hook swung around from the desk to smile cordially at the lawyer.

"How delightful to see you! What will you have to drink?"

"Rye," Malone said, "and it's nice to see you too. Only this isn't exactly a social call."

He knew better, though, than to get down to business before the drinks had arrived. (Max Hook stuck to pink champagne.) That wasn't the way Max Hook liked to do things. But when the rye was down, and the gambling boss had lighted a slender, tinted (and,

Malone suspected, perfumed) cigarette in a rose quartz holder, he plunged right in.

"I suppose you read in the papers about what happened to my client, Palmer," he said.

"I never read the papers," Max Hook told him, "but one of my boys informed me. Tragic, wasn't it?"

"Tragic is no name for it," Malone said bitterly. "He hadn't paid me a dime."

Max Hook's eyebrows lifted. "So?" Automatically he reached for the green metal box in the left-hand drawer. "How much do you need?"

"No, no," Malone said hastily, "that isn't it. I just want to know if one of your boys—Little Georgie La Cerra—smuggled the rope in to him. That's all."

Max Hook looked surprised, and a little hurt. "My dear Malone," he said at last, "why do you imagine he'd do such a thing?"

"For money," Malone said promptly, "if he did do it. I don't care, I just want to know."

"You can take my word for it," Max Hook said, "he did nothing of the kind. He did deliver a note from a certain young lady to Mr. Palmer, at my request—a bit of a nuisance, too, getting hold of that admittance order signed by the warden. I assure you, though, there was no rope. I give you my word, and you know I'm an honest man."

"Well, I was just asking," Malone said. One thing about the big gangster, he always told the truth. If he said Little Georgie La Cerra hadn't smuggled in that rope, then Little Georgie hadn't. Nor was there any chance that Little Georgie had engaged in private enterprises on the side. As Max Hook often remarked, he liked to keep a careful watch on his boys. "One thing more, though," the lawyer said, "if you don't mind. Why did the young lady come to you to get her note delivered?"

Max Hook shrugged his enormous shoulders. "We have a certain—business connection. To be exact, she owes me a large sum of money. Like most extremely mercenary people she loves gambling, but she is not particularly lucky. When she told me that the only chance for that money to be paid was for the note to be delivered, naturally I obliged."

"Naturally," Malone agreed. "You didn't happen to know what was in the note, did you?"

Max Hook was shocked. "My dear Malone! You don't think I read other people's personal mail!"

No, Malone reflected, Max Hook probably didn't. And not having read the note, the big gambler probably wouldn't know what kind of "terrible trouble and danger" Madelaine Starr was in. He decided to ask, though, just to be on the safe side.

"Trouble?" Max Hook repeated after him. "No, outside of having her fiancé condemned to death, I don't know of any trouble she's in."

Malone shrugged his shoulders at the reproof, rose and walked to the door. Then he paused, suddenly. "Listen, Max. Do you know the words to a tune that goes like this?" He hummed a bit of it.

Max Hook frowned, then nodded. "Mmm—I know the tune. An entertainer at one of my places used to sing it." He thought hard, and finally came up with a few lines.

"He was leaning against the prison bars,
Dressed up in his new prison clothes—"

"Sorry," Max Hook said at last, "that's all I remember. I guess those two lines stuck in my head because they reminded me of the first time I was in jail."

Outside in the taxi, Malone sang the two lines over a couple of times. If he kept on, eventually he'd have the whole song. But Paul Palmer hadn't been leaning against the prison bars. He'd been hanging from the water pipe.

Damn, and double damn that song!

It was well past eight o'clock, and he'd had no dinner, but he didn't feel hungry. He had a grim suspicion that he wouldn't feel hungry until he'd settled this business. When the cab paused for the next red light, he flipped a coin to decide whether he'd call first on Madelaine Stan or Lillian Claire, and Madelaine won.

He stepped out of the cab in front of the small apartment building on Walton Place, paid the driver, and started across the sidewalk just as a tall, white-haired man emerged from the door. Malone recognized Orlo Featherstone, the lawyer handling Paul Palmer's estate, considered ducking out of sight, realized there wasn't time, and finally managed to look as pleased as he was surprised.

"I was just going to offer Miss Starr my condolences," he said.

"I'd leave her undisturbed, if I were you," Orlo Featherstone said coldly. He had only one conception of what a lawyer should be, and Malone wasn't anything like it. "I only called myself because I am, so to speak and in a sense, a second father to her."

If anyone else had said that, Malone thought, it would have called for an answer. From Orlo Featherstone, it sounded natural. He nodded sympathetically and said, "Tragic affair, wasn't it."

Orlo Featherstone unbent at least half a degree. "Distinctly so. Personally, I cannot imagine Paul Palmer doing such a thing. When I visited him yesterday, he seemed quite cheerful and full of hope."

"You—visited him yesterday?" Malone asked casually. He drew a cigar from his pocket and began unwrapping it with exquisite care.

"Yes," Featherstone said, "about the will. He had to sign it, you know. Fortunate for her," he indicated Madelaine Starr with a gesture toward the building, "that he did so. He left her everything, of course."

"Of course," Malone said. He lighted his cigar on the second try. "You don't think Paul Palmer could have been murdered, do you?"

"Murdered!" Orlo Featherstone repeated, as though it was an obscene word. "Absurd! No Palmer has ever been murdered."

Malone watched him climb into a shiny Cadillac, then started walking briskly toward State Street. The big limousine passed him just as he reached the corner; it turned north on State Street and stopped. Malone paused by the newsstand long enough to see Mr. Orlo Featherstone get out and cross the sidewalk to the corner drugstore. After a moment's thought he followed and paused at the cigar counter, from where he could see clearly into the adjacent telephone booth.

Orlo Featherstone, in the booth, consulted a little notebook. Then he took down the receiver, dropped a nickel in the slot, and began dialing. Malone watched carefully. D-E-L—9-6-0—It was Lillian Claire's number.

The little lawyer cursed all soundproof phone booths, and headed for a bar on the opposite corner. He felt definitely unnerved.

After a double rye, and halfway through a second one, he came to the heartening conclusion that when he visited Lillian Claire, later in the evening, he'd be able to coax from her the reason why Orlo Featherstone, of all people, had telephoned her, just after leaving the late Paul Palmer's fiancée. A third rye braced him for his call on the fiancée herself.

Riding up in the self-service elevator to her apartment, another heartening thought came to him. If Madelaine Starr was going to inherit all the Palmer dough—then it might not be such a trick to collect his five thousand bucks. He might even be able to collect it by a week from Thursday.

And he reminded himself, as she opened the door, this was going to be one time when he wouldn't be a sucker for a pretty face.

Madelaine Starr's apartment was tiny, but tasteful. Almost too tasteful, Malone thought. Everything in it was cheap, but perfectly correct and in exactly the right place, even to the Van Gogh print over the midget fireplace. Madelaine Starr was in exactly the right taste, too.

She was a tall girl, with a figure that still made Malone blink, in spite of the times he'd admired it in the courtroom. Her bronze-brown hair was smooth and well-brushed, her pale face was calm and composed. Serene, polished, suave. Malone had a private idea that if he made a pass at her, she wouldn't scream. She was wearing black house pajamas. He wondered if they were her idea of mourning.

Malone got the necessary condolences and trite remarks out of the way fast, and then said, "What kind of terrible trouble and danger are you in, Miss Starr?"

That startled her. She wasn't able to come up with anything more original than "What do you mean?"

"I mean what you wrote in your note to Paul Palmer," the lawyer said.

She looked at the floor and said, "I hoped it had been destroyed."

"It will be," Malone said gallantly, "if you say so."

"Oh," she said. "Do you have it with you?"

"No," Malone lied. "It's in my office safe. But I'll go back there and burn it." He didn't add when.

"It really didn't have anything to do with his death, you know," she said.

Malone said, "Of course not. You didn't send him the rope too, did you?"

She stared at him. "How awful of you."

"I'm sorry," Malone said contritely.

She relaxed. "I'm sorry too. I didn't mean to snap at you. I'm a little unnerved, naturally." She paused. "May I offer you a drink?"

"You may," Malone said, "and I'll take it."

He watched her while she mixed a lot of scotch and a little soda in two glasses, wondering how soon after her fiancé's death he could safely ask her for a date. Maybe she wouldn't say "Yes" to a broken-down criminal lawyer, though. He took the drink, downed half of it, and said to himself indignantly, "Who's broken-down?"

"Oh, Mr. Malone," she breathed "you don't believe my note had anything to do with it?"

"Of course not," Malone said. "That note would have made him want to live, and get out of jail." He considered bringing up the matter of his five thousand dollar fee, and then decided this was not the time. "Nice that you'll be able to pay back what you owe Max Hook. He's a bad man to owe money to."

She looked at him sharply and said nothing. Malone finished his drink, and walked to the door.

"One thing, though," he said, hand on the knob. "This—terrible trouble and danger you're in. You'd better tell me. Because I might be able to help, you know."

"Oh, no," she said. She was standing very close to him, and her perfume began to mingle dangerously with the rye and scotch in his brain. "I'm afraid not." He had a definite impression that she was thinking fast. "No one can help, now." She looked away, delicately. "You know—a girl—alone in the world—"

Malone felt his cheeks reddening. He opened the door and said, "Oh." Just plain Oh.

"Just a minute," she said quickly. "Why did you ask all these questions?"

"Because," Malone said, just as quickly, "I thought the answers might be useful—in case Paul Palmer was murdered."

That, he told himself, riding down the self-service elevator, would give her something to think about.

He hailed a cab and gave the address of the apartment building where Lillian Claire lived, on Goethe Street. In the lobby of the building he paused long enough to call a certain well-known politician at his home and make sure that he was there. It would be just as well not to run into that particular politician at Lillian Claire's apartment, since he was paying for it.

It was a nice apartment, too, Malone decided, as the slim mulatto maid ushered him in. Big, soft modernistic divans and chairs, paneled mirrors, and a built-in bar. Not half as nice, though, as Lillian Claire herself.

She was a cuddly little thing, small, and a bit on the plump side, with curly blonde hair and a deceptively simple stare. She said, "Oh, Mr. Malone. I've always wanted to get acquainted with you." Malone had a pleasant feeling that if he tickled her, just a little, she'd giggle.

She mixed him a drink, lighted his cigar, sat close to him on the biggest and most luxurious divan, and said, "Tell me, how on earth did Paul Palmer get that rope?"

"I don't know," Malone said. "Did you send it to him, baked in a cake?"

She looked at him reprovingly. "You don't think I wanted him to kill himself and let that awful woman inherit all that money?"

Malone said, "She isn't so awful. But this is tough on you, though. Now you'll never be able to sue him."

"I never intended to," she said. "I didn't want to be paid off. I just thought it might scare her away from him."

Malone put down his glass, she hopped up and refilled it. "Were you in love with him?" he said.

"Don't be silly." She curled up beside him again. "I liked him. He was much too nice to have someone like that marry him for his money."

Malone nodded slowly. The room was beginning to swim—not unpleasantly—before his eyes. Maybe he should have eaten dinner after all.

"Just the same," he said, "you didn't think up that idea all by yourself. Someone put you up to asking for money."

She pulled away from him a little—not too much. "That's perfect nonsense," she said unconvincingly.

"All right," Malone said agreeably. "Tell me just one thing—"

"I'll tell you this one thing," she said. "Paul never murdered his uncle. I don't know who did, but it wasn't Paul. Because I took him home that night. He came to see me, yes. But I didn't put him in a cab and send him home. I took him home, and got him to his own room. Nobody saw me. It was late—almost daylight." She paused and lit a cigarette. "I peeked into his uncle's room to make sure I hadn't been seen, and his uncle was dead. I never told anybody because I didn't want to get messed up in it worse than I was already."

Malone sat bolt upright. "Fine thing," he said, indignantly and a bit thickly. "You could have alibied him and you let him be convicted."

"Why bother?" she said serenely. "I knew he had you for a lawyer. Why should he need an alibi?"

Malone shoved her back against the cushions of the davenport and glared at her. "A'right," he said. "But that wasn't the thing I was gonna ask. Why did old man Featherstone call you up tonight?"

Her shoulders stiffened under his hands. "He just asked me for a dinner date," she said.

"You're a liar," Malone said, not unpleasantly. He ran an experimental finger along her ribs. She did giggle. Then he kissed her. . . .

All this time spent, Malone told himself reprovingly, and you haven't learned one thing worth the effort. Paul Palmer hadn't killed his uncle. But he'd been sure of that all along, and anyway it wouldn't do any good now. Madelaine Starr needed money, and now she was going to inherit a lot of it. Orlo Featherstone was on friendly terms with Lillian Claire.

The little lawyer leaned his elbows on the table and rested his head on his hands. At three o'clock in the morning, Joe the Angel's was a desolate and almost deserted place. He knew now, definitely, that he should have eaten dinner. Nothing, he decided, would cure the way he felt except a quick drink, a long sleep, or sudden death.

He would probably never learn who had killed Paul Palmer's uncle, or why. He would probably never learn what had happened to Paul Palmer. After all, the man had hanged himself. No one else could have got into that cell. It wasn't murder to give a man enough rope to hang himself with.

No, he would probably never learn what had happened to Paul Palmer, and he probably would never collect that five thousand dollar fee. But there was one thing he could do. He'd learn the words of that song.

He called for a drink, the janitor, and the janitor's guitar. Then he sat back and listened.

"As I passed by the ol' state's prison,
Ridin' on a stream-line' train—"

It was a long rambling ballad, requiring two drinks for the janitor and two more for Malone. The lawyer listened, remembering a line here and there.

"When they hanged him in the mornin'
His last words were for you,
Then the sheriff took his shiny knife
An' cut that ol' rope through."

A sad story, Malone reflected, finishing the second drink. Personally, he'd have preferred "My Wild Irish Rose" right now. But he yelled to Joe for another drink and went on listening.

"They hanged him for the thing you done,
You knew it was a sin,
How well you knew his heart could break,
Lady, why did you turn him in—"

The little lawyer jumped to his feet. That was the line he'd been trying to remember! And what had Paul Palmer whispered? "*It wouldn't break.*"

Malone knew, now.

He dived behind the bar, opened the cash drawer and scooped out a handful of telephone slugs.

"You're drunk," Joe the Angel said indignantly.

"That may be," Malone said happily, "and it's a good idea too. But I know what I'm doing."

He got one of the slugs into the phone on the third try, dialed Orlo Featherstone's number, and waited till the elderly lawyer got out of bed and answered the phone.

It took ten minutes, and several more phone slugs to convince Featherstone that it was necessary to get Madelaine Starr out of bed and make the three-hour drive to the state's prison, right now. It took another ten minutes to wake up Lillian Claire and induce her to join the party. Then he placed a long-distance call to the sheriff of Statesville County and invited him to drop in at the prison and pick up a murderer.

Malone strode to the door. As he reached it, Joe the Angel hailed him.

"I forgot," he said. "I got sumpin' for you." Joe the Angel rummaged back of the cash register and brought out a long envelope. "That cute secretary of yours was looking for you all over town to give you this. Finally she left it with me. She knew you'd get here sooner or later."

Malone said "Thanks," took the envelope, glanced at it, and winced. "First National Bank." Registered mail. He knew he was overdrawn, but—

Oh, well, maybe there was still a chance to get that five thousand bucks.

The drive to Statesville wasn't so bad, in spite of the fact that Orlo Featherstone snored most of the way. Lillian snuggled up against Malone's left shoulder like a kitten, and with his right hand he held Madelaine Starr's hand under the auto robe. But the arrival, a bit before seven A.M., was depressing. The prison looked its worst in the early morning, under a light fog.

Besides, the little lawyer wasn't happy over what he had to do.

Warden Garrity's office was even more depressing. There was the warden, eyeing Malone coldly and belligerently, and Madelaine Starr and her uncle, Dr. Dickson, looking a bit annoyed. Orlo Featherstone was frankly skeptical. The sheriff of Statesville county was sleepy and bored. Lillian Claire was sleepy and suspicious. Even the guard, Bowers, looked bewildered.

And all these people, Malone realized, were waiting for him to pull a rabbit out of his whiskers.

He pulled it out fast. "Paul Palmer was murdered," he said flatly.

Warden Garrity looked faintly amused. "A bunch of pixies crawled into his cell and tied the rope around his neck?"

"No," Malone said, lighting a cigar. "This murderer made one try—murder by frame-up. He killed Paul Palmer's uncle for two reasons, one of them being to send Paul Palmer to the chair. It nearly worked. Then I got him a new trial. So another method had to be tried, fast, and that one did work."

"You're insane," Orlo Featherstone said, "Palmer hanged himself."

"I'm not insane," Malone said indignantly, "I'm drunk. There's a distinction. And Paul Palmer hanged himself because he thought he wouldn't die, and could escape from prison." He looked at Bowers and said, "Watch all these people, someone may make a move."

Lillian Claire said, "I don't get it."

"You will," Malone promised. He kept a watchful eye on Bowers and began talking fast. "The whole thing was arranged by someone who was mercenary and owed money. Someone who knew Paul Palmer would be too drunk to know what had happened the night his uncle was killed, and who was close enough to him to have a key to the apartment. That person went in and killed the uncle with Paul Palmer's gun. And, as that person had planned, Paul Palmer was tried and convicted and would have been electrocuted, if he hadn't had a damn smart lawyer."

He flung his cigar into the cuspidor and went on. "Then Paul Palmer was granted a new trial. So the mercenary person who wanted Paul Palmer's death convinced him that he had to break out of prison, and another person showed him how the escape could be arranged—by pretending to hang himself, and being moved to the prison hospital—*watch her, Bowers!*"

Madelaine Starr had flung herself at Dr. Dickson. "Damn you," she screamed, her face white. "I knew you'd break down and talk. But you'll never talk again—"

There were three shots. One from the little gun Madelaine had carried in her pocket, and two from Bowers' service revolver.

Then the room was quite still.

Malone walked slowly across the room, looked down at the two bodies, and shook his head sadly. "Maybe it's just as well," he said. "They'd probably have hired another defense lawyer anyway."

"This is all very fine," the Statesville County sheriff said. "But I still don't see how you figured it. Have another beer?"

"Thanks," Malone said. "It was easy. A song tipped me off. Know this?" He hummed a few measures.

"Oh, sure," the sheriff said. "The name of it is, 'The Statesville Prison.'" He sang the first four verses.

"Well, I'll be double-damned," Malone said. The bartender put the two glasses of beer on the table. "Bring me a double gin for a chaser," the lawyer told him.

"Me too," the sheriff said. "What does the song have to do with it, Malone?"

Malone said, "It was the crank on the adding machine, pal. Know what I mean? You put down a lot of stuff to add up and nothing happens, and then somebody turns the crank and it all adds up to what you want to know. See how simple it is?"

"I don't," the sheriff said, "but go on."

"I had all the facts," Malone said, "I knew everything I wanted to know, but I couldn't add it up. I needed one thing, that one thing." He spoke almost reverently, downing his gin. "Paul Palmer said '*It wouldn't break*'—just before he died. And he looked terribly surprised. For a long time, I didn't know what he meant. Then I heard that song again, and I did know." He sang a few lines. "*The sheriff took his shiny knife, and cut that of rope through.*" Then he finished his beer, and sang on, "*They hanged him for the thing you done, you knew it was a sin. You didn't know his heart could break, Lady, why did you turn him in.*" He ended on a blue note.

"Very pretty," the sheriff said. "Only I heard it, '*You knew that his poor heart could break.*'"

"Same thing." Malone said, waving a hand. "Only, that song was what turned the crank on the adding machine. When I heard it again, I knew what Palmer meant by '*it wouldn't break.*'"

"His heart?" the seriff said helpfully.

"No," Malone said, "the rope."

He waved at the bartender and said "Two more of the same." Then to the sheriff, "He expected the rope to break. He thought it would be artfully frayed so that he would drop to the floor unharmed. Then he could have been moved to the prison hospital—from which there had been two escapes in the past six months. He had to escape, you see, because his sweetheart had written him that she was in terrible trouble and danger—the same sweetheart whose evidence had helped convict him at the trial.

"Madelaine Starr wanted his money," Malone went on, "but she didn't want Paul. So her murder of his uncle served two purposes. It released Paul's money, and it framed him. Using poor old innocent Orlo Featherstone, she planted in Lillian Claire's head the idea of holding up Paul for money, so Paul would be faced with a need for ready cash. Everything worked fine, until I gummixed up the whole works by getting my client a new trial."

"Your client shouldn't of had such a smart lawyer," the sheriff said, over his beer glass.

Malone tossed aside the compliment with a shrug of his cigar. "Maybe he should of had a better one. Anyway, she and her uncle, Dr. Dickson, fixed it all up. She sent that note to Paul, so he'd think he had to break out of the clink. Then her uncle, Dickson, told Paul he'd arrange the escape, with the rope trick. To the world, it would have looked as though Paul Palmer had committed suicide in a fit of depression. Only he did have a good lawyer, and he lived long enough to say '*It wouldn't break.*'"

Malone looked into his empty glass and lapsed into a melancholy silence.

The phone rang—someone hi-jacked a truck over on Springfield Road—and the sheriff was called away. Left by himself, Malone cried a little into his beer. Lillian Claire had gone back to Chicago with Orlo Featherstone, who really had called her up for a date, and no other reason.

Malone reminded himself he hadn't had any sleep, his head was splitting, and what was left of Joe the Angel's hundred dollars would just take him back to Chicago. And there was that letter from the bank, probably threatening a summons. He took it out of his pocket and sighed as he tore it open.

"Might as well face realities," Malone said to the bartender. "And bring me another double gin."

He drank the gin, tore open the envelope, and took out a certified check for five thousand dollars, with a note from the bank to the effect that Paul Palmer had directed its payment. It was dated the day before his death.

Malone waltzed to the door, waltzed back to pay the bartender and kiss him goodbye.

"Do you feel all right?" the bartender asked anxiously.

"All right?" Malone said. "I'm a new man!"

What was more, he'd just remembered the rest of that song. He sang it, happily, as he went up the street toward the railroad station.

"As I passed by the ol' state's prison,
   Ridin' on a streamline' train,
I waved my hand, and said out loud,
I'm never comin' back again,
I'm never comin' back a—gain!"

MURDER AMONG MAGICIANS
Manley Wade Wellman

The versatile Manley Wade Wellman (1903-1986) began writing in the 1920s and, by the 1930s, was selling stories to the leading pulps in the horror and supernatural genres: *Weird Tales*, *Wonder Stories*, and *Astounding Stories*. He had three series running simultaneously in *Weird Tales*.

One featured Silver John, also known as John the Balladeer, the backwoods minstrel with a silver-stringed guitar, and the other two starred in the challenging sub-genre of psychic and occult detection, combining supernatural elements with the tropes of the detective story with John Thunstone, the New York playboy and adventurer, and tales of the elderly Judge Keith Hilary Persuivant, which he wrote under the pseudonym Gans T. Fields.

His short story, "A Star for a Warrior," won the Best Story of the Year award from *Ellery Queen's Mystery Magazine* in 1946, beating out William Faulkner, who wrote an angry letter of protest to Frederic Dannay, the editor of the magazine. Other major honors include Lifetime Achievement Awards from the World Fantasy Writers (1980) and the British Fantasy Writers (1986), and the World Fantasy Award for Best Collection for *Worse Things Waiting* (1975).

In the mystery category, he wrote *A Double Life* (1947), a novelization of the George Cukor-directed film, *Find My Killer* (1947), and *The School of Darkness* (1985), set in the world of academia.

Several of Wellman's stories have been adapted for television, including "The Valley Was Still" for *The Twilight Zone* (1961), "The Devil is Not Mocked" for *Night Gallery* (1971), and two episodes of *Lights Out*, "Larroes Catch Meddlers" (1951) and "School for the Unspeakable" (1952).

Wellman also wrote for the comic books, producing the first *Captain Marvel* issue for Fawcett Publishers. When D.C. Comics sued Fawcett for plagiarizing their Superman character, Wellman testified against Fawcett, and D.C. won the case after three years of litigation.

"Murder Among Magicians" was originally published in the December 1939 issue of *Popular Detective.*

Murder Among Magicians
Manly Wade Wellman

SECUTORIS, FOREMOST stage magician and escape artist of his day, flashed white teeth between spiky beard and spiky moustaches at his guests. Full-bodied, vigorous, ungrayed despite his fifty-odd years, in the flame-colored evening suit he affected, he dominated the living room of Magic Manor, his sea-girt miniature castle.

The five guests, four men and a woman, were magicians like himself—four of them the best in the profession after him. Three of the men wore formal black; the fourth wore tweeds. The slender woman wore a sheathlike low-cut evening frock of lemon silk.

"*If* there is a life after death, and *if* my spirit returns," Secutoris was continuing a discussion, "it will speak a word for you to recognize."

"What word?" asked Hugh Drexel.

Young Drexel was a newspaperman; not a professional magician. But his sleight-of-hand hobby had gained for him the job of ghost-writing Secutoris' memoirs, which in turn won the tall, light-haired, strong-featured young man the entree to such gatherings as this.

"I'll say the word 'free.' 'Free!'" Secutoris' sonorous voice tossed the word exultantly, and he added sardonically "Of course, Wiggins here will sell the information to some skulking medium the day I die. It will be up to you others to expose him, if he does."

Few would have had the nerve so to gash the feelings of Arouj, finest fire juggler in America, a hot-tempered, swarthy man who claimed Arab descent, though rumor had it that he was a New York waif, born Wiggins. He it was who had not bothered with formal attire.

"How many times," Arouj demanded shrilly, "have I asked you not to call me Wiggins?"

"Hundreds," Secutoris chuckled, unabashed. "Isn't it your name?"

"You changed your name for the stage, didn't you?" challenged Arouj. "What if I called you—Delivuk, isn't it?"

"I wouldn't mind in the least, Secutoris suavely assured. "Delivuk, is an honored name in my native Hungary."

A sudden puff of wind whined around the house, and then came the sound of big waves tugging at the rock in Bennington Harbor on which Magic Manor stood.

"That wind heralds a storm," commented old Roheim, in his cultured voice.

Skeleton-lean, bald, and grim as a mummy, Roheim always spoke with deliberation and precision. Some said that he had served his apprenticeship in magic under Robert-Houdin in France. His friendship with Secutoris brought more comment, however, for the black-bearded "Handcuff King" had married, then divorced Roheim's daughter, who had since died.

"If it should storm," said Secutoris, smiling hospitably, "you may all have to stay the night. It would not be safe to trust a launch on that sea in the dark."

"We'd crowd you," murmured Stefan Delivuk, Secutoris' half brother.

Known professionally as Stephano, Delivuk was thin and mouseg-ray, and appeared shabby even in evening dress. A critic had once called him more skillful than Secutoris, though overshadowed by his brother's spectacular showmanship.

"We men could sleep anywhere, of course," he went on, "but Cassa—"

He smiled at the woman in the lemon gown, who smiled back at him and shook her head.

Cassa, as she was known professionally, had been born Zita Lewis-sohn. She was a gypsy beauty, with her cloud of storm-black hair. Hugh Drexel could not keep his eyes from her. Neither, it seemed, could Se-cutoris. Old Roheim's burning gaze sometimes rested on her, as well.

"I mustn't stay," she said quickly. "I must leave before it's late. Lend me the launch now, Secutoris."

Secutoris shrugged slightly.

"Oh, it may clear off—it's only the shank of the evening," he said. "Half an hour to witching midnight. Have a drink?"

He snapped his fingers toward a dark alcove. A fringe of tiny lights blazed up around the opening, and a figure materialized behind them—Roget, Secutoris' bald manservant, with a tray of cocktails. He stepped into the room amid applause.

"The old black art gag," Arouj sniffed disdainfully, though he accepted a drink. "Lights to keep us from seeing in, and a panel drawn back to reveal Roget."

"Quite true," Secutoris acknowledged readily. "But here *is* a new one."

He took a deck of cards from a sideboard and quickly selected the kings and aces.

"Don't draw one," he said. "You'll say I forced it. Think of a card, Wiggins—only think."

Shuffling the eight cards, he laid them face down on the center table.

"Now touch four," he said.

Scornfully Arouj did so. Secutoris discarded the pasteboards he indicated.

"Now two more," urged Secutoris, and two cards were left. "One," he said next, and a third time removed the card Arouj touched.

A single pasteboard remained.

"What was your choice?" he asked.

"Ace of hearts," muttered Arouj.

Slowly and impressively, Secutoris turned the remaining card face up. It was the ace of hearts.

"Ten dollars for that trick," Stephano offered quickly.

"I wouldn't give a dime for it," sneered Arouj.

"Wiggins wouldn't give a dime to see the Supreme Court play marbles," observed Secutoris, chuckling, then shook his head at Stephano. "No sale, old boy. I've willed you all my effects—including my magic. Wait until I die."

"Stephano needs new tricks badly in his act," Drexel murmured to Cassa, "but Secutoris won't help, not even with that little ruffle."

"And he has been speaking of dying," she whispered back. "Why doesn't he do it?"

"You don't like him, do you?" said Drexel.

She shook her head.

"I quit his show because he got too—friendly. Now he's starting it again."

In her lovely dark eyes was scornful distaste.

Secutoris, blandly unconscious that he was the subject of discussion, was unlocking a closet door.

"Want to see my apparatus for next season's show?" he invited, and stepping inside, began to lift glittering paraphernalia from a shelf.

With a quick, taunting laugh, Arouj scuttled forward, and

slammed the closet door, turning the key hurriedly. In his eyes gleamed impish delight.

"There, Secutoris!" he cried. "You are the escape artist—let's see you escape from that!"

Insistent rapping came from inside.

"Open up," called Secutoris in a muffled voice.

"No, *you* open it!" Arouj grimaced joyfully at the others.

"I'll make you sweat for this, Wiggins!" Secutoris promised balefully, thumping louder.

"Look here," interposed Stephano. "I've an interest in my brother's tricks. I don't want you others to see how he escapes."

"Should he escape," said Roheim.

"I'll escape, all right!" growled Secutoris from within.

"Suppose we give him ten minutes," said Roheim, in his carefully enunciated tones.

"Hear that, Secutoris?" crowed Arouj, taking the key from the lock. "You've got ten minutes to get out—if you can."

They went into the adjoining study and the little fire juggler tossed the key on a desk. Interested mainly in their profession, shop talk was quickly under way again. They were deep in a discussion of illusions, audiences, triumphs—when abruptly the room was plunged into darkness.

"Every heavy sea jams those light wires," groaned Stephano. "Why did he build out here in mid-ocean, anyway?"

Groping toward the wall of the blackened study to the light switch, Drexel rammed the desk and his hand touched the key Arouj had laid down. For a moment he was tempted to creep noiselessly into the living room and free Secutoris, for a joke. But why help Secutoris, who was annoying Cassa? Drexel stepped back from the desk, pocketing the key. As good a joke one way as the other, he decided.

Behind Drexel someone clicked vainly at the switch. Voices were mumbling complaints about the darkness when at last a glow appeared, touching faces into strange live masks. Roget was entering with two candles in sticks.

"How long do you suppose the lights have been out?" Cassa asked at Drexel's elbow.

Roheim produced a watch, his hawklike profile bending close above it.

"I should judge that Secutoris has been locked in for at least fifteen minutes now," he pronounced weightily. He took a candlestick from Roget. "Where is the key?"

"I have it," responded Drexel, and Roget led the way into the living room.

The candle made strange shadows dance on wall and ceiling as the group clustered around the closet door. It was shut and locked, as they had last seen it.

"Give up, Secutoris?" called Arouj maliciously.

No answer came from inside the closet.

"He's probably out of there, lying in wait for you in the shadows," suggested Stephano.

Arouj looked hurriedly behind him, as the others all laughed. But there was a slight nervousness in the laughter.

"He's not in sight," said Drexel. "Let's open up."

He put the key in the lock, turned it—and like a great red bottle tumbling from a shelf Secutoris pitched out, thudded down on his face, and lay still. . .

When the harbor police boat arrived from Bennington, it stopped at the very front door, for the tide covered the rocks up to the foundations of Magic Manor. The occupants of the miniature castle, gathering at the entry, could barely make out the lights of the mainland, for a heavy rain fell, whipping the waves to a black snarl.

A giant figure emerged from the cockpit and strode in, water streaming from a huge slicker and a soaked felt hat.

"Grinstead—Homicide detail," the rain-soaked man introduced himself tersely. "Who owns this place?"

"It belonged to Secutoris, the magician," answered Stephano. "He's the dead man I telephoned the police about."

Grinstead doffed his wet hat and they got a better view of his wide mouth, heavy brows and broken nose.

"Any of his family here?" he asked crisply.

Roget turned and walked silently into the back of the house.

"I suppose I'm next of kin," Stephano volunteered. "I'm his half brother."

Grinstead stalked into the candlelit parlor and lifted the sheet from the still form in the corner. He studied the distorted, bearded features, the purple weal around the throat, the rumpled red garments.

"Strangled," he grunted.

Drexel handed him a joined pair of metal rings that lay on the center table.

"These were leg irons from the display in his study," he explained. "Stuff he used in his act. One of them was clamped around his neck to choke him."

Grinstead snatched the irons.

"And you took them off?" he roared.

"Of course I took them off," Drexel said stoutly. "I tried to revive him—gave him artificial respiration."

"And everybody else pawed these irons, of course," the huge detective growled. "Covered 'em with prints. How do you expect me to catch the murderer?"

"Murderer?" echoed Cassa, shuddering. "He was—murdered?"

"Of course not, lady," Grinstead said witheringly. "This shackle just sneaked up all by itself and coiled lovingly around his neck."

Cassa's wide eyes were fearstricken.

"I thought perhaps suicide—" she began faintly.

"Not a chance." Kneeling ponderously, Grinstead touched the dead man's crown with his huge forefinger. "See that bruise? He couldn't have done it himself without diving headfirst onto something. No, somebody biffed him right on top of the head, then clamped the ring around his throat and let him choke."

He covered the body again.

"You, half brother," he addressed Stephano. "Tell me about it."

As Stephano talked, the officer wrote hurriedly in a notebook. Then he made a heavy-footed tour of the castle, peering into all corners of the living room, the study, the kitchen-workshop, and the room where Secutoris and Roget sometimes slept. Finally he motioned Drexel into the study.

"I'll start with you," he announced gruffly.

The door closed, they sat down. Grinstead took the telephone from the desk and dialed a number.

"Murder, Chief," he said into the transmitter, when he got his call. "Won't be back till tomorrow. It's drowning weather."

He hung up and then turned to face Drexel.

"That half brother said you were a newspaper reporter. What are you doing here?"

Drexel explained, and Grinstead nodded.

"So Secutoris was the Handcuff King?" he said at last. "Was this strangling shackle some kind of a phony?"

Drexel took it from the desk between them, studied it and shook his head.

"Hardly," he said. "Secutoris didn't need fake irons. The real ones just fell off of him when he wanted them to. He must have been completely knocked out, as you say, or he'd have shucked this one."

"How long does it take a magician to pick a lock?"

Drexel thought. "Two minutes and up, depending on how good he is. And Secutoris was the best, since the death of Houdini."

Grinstead digested the information.

"How long between the time the lights blinked out and the time the candles were brought in?" he asked then.

"About eight minutes," guessed Drexel.

"During which somebody unfastened the door, laid Secutoris out, put the iron to him, locked up again, and came back in here," Grinstead summed up. He pursed his wide, hard lips. "Could anybody besides Secutoris pick that lock, do the job, and unpick it again, in the dark, as quick as that?"

"I can't say."

Drexel did not volunteer the information that Cassa had once been Secutoris' stage assistant.

"Where did you get the key to unlock the closet?"

"Why, off this desk, where Arouj put it down," said Drexel.

Grinstead changed the subject.

"This Stephano, now. With his brother's tricks he'd be a big success instead of just getting by, eh?"

"He would."

Grinstead made notes in his book.

"You can go now," he said, and as he opened the door he called to Stephano: "Come in here, you, half brother."

Drexel sat down beside Cassa as Stephano entered the study. Everyone tried not to look at the sheeted corpse in the corner, and faces were pale and strained in the candlelight. Bits of small talk trailed off awkwardly, with long silences between.

Finally Grinstead opened the door again.

"Give me the little guy who locked Secutoris in," he called, and Arouj got up and went forward.

More silence followed Arouj's departure.

"Have you seen my new cigarette-case illusion?" asked Roheim irrelevantly, and the others sighed with relief, thankful for any distraction from their gloom-ridden thoughts.

With one claw-hand the withered old magician drew a silver case from a side pocket, passing it around for examination.

"Will someone lend me a cigarette?" he asked calmly.

Cases or packages were proffered. Roheim accepted from Cassa a long, violet-tinted cigarette with gold lettering. He clipped the butt end between the two halves of the case, and touched the tip to the candle that stood on the table.

"Now puff," he ordered, and the cigarette case expelled a cloud of smoke. "Puff," he repeated, and again it obeyed.

"Clever," cried Stephano, forgetting his horror in his professional interest. "I'll give you five dollars for the trick."

"And I accept," Roheim said cordially. "I shall diagram the case for you, showing the secret bellows. But will you not have all the effects you need, better than this, since your brother has left his secrets to you?"

"Thunder, that's so!" said Stephano.

Drexel wondered if he had really forgotten that.

"Come in, Roheim," growled Grinstead as he released Arouj.

Fired by the old conjuror's example, Cassa took Roheim's place and entertained with legerdemain, and Arouj took his turn when Grinstead summoned her.

Idly, Drexel picked up the cigarette case Roheim had laid on the table. He studied it for a hint of its mechanism, then scrutinized the violet cigarette. It seemed as smart, exotic and distinctive as the girl herself. He tried a puff. The tobacco was subtly flavored with rose perfume.

Grinstead called in Roget, the manservant, last of all.

"Miss me?" asked the girl, trying to be cheerful as she sat down beside Drexel.

"Terribly." He squashed out the coal of the cigarette in an ash tray.

"Don't you like my fancy cigarettes?" she asked, then laughed. "To tell the truth, I don't, either. They're just swank."

Drexel caught Roheim's hostile sideward stare, and the sudden flash of enmity he saw startled him. Was Roheim jealous of him? Old men's love was sometimes fiercest, he knew, because most hopeless.

Again Grinstead emerged from the study, an envelope in his hand.

"Gather around," he commanded. "Here is Secutoris' will. Might as well read it now as wait for any lawyers. I've got to solve this case."

His voice was gruffly official as he seated himself at the candle-lighted table. The two flickering flames of the candles made distorted figures on the walls, as though stealthy specters had also gathered.

"Roget got this out of the safe for me," Grinstead informed, displaying the envelope. On it was written:

IN THE EVENT OF MY DEATH, THE TERMS OF MY WILL, HEREIN ENCLOSED, ARE TO BE READ ALOUD TO MY HALF BROTHER STEFAN DELIVUK, MY CONFIDENTIAL SERVANT AARON ROGET, AND MISS ZITA LEWISSOHN, WITH RESPONSIBLE WITNESSES ATTENDING.

"What's his will doing out in this sea-going coop?" put in Drexel.

"It's a copy, sir," volunteered Roget. "The original is, of course, with his New York attorneys."

Grinstead tore open the envelope and extracted a folded sheet of typewriting.

Drexel, settling in his chair beside the half open closet door, happened to glance downward into the gloomy niche where Secutoris had met death. A pale speck on the floor caught his eye. He looked around quickly. The others were all listening as Grinstead read the will's formal opening. His hand reached down, his fingers clipped the object and brought it out.

It was the butt of a cigarette—gold-lettered, violet-tinted, rose-perfumed!

He dared not look at Cassa or the others. Grinstead was reading in a mechanical tone from the copy of the will:

"'All of my property, with the exception of specific bequests hereinafter mentioned, I bequeath to my half brother Stefan, known professionally as Stephano; and in particular do I give him all apparatus used in my magical and escape illusions on the stage, with my sealed notebooks describing their use'."

Drexel still held the cigarette butt that Roheim had used in his cigarette case trick. Stealthily he compared it with the one he had found in the closet. They were identical, save that the one from the closet floor was flicked with raspberry lipstick—Cassa's.

She had smoked it, and it had been dropped in the closet where Secutoris had died. And Cassa knew many of Secutoris' lock-forcing tricks!

A chill wave swept over Drexel as he thrust the stubs into his coat pocket. He hardly heard Grinstead's voice rasping on until one phrase suddenly startled him.

"'I bequeath to Zita Lewissohn, professionally known as Cassa, my house Magic Manor located on a rock in the harbor of—'"

"Wait!" Stephano sharply interrupted. "Why, Cassa, should my brother leave you this place?"

"As if you had to ask that!" jeered Arouj.

"I resent that!" cried Cassa hotly, and Drexel started to get up from his chair.

"Take it easy, you people!" Grinstead bleakly overrode them. "Get this: To Aaron Roget I bequeath the sum of five hundred dollars, and should he make further claim against my estate, alleging kinship or other right, I direct that the enclosed sealed paper be opened and its contents made public. Should he agree to the terms of this, my will, then I direct that said paper be burned unopened."

"Where's the paper?" inquired Arouj officiously.

"Probably with the original will," said Grinstead. "We'll get hold of it later."

"No!" Roget had sprung to his feet. He was white as milk, all the way to the top of his bald skull. "I call everyone to witness that I accept the terms! Let the paper be burned."

"If I was you," said the detective, "I wouldn't try to hold anything out."

"I'll tell this much, then," chattered Roget breathlessly. "That sealed document concerns my birth. It's a secret, and Secutoris always could make me do whatever he wanted by threatening to tell." His voice rose hysterically. "My mother has suffered enough without—"

"That sounds like a murder motive," sniffed Stephano, and Roget, breaking off, glared at him.

"Let me make my own pinches," Grinstead snapped, folding the document. "Well, that's all the will. Anybody got anything to say?"

"I have," said Roheim, rising to his gaunt height. He leveled a skeleton forefinger at Drexel, his eyes glittering. "Search that man!"

Everybody whipped around to stare.

"I saw him pick up something from the closet floor and hide it in his pocket," accused the old man coldly. "Secutoris died in that closet, If Mr. Drexel found anything, he should produce it."

Drexel rose from his chair.

"You're dreaming," he protested lamely.

"If you found anything, turn it over," commanded Grinstead.

Drexel let the big detective probe in his pocket and bring out the two stubs. Roheim's eyes glittered.

"They are Cassa's," contributed Arouj, craning his thin neck to see.

Drexel made a feeble effort to defend his action.

"—well, I admire Cassa," he said, feeling foolish. "I wanted a souvenir—"

"I think he took that one from Roheim's case," Stephano informed Grinstead, pointing to one stub. "The other has lipstick on it. She must have been smoking it."

"Then she must have dropped it in the closet," Roheim charged austerely.

Cassa's cheeks were glowing.

"I did nothing of the sort!" she snapped. "I've been smoking all over the place, but I wasn't once near the closet. Only when Secutoris went in, and when he"—she faltered—"came out."

"You actually think she could overpower a strong man like Secutoris?" demanded Drexel loyally.

"He was stunned," reminded Grinstead. "She could have swung

those irons hard enough to knock out Joe Louis." He peered into the closet. "Funny I didn't notice that butt in there."

"Why did my brother will this house to you?" Stephano again demanded of Cassa.

"He and I were friends once." Cassa sounded exasperated. "He wanted a quiet place where he could work out new effects, rest, and give a few parties. I helped him plan Magic Manor. As he was out of ready cash at the time, I lent him enough to start building. He couldn't pay me back at once—you know how money slipped through his fingers—so he put me in his will for protection."

"If you were his friend, why did you leave his act?" insisted Stephano, his eyes glaring.

"He—" Her voice stumbled, as if in confused rage at the memory. "Well, he was always suggesting—he tried to force me to marry—"

"Don't insult my dead brother!" Stephano shouted furiously. He whirled toward Grinstead. "Why don't you put her under arrest?"

Drexel's last thread of restraint snapped. He bounded at Stephano, hurled his right fist to the chin. Cassa's accuser went reeling, then recovered and charged back. But he missed a swing, and floundered on his knees before a second smashing right from Drexel. As he rose, Grinstead sprang in, caught the two men by their collars like fighting terriers, held them, struggling at arm's length.

"Drexel's her accomplice," panted Stephano. "He was jealous—"

"You cheap grifter!" yelled Hugh Drexel. "You're hanging it on Cassa because she told the truth about your chiselling brother!"

"Bottle it!" roared Grinstead. With a sudden effort he shoved them in opposite directions. "Another outbreak like that, and I'll lick you both—and don't think I can't!"

He turned heavily to Cassa.

"Unless you can explain this cigarette business," he said flatly, "I'll have to hold you."

"Don't say a word, Cassa," counseled Drexel hurriedly. "Let a lawyer do all the talking for you. Grinstead, you feel sure that the closet door couldn't be opened without a key?"

"That's the way it looks." Grinstead nodded. "Why?"

"Well, I picked up the key as the lights went out. I never let go of it until it was in the lock again. If you have to arrest someone, arrest me!"

Drexel thought it over when Grinstead, weary after an hour of fruitless questioning, left him alone in the study. Sitting at the desk, he stared at the shelves of manacles and other apparatus, at the framed photographs of Houdini, Harry Kellar and Bautier de Kolta, at the fluttering flame-point of the candle on the desk before him.

He had not admitted guilt, nor had he been too emphatic in protesting innocence. He would give Cassa some hours, at least, to marshal her defences before he set about clearing himself.

But how, he kept asking in his mind, could the door have been opened and Secutoris killed, save by someone who forced the lock quickly and blindly? There had been only one way to reach him.

Or was that true?

"Fool!" Drexel accused himself.

This was a magician's house. If Secutoris had designed it, undoubtedly it had been built like a glorified trick cabinet full of secret traps, masked exits, and the like. That shadowy nook where Roget had appeared with the cocktails should have been clue enough.

Drexel rose, lifted the candle, and approached the wall that divided the study from the living room.

It sounded solid to his tappings until he came to the rear of Secutoris' closet. There, of course, it rang hollow. Drexel examined the wall at that point, first closely, then from two paces' distance.

The wall paper, he saw, was arranged in vertical strips about forty-five inches wide. He resumed his tapping across the particular strip which backed the closet. The hollow ringing sound answered him all the way from edge to edge—no further, and no less far. He fingered the edges. The paper did not overlap the strips to left and right, but showed a hairline of clearance, like a black line drawn with ink.

Opening his penknife Drexel thrust its point into one of the hairlines. It entered to the depth of a quarter of an inch. Then he prodded the substance beneath the paper. It was not plaster but wallboard—wallboard that, in all probability, covered a wooden framework, designed to move in one piece.

Here, Drexel was satisfied, would be a back door to the closet. It was a device right out of a crime thriller. Only a conjuror would think of building it. Through it the murderer . . . But who was the murderer?

Cassa had helped design Magic Manor. She must know of this secret panel. But Drexel resolutely banished the thought. Roget knew, of course. Probably Stephano: perhaps Roheim. Arouj may have shared the secret, or may have guessed it as he, Drexel, had done.

He turned his attention to the panel again, searching in vain for a button, a projection that might house a spring, or a crack wide enough to pry into. The only marks were two irregular dark spots or stains, such as might come from the frequent pressure of naked, sweaty palms. They were just inside the two edges of the panel, at shoulder height. Drexel pressed upon them, but there was no movement.

The living room door opened and he pivoted to confront Grinstead and Roheim.

"What are you up to?" demanded the detective.

Drexel beckoned him eagerly. "Look, here's how the killer worked without a key! See how the panel is set in? Secutoris was going to come out this way. But someone knew and was waiting for him. Whoever it was biffed Secutoris, let him fall back against the front closet door, and then used the iron to choke him."

He spoke excitedly, forgetting that he was suspected of the very crime he outlined.

Grinstead bent close, stared and nodded.

"You know all about this family entrance, huh?" he commented very shrewdly, and Drexel's forgetfulness was banished.

"I know," he groaned in disgust. "I suppose I shot Lincoln, too."

Roheim laid a bony hand on the detective's huge shoulder.

"If Mr. Drexel knows, might not others?" he purred. "Let me try my plan."

"This old guy says he's a hypnotist," Grinstead explained to Drexel, "and says that anybody under his spell will tell the truth. Want to take a whack at it to show if you're innocent or not?"

"Certainly not," said Drexel disdainfully.

"Others have consented," Roheim said to the detective pointedly. "Allow me to begin with Cassa."

"Okay," mumbled the big man.

Drexel started to protest, then subsided, glaring silently at the angular shadows in the corners of the study. What foolishness had prompted Cassa to submit to hypnosis? What made Roheim so anxious to offer his assistance? Drexel could think of no answer.

In a few moments Cassa entered on the arm of Roheim. Her slow, mechanical movements and fixed expression showed that she was in a trance. At the heels of the pair came Grinstead, with Arouj and Stephano close behind.

"Cassa," murmured Roheim monotonously, "are you able to understand?"

"Yes," she whispered.

"Are you acquainted with this house?" droned the hypnotist.

"I helped to design it."

"You know the closet where Secutoris' body was found?"

"I know it."

"How many ways lead into that closet, Cassa?"

"Two," she replied, in a voice no louder than a sigh. "One visible— one hidden."

Someone gasped. Grinstead motioned for silence.

"You know the hidden way, Cassa?" was Roheim's next soft, insistent suggestion.

"Yes."

"Show us."

Slowly she faced the wall where the panel was, and walked haltingly toward it. Roheim kept pace with her. She put her slim hands upon the stained spots, and pushed upward. The panel rose like a window sash, vanishing into a recess above the level of the ceiling. The interior of the closet stood exposed.

Roheim snapped his twiglike fingers at Cassa's ear and whistled shrilly. She breathed deeply, as if waking. Then she stared into the black recess. She screamed and wilted to the floor, eyes closed and face as pallid as wax. Roheim pivoted triumphantly to face Grinstead.

"Well?" he smiled. "Is she not guilty?"

Drexel had sprung forward and was lifting Cassa. With her in his arms, he glared at the hypnotist.

"Still framing," he shot out, then laid Cassa on a divan.

Arouj caught a carafe of wine from a table and Drexel forced some between Cassa's lips. She moaned and stirred, then opened her eyes. Drexel turned to Roheim, his wrath exploding like a bomb.

"Your howl about cigarette stubs couldn't railroad her, so you put her into a trance," he accused. "Of course she fainted when she woke up looking into that dark closet! Any overwrought woman would. If you knew she'd tell the truth under hypnosis, why didn't you ask her outright if she killed Secutoris?"

He advanced menacingly. Roheim faced him, his old body tense but unafraid.

"You knew she'd clear herself," Drexel raged on, "and you can't afford that, Roheim. Because you killed Secutoris yourself!"

Roheim shook his head. "No," he said in slow, exact defiance.

Cassa sat up. "Look," she muttered weakly. "The body's gone."

Every eye sought the corner where the dead Secutoris had lain. Only a crumpled sheet remained.

"Free!" came a sudden, exultant cry. "Free!"

From the darkened back of the house strode a figure—robust, swaggering, clad in flame-colored evening clothes.

"May I come in? That's a good one, asking to come into my own living room."

Then they knew. It was Secutoris' voice coming from the lips of that flame-attired apparition. Teeth flashed between spiky mustache and spiky chin-tuft. Glowing eyes mocked.

Chilled, all who saw, shrank back before the apparition. Drexel caught Cassa's hand and held it tightly. Roheim began to mutter prayers.

"You wonder why I'm here," went on the voice of Secutoris. "You wonder, too, who killed me. No, one of you doesn't have to wonder. Won't that one confess—before I drag the story out?"

A pause. Nobody broke the silence. The brilliant eyes singled out Arouj.

"Don't you wish you hadn't locked me up, Wiggins? Your evening's been ruined, and you didn't humiliate me, after all. I've made the most spectacular escape of my career. But you wouldn't give a dime for this trick, either, would you, Wiggins?"

"Don't call me Wiggins!" wailed Arouj.

A quiet taunting chuckle mocked him. The pale, bearded face floated toward Drexel, who steadied his own gaze.

"Shaky?" inquired the voice of Secutoris. "Were you really trying to help me with your artificial respiration? Or only—shall we say—stalling?"

"I did my best," Drexel forced himself to say through dry lips. "It wasn't much."

"No, it wasn't much." The eyes slid to Cassa. The voice was caressingly gentle. "Still afraid, my dear?"

"Never afraid of you, Secutoris." Cassa spoke bravely, but she gripped Hugh Drexel's hand with desperate strength. "Only repelled."

"Repelled?" He seemed to wish that she would unsay that. "Do you hold ill will against me?"

"Not against the dead," she replied, her voice steady.

A slow, sad smile revealed the teeth under the mustache. The brilliant eyes left Cassa and fastened upon Roheim.

"You're old," came the soft voice. "Are you ready to lay life down?"

"I did not kill you," said Roheim, tightly and defiantly.

"Why did you do your best to make Cassa seem guilty?"

Roheim made his stare meet that of Secutoris.

"I tried because—let me say it this way. My daughter died because you left her. Could I have any good will toward this other woman whom you wanted?" Pulses throbbed in the bony temples. "I tried to make her seem guilty by planting the cigarette butt, and by sending her, hypnotized, to reveal the secret of the closet." The old man's voice began to shake. "I—I hated her. I tried—to hurt her. But I did not kill you, I say."

Now the eyes were on Stephano.

"Brother, are you glad to have inherited my tricks?"

"N-no," mumbled Stephano wretchedly. "Not when—"

"Enough of this comedy."

Secutoris' voice lost its tone of mockery and took on a steely hardness. The brilliant eyes swept commandingly over the group. As though assailed by a gust of icy wind, that group huddled closer. Secutoris brought his right hand from behind his back. It held two metal rings.

"These irons failed once tonight. They won't fail again."

One ring sprang open in his hand, gaping like a pair of lean, starved jaws.

"I know the killer, and the killer knows I know!" rang out Secutoris' voice. "That killer shall strangle—and shall not return from the dead!"

The very candle flame trembled, the shadows on wall and ceiling writhed.

"Now!" bawled the thing in flame-colored garments.

The hand lifted the yawning iron. Secutoris took a step forward. Another.

Then a scream tore the drum-taut air. Limbs struggled in the press of horrified bodies. Grinstead grunted in satisfaction, and shoved forward into the open. Writhing and fluttering in his grip was Arouj.

"No, no!" shrieked the frantic fire juggler. "Don't give me to him!"

"Then you did it," accused Grinstead.

"I couldn't stand his insults!" Arouj twisted around, clawing the detective's coat. "Once he locked me in that closet for an hour, then let me out through the panel, laughing. He forgot—I remembered." His words gushed over each other in his hysteria. "After locking him in tonight, I knew he'd turn off the lights with a hidden switch inside. When he did, and came out into the room back of the panel I was waiting for him with a blackjack, and then I put the iron—"

He collapsed, half fainting. Grinstead eased him into a chair.

"My job is over," said the man in flame-colored clothes, in a new voice. He plucked away beard and mustache and lifted the bushy wig from his bald pate.

"Roget!" came the chorus.

"Right." Grinstead nodded. "He told me how he'd doubled for his master in escape tricks and such, with makeup, costume, and voice. So I got him to help. When he came at the bunch with that iron, I watched from behind. All of you were scared almost screwy—but only this little Arouj guy tried to run. And I grabbed him."

Everyone began to chatter and gesticulate. Everyone but Cassa and Drexel. They moved toward the front window, his arm around her shoulder, and saw that, as the dawn came, the storm was ceasing.

Perhaps Harry Houdini, in his desire to hear a special code word from beyond the grave, inspired Secutoris. Bessie Houdini, Harry's widow, waited six years to hear her mother-in-law's maiden name spoken by a spirit medium. She never did.

Magic Manor seemed to harbor a peculiar bunch of characters, but any gathering of magicians is a little frightening to a non-magically oriented onlooker. Just ask a hotel manager who has been host to a magicians' convention! Next time you see a lone figure swaddled in a straitjacket, struggling bravely to free himself while suspended head down from a rope attached to your local Safeway Store, this is a sure sign that a magicians' meeting is in town. Avert your eyes, take a side street, and remember Secutoris—there might be a "Murder Among Magicians"!

MURDER AT THE AUTOMAT
Cornell Woolrich

Rightly known as the greatest writer of suspense fiction of the twentieth century, the long and prolific career of Cornell (George Hopley) Woolrich (1903-1968) embraced many kinds of fiction.

His first novel, *Cover Charge* (1926) was a romance, as was his second, *Children of the Ritz* (1927), which won a $10,000 prize (a staggering sum at that time) jointly offered by *College Humor* magazine and First National Pictures, which produced a film based on the book two years later. His next four books were also romantic novels and were so well received that critics compared him to F. Scott Fitzgerald.

He found magazines eager to buy his varied fiction in the 1920s and 1930s, including humor, western and adventure fiction and, finally, in 1934, his true forte, the noir stories for which he is properly revered today. Many of his greatest works, written as by Cornell Woolrich, William Irish, and George Hopley, have been adapted for motion pictures, including *The Bride Wore Black* (1940, filmed by Francois Truffaut in 1967), *Phantom Lady* (1942, under the Irish name, filmed in 1944), "It Had to Be Murder" (1942, filmed by Alfred Hitchcock as *Rear Window* in 1954), *Black Alibi* (1942, filmed as

The Leopard Man in 1943), *The Black Angel* (1943, filmed in 1946) and *Night Has a Thousand Eyes* (1945, filmed in 1948).

While the noir and suspense novels and stories that Woolrich produced over four decades placed him in the pantheon of the greatest of the great mystery writers of all time, he also wrote detective stories that were meticulously plotted. He even took on the great challenge of the locked room puzzle on three occasions: "The Screaming Laugh" (1938), which has a better title than plot, "The Room with Something Wrong" (1938), a tour-de-force published in *Golden Age Detective Stories*, and the present story, which sets up a tantalizing premise and may be the best-plotted crime story of his career.

"Murder at the Automat" was first published in the August 1937 issue of *Dime Detective Magazine*; it was first collected in *Nightwebs* (New York, Harper & Row, 1971).

Murder at the Automat
Cornell Woolrich

NELSON PUSHED through the revolving door at twenty to one in the morning, his squadmate, Sarecky, in the compartment behind him. They stepped clear and looked around. The place looked funny. Almost all the little white tables had helpings of food on them, but no one was at them eating. There was a big black crowd ganged up over in one corner, thick as bees and sending up a buzz. One or two were standing up on chairs, trying to see over the heads of the ones in front, rubbering like a flock of cranes.

The crowd burst apart, and a cop came through. "Now, stand back. Get away from this table, all of you," he was saying.

"There's nothing to see. The man's dead—that's all."

He met the two dicks halfway between the crowd and the door. "Over there in the corner," he said unnecessarily. "Indigestion, I guess." He went back with them.

They split the crowd wide open again, this time from the outside.

In the middle of it was one of the little white tables, a dead man in a chair, an ambulance doctor, a pair of stretcher—bearers, and the automat manager.

"He gone?" Nelson asked the interne.

"Yep. We got here too late." He came closer so the mob wouldn't overhear. "Better send him down to the morgue and have him looked at. I think he did the Dutch. There's a white streak on his chin, and a half eaten sandwich under his face spiked with some more of it, whatever it is. That's why I got in touch with you fellows. Good night," he wound up pleasantly and elbowed his way out of the crowd, the two stretcher-bearers tagging after him. The ambulance clanged dolorously outside, swept its fiery headlights around the corner, and whined off.

Nelson said to the cop: "Go over to the door and keep everyone in here, until we get the three others that were sitting at this table with him."

The manager said: "There's a little balcony upstairs. Couldn't he be taken up there, instead of being left down here in full sight like this?"

"Yeah, pretty soon," Nelson agreed, "but not just yet." He looked down at the table. There were four servings of food on it, one on each side. Two had barely been touched. One had been finished and only the soiled plates remained. One was hidden by the prone figure sprawled across it, one arm out, the other hanging limply down toward the floor.

"Who was sitting here?" said Nelson, pointing to one of the unconsumed portions. "Kindly step forward and identify yourself." No one made a move. "No one," said Nelson, raising his voice, "gets out of here until we have a chance to question the three people that were at this table with him when it happened."

Someone started to back out of the crowd from behind. The woman who had wanted to go home so badly a minute ago, pointed accusingly. "*He* was—that man there! I remember him distinctly. He bumped into me with his tray just before he sat down."

Sarecky went over, took him by the arm, and brought him forward again. "No one's going to hurt you," Nelson said, at sight of his pale face. "Only don't make it any tougher for yourself than you have to."

"I never even saw the guy before," wailed the man, as if he had already been accused of murder, "I just happened to park my stuff at the first vacant chair I—" Misery liking company, he broke off short and pointed in turn. "*He* was at the table, too! Why doncha hold him, if you're gonna hold me?"

"That's just what we're going to do," said Nelson dryly. "Over here, you," he ordered the new witness. "Now, who was eating spaghetti on his right here? As soon as we find that out, the rest of you can go home."

The crowd looked around indignantly in search of the recalcitrant witness that was the cause of detaining them all. But this time no one was definitely able to single him out. A white-uniformed busman finally edged forward and said to Nelson: "I think he musta got out of the place right after it happened. I looked over at this table a minute before it happened, and he was already through eating, picking his teeth and just holding down the chair."

"Well, he's not as smart as he thinks he is," said Nelson. "We'll catch up with him, whether he got out or didn't. The rest of you clear out of here now. And don't give fake names and addresses to the cop at the door, or you'll only be making trouble for yourselves."

The place emptied itself like magic, self-preservation being stronger than curiosity in most people. The two tablemates of the dead man, the manager, the staff, and the two dicks remained inside.

An assistant medical examiner arrived, followed by two men with the usual basket, and made a brief preliminary investigation. While this was going on, Nelson was questioning the two witnesses, the busman, and the manager. He got an illuminating composite picture.

The man was well-known to the staff by sight, and was considered an eccentric. He always came in at the same time each night, just before closing time, and always helped himself to the same snack—coffee and a bologna sandwich. It hadn't varied for six months now. The remnants that the busman removed from where the man sat each time, were always the same. The manager was able to corroborate this. He, the dead man, had raised a kick one night about a week ago, because the bologna sandwich slots had all been emptied before he came in. The manager had had to remind him that it's first come, first served, at an automat, and you can't reserve your food ahead of time. The man at the change booth, questioned by Nelson, added to the old fellow's reputation for eccentricity. Other, well-dressed people came in and changed a half dollar, or at the most a dollar bill. He, in his battered hat and derelict's overcoat, never failed to produce a ten and sometimes even a twenty.

"One of these misers, eh?" said Nelson. "They always end up behind the eight ball, one way or another."

The old fellow was removed, also the partly consumed sandwich. The assistant examiner let Nelson know: "I think you've got something here, brother. I may be wrong, but that sandwich was loaded with cyanide."

Sarecky, who had gone through the man's clothes, said: "The name was Leo Avram, and here's the address. Incidentally, he had seven hundred dollars, in Cs, in his right shoe and three hundred in his left. Want me to go over there and nose around?"

"Suppose I go," Nelson said. "You stay here and clean up."

"My pal," murmured the other dick dryly.

The waxed paper from the sandwich had been left lying under the chair. Nelson picked it up, wrapped it in a paper napkin, and put it in his pocket. It was only a short walk from the automat to where Avram lived, an outmoded, walk-up building, falling to pieces with neglect.

Nelson went into the hall and there was no such name listed. He thought at first Sarecky had made a mistake, or at least been misled by whatever memorandum it was he had found that purported to give the old fellow's address. He rang the bell marked "Superintendent," and went down to the basement entrance to make sure. A stout blond woman in an old sweater and carpet slippers came named out.

"Is there anyone named Avram living in this building?"

"That's my husband—he's the superintendent. He's out right now, I expect him back any minute."

Nelson couldn't understand, himself, why he didn't break it to her then and there. He wanted to get a line, perhaps, on the old man's surroundings while they still remained normal. "Can I come in and wait a minute?" he said.

"Why not?" she said indifferently.

She led him down a barren, unlit basement-way, stacked with empty ashcans, into a room green-yellow with a tiny bud of gaslight. Old as the building upstairs was, it had been wired for electricity, Nelson had noted. For that matter, so was this basement down here. There was a cord hanging from the ceiling ending in an empty socket. It had been looped up out of reach. "The old bird sure was a miser," thought Nelson. "Walking around on one grand and living like this!" He couldn't help feeling a little sorry for the woman.

He noted to his further surprise that a pot of coffee was boiling on a one-burner gas stove over in the corner. He wondered if she knew that he treated himself away from home each night. "Any idea where he went?" he asked, sitting down in a creaking rocker.

"He goes two blocks down to the automat for a bite to eat every night at this time," she said.

"How is it," he asked curiously "he'll go out and spend money like that, when he could have coffee right here where he lives with you?"

A spark of resentment showed in her face, but a defeated resentment that had long turned to resignation. She shrugged. "For himself, nothing's too good. He goes there because the light's better, he says. But for me and the kids, he begrudges every penny."

"You've got kids, have you?"

"They're mine, not his," she said dully.

Nelson had already caught sight of a half grown girl and a little boy peeping shyly out at him from another room. "Well," he said, getting up, "I'm sorry to have to tell you this, but your husband had an accident a little while ago at the automat, Mrs. Avram. He's gone."

The weary stolidity on her face changed very slowly. But it did change—to fright. "Cyanide—what's that?" she breathed, when he'd told her.

"Did he have any enemies?"

She said with utter simplicity, "Nobody loved him. Nobody hated him that much, either."

"Do you know of any reason he'd have to take his own life?"

"Him? Never! He held on tight to life, just like he did to his money."

There was some truth in that, the dick had to admit. Misers seldom commit suicide.

The little girl edged into the room fearfully, holding her hands behind her. "Is—is he dead, Mom?"

The woman just nodded, dry-eyed.

"Then, can we use this now?" She was holding a fly-blown electric bulb in her hands.

Nelson felt touched, hardboiled dick though he was. "Come down to headquarters tomorrow, Mrs. Avram. There's some money there you can claim. G'night." He went outside and clanged the basement-gate shut after him. The windows alongside him suddenly bloomed feebly with electricity, and the silhouette of a woman standing up on a chair was outlined against them.

"It's a funny world," thought the dick with a shake of his head, as he trudged up to sidewalk-level.

It was now two in the morning. The automat was dark when Nelson returned there, so he went down to headquarters. They were questioning the branch manager and the unseen counterman who prepared the sandwiches and filled the slots from the inside.

Nelson's captain said: "They've already telephoned from the chem lab that the sandwich is loaded with cyanide crystals. On the other hand, they give the remainder of the loaf that was used, the leftover bologna from which the sandwich was prepared, the breadknife, the cutting board, and the scraps in the garbage receptacle—all of which we sent over there—a clean bill of health. There was clearly no slip-up or carelessness in the automat pantry. Which means that cyanide got into that sandwich on the consumer's side of the apparatus. He committed suicide or was deliberately murdered by one of the other customers."

"I was just up there," Nelson said. "It wasn't suicide. People don't worry about keeping their light bills down when they're going to take their own lives."

"Good psychology," the captain nodded. "My experience is that miserliness is simply a perverted form of self-preservation, an exaggerated clinging to life. The choice of method wouldn't be in character, either. Cyanide's expensive, and it wouldn't be sold to a man of Avram's type, just for the asking. It's murder, then. I think it's highly important you men bring in whoever the fourth man at the table was tonight. Do it with the least possible loss of time."

A composite description of him, pieced together from the few scraps that could be obtained from the busman and the other two at the table, was available. He was a heavy-set, dark-complected man, wearing a light-tan suit. He had been the first of the four at the table, and already through eating, but had lingered on. Mannerisms—had kept looking back over his shoulder, from time to time, and picking his teeth. He had had a small black satchel, or sample case, parked at his feet under the table. Both survivors were positive on this point. Both had stubbed their toes against it in sitting down, and both had glanced to the floor to see what it was.

Had he reached down toward it at any time, after their arrival, as if to open it or take anything out of it?

To the best of their united recollections—no.

Had Avram, after bringing the sandwich to the table, gotten up again and left it unguarded for a moment?

Again, no. In fact the whole thing had been over with in a flash. He had noisily unwrapped it, taken a huge bite, swallowed without chewing, heaved convulsively once or twice, and fallen prone across the tabletop.

"Then it must have happened right outside the slot—I mean the inserting of the stuff—and not at the table, at all," Sarecky told Nelson privately. "Guess he laid it down for a minute while he was drawing his coffee."

"Absolutely not!" Nelson contradicted. "You're forgetting it was all wrapped up in wax paper. How could anyone have opened, then closed it again, without attracting his attention? And if we're going to suspect the guy with the satchel—and the cap seems to want us to— he was already at the table and all through eating when Avram came over. How could he know ahead of time which table the old guy was going to select?"

"Then how did the stuff get on it? Where did it come from?" the other dick asked helplessly.

"It's little things like that we're paid to find out," Nelson reminded him dryly.

"Pretty large order, isn't it?"

"You talk like a layman. You've been on the squad long enough by now to know how damnably unescapable little habits are, how impossible it is to shake them off, once formed. The public at large thinks detective work is something miraculous like pulling rabbits out of a silk-hat. They don't realize that no adult is a free agent— that they're tied hand and foot by tiny, harmless little habits, and held helpless. This man has a habit of taking a snack to eat at midnight in a public place. He has a habit of picking his teeth after he's through, of lingering on at the table, of looking back over his shoulder aimlessly from time to time. Combine that with a stocky build, a dark complexion, and you have him! What more d'ya want—a spotlight trained on him?"

It was Sarecky, himself, in spite of his misgivings, who picked him up forty-eight hours later in another automat, sample case and all, at nearly the same hour as the first time, and brought him in for questioning! The busman from the former place, and the two customers, called in, identified him unhesitatingly, even if he was now wearing a gray suit.

His name, he said, was Alexander Hill, and he lived at 215 Such-and-such a street.

"What business are you in?" rapped out the captain.

The man's face got livid. His Adam's apple went up and down like an elevator. He could barely articulate the words. "I'm—I'm a salesman for a wholesale drug concern," he gasped terrifiedly.

"Ah!" said two of his three questioners expressively. The sample case, opened, was found to contain only tooth powders, aspirins, and headache remedies.

But Nelson, rummaging through it, thought: "Oh, nuts, it's too pat. And he's too scared, too defenseless, to have really done it. Came in here just now without a bit of mental build-up prepared ahead of time. The real culprit would have been all primed, all rehearsed, for just this. Watch him go all to pieces. The innocent ones always do."

The captain's voice rose to a roar. "How is it everyone else stayed in the place that night, but you got out in such a hurry?"

"I—I don't know. It happened so close to me, I guess I—I got nervous."

That wasn't necessarily a sign of guilt, Nelson was thinking. It was his duty to take part in the questioning, so he shot out at him: "You got nervous, eh? What reason d'you have for getting nervous? How'd you know it wasn't just a heart attack or malnutrition—unless you were the cause of it?"

He stumbled badly over that one. "No! No! I don't handle that stuff! I don't carry anything like that—"

"So you know what it was? How'd you know? We didn't tell you," Sarecky jumped on him.

"I—I read it in the papers next morning," he wailed.

Well, it had been in all of them, Nelson had to admit.

"You didn't reach out in front of you—toward him—for anything that night? You kept your hands to yourself?" Then, before he could get a word out, *"What about sugar?"*

The suspect went from bad to worse. "I don't use any!" he whimpered.

Sarecky had been just waiting for that. "Don't lie to us!" he yelled, and swung at him. "I watched you for ten full minutes tonight before I went over and tapped your shoulder. You emptied half the container into your cup!" His fist hit him a glancing blow on the side of the jaw, knocked him and the chair he was sitting on both off balance. Fright was making the guy sew himself up twice as badly as before.

"Aw, we're just barking up the wrong tree," Nelson kept saying to himself. "It's just one of those fluke coincidences. A drug salesman happens to be sitting at the same table where a guy drops from cyanide poisoning!" Still, he knew that more than one guy had been strapped into the chair just on the strength of such a coincidence and nothing more. You couldn't expect a jury not to pounce on it for all it was worth.

The captain took Nelson out of it at this point, somewhat to his relief, took him aside and murmured: "Go over there and give his place a good cleaning while we're holding him here. If you can turn up any of that stuff hidden around there, that's all we need. He'll break down like a stack of cards." He glanced over at the cowering figure in the chair. "We'll have him before morning," he promised.

"That's what I'm afraid of," thought Nelson, easing out. "And then what'll we have? Exactly nothing." He wasn't the kind of a dick that would have rather had a wrong guy than no guy at all, like some of them. He wanted the right guy—or none at all. The last he saw of the captain, he was stripping off his coat for action, more as a moral threat than a physical one, and the unfortunate victim of circumstances was wailing, "I didn't do it, I didn't do it," like a record with a flaw in it.

Hill was a bachelor and lived in a small, one-room flat on the upper West Side. Nelson let himself in with the man's own key, put on the lights, and went to work. In half an hour, he had investigated the place upside down. There was not a grain of cyanide to be found, nor anything beyond what had already been revealed in the sample case. This did not mean, of course, that he couldn't have obtained some either through the firm he worked for, or some of the retail druggists whom he canvassed. Nelson found a list of the latter and took it with him to check over the following day.

Instead of returning directly to headquarters, he detoured on an impulse past the Avram house, and, seeing a light shining in the basement windows, went over and rang the bell.

The little girl came out, her brother behind her. "Mom's not in," she announced.

"She's out with Uncle Nick," the boy supplied.

His sister whirled on him. "She told us not to tell anybody that, didn't she!"

Nelson could hear the instructions as clearly as if he'd been in the room at the time, "If that same man comes around again don't you tell him I've gone out with Uncle Nick, now!"

Children are after all very transparent. They told him most of what he wanted to know without realizing they were doing it. "He's not really your uncle, is he?"

A gasp of surprise. "How'd you know that?"

"Your ma gonna marry him?"

They both nodded approvingly. "He's gonna be our new Pop."

"What was the name of your real Pop—the one before the last?"

"Edwards," they chorused proudly. "What happened to him?"

"He died."

"In Dee-troit," added the little boy.

He only asked them one more question. "Can you tell me his full name?"

"Albert J. Edwards," they recited.

He gave them a friendly push. "All right, kids, go back to bed."

He went back to headquarters, sent a wire to the Bureau of Vital Statistics in Detroit, on his own hook. They were still questioning Hill down to the bone, meanwhile, but he hadn't caved in yet. "Nothing," Nelson reported. "Only this accountsheet of where he places his orders."

'I'm going to try framing him with a handful of bicarb of soda, or something—pretend we got the goods on him. I'll see if that'll open him up," the captain promised wrathfully. "He's not the pushover I expected. You start in at seven this morning and work your way through this list of retail druggists. Find out if he ever tried to contract them for any of that stuff."

Meanwhile, he had Hill smuggled out the back way to an outlying precinct, to evade the statute governing the length of time a prisoner can be held before arraignment. They didn't have enough of a case against him yet to arraign him, but they weren't going to let him go.

Nelson was even more surprised than the prisoner at what he caught himself doing. As they stood Hill up next to him in the corridor, for a minute, waiting for the Black Maria, he breathed over his shoulder, "Hang on tight, or you're sunk!"

The man acted too far gone even to understand what he was driving at.

Nelson was present the next morning when Mrs. Avram showed up to claim the money, and watched her expression curiously. She had the same air of weary resignation as the night he had broken the news to her. She accepted the money from the captain, signed for it, turned apathetically away, holding it in her hand. The captain, by prearrangement, had pulled another of his little tricks—purposely withheld one of the hundred-dollar bills to see what her reaction would be.

Halfway to the door, she turned in alarm, came hurrying back. "Gentlemen, there must be a mistake! There's—there's a hundred-dollar bill here on top!" She shuffled through the roll hastily. "They're all hundred-dollar bills!" she cried out aghast. "I knew he had a little money in his shoes—he slept with them under his pillow at nights—but I thought maybe, fifty, seventy dollars—"

"There was a thousand in his shoes," said the captain, "and another thousand stitched all along the seams of his overcoat."

She let the money go, caught the edge of the desk he was sitting behind with both hands, and slumped draggingly down it to the floor in a dead faint. They had to hustle in with a pitcher of water to revive her.

Nelson impatiently wondered what the heck was the matter with him, what more he needed to be convinced she hadn't known what she was coming into? And yet, he said to himself, how are you going to tell a real faint from a fake one? They close their eyes and they flop, and which is it?

He slept three hours, and then he went down and checked at the wholesale drug concern Hill worked for. The firm did not handle cyanide or any other poisonous substance, and the man had a very good record there. He spent the morning working his way down the list of retail druggists who had placed their orders through Hill, and again got nowhere. At noon he quit, and went back to the automat where it had happened—not to eat but to talk to the manager. He was really working on two cases simultaneously—an official one for his captain and a private one of his own. The captain would have had a fit if he'd known it.

"Will you lemme have that busman of yours, the one we had down at headquarters the other night? I want to take him out of here with me for about half an hour."

"You're the Police Department," the manager smiled acquiescently.

Nelson took him with him in his streetclothes. "You did a pretty good job of identifying Hill, the fourth man at that table," he told him. "Naturally, I don't expect you to remember every face that was in there that night. Especially with the quick turnover there is in an automat. However, here's what you do. Go down this street here to Number One-twenty-one—you can see it from here. Ring the super-intendent's bell. You're looking for an apartment, see? But while you're at it, you take a good look at the woman you'll see, and then come back and tell me if you remember seeing her face in the automat that night or any other night. Don't stare now—just size her up."

It took him a little longer than Nelson had counted on. When he finally rejoined the dick around the corner, where the latter was wait-ing, he said: "Nope, I've never seen her in our place, that night or any other, to my knowledge. But don't forget—I'm not on the floor every minute of the time. She could have been or and out often without my spotting her."

"But not," thought Nelson, "without Avram seeing her, if she went anywhere near him at all." She hadn't been there, then. That was prac-tically certain. "What took you so long?" he asked him.

"Funny thing. There was a guy there in the place with her that used to work for us. He remembered me right away."

"Oh, yeah?" The dick drew up short. "Was he in there that night?"

"Naw, he quit six months ago. I haven't seen him since."

"What was he, sandwich maker?"

"No, busman like me. He cleaned up the tables."

Just another coincidence, then. But, Nelson reminded himself, if one coincidence was strong enough to put Hill in jeopardy, why should the other be passed over as harmless? Both cases—his and the captain's—now had their coincidences. It remained to be seen which was just that—a coincidence and nothing more—and which was the McCoy.

He went back to headquarters. No wire had yet come from Detroit in answer to his, but he hadn't expected any this soon—it took time. The captain, bulldog-like, wouldn't let Hill go. They had spirited him away to still a third place, were holding him on some technicality or other that had nothing to do with the Avram case. The bicarbonate of soda trick hadn't worked, the captain told Nelson ruefully.

"Why?" the dick wanted to know. "Because he caught on just by looking at it that it wasn't cyanide—is that it? I think that's an important point, right there."

"No, he thought it was the stuff all right. But he hollered blue murder it hadn't come out of his room."

"Then if he doesn't know the difference between cyanide and bicarb of soda at sight, doesn't that prove he didn't put any on that sandwich?"

The captain gave him a look. "Are you for us or against us?" he wanted to know acidly. "You go ahead checking that list of retail druggists until you find out where he got it. And if we can't dig up any other motive, unhealthy scientific curiosity will satisfy me. He wanted to study the effects at first hand, and picked the first stranger who came along."

"Sure, in an automat—the most conspicuous, crowded public eating place there is. The one place where human handling of the food is reduced to a minimum."

He deliberately disobeyed orders, a thing he had never done before—or rather, postponed carrying them out. He went back and commenced a one-man watch over the basement entrance of the Avram house.

In about an hour, a squat, foreign-looking man came up the steps and walked down the street. This was undoubtedly "Uncle Nick," Mrs. Avram's husband-to-be, and former employee of the automat. Nelson tailed him effortlessly on the opposite side, boarded the same bus he did but a block below, and got off at the same stop. "Uncle Nick" went into a bank, and Nelson into a cigar store across the way that had transparent telephone booths commanding the street through the glass front.

When he came out again, Nelson didn't bother following him any more. Instead, he went into the bank himself. "What'd that guy do— open an account just now? Lemme see the deposit slip."

He had deposited a thousand dollars cash under the name of Nicholas Krassin, half of the sum Mrs. Avram had claimed at headquarters only the day before. Nelson didn't have to be told that this by no means indicated Krassin and she had had anything to do with the old man's death. The money was rightfully hers as his widow, and, if she wanted to divide it with her groom-to-be, that was no criminal offense. Still, wasn't there a stronger motive here than the "unhealthy scientific curiosity" the captain had pinned on Hill? The fact remained that she wouldn't have had possession of the money had Avram still been alive. It would have still been in his shoes and coat seams where she couldn't get at it.

Nelson checked Krassin at the address he had given at the bank, and, somewhat to his surprise, found it to be on the level, not fictitious. Either the two of them weren't very bright, or they were innocent. He went back to headquarters at six, and the answer to his telegram to Detroit had finally come. "Exhumation order obtained as per request stop Albert J. Edwards deceased January 1936 stop death certificate gives cause fall from steel girder while at work building under construction stop—autopsy—"

Nelson read it to the end, folded it, put it in his pocket without changing his expression.

"Well, did you find out anything?" the captain wanted to know.

"No, but I'm on the way to," Nelson assured him, but he may have been thinking of that other case of his own, and not the one they were all steamed up over. He went out again without saying where.

He got to Mrs. Avram's at quarter to seven, and rang the bell.

The little girl came out to the basement entrance. At sight of him, she called out shrilly, but without humorous intent, "Ma, that man's here again."

Nelson smiled a little and walked back to the living quarters. A sudden hush had fallen thick enough to cut with a knife. Krassin was there again, in his shirtsleeves, having supper with Mrs. Avram and the two kids. They not only had electricity now but a midget radio as well, he noticed. You can't arrest people for buying a midget radio. It was silent as a tomb, but he let the back of his hand brush it, surreptitiously, and the front of the dial was still warm from recent use.

'Tm not butting in, am I?" he greeted them cheerfully.

"N-no, sit down," said Mrs. Avram nervously. "This is Mr. Krassin, a friend of the family. I don't know your name—"

"Nelson."

Krassin just looked at him watchfully.

The dick said: "Sorry to trouble you. I just wanted to ask you a couple questions about your husband. About what time was it he had the accident?"

"You know that better than I," she objected. "You were the one came here and told me."

"I don't mean Avram, I mean Edwards, in Detroit—the riveter that fell off the girder."

Her face went a little gray, as if the memory were painful. Krassin's face didn't change color, but only showed considerable surprise.

"About what time of day?" he repeated.

"Noon," she said almost inaudibly.

"Lunch time," said the dick softly, as if to himself. "Most workmen carry their lunch from home in a pail—" He looked at her thoughtfully. Then he changed the subject, wrinkled up his nose appreciatively. "That coffee smells good," he remarked.

She gave him a peculiar, strained smile. "Have a cup, Mr. Detective," she offered. He saw her eyes meet Krassin's briefly.

"Thanks, don't mind if I do," drawled Nelson.

She got up. Then, on her way to the stove, she suddenly flared out at the two kids for no apparent reason: "What are you hanging around here for? Go in to bed. Get out of here how, I say!" She banged the door shut on them, stood before it with her back to the room for a minute. Nelson's sharp ears caught the faint but unmistakable click of a key.

She turned back again, purred to Krassin: "Nick, go outside and take a look at the furnace, will you, while I'm pouring Mr. Nelson's coffee? If the heat dies down, they'll all start complaining from upstairs right away. Give it a good shaking up."

The hairs at the back of Nelson's neck stood up a little as he watched the man get up and sidle out. But he'd asked for the cup of coffee, himself.

He couldn't see her pouring it—her back was turned toward him again as she stood over the stove. But he could hear the splash of the hot liquid, see her elbow motions, hear the clink of the pot as she replaced it. She stayed that way a moment longer, after it had been poured, with her back to him—less than a moment, barely thirty seconds. One elbow moved slightly. Nelson's eyes were narrow slits. It was thirty seconds too long, one elbow motion too many.

She turned, came back, set the cup down before him. 'I'll let you put your own sugar in, yes?" she said almost playfully. "Some like a lot, some like a little." There was a disappearing ring of froth in the middle of the black steaming liquid.

Outside somewhere, he could hear Krassin raking up the furnace.

"Drink it while it's hot," she urged.

He lifted it slowly to his lips. As the cup went up, her eyelids went down. Not all the way, not enough to completely shut out sight, though.

He blew the steam away. "Too hot—burn my mouth. Gotta give it a minute to cool," he said. "How about you—ain't you having any? I couldn't drink alone. Ain't polite."

"I had mine," she breathed heavily, opening her eyes again. "I don't think there's any left."

"Then I'll give you half of this."

Her hospitable alarm was almost overdone. She all but jumped back in protest. "No, no! Wait, I'll look. Yes, there's more, there's plenty!"

He could have had an accident with it while her back was turned a second time, upset it over the floor. Instead, he took a kitchen match out of his pocket, broke the head off short with his thumbnail. He threw the head, not the stick, over on top of the warm stove in front of which she was standing. It fell to one side of her, without making any noise, and she didn't notice it. If he'd thrown stick and all, it would have clicked as it dropped and attracted her attention.

She came back and sat down opposite him. Krassin's footsteps could be heard shuffling back toward them along the cement corridor outside.

"Go ahead. Don't be bashful—drink up," she encouraged.

There was something ghastly about her smile, like a death's head grinning across the table from him.

The match head on the stove, heated to the point of combustion, suddenly flared up with a little spitting sound and a momentary gleam. She jumped a little, and her head turned nervously to see what it was. When she looked back again, he already had his cup to his lips. She raised hers, too, watching him over the rim of it. Krassin's footfalls had stopped somewhere just outside the room door, and there wasn't another sound from him, as if he were standing there, waiting.

At the table, the cat-and-mouse play went on a moment longer. Nelson started swallowing with a dry constriction of the throat. The woman's eyes, watching him above her cup, were greedy half moons of delight. Suddenly, her head and shoulders went down across the table with a bang, like her husband's had at the automat that other night, and the crash of the crushed cup sounded from underneath her.

Nelson jumped up watchfully, throwing his chair over. The door shot open, and Krassin came in, with an ax in one hand and an empty burlap bag in the other.

'I'm not quite ready for cremation yet," the dick gritted, and threw himself at him.

Krassin dropped the superfluous burlap bag, the ax flashed up overhead. Nelson dipped his knees, down in under it before it could fall. He caught the shaft with one hand, midway between the blade and Krassin's grip, and held the weapon teetering in mid-air. With his other fist he started imitating a hydraulic drill against his assailant's teeth. Then he lowered his barrage suddenly to solar-plexus level, sent in two body blows that caved his opponent in—and that about finished it.

Out in the wilds of Corona, an hour later, in a sub-basement locker room, Alexander Hill—or at least what was left of him—was saying: "And you'll lemme sleep if I do? And you'll get it over real quick, send me up and put me out of my misery?"

"Yeah, yeah!" said the haggard captain, flicking ink out of a fountain pen and jabbing it at him. "Why dincha do this days ago, make it easier for us all?"

"Never saw such a guy," complained Sarecky, rinsing his mouth with water over in a corner.

"What's that man signing?" exploded Nelson's voice from the stairs.

"Whaddye think he's signing?" snarled the captain. "And where you been all night, incidentally?"

"Getting poisoned by the same party that croaked Avram!" He came the rest of the way down, and Krassin walked down alongside at the end of a short steel link.

"Who's this guy?" they both wanted to know.

Nelson looked at the first prisoner, in the chair. "Take him out of here a few minutes, can't you?" he requested. "He don't have to know all our business."

"Just like in the storybooks," muttered Sarecky jealously. "One-Man Nelson walks in at the last minute and cops all the glory."

A cop led Hill upstairs. Another cop brought down a small brown paper parcel at Nelson's request. Opened, it revealed a small tin that had once contained cocoa. Nelson turned it upside down and a few threads of whitish substance spilled lethargically out, filling the close air of the room with a faint odor of bitter almonds.

"There's your cyanide," he said. "It came off the shelf above Mrs. Avram's kitchen stove. Her kids, who are being taken care of at headquarters until I can get back there, will tell you it's roach powder and they were warned never to go near it. She probably got it in Detroit, way back last year."

"She did it?" said the captain. "How could she? It was on the automat sandwich, not anything he ate at home. She wasn't at the automat that night, she was home, you told us that yourself."

"Yeah, she was home, but she poisoned him at the automat just the same. Look, it goes like this." He unlocked his manacle, refastened his prisoner temporarily to a plumbing pipe in the corner. He took a paper napkin out of his pocket, and, from within that, the carefully preserved waxpaper wrapper the death sandwich had been done in.

Nelson said: "This has been folded over twice, once on one side, once on the other. You can see that, yourself. Every crease in it is double-barreled. Meaning what? The sandwich was taken out, doctored, and rewrapped. Only, in her hurry, Mrs. Avram slipped up and put the paper back the other way around.

"As I told Sarecky already, there's death in little habits. Avram was a miser. Bologna is the cheapest sandwich that automat sells. For six months straight, he never bought any other kind. This guy here used to work there. He knew at what time the slots were refilled for the last time. He knew that that was just when Avram always showed up. And, incidentally, the old man was no fool. He didn't go there because the light was better—he went there to keep from getting poisoned at home. Ate all his meals out.

"All right, so what did they do? They got him, anyway—like this. Krassin, here, went in, bought a bologna sandwich, and took it home to her. She spiked it, rewrapped it, and, at eleven thirty, he took it back there in his pocket. The sandwich slots had just been refilled for the last time. They wouldn't put any more in till next morning. There are three bologna slots. He emptied all three, to make sure the victim wouldn't get any but the lethal sandwich. After they're taken out, the glass slides remain ajar. You can lift them and reach in without inserting a coin. He put his death sandwich in, stayed by it so no one else would get it. The old man came in. Maybe he's near sighted and didn't recognize Krassin. Maybe he didn't know him at all—I haven't cleared that point up yet. Krassin eased out of the place. The old man is a miser. He sees he can get a sandwich for nothing, thinks something went wrong with the mechanism, maybe. He grabs it up twice as quick as anyone else would have. There you are.

"What was in his shoes is this guy's motive. As for her, that was only partly her motive. She was a congenital killer, anyway, outside of that. He would have married her, and it would have happened to him in his turn some day. She got rid of her first husband, Edwards, in Detroit that way. She got a wonderful break. He ate the poisoned lunch she'd given him way up on the crossbeams of a building under construction, and it looked like he'd lost his balance and toppled to his death. They exhumed the body and performed an autopsy at my request. This telegram says they found traces of cyanide poisoning even after all this time.

"I paid out rope to her tonight, let her know I was onto her. I told her her coffee smelled good. Then I switched cups on her. She's up there now, dead. I can't say that I wanted it that way, but it was me or her. You never would have gotten her to the chair, anyway. She was unbalanced of course, but not the kind that's easily recognizable. She'd have spent a year in an institution, been released, and gone out and done it all over again. It grows on 'em, gives 'em a feeling of power over their fellow human beings.

"This louse, however, is not insane. He did it for exactly one thousand dollars and no cents—and he knew what he was doing from first to last. So I think he's entitled to a chicken-and-ice cream dinner in the death house, at the state's expense."

"The Sphinx," growled Sarecky under his breath, shrugging into his coat. "Sees all, knows all, keeps all to himself."

"Who stinks?" corrected the captain, misunderstanding. "If anyone does, it's you and me. He brought home the bacon!"

DISCUSSION QUESTIONS

- Reading this anthology, did you learn anything about the Golden Age locked room mystery story that you didn't already know? If so, what?

- Which story's puzzle did you find the most perplexing?

- Did any of the solutions stretch credibility?

- Were you able to solve any of the mysteries before the main character? If so, which ones?

- How did the cultural history of the era play into these stories? Did anything help date them for you?

- Did any stories surprise you in terms of subject, character, or setting? If so, which ones?

- Did any stories remind you of work from authors today? If so, which ones?

- What characteristics do you think made these authors so popular in their day? Do you think readers today still want the same things from their reading material?

H.F. Heard, *A Taste for Honey*

Dolores Hitchens, *The Cat Saw Murder*
Introduced by Joyce Carol Oates

Dorothy B. Hughes, *Dread Journey*
Introduced by Sarah Weinman
Dorothy B. Hughes, *Ride the Pink Horse*
Introduced by Sara Paretsky
Dorothy B. Hughes, *The So Blue Marble*

W. Bolingbroke Johnson, *The Widening Stain*
Introduced by Nicholas A. Basbanes

Baynard Kendrick, *The Odor of Violets*

Jonathan Latimer, *Headed for a Hearse*
Introduced by Max Allan Collins

Frances and Richard Lockridge, *Death on the Aisle*

John P. Marquand, *Your Turn, Mr. Moto*
Introduced by Lawrence Block

Stuart Palmer, *The Puzzle of the Happy Hooligan*

Otto Penzler, ed., *Golden Age Detective Stories*

Ellery Queen, *The American Gun Mystery*
Ellery Queen, *The Chinese Orange Mystery*
Ellery Queen, *The Dutch Shoe Mystery*
Ellery Queen, *The Egyptian Cross Mystery*
Ellery Queen, *The Siamese Twin Mystery*

Patrick Quentin, *A Puzzle for Fools*